Dust in the Wind

Dust in the Wind

A Story of the Wheat Harvest

Tom Morrow

iUniverse, Inc.
Bloomington

Dust in the Wind
A Story of the Wheat Harvest

iUniverse books may be ordered through booksellers or by contacting:

iUniverse
1663 Liberty Drive
Bloomington, IN 47403
www.iuniverse.com
1-800-Authors (1-800-288-4677)

ISBN: 978-1-4697-9081-7 (sc)
ISBN: 978-1-4697-9082-4 (hc)
ISBN: 978-1-4697-9083-1 (e)

Printed in the United States of America

iUniverse rev. date: 04/09/2012

CHAPTER 1

Crane, Oklahoma. June, 1960.

I looked into the faded blue eyes, almost buried in the gaunt, seamed face of Early Dean. He was taller than my five-seven, broader too, heavier than my one-forty, but stoop-shouldered and work worn. He shuffled his feet and a worried look wrinkled his face even more. "I'm sorry, Dave," his voice came from deep in his chest. "You been a good hand and I got no complaints, but Troy here," he motioned with his head to the battered truck in the driveway and the rawboned man, sitting next to the tousle-haired girl. "Why he's got a wife and kids to feed and you know as good as any how hard times are."

I studied the gravel of the road, then looked up, "I know, Early. But I need a job too." Hauling hay wasn't much of a job but I had counted on it for the whole summer.

"I know you do Dave. But you know I can't use both of you." He glanced up at the mockingbird that was calling his war cry from the oak tree, close by. "I'm gonna have trouble just keeping Troy working." Anger crept into his voice now, and he growled. "You're just a kid, Dave. Troy here's, he's got a family to feed, kids... You know how it is."

"Yeah, Early, I know how it is," I looked away from the eyes that had grown hard, "I just wish..."

"I do too Dave," his voice softened. "I hate to let you go, but..."

"But Troy's got a family to feed." I smiled at Kathy. She was Early's sixteen-year-old daughter who drove the truck in the hay fields when she wasn't running the tractor, cutting, raking, and bailing the hay we hauled for the farmers and ranchers in the area. The ones that couldn't afford their own equipment. I looked back at Early. "It's alright, I ain't got no hard feelings, but maybe if things get better…"

"You'll be the first I call, Dave."

"And maybe, if you hear of someone else needing help, maybe you can…"

"I'll sure tell them to get hold of you. Call you here at your Daddy's."

"I'd appreciate it. I sure would."

"I'll do it," he held out a weather and work-battered hand.

I took it in a firm grip, the way Dad had taught me to shake hands. "It's been good, Early. You're a good man to work for."

"I appreciate that and I'm sorry I can't use the both of you," he said as he pulled a tattered billfold out of his faded blue jeans. "I figure you got twenty-six dollars coming for the last two days," he smiled. "Tell you what. I'll just make that an even thirty, for your trouble." He held out three tens.

"I thank you Early, for the bonus too. It wasn't necessary though."

He glanced away. "It was to me Dave, I hate to do things like this."

He scruffed the gravel under his feet purposely and I looked back at him, "I guess that's all that needs saying," I said and turned.

The door slammed on the battered truck. The engine started. I was almost to the house when Kathy yelled, "bye Dave, I'll see you around."

I waved at her as they drove off, took out my billfold and put the thirty dollars that represented two days of back-breaking, slave labor to move seventeen-hundred, thirty-some-odd, forty to sixty pound bales of hay. We loaded the bales on the truck in the sun-blistered fields, then unloaded and stacked them neatly in the top of an airless, overheated barn somewhere for a cent and a half a bale. But it was a damn sight better job than I had now.

I'd hoped to work the whole summer for Early, hauling, cutting and raking hay. I had my eye on a little 1953, Ford Coupe, a ticket to freedom that I could buy for two-hundred and fifty dollars. But now I had to find another job and I knew that might be tough.

Mom opened the screen door for me. "What's happened Davie?" Lines of worry wrinkled her forehead and eyes.

There was no easy way to say it. "I lost my job to Troy Calendar. He's got kids to feed." I walked on through the living room to the kitchen. The smell of the breakfast we had eaten still lingered in the air.

"That's too bad, Davie," Mom said from behind me, "But times is hard."

"I know how hard times are Momma, but I need a job too. I got things to buy, school clothes, and I'd like to have a car."

"I know, Davie," she poured two cups of coffee and sat with me at the metal-legged table. "They even made up a new word for how hard times is. They call it a 'recession' now instead of a depression, like when me and your father was young. But it means the same thing. People's out of work all over the country, not just here."

She touched my arm, "Davie, you ain't but seventeen. I know you need the work but Troy's got kids to feed. It's hard when you got kids to feed and you can't. It's hard watching your kids go hungry. It's something I hope you don't ever know."

I lit a cigarette, watching a fly crawl across the table. "I know, Momma. I'm not saying he didn't need the work more than me. I'm just saying I needed it too." My voice almost broke at the end.

She smiled then, "You'll find something else, Davie. I'll listen out for you and I'll tell Sara to listen too."

The fly reached a clear spot. I crushed it with a wire swatter, glad to hurt something. "Momma, you know I was lucky to get that job. You know there wasn't that much work around here, and now, what work there was is taken."

She gently patted my arm. "You found that job. You've worked every summer for the last four, you'll find something else. Just you wait and see. Your father found work. Things are beginning to open up a little. You'll find something."

I had to smile, but she was right. Dad had found work with the county, rebuilding the road to Madill. Who knows? I might even find something better than hauling hay. Anything I found would be easier for sure. The thirty dollars in my pocket came to my mind and the eighty I had saved from the last two weeks. One hundred-ten dollars, almost half what Fred Means wanted for the little Ford.

I smiled. "Yeah, Mom, I'll find something else. I got to find something else."

Her face lit up, "sure you will Davie." She brushed a strand of her dark brown hair, that was rapidly becoming salt and pepper with gray, behind her ear and looked at the clock. "Goodness, it's almost eight o'clock and I haven't even started on my housework."

She stood, "Davie, it would do your father proud if you was to do up some of the work around here today."

"Yeah, I guess I could start working the garden out, turning it and laying out a few more rows."

"That would be real good, Davie. Your father would like that."

My gaze traveled to the old elm tree that had fallen across the fence last winter in a high wind and generally messed things up. Dad and I had been cutting on it for a couple of weeks now but there was still a lot of work there. "I might even cut some on the old tree."

Mom looked that way, "just something. Your father will be disappointed if you don't do something."

"Yeah, I know." I took the coffee cups to the sink and went outside to the pump house. I got the shovel, then went to the far end of the garden. We had worked the ground here once but the Bermuda grass had almost taken it again and Dad wanted to plant a late crop here. I took off my shirt and started turning the ground. The moist, earthy smell of it came to me as I chopped the loamy clods into fine pieces. The work wasn't hard but it was boring and my mind went to the Blue River bottom where Early was working today. It would be hotter than blazes in there and the surrounding trees blocked what wind there was. Maybe Troy wouldn't think too much of hay hauling after today. But then, my mind went to his three ragged, big-eyed kids and I knew my job was gone. He'd do whatever it took to put food on his table, even stealing another man's job. Well, I'd go to town this afternoon and ask around. Maybe something would come up.

The next shovel turned up three fat earthworms so I got a can to put them in. A couple of more shovels full and I had a half-dozen. I crumbled some dirt on them and put them in the shade then turned my mind off, concentrating on the shovel work.

I'd finished turning the ground once after about two hours. It would take at least one more turning before it was ready to plant but it would have to set for a couple of days till the grass roots died. I put the shovel away and went into the kitchen, poured a glass of ice water from the jug we always kept in the refrigerator and sat at the table.

Mom came in and sat down with me. "Hot today?"

"Not too bad right now but it's going to be this afternoon. I think I'll go to town, just to ask around about work."

"Did you get the garden work done?"

"I got that piece at the far end turned again but it's going have to be done again before it's ready. I sure wish we had a rototiller." And remembering the old tree again, "and a chain saw. It sure would make things easier around here."

"We could use a lot of things around here, Davie, but we don't have the money for them."

"I know, I was just wishing. I dug some worms. I'll try to get me and dad a big catfish for supper after while."

"That would be nice. Do you want some dinner now?"

"No, I'm going to go on downtown." I went to the bathroom to clean up.

"You sure you don't want to eat?" Mom said over the rush of the water. "I'll fix you something."

"No, I'll be by the café after while and grab a hamburger."

"Okay," she said as I walked through the house to my bedroom. At least it was mine now. It had been both of my sisters, then mine and my brother's but they had left home to make lives of their own. Now, it was mine.

The ceiling was white, the walls blue. There was a girl's dresser and a mirror, left by my sister Ginger. A chest of drawers that didn't match, left by Betty. I had a double bed and a night stand with a radio and a reading lamp that I had bought. A gun rack, that I had built, hung on one wall and was adorned with a homemade Bois d' arc bow, a .22 rifle and a hunting knife. Several boxes of ammo sat on the shelf. A hunting vest, studded with shotgun shells, hung from a corner of the rack. A large picture of several mountains peaks, glaciers, a small lake and an old cabin hung on the opposite wall. I had found the picture out back of a five-and-dime store that had gone out of business and brought it home. I looked at it often with an empty longing. I loved mountains, and especially this picture of them. It was bleak in its starkness, lonely looking. I had made the frame myself.

I took the thirty dollars out of my billfold and pulled out the eighty I had saved, wondering if I'd ever get the chance to actually see a mountain glacier or anything outside of Crane, Oklahoma. Losing the job with Early wasn't the end of the world, but it was sure close.

I put the money away, keeping out ten. I grabbed a clean tee shirt, and hollered, "I'm gone, Mom."

"Okay, Dave," she said from the other bedroom and I crossed the yard to the road. The gravel crunched under my boots as I walked steadily down the hill. A breeze played across the narrow field on my right, bringing the dank smell of deep woods, spiced with the sharp tang of cedar from the trees farther over. The locusts were shrilling steadily now that the day had heated up and from a distance I could hear the rasping caw of a crow. The woods thinned giving way to grassland that had a lighter, dusty smell of grass withering in the still heat.

I topped the last hill then left the gravel road for the asphalt highway. A few minutes later I was walking through a tree-shrouded residential area with big houses that sat way back from the highway. Squirrels played on the yards that had been neatly clipped, almost manicured, by someone that didn't live there, and I wondered what it would be like to live in a house with more than five rooms.

Crane was practically deserted but it always was during the week. The clock and thermometer at the bank said it was eleven-thirty and ninety-four degrees but it seemed hotter with the sun radiating off the brick buildings. Only two old men sat on the concrete benches by the corner. On Saturday, there would be fifteen or twenty of them arguing about religion or politics or whatever old men argued about.

I crossed the street and went in the pool hall. My eyes took a second to adjust after the bright sunlight. The combined odors of chalk, leather, man-sweat, cigar and cigarette smoke, tobacco juice and dusty old building came to me. The sharp click of two ivory balls hitting was drowned by the crash of a rack breaking. There were four snooker tables close to the door, four pool tables farther back. All the way to the rear of the narrow building were the domino tables where some of the old men played. No matter what day it was there were always at least two domino games going on. Today was no exception. What was the exception was the number of men playing pool, snooker and dominos. Almost every table was full.

Denver, sat on one of the high stools that lined the wall. I went over and sat beside him. He was a tall, lanky guy who had ridden bulls in the rodeo before one of them fell on him, crushing his right leg, crippling him for life. He limped badly, but he worked out his arms and upper body constantly. He was terribly strong and terribly proud of it, making up, I guess, for his handicap. He glanced at me as if I wasn't worthy of the spoken greeting, but I said, "how's it going," anyway.

He nodded slowly, lighting a small, brown cigar, then drawled, "why ain't you working today?"

"Lost my job to Troy Calendar." I shrugged as if it didn't matter.

"Heard you was going too, day before yesterday," Denver grunted. He was a guy who knew everything that went on in town. "Don't feel bad about it," he added. "Early said you was a good hand but times is hard and Troy's got a family to feed."

I mumbled, "If I hear one more time about how hard times is and how Troy Calendar's got kids to feed, I think I'm gonna puke."

Denver scorched me with a glare. "Boy, times is hard!" he growled. "They're calling it a recession now, but if Hoover was President instead of Eisenhower, they'd call it by another name. And, no, I don't know of anyone that needs any help," he snapped in answer to my unasked question. "You see them boys playing pool back there?" He pointed with his chin.

I nodded.

"Well, them's the Perkins boys from Filmore. They been working up to the City for a couple of years. Now, they done come back here cause there ain't no work, even up there. And they got families to feed too. All you got is a car to buy."

I started to tell him that I had more than a car to buy. That car would eventually take me away from this one-horse town that seemed to be smothering me but I needed Denver and I had no need to make him mad.

Someone hollered, "rack!" from one of the pool tables and Denver limped to the table. He racked all the tables after each game and collected the money. If anyone got caught racking their own table they got kicked out and barred for a month. That was serious because the pool hall and the picture show were the only entertainment in the whole town.

While he was gone, Rocky Cobb came in and sat beside me on Denver's stool. He took out a comb, running it through his greasy black hair then cut his narrow eyes to me and said, "what do you know White? Say, you got a cigarette?"

I grinned, shaking one out to him. "I know you're sitting in Denver's place and he's gonna pull your arm off when he gets back."

"Piss on Denver," Rocky growled as he got up. "You want to play a game of snooker?"

"Yeah, might as well. There ain't nothing else going on. Go ahead and break them." I walked to the wooden rack that held the cue sticks and selected one. Denver limped back to his stool as the crash told me Rocky had broken the rack of balls. "Say, Denver," I said. "I'd appreciate if you kept an ear open for me."

He looked at me hard then nodded slightly. "I ain't never heard too much bad about you, Dave White. Everyone you ever worked for says you made them a hand. 'Sides, I like your mother. She's the best cook in this town. I'll keep an ear out for you." He turned, climbing back on his stool.

"Your shot, White," Rocky said, and I turned to the snooker table. "I made one on the break," he said as I bent over the table, lining up the white cue ball on a red ball near a corner pocket. "I thought you was working, hauling hay for Early Dean," Rocky said as I made the red ball and lined up on the six.

"I was, till today." I made the six, respotted it and took aim on another red ball. "Lost my job." The red ball dropped into the center pocket and I lined up on the four.

"You out of work then?" Rocky asked as I missed the shot.

"Yeah," I wrote my score on the small black board hanging on the wall. "But I'm looking for something else."

"We ought to go out West and cut wheat then." Rocky missed his shot.

I studied him curiously, "what are you talking about Rocky?"

He looked up slyly as if he had a great secret. "The wheat harvest, Man. All you got to do is drive a truck or a combine and keep them serviced. And they pay good money out West."

"Won't do me no good. I can't drive a truck." I made another red ball then missed the six. "Early or Kathy did all the driving. I just humped the bales."

"Well, whatever. I don't reckon you're wanting a job too bad." He made a red ball, then missed the seven.

"I'm wanting work bad, Rocky, but not bad enough to go chasing all over the country for a job I can't do."

"Okay, okay, it ain't no problem. It's just that I'm going out there soon and I wouldn't mind some company."

I looked up from the table. "Reckon you better find you someone else then. I got better sense than that." I made the red ball then the seven. I respotted the seven, and then missed a red ball.

"I'm telling you Dave, the money's good and the work ain't that bad."

I shook my head but then had second thoughts. "Tell you what, I'll think on it."

Rocky leaned on his cue stick. "Don't think on it too long, I'm leaving in a couple of days."

"Y'all gonna shoot snooker or jaw, jack all day?" Denver yelled. "I got people waiting on that table."

"You just hold on to yourself there." Rocky yelled back at him.

"How'd you like me coming over there and slapping shit out of you, Rocky Cobb," Denver said with an evil-looking smile.

Rocky bent over to shoot and I shut up. We finished the game and played one more before I decided to walk down to the café.

The heat outside was like a hammer now even under the shade of the store awnings and I was almost soaked with sweat by the time I had walked the two blocks to the other end of town.

The Crane café sat next to the Ford dealership and across the street from the picture show. Sara's old green Chevrolet was parked in its usual spot so I knew Mom got to work alright. Sara was the waitress and cashier, Mom was the cook. Together, they made up the two till ten shift of the café. Sara always picked Mom up at home to bring her to work. Mom was always trying to pay Sara for her trouble, but she wouldn't take the money. So Mom filled her car up with gas once a month.

Sara was only eighteen but she seemed older. She'd dropped out of school her junior year when she was sixteen, got married and moved to Ardmore. She came back about six months later and started working at the café. That had been just over a year ago. She lived alone now and dated grown men. Not that I blamed them. She was about five-two and only weighed about a hundred pounds, all in the right places. She had dark hair and green eyes with flecks of gold in them. Her teeth were tiny and straight and the purest white I'd ever seen. Her only flaw, that I knew of, was freckles. She had thousands of them on her arms and her face. I always wondered if they were all over the rest of her, but I knew, for sure, my chances of finding out were as remote as the stars I looked at from the top of the house on the nights I climbed up there to be alone.

She was sitting at her usual place in the back booth, facing the door. The smell of burned coffee was strong in the air combined with the smell of food being cooked. I got a pack of cigarettes from the machine then a Coke from the box behind the counter. Marty Robbins, moaning about a white sports coat, came from the big jukebox on which a large fan stirred the hot air.

Sara grinned, looking up from the crossword puzzle as I slid into the booth with her. "What's going on Kid?" Her voice had a musical tone with an underlying huskiness.

"Nothing but the heat."

She smiled, "I heard about your job. Too bad. I haven't heard anything, but I'll keep an ear out for you."

"I'd appreciate that Sara. Just about anything will do."

"How much do you have saved?"

"A hundred. I need two-fifty."

She grinned again. "That's a good price, and it's a good little car. I'll bet Gayle will like it. How is your love life anyway?"

"She was alright the last time I saw her but that was Sunday night. I thought I might get Dad's car and go over there tonight."

She shook her head, "not in your daddy's car you won't. There's a poker game tonight. I heard one of the mechanics at the Ford house talk about it."

"Are you sure?"

She smiled knowingly, "not positive, but that's what I heard. Maybe Robert will win enough to buy you that car." The jukebox went silent, Sara slid out of the booth, punched some buttons and Del Shannon, began singing, *Runaway.*

"Yeah, and maybe the sun will come up in the south tomorrow." I said over the music. "You know what kind of bills we ran up while Dad was out of work."

Sara smoothed her uniform and slid back in the booth. "Yeah, I know. And I know how tough it is, but things will get better." The door opened and a couple of men came in. Sara grinned at them.

"Just a cup of coffee, Sara," one of them said, "And, say, dump that out and make a fresh pot, if you would."

"Sure, thing Joe," Sara slid out of the booth. I watched her tugging her blue uniform into place as she walked to the counter. She had freckles on her lower legs too.

She joked with the men a second then went to the jukebox, which was silent again and dropped in a quarter. Sam Cooke started moaning about working on a chain gang.

One of the men watched her walk away. "Sara, when are me and you gonna run away from here?" Then he laughed.

Her laugh was a husky tinkling, "just as soon as you come up with about a million dollars and divorce your wife."

He grinned, "that's about what I thought. Never."

She laughed again. "Hell, Joe, you never know. You might make it someday, but give me a day or so warning before we have to leave."

"I'll do it Honey," he laughed then turned to the other guy while Sara poured their coffee. She came back to the booth, going back to her crossword puzzle.

Mom came out of the kitchen. A food splattered apron covered her white uniform. "Well, did you hear of anything?"

"Not really. But I've got Denver and Sara listening out for me. Between the two of them, they know everyone and everything that happens in this part of the state."

Sara laughed and added, "and most everything that is going to happen."

Mom laughed, "You hungry? You want something to eat?"

I glanced at the big clock over the jukebox. It was three o'clock. "Yeah, why don't you fix me a hamburger then I'm going back out to the house."

Mom nodded and went back to the kitchen. A second later I heard the sizzle of frying meat. Two highway patrolmen came in and Sara got up to wait on them. I turned the paper around opening it to the auto sales page, feeling my chances of getting a car this summer were pretty slim and getting slimmer.

Sara came back to the booth and lit a cigarette, looking at me. "You can use my car tonight, Dave, if you want to."

I grinned, "I'd sure appreciate that, Sara. I'll ask Dad first, but I'd sure like to see Gayle tonight. I'm feeling pretty low."

She patted my arm, "I can tell you do."

Mom came out with my hamburger and sat beside me again. I ate the burger, wishing I'd ordered two. When I finished I said, "I think I'm going on home."

Mom got up, "yes, it's getting pretty late. Your father will be home by five-thirty."

"I hate to tell him about the job. " I slid out of the booth.

"It's not your fault, Davie. You had no control over it," Mom said.

"I don't care. I still hate to tell him about it. I'm going home. I'll see you tonight." I walked to the door and outside. The heat was even worse as I started down the street. Both the old men were gone when I turned at the bank. It was an even one, hundred degrees.

When I got home, I went into my room and changed clothes, putting on my oldest and most ragged pair of jeans. I took down the .22 rifle and went back outside. I got two cane fishing poles from the pump house and the can of worms I'd left in the shade then started to the big pond across the road.

A bullfrog, big from the sound of him, was 'barumping' his love call and a great blue heron clumsily took flight then soared high into the light-blue sky as I started across the earthen tank dam. I baited both poles and set them in the deepest water, jamming the sharp ends into the soft ground to secure them. Then I lit a cigarette and sat in the shade of a huge oak tree to let the animals settle down some. After about ten minutes one line began jerking and I landed a nice three pound catfish. I killed and cleaned him then took the rifle and made a circle around the pond killing four big bull frogs as I went. When I returned to the poles, both were jerking. I had another three pounder and a smaller catfish on the lines. I turned the smaller one loose and cleaned the frogs and the other fish, then walked home.

I washed everything, put all of it in a pan of salt water to soak and turned on the TV to watch the last of *American Bandstand'*, 'The Mickey Mouse Club,' came on after that and when it was about half over, Dad walked in, sweat-soaked and flushed with the heat.

"What are you doing home so soon?" He was about my same height but forty pounds heavier, dressed in stripped overalls, a cotton shirt, and a red ball cap. He took off his cap, wiped his forehead with his shirt sleeve then replaced the cap in one easy motion. The sleeve was dark, almost dripping with sweat.

I followed him into the kitchen telling him what had happened. He nodded as he sat. "Well, it ain't no good deal, but you can't help that. You made Early a hand and that's all a mule can do."

I poured both of us a glass of water. "I caught some nice fish and killed four big bullfrogs for supper."

"You do any work around here today?" The tone of his voice was questioning, hard.

"Yeah, I turned the far end of the garden over again."

"That's good, long as you do something. I'll cook supper after I rest a bit." He took a bottle of whiskey out of the refrigerator and took a gurgling drink.

"Damn, it was hotter than a bitch out there today."

I nodded silently.

"I never knew a little old flag could get so heavy, and standing on the fresh asphalt is worse than having both feet stuck in a fire. I used to laugh at them old boys flagging traffic but it's just about the worse job I've ever had."

He took another drink of whiskey, then put the bottle back in the refrigerator.

"You gonna need the car tonight?" I asked, hoping against hope, knowing Sara was seldom wrong.

"Yeah, I got something to do tonight, why?" He took off his ball cap, wiping his forehead with his sleeve again.

"I thought I might run over to Connerville for a while to see Gayle."

"Maybe tomorrow night. I got things to do tonight." His tone said there was no need to ask further.

"Sara offered to let me use her car. How about that?"

He shook his head slightly. "I don't like you using her car Dave, but I guess it'll be alright. You put her some gas in, you hear?" He stood, "Now, get out of here while I fix supper."

"Alright." I headed to the bathroom to clean up and change clothes again. The food was ready by the time I finished.

Dad had rolled the catfish and frog legs in corn meal, and dropped them into deep grease that was hot enough to light a match. He broke an egg in the corn meal, added a little milk, salt and pepper. He rolled it into balls with diced onions and garlic then dropped them into the same grease, and fried up a plate full of sliced potatoes. He'd warmed the red beans left from supper last night and sliced up a side dish of pickles and onions.

When he finished eating, he pushed his chair back grinned and lit a cigarette. "Damn," he said, "I wonder what the poor folks is eating tonight."

I just shook my head, too full to talk. The hushpuppies had been crunchy on the outside, moist within. The catfish was flaky moist and not overdone, the potatoes, the same. The frog legs added a muddy, wild flavor, and the day-old beans were just the right addition to a full meal. I groaned, wondering if I'd ever be able to stand again when Dad said, "You want a ride to town, you better get them dishes done."

I groaned again as he walked into the bathroom to clean up. Finally, I got up, made dishwater and began cleaning the kitchen. I was finished by the time he was, leaving the dishes to drip dry. He'd changed into khaki pants and shirt and traded his ball cap for a Stetson. I noticed too the bulge in his right front pocket. He was evidently playing with the wild bunch tonight. He usually didn't carry his pistol.

We rode to town in silence, an old Hank Williams song, *Hey Goodlookin',* was playing on the radio and the late afternoon sun was glaring through the windshield. Dad let me off at the café. "Don't forget to be back about ten-thirty. Sara and your mother will be tired and ready to go home. And you be careful with that car."

"Okay, Dad. You be careful too."

He just grunted and drove away.

I went in the café, several people were eating, Mom and Sara were both busy, so I sat in the back booth alone. The paper was still open to the half-finished crossword puzzle. Sara got a break about then and sat beside me. She smelled musky, sort of a mixture of sweat and perfume that immediately made me wonder about those freckles, which made me start getting hard.

I smiled at her as she bumped me with her shoulder. "You still need the car tonight?"

"Yeah, if it's okay."

"Dave, if it hadn't been okay, I'd never offered it. You just mind your manners though and drive it right. Be sure to check the oil too. It burns a lot. And for God's sake, be careful, okay?"

"Okay Sara. I know how to drive."

She nodded but didn't smile. "Yeah, I know you know how to drive but that ain't all I'm talking about. You be careful with Gayle too. You two have been getting pretty chummy here lately and you're too way young to be saddled with a wife and a kid."

I could feel myself turning purple. "Sara! Gayle ain't like that," I choked out.

"Bullshit, Dave," she said low. "We're all like that. And if I didn't care, I wouldn't say anything but you're too good of a kid to get messed up. I don't know why, you little shit, but I like you. Now, I've got an order. The keys are in my purse. You do like I tell you, okay?" Her tone was joking but the look in her eye was dead serious as she smiled and squeezed my arm. "Dammit, I said, okay?"

"Okay, Sara," I finally said.

She slid out of the booth. "Sara." I said low, she turned. "I like you too, a lot."

She smiled softly, "I know you do," then she walked away.

I sat there a second, trying to figure out what had just happened. Then I decided that she and Mom had been talking and Mom was worried about me but she would never mention it. Dad neither. We didn't talk about sex around the house. Then I heard Sara laugh and crackwise to some guy at the counter and I knew she'd been thinking of me as a little brother or something and nothing more. It was a terrible let-down because, there for a second, I thought she might be jealous.

I got up slowly and went to the kitchen. Mom was working over the large grill and there was a whole sink full of dirty dishes. She smiled and wiped the sweat off her forehead with the back of her hand. I should stay and help her, I thought, but I heard myself say, "Sara said I could use her car, Mom. I'm going over to Gayle's."

"Be careful in Sara's car, Davie, and be sure to be back by nine-thirty."

"Okay, Mom," I fumbled in Sara's purse for the keys then walked out.

CHAPTER 2

The little Chevy ran smoothly at fifty but started straining at sixty so I held it down as I headed through the wooded hills north of town. Elvis was blaring a wild song about someone's little sister over the rushing wind noise but I wasn't paying any attention to it. My mind was on Gayle. She was about five-three and slender but strong, her body was hardened by doing the work of a man. Her hair was shoulder length and dark blond at the roots fading to almost platinum at the ends where it had been bleached by the sun. Her eyes were the dark violet of the sky in the east at sunset and twinkled when she smiled giving a bright contrast to her sun-tanned face and beautiful teeth. We'd been dating eight months. She wore my class ring on a chain around her neck.

The dying sun streamed in the car window. The wooded hills gave way to the flats, land that had been cleared and was once productive till it wore out. Now it grew native grass that was used for grazing cattle and cut for hay.

I left the highway at LeRoy's Bar, starting through a maze of gravel roads. I noticed there were hardly any cars parked out back as I passed the bar. LeRoy's was the local watering hole for all of the teenagers in the area and the place had only one rule: if you could see over the bar and thought you were bad enough to come in, you could drink.

LeRoy was a huge man, standing almost seven feet and weighing close to three hundred pounds. He had very little trouble at his place no matter who came in.

The sunset lit the whole sky with streaks of red, gold, pink, and blue as I crossed the pipe cattle guard under the fancy wrought iron sign of the Davis ranch. The road changed from cheap county gravel to high-dollar, crushed limestone but Davis could afford it. He was a millionaire out of Dallas that had bought several smaller adjoining places to make one of twenty-six hundred acres. Phil Stone, Gayle's dad, was his foreman and they lived on the place.

Phil looked like anything in the world but a ranch foreman. He was only five-four, and weighed about one-forty. His face was sunburned a fiery red instead of brown but it matched his thinning red hair. He wore a ball cap constantly instead of a cowboy hat and the top of his balding head was fish-belly white. It gave him a weird two-toned look the few times I'd seen him without the cap. He was said to know more about horses and cattle than any man in the whole county. Since the closes vet was thirty miles over to Durant, people with sick animals called on him constantly.

The Davis house loomed out of the twilight in front of me. It was a huge, rambling, Spanish type, two-story, built from native stone. Someone said it'd cost a quarter of a million dollars and I believed them.

I hated that house. I hated even driving past it, especially in a borrowed car. I hated the arrogance it oozed, the power that only big money can command. Mostly though, I hated it because it made me feel exactly how it was supposed to make me feel, small.

The last rays of the sun glinted on the fancy leaded windows, the ten foot, double door and the wrought iron that covered every opening. It was made to look decorative instead of the bars it really was. The sign in the drive said, *'Ranch Headquarters,'* and that got a good laugh from everyone that lived around here. Because everyone around here knew that all the decisions concerning this ranch were made in the modest white frame house a quarter-mile down the drive. The one with Phil Stone sitting on the front porch.

"Get in this house," Phil hollered as I got out of the car. "Wasn't expecting you over tonight or we'd have saved supper." He turned in his chair, yelling through the door. "Gayle, Gayle! Dave's here." Then he turned back to me.

"You hungry, Dave? They're just now cleaning the table."

I held my hand out, palm toward him. "No, thanks, Phil. I'm about to bust right now."

"Well then, how about a glass of tea?"

"I'll take that." I sat on the scuffed, bare porch beside his chair.

"Gayle, bring this boy some tea," Phil yelled, as she came through the door with a glass. She was wearing blue jeans and a sleeveless boys shirt, filling both of them out in all the right places. Her usual ponytail swung free behind her and she smiled, touching my hand as she handed me the tea.

"I didn't expect you over tonight," she sat beside me.

"I hadn't planned on coming over tonight til I lost my job today."

"Lost your job?" Gayle said with a rush.

I nodded, noticing Phil's cocked eyebrow. "Early hired Troy Calendar and let me go. He said Troy needed the work."

Phil shrugged, "that's tough Dave. I'm real sorry but...."

"Yeah," I cut in. "Times is hard and Troy's got a family, but that don't help me none."

Gayle put her hand on my shoulder. "I'm real sorry, Dave. You were counting on that job to buy your car."

"Don't look like I'll be able to now." I shrugged again. "It don't matter none."

Phil smiled, "I guess not. That car is all you've been able to talk about for the last couple of months."

A whippoorwill called from a distance. Another one answered him from closer. "Well, maybe something will turn up. I've got everyone in town looking for me."

"I'll keep my ear out for you too," Phil said. "I wish I could use you here on the ranch, but I'm full up right now."

"It wouldn't matter, Phil. I don't have no way of getting out here."

He stood, "I guess that would be a problem at that." He walked in the house.

I kissed Gayle lightly on the lips. "You think we might be able to go somewhere for a little while? I've got to be back at nine-thirty."

She nodded, "I'll go ask." She went into the house, banging the screen door. The evening star hung low in the west over the last purple of the sunset. A gentle breeze blew across the meadow cooling the parched earth as I sipped my tea. Gayle came out smiling a second later. "Dad said we could go for a little while."

I stood, "alright, at least something good is going to happen today." The whippoorwill hollered again as we walked to the car.

Gayle snuggled close to me after we got away from the house and as we passed the big house she looked up dreamily. "I want a place like that someday."

"What for?" I said over Ben E. King, sighing, *Stand by Me,* from the radio.

"I don't know. I just want to be important someday. You know, have a big house, lot's of money and then people would look up to me."

That statement went all through me. "I don't like people who live like that, people who have big houses, four times what they need and expect other people to look up to them cause they're rich. I met Davis once, he's an overbearing son of a bitch and that sign, 'Ranch Headquarters,' proves it. He don't know which end a cow pisses from."

Gayle laughed. "You're just jealous because Harland brings me nice things when he comes."

"Oh, so it's Harland now!" I slammed on the brakes to avoid hitting a rabbit and skidded to a full stop. "And you think I'm jealous of a sixty-five-year-old man screwing around with a fifteen-year-old girl?"

I pulled her to me kissing her hard. She melted against my chest, running her fingers through my hair. I broke the kiss, looking deep in her eyes. "When Harland gets to do that, I'll be jealous."

She smiled coyly, "and how do you know he hasn't?"

I laughed, pushing her away and driving on. "He's still alive. If Phil Stone even thought such a thing, he'd have that old man's balls for breakfast."

Her laugh was a musical tinkle over the radio. "Maybe it's already happened and neither of you know it."

I knew instinctively she was baiting me. That was the one thing about her I hated and she did it constantly. She was the prettiest girl I'd ever dated and one of the prettiest in the whole county, but she knew it and she flaunted it. But she was still the prettiest girl I'd ever dated and I was crazy about her so I put up with it.

"Well?" she said, when I didn't answer.

"Well, what?" I pulled onto the gravel road with a bump.

"What if it's already happened?" Her voice had a hidden laugh.

"I don't guess there's a helluve a lot I can do about it. If you want that old son of a bitch kissing on you, that's your business."

She laughed but then her face went hard in the lights of the dashboard. "Well, I haven't but if I thought it would get me away from cow shit and horses, I would."

"I thought you liked horses." I pulled in behind LeRoy's just as a big eighteen-wheeled, road rig thundered by on the highway, drowning out the honky-tonk jukebox. I couldn't help watching his lights disappear into the darkness, wondering where he was going.

"I do like horses," she said. "As long as someone else has to feed'em and muck out the barn. I like to ride the things, that's all. Someday though, I'll have someone else to do the nigger work. You'll see."

"Yeah, I'll see. Someday I'll hire that someone else for you. How about that?"

She smiled at me, "and buy me a big house like Harland's?"

"And buy you a big house like Harland's. And get us away from Crane, Oklahoma." I heard myself saying the words but I didn't believe them anymore than she did. Then another truck roared by and the trapped feeling I had, grew until it almost swallowed me. I mean, who was I trying to kid? "Come on let's go in," and I took her by the arm, leading her to the door.

LeRoy's Bar was a lean-to shed built on the back of a house. There were two, coin-operated, pool tables in the center of the room, a full-sized shuffleboard table against one wall, a half-dozen tables and chairs scattered about. A big, thumping jukebox took up one whole corner. A homemade bar blocked the entrance to the back portion of the house where LeRoy lived with whomever he could entice to live with him. Usually it was the extra girl he had working at the bar but now only old Mable was working. And Mable looked like she had crawled out from under the house after it had been built a while. Beside the bar was a huge recliner from which LeRoy surveyed his domain when he was here. Tonight he wasn't but that didn't surprise me any, knowing about the poker game.

Mable eyed us boredly from behind the bar. I ordered a beer for me and a soft drink for Gayle, nodding to the one old man at the bar. Other than him the place was empty. I sat beside Gayle in one of the booths and drank half the beer in a guzzle, a feeling of hopelessness and frustration growing in me. Gayle put her hand on my arm. "What's wrong tonight Dave?"

I shook my head wondering about Gayle. "I've lost my job and I've got no chance of finding another. I'm sick of Crane. I'm sick of this whole part of the country and I have no chance of getting out until I graduate. Maybe I can go up to the City then and get away from here. Maybe I can get a car then."

"I know it's rough, Dave, but you'll find something. Maybe Dad will have some work in a week or so. Besides, you can still drive your dad's car."

Her seriousness surprised me. "Hey, aren't you the one that wanted the big house with the nigger to hold your horse?"

"Well, I still have Harland Davis for that. I have you for other things." She ran her hand along the inside of my thigh, whispering, "why don't we get out of here?"

She smiled openly when I cocked an eyebrow, slid out of the booth and we walked out into the night.

The Big Dipper stood out brightly in the north, a waxing moon was directly overhead. A dog barked from somewhere in the distance and another truck roared by on the highway, its tires singing a lonely whine.

Gayle snuggled close to me in the car as I drove away. The night was alive with movement, bull bats dived at the headlights and night bugs smacked against the windshield. A possum scurried across the road then a rabbit froze at the road's edge, trapped in the headlights. The night breeze was cool making the heat from Gayle's body seem more apparent as she moved even closer to me. After about a mile I stopped and killed the engine leaving the radio playing. I pulled her close to me, kissing her deeply. Gayle kissed me long and slow, moving slightly when I slipped my hand inside her shirt.

"This makes me almost glad you lost your job," she whispered huskily, moving slightly. "That feels

good."

"I don't mind losing the job as much as I mind not being able to buy the car. Fred won't hold it forever."

"That's all you can talk about anymore, just that old car." She tried to sit up but was trapped by my hand inside her shirt. "Here," she struggled briefly. "Help me undo this thing."

I moved my hand and she sat up, unbuttoning the shirt. I fumbled one-handedly with the clasp on her bra, then snapped it open. She turned, lying across me, cradled by my left arm.

She smiled, closing her eyes, whispering. "That feels good."

"Why don't you take it all the way off?" I pulled at her loose bra.

I looked out at the stars. "Gayle, you know I love you."

"I know you do, Dave, and I love you too. But this is far enough."

I shrugged silently, looking back at the stars cold and remote in the moonlit sky. "Do you ever just want to go---somewhere?" The moonlight playing shadows gave her a soft sensuous look, almost glowing in the half-light.

She smiled. "Sometimes, but I don't let it bother me."

"Why not? It bothers me."

Her face wrinkled in thought. "Because, well...I don't know. I'd like to have a big house, like Davis's, but I want it here."

"Why here, for God's sake?"

She moved slightly. "It's scary out there. Besides, Daddy's here and you're here. Why would I want to leave?"

"Just to see what's out there. Just to see the other side of that hill over there. I can't explain it."

She hugged me close. "Isn't here good enough? Your folks are here, your home, me."

I kissed her lightly, hearing the whippoorwill's lonely call. "Sometimes it's enough, but sometimes … I feel like I have to go. But I don't know where and I don't know how, much less why. Sometimes I spend hours just looking at road maps wondering what's there, who's there, what it looks like."

"Aren't you happy with me Dave?"

"Sure, I'm happy with you. I love you, Gayle, but--I guess that's it, just but… I can't explain it."

She touched my face. "You'll get to go someday. I can feel it in you."

"Someday isn't good enough. I'll be dead someday. I had it all planned. I could buy that car this summer and next summer I'd be free. I could go anywhere I wanted."

"How about me? What am I going to do when you leave?"

"I hadn't thought that far ahead, Hon. You still have three years of school. By then, I'd have a good job up in the mountains and I could come back for you. We could be married then."

She smiled. "I may not be here when you come back. I may not want to waste my time sitting around the house. There are other boys, you know."

I felt my whole body stiffen against my will but then she pulled my head down, kissing me long and deep. I slid my hand down her stomach unbuttoning the top button of her blue jeans. She let me unbutton the second one before she touched my hand. I nodded, slipping my hand inside her panties, feeling the silky curve of her belly, my fingers stretching further than I'd ever gone before.

She moaned softly, then touched my hand again whispering. "Dave, please…. I'm sorry." Her voice was husky with emotion, her face strained in the moonlight, her eyes searching mine. "I want you too," she whispered. "But I'm afraid."

"It's okay, Gayle," I heard myself say tonelessly. "We're going to have to leave in a minute anyway. It's after nine-thirty."

"You're not mad at me, are you?"

I shook my head. "No, I'm not mad at you."

"I'm afraid you wouldn't like me anymore if we went any farther. What if someone found out? What would I do then?"

"Who the hell is going to find out?" My voice was harder than I had meant it to be. "I love you. Do you think I'd blab it to the world? Is that what you think?"

Her eyes grew worried. "You're mad at me, aren't you?" her voice quavered.

"No, I'm not mad. This has just been a bad day, all the way around."

"I love you." She moved my hand back to her stomach, smiling at me. When I didn't go any further, the worried look came back to her eyes. She moved her pelvis, whispering low. "You can do it now, if you want too."

But it was too late. "No Gayle, we have to go. I have to pick up Mom and Sara. And I need to go down the road a minute before we leave." I moved and she sat up.

"Dave, I was just teasing you tonight, you know, about Harland and all, and going out with other guys. I wouldn't do that. You know that, don't you?"

I got out of the car. "I know you were, but it's getting a little old." I walked down the road a hundred feet or so and breathed a sigh of relief as my painful erection shrank while I urinated, looking at the stars.

She smiled at me as I got in. Then she moved to me, kissing me. "I love you, Dave. Don't be mad at me. Okay?"

I held her close kissed her softly. "I love you too, Gayle Stone, but sometimes you're a pain." I started the car and drove her home.

The windows on the big house glinted evilly in the moonlight as I drove back past, almost as if they were smiling, causing a sudden jealous rage to fill me. A rage that passed just as suddenly into emptiness. By the time I got back to Crane, the emptiness had changed to total depression bordering on despair and I was almost crying.

Sara noticed it as soon as I walked in the empty café. She touched my arm, "What's wrong Dave?" Her voice was full of real concern.

I shook my head. "Nothing really."

"Sure, there is. Did you and Gayle have a fight?"

"No, that's not it."

"What is it then?" Her eyes searched mine.

I sat in a booth. She sat beside me. "I don't know Sara. Everything just seemed to fall in on me. I just feel like I'm trapped here and I'll never be able to get out."

Suddenly I felt as if I sounded like a whining kid and looked at her, half expecting to see her laugh, but she touched my hand again. "Things will work out. I know you feel bad but it's not the end of the world. Things will get better. You've only been out of work a day. Give it some time, something will turn up."

"I just don't feel like I have time."

"I know it seems that way but really, you've got your whole life ahead of you. Don't try to grow up so fast or you'll wind up like me." Her voice turned hard at the last and her green eyes turned sad.

I thought about what she'd said a second while Kitty Wells sang, *Touch and go Heart.* "What's wrong with you? You seem to be in pretty good shape to me."

She frowned, wrinkling her forehead. "I'm too old for myself. I grew up too fast. I was married at sixteen and divorced at sixteen. I missed out on the fun of growing up and now, I'm eighteen, going on thirty. I'm too young for the ones I run with and too old for the ones I should be running with." She looked perplexed, "do you understand what I'm trying to say?"

I shook my head. "No, not really." A big truck passed the café, exhaust pipes roaring as he built up speed to climb the hill out of town.

"Well, it's good in a way that you don't," Sara continued. "What I'm trying to say is that I should still be going to school dances and out parking with boys when instead, I'm going to nightclubs over at Ardmore and to bed with grown men. I've seen too much and I've done too much to be only eighteen. Now, do you understand?"

I could feel myself blushing as I nodded, "Sort of, but not really. It really sounds like fun to me."

She smiled sadly. "It did me too, when I was sixteen, but I missed out on a lot of fun. Don't let that happen to you okay? Losing that job may be the best thing that ever happened to you." The gold flecks sparkled in those fantastic eyes of hers that showed worry and concern.

"How do you figure that?"

She shook her head. "You've been working since you were thirteen. Maybe this summer you can have a little fun."

"How can I have fun with no car and no money?"

She shrugged, "that's a problem and you're right. There is not much way to have fun without money, not here anyway. Well, I've got to get this place cleaned up and get the hell out of here." She looked at me, "You feel any better?"

"No, not really," but then I saw the disappointment cloud her face and I said, "yeah, I guess so." I nodded, "yeah, I feel better. Just knowing you care makes me feel better."

She smiled broadly and suddenly kissed me on the cheek. "Thanks, Dave, and I do care." She slid out of the booth and began clearing the cash register.

I swept and mopped the floor while mom finished in the kitchen. Sara met us at the front door. As I pulled it closed, Sara bumped me with her hip. "Goodnight Asshole," she whispered, then giggled.

I squeezed her arm. "Thanks for letting me use your car."

"No problem. Anytime."

Mom and I got in the car and Sara drove us home in silence. Dad was still gone. Mom went on in the house but I stayed outside sitting on the porch swing, listening to the crescendo of crickets, tree frogs and other animals and insects that filled the night. From far away I heard the shriek of a dying rabbit, the only sound a rabbit ever makes. A coyote yapped from the woods in back of the house and from way down on the creek came the rarely heard, long-drawn, howl of a wolf that sent shivers up my back. Pretty soon Mom's bedroom light went out and I climbed up on the roof.

The waxing moon hung low in the west giving the stars more brilliance in the dark sky. The great arc of the Milky Way split the sky from north to south and Polaris gleamed coldly in line with the Big Dipper pointing the way north. My mind had wandered, flitting over the happenings of the day when I heard the truck climbing the hill on the highway a half-mile away. The engine strained, then died, revved and came back louder and more throaty as the driver down-shifted. It made a sad, lonely sound in the night and I wished I was riding shotgun with him, going? It didn't matter where. I figured anywhere was better than being here.

Pretty soon I climbed down and went to bed.

CHAPTER 3

The next couple of days passed slowly with me turning the garden twice more. Mostly, I hung around the phone waiting with a growing desperation but to no avail. Oh, it rang a few times but there was never any mention of work. There was no need for me to go looking for a job. If anyone was needing help either Sara or Denver would hear about it and contact me.

Dad had been real edgy since the poker game so I figured he'd lost. He never said and I was smart enough not to ask. Mostly, I just stayed out of his way. He was easy enough to get along with most of the time especially when things were good but when they weren't, he could be like a bear with a sore tooth. The problem was I never really knew how to tell his moods and even at that, they could change in the wink of an eye. So by the time Saturday rolled around I was ready for a break.

Crane was totally different when I walked down the big hill about noon or so. All the parking places on Main street were filled and people crowded the sidewalks. The concrete benches by the bank had a full load of old men, spitting tobacco juice and arguing. The pool hall was full too. Every table was occupied and had a waiting list. Mose Wall, an old Negro, was helping Denver rack the tables and the domino tables were three deep in watchers. I waited until a stool came empty, then grabbed it and just watched. Denver limped by nodding at me but it was just a hello nod. If he had heard anything I would have known. I nodded back, knowing better than to bug him. Denver was real touchy too.

A couple of guys my age came in and walked to me. We talked a second, trying to decide whether to wait on a snooker table or to go swimming in the creek that ran through town,

I heard someone holler, "Rack," and a table came open so me and a guy named Rick took it. I lost two games before I climbed back on the high stool and watched the crowd slowly change from farmers and ranchers in town to do their shopping to younger men and kids like myself, in town because it was Saturday night. Pretty soon I got tired of that and started down to the café.

Just as I walked outside I saw Dad's car parked in front of the Soldiers' Tavern so on a wild chance, I went in. The place smelled of stale beer and cigarettes. A honky-tonk jukebox was thumping, *Big Bad John,* by Jimmy Dean, from a corner. Several people, men and women, were drinking. A few were playing pool. Dad was setting at the bar and smiled as I sat beside him. His face was flushed and his eyes were beginning to glaze. "What's going on Davie?" he said.

"Not much. I was just wondering if I could use the car tonight."

He nodded slightly. "I don't see why not. You been doing some good work this week. Have you heard anything about a job?"

"No, but I still got everyone looking for me."

"That's good. You keep looking. Maybe something will turn up."

The waitress, a young woman, pretty in a hard fashion, stopped singing with the jukebox. "You want anything Dave?"

I shook my head and she went back to her singing, *Night Life,* along with Patsy Cline. Dad nodded, "Yep, you been working real smart out there this week." He handed me the car keys. "Here you go, I reckon I can find me a way home."

"You sure now?"

"Yeah, no problem. You go on and have your fun. Tell Phil I said hi."

"I will, Dad," turned to leave wondering about my luck. It wasn't often I got the car at three o'clock in the afternoon.

I drove on down to the café which was practically empty. Sara was in her usual station, working on the crossword puzzle. She looked up briefly as I sat down. "What's happening Dip Shit?"

"Nothing but the heat. Dad's feeling good though. He already let me have the car."

She didn't look up. "He lost about a hundred the other night."

"I figured as much. He's been real touchy all week."

"There's another game tonight, out at your house. A small one though."

"Maybe he'll win it back."

"Could be," she smiled nervously. "Dave, I haven't heard a thing about a job. I mean, nothing of any kind." She took a deep breath. "Fred sold the car."

The disappointment went through me like a knife. "You--you sure?"

She nodded, touching my hand. "A guy heard about it and offered him three hundred. He took it. Dave, he had to take it. I'm sorry."

I felt the tears coming and tried to blink them back but I missed a couple. Sara smiled, squeezing my hand, blinking hard too. "Dammit, stop that," she said roughly. "It ain't the end of the world."

"It's damn close. No job, no car, no chance of either. My God! I hate this town."

She smiled, "I know Dave. I know you do. I do too."

"Well, why did you come back then?"

"I don't know. This place is weird like that. Almost everybody that leaves, comes back."

"If I ever get away, I damn sure won't."

She squeezed my hand again, just smiling at me. "Why don't you go on out to Gayle's. Maybe she can help you."

"Maybe she can but I doubt it. I don't think anything can help me now, unless you have a couple of million you can give me."

She laughed, causing her freckles to stand out. "Fat chance of that. I can't even pay attention. But I can take your mother home tonight though, so you go on and have a good time." A couple state troopers came in and she got up to wait on them, stopping at the jukebox first. One of the troopers, an older guy, looked at me. I nodded to him, turned the paper around and opened it to the auto sales page, trying not to cry.

Tommy Mullen came in just then and sat beside me saying, "how's it going?" His mom and step-dad owned the café.

I shook my head and told him what had happened since I'd seen him last.

"Man, that's rough. That was a nice little car. Say, April and Lester are in. They're out at the house. You want to run out there for a while?"

I shrugged. Normally I would have jumped at the chance. I'd been in love with Tommy's sister, April Rose, half my life and her husband, Lester was a professional rodeo rider. They lived on the road going from city to city, rodeo to rodeo. And they could tell some tales about places I'd only heard of, cities like Prescott, and Cheyenne, Phoenix, Dallas, Denver, Helena, and the biggest rodeo of all, Madison Square Garden, in New York City, where Lester had finished second last year in the National Finals.

"Yeah," I said. "Yeah, let's go." We walked out.

We took his car, a little '50 Ford Coupe, and drove to his step-dad's, Louis Jorden's place about three miles from town, talking about nothing on the way. Tommy had been my best friend since we had started the first grade and I'd spent the night at his house at least once a week since then. Until the trouble started that is.

April Rose was five years older than Tommy. They'd had some real problems about nine years ago, real problems. She and her mother had been accused of being witches by half the town. Dad had got a big laugh out of that but it got serious enough to get them kicked out of the church they attended. That was enough to cause them to lose the crop they had planted because they had no help at harvest time. Tommy's dad committed suicide right after that. And right after that there was a lot of talk about April Rose being real loose. She left home then. She walked away one night when she was only fourteen and just disappeared for about eight years.*(A Minor Occurrence)* The sheriff found her bloody dress out on the twelve-mile-prairie. Everyone except her mother thought she was dead.

I had heard a lot of talk when she showed up again about a year ago, married to Lester. Some said she had been working in a whorehouse. Some said she'd been driving a truck. She said she'd been working in a bar. I believed her. She talked about the bar some but she also talked about driving eighteen wheeled trucks. The big road-rigs that I loved to hear go by on the highway.

We had never paid much attention to all the talk back then. Tommy practically lived at my house after his dad killed himself and April left. After that, his Mom and Louis got married and things turned out alright for him, better for him than I had it.

He had a car.

We turned off the Bullet Prairie road onto the road leading to Tommy's house and by now I was feeling some better. Tommy was quite a guy. He was four inches taller than my five-seven and weighed about one-eighty. He took after his mother who was five-eleven and weighed over two hundred pounds. But he was a happy guy, one that was nice to be around. He was always laughing and joking and cutting up. Gayle and I double-dated sometimes with him and Carol, his girl. She was just like him, a lot of fun to be around.

Sometimes I wished I was more like Tommy instead of like I was. He was happy in Crane and wanted nothing more than to stay here and raise cattle. I, on the other hand, went a little crazy just listening to the geese fly over in the spring hearing them call to each other, wishing I could go with them. I knew where they went in the fall. A lot of them wintered on the game refuge just outside of town. But in the spring when they headed back north they seemed to call to me. And their call seemed to reach down deep inside me where it touched something primitive. Something that told me it was time to move on, to go somewhere, anywhere, just go.

I'd read that America was the home of the wanderers, the restless people. The ones that hadn't been satisfied where they were and had moved on to something, somewhere, else. I knew that every person in this country, including the Indians, had come here from somewhere else. I guess I was one of the rovers and it ran deeper in me than most. I didn't know why, and it was really a curse.

Tommy stopped the car, bringing me back to here and now. We walked to the large, rambling wood frame house. Lester, April Rose, Louis and Reba were sitting on the wide, covered porch that ran around two sides of the house. April stood and walked to me. She was a tiny thing, only about five-one and didn't weigh even a hundred pounds. She was wearing blue jeans, boots and a western-style shirt with snaps instead of buttons. Her hair was long and pale blond and when she grinned at me her bright blue eyes sparkled and danced with lights.

She hugged me, saying, "Dave, it's good to see you." And she meant it, cause then she kissed my cheek. There had been a time when my house was the only one in town open to her brother. Neither of them had forgotten.

Reba got up. She and April went in the house while Lester stood and shook my hand. He was half-Chickasaw, dark-complected with jet-black hair just going to gray over his ears, and had pale blue eyes that could freeze a man. Word had it that he killed his best friend in Korea to keep from leaving him wounded and freezing on the battlefield. I didn't know for sure, but somehow I didn't doubt it. *(A Minor Occurrence)*

The town had been named after his great, grizzled, grandfather, Standing Crane, who had been the last war chief of the Chickasaws. He'd died on the Trail of Tears, back in the early eighteen-hundreds when the Federal Government had moved all the Indians from Mississippi, Georgia and Tennessee to Oklahoma. His family had lived in Crane ever since.

"How's it been going, Dave?" Lester said, sitting back down.

"Pretty good. How's it been with you?"

"Pretty good. We drove in from Denver last night. Got another rodeo in Fort Smith, in about three days."

"What's Denver like?"

"It's pretty up there. Snowcapped mountains to the west and prairie to the east. We came down through the mountains from Santa Fe. It's sure a pretty drive. Lot's of snow still on the mountains. Some on the road."

"How did you do in the rodeo?'

"Okay," he said. "I took first in the bareback and saddle bronc, but I lost out on the bulls to an old boy named Jim Shoulders. Now, that boy can ride bulls."

Reba and April came back out just then with glasses of tea and I noticed the bulge in April's back pocket. I knew what it was, a big, switch-bladed knife that she was never without.

She and Reba sat just as Louis said, "I don't know why you want to live like you do. Just roaming from pillar to post, never staying in one place long enough hardly to eat."

"I'll settle someday," Lester said. "But right now," he reached out, taking April by the hand. "We're happy just seeing the country. I'm good at what I do and I like doing it. We'll come home someday, settle and maybe have a kid or two. Right now this is good enough."

And I felt something in me tear, leaving a gaping wound. Coming out here, right now, had not been the good idea I'd thought it was. Both of them started then, telling of the places they had been, the things they had seen. And for the next hour or so all I heard were tales of exactly what I wanted to do. I just didn't know how I was going to do it.

Tommy and I left after a couple of hours with the names still ringing in my ears. Calgary, Billings, Great Falls, Boise and the restlessness in me had re-doubled to the point I thought I would burst.

Tommy dropped me off at the café and I got in my car, without going in, and drove out to Gayle's.

CHAPTER 4

$$\sim\!\!\!\!\!\!-\!\!\!\!\!-$$

The moon was beginning to dip in the west and the late-night was filled with a total stillness. The cigarette I flipped out the open window streaked in a fiery arc until it smashed in a silent explosion of sparks on the high-dollar, crushed-rock driveway. Gayle's white blouse gleamed in the dark on her side of the car ending abruptly at her dark skirt. She stared straight ahead, not speaking.

Finally I said, "Look, Gayle, I said I was sorry."

"Well you should be. I'll swear, Dave White. I thought you had four hands tonight." Her voice was hard, her tone strident.

"I stopped when you said to." I put my hand on her shoulder.

"You didn't stop trying though!" was her sullen reply.

I moved my hand back to the steering wheel. "No, I didn't. I don't know why I didn't. It's just like I can't tell you how I feel." I hit the steering wheel.

"If you're going to start that again, you can just take me home." Her eyes flashed in the dark. "I'm tired of hearing about how bad you feel."

"And you still don't understand, do you?"

"I'm just tired of hearing about it."

"Gayle, it's more than a feeling." I touched her shoulder again. "I needed something tonight, maybe some kind of reassurance. I feel like everything is caving in on me. Don't be like this, not right now. I need you tonight." I pulled at her shoulder.

She smiled slightly. "Promise to keep your hands to yourself?"

I let go of her shoulder and started the car. "I feel like I'm talking to a friggin brick wall. You haven't heard a word I've said. Nothing I've said all night. And if you did hear, you damn sure didn't understand." I pulled the car in gear and drove away.

She slid across the seat as I drove away. "Dave, stop the car. I didn't mean it. Don't be mad at me."

"I'm not mad Gayle," I drove on. "I'm just tired."

She rubbed my shoulder, "Are you tired of me. Is that it?"

"I'm just tired of trying to talk to you. I'm tired of trying to explain things you don't care about, much less understand."

"I love you, Dave. I really do," her voice trembled.

"I know you do. I guess I'm just not good company tonight and I'm sorry I went so far. I just--just--I can't explain it tonight." The big house passed in the dark. Her white house gleamed in the moonlight.

"Can you come over tomorrow?" Now her tone was almost pleading.

"I don't know."

I wish you would stop the car. They haven't seen us yet."

"It doesn't matter." I drove on.

"I don't want you to go home mad at me."

"I told you, I'm not mad. I'm just tired."

"Will you come over tomorrow?"

I stopped in front of her house, "Yeah, I'll be over tomorrow." I walked her to the door. "I'm sorry about tonight. I just…I'm just sick over all of it."

She kissed me softly covering her breast with my hand. "I acted real bad too, but it will be better next time." She smiled, "you'll see."

"That doesn't matter anymore. It just doesn't matter."

"It'll be better," she smiled again. "You'll see." She kissed me again, then turned and went in.

I walked back to the car shaking my head, wondering if she'd heard anything I'd said all night. I'd tried to tell her about what I felt but either I didn't have the words or her head was somewhere else. But then she was one who didn't feel the pull of the tides and the calling of the moon. One that didn't climb up on the house like I did, to watch the clouds swirl and roil, piling into each other until the great thunderheads grew tall and flat on top when the massive storms were building. She feared the thunder and lighting whereas I loved it when the Gods cracked their knuckles so loud the ground shook with the roar and the whole sky was lighted with fiery bolts that sometimes walked the earth.

I started the car and backed out still wondering how someone couldn't stand in awe of the rolling thunder. I wondered how people could be content to spend their lives in the same spot. The big house grinned evilly at me as I passed. I gave it the finger.

It understood how I felt, even if she didn't.

*   *   *

The poker game was still in progress when I got home. We had a real nice chicken house but no chickens anymore so it made a good place to play poker or whatever. Sometimes I would go in and watch them play, but not tonight. Tonight, the frustration and despondency I'd been feeling all week was worse than ever and seeing Gayle had only added to it. Talking to April and Lester hadn't helped either, so tonight I went straight to the roof.

I don't remember when I started climbing on the roof, or even why. I did it now to be alone, to be able to think. The moon was all but gone in the west and the stars were alive in the inky blackness of space, tens of hundreds of millions of them burning bright pinpoints of light that I never tired looking at. I felt the same when I looked deep into a flickering fire. I could just let my mind go, to wander or remember or to plan. Tonight, there was no need to remember or plan so I just let it wander. A meteor streaked across the western sky and I almost made a wish but then smiled at myself for being so childish. I'd learned early on that work, not wishing, got things accomplished. But still, it didn't cost anything, so I wished for a job. After that I just let go, cleared my head and roamed the stars for a long time, wondering what was there and wishing I could go. Then I climbed back down and went to bed. The poker game was still going strong.

Dad woke me the next morning like he always woke me, by standing in the door and yelling. I hated to be woke up like that but if he knew, he didn't let it bother him. I stumbled to the kitchen, still half asleep, and poured a cup of coffee while Mom put breakfast on the table. A look from Dad would curdle milk and I had a feeling this wasn't going to be a very good day.

Then Dad said, "just forget whatever you got planned for today. Me and you are gonna get some of this work done around here..."

I said, "Fred Means sold the car."

He snapped out. "I don't give a damn what Fred Means done. Besides, that's a good thing anyway. We can't afford two cars." His tone said, 'don't talk back,' but I couldn't let it go.

"I was going to pay for it," I tried to keep my voice calm.

"Yeah, but you ain't got no job now." His words dripped with sarcasm.

"I'll get one!" I hissed, trying not to raise my voice.

"Well, until you do, you can work around here some. Me and you is gonna cut up that old tree today. How do you like that?" His tone and his eyes dared me to say something back.

Which I didn't, knowing that anything I said would come out wrong and cause more trouble that I would be sorry for later.

But Dad wouldn't let it alone. "Well! I asked you a question young man. I said, '*how do you like that!*'" There was no question in the statement he had growled.

"I guess that will be alright, Dad," I said low, biting my lip. "I didn't have anything planned for today anyway." I had learned long ago that the best way to handle him was to just keep quiet and do what I was told. Nothing else would work and today was no exception. I'd go along with whatever he said and it would blow over.

"Well," he growled, going back to his paper. "It's a damn good thing."

Mom smiled and squeezed my shoulder as she put breakfast on the table so I knew I'd done good. But, as I ate, I couldn't help wonder just how much money he had lost last night.

Nothing else was said while we ate but just afterwards, I went to the pump house and got the old two-man, cross-cut-saw that my grandfather had bought fifty years ago. The sun was well up and hot already so I didn't figure we'd work long, and I was right. The old tree was four feet thick and seasoned out hard as a rock. After we had sawed through it four times then split and stacked what we had cut, Dad wiped his brow with his sleeve and said that was enough. I put the saw back and went on in the house.

Sara had already picked Mom up so after I cleaned up and changed clothes, I figured, what the hell, I had nothing to lose and asked Dad for the car.

He was tired but not over his mad yet.

"I don't see any reason for you to need the car."

"I'd like to go see Gayle today."

"You seen her. just yesterday and again the other night when you borrowed Sara's car."

"I know I did, but I told her I'd come out again today."

He glared at me. "Well, you told her wrong then. I ain't got money for gas for you to be chasing pussy all over creation. Why don't you go out with someone that lives closer to you?"

"I don't like anyone that lives in town."

"Well, you ain't running to Connersville every day, I guess you know. Hell, it's twenty miles up there."

"I know how far it is. I got money for gas." This was a tired argument that I got thrown in my face every since Gayle and I had started dating.

His face was chiseled out of stone. "I reckon you'll need that money for other things pretty soon. You got school coming up. No, you ain't going today and don't let me hear of you begging Sara's car neither."

And that was that. Both outs were blocked and I was trapped. "Well, how about if I just walk to town?"

He glared up at me. "You just got to be going all the time, don't you? Why don't you stay home?"

I started to answer, but he cut me off. "Go on, dammit! If you just have to, then go on. I just don't understand why you feel like you have to."

I couldn't answer that simply because I didn't know why I felt like I had to. I couldn't tell him anymore than I could tell Gayle.

"Well, if you don't care I'm going on in."

There was a flash of real anger in his eyes for a second then he said low. "I done told you I don't mind. Go on to town." But the anger was gone and a tiredness came through, a resignation, as if he'd just realized it wasn't me he was really mad at. He was mad at himself.

I walked on out. I could have said more but there was no need and it would've only made things worse. But after I got away from the house I told the whole world what I thought, all the way to town.

The pool hall was closed on Sunday, so was everything else in town except the café and the picture show. I'd seen the show and a couple of state troopers were flirting with Sara so I sat on the bicycle rack in front of the show and watched the dust blow in ropes up the empty street. I'd been there about a half-hour when Rocky Cobb came walking up, combing his greasy hair. I made a mental bet as to the first thing he'd say to me. I made a mental note to pay myself when he said, "say White, you got a cigarette?"

I shook one out to him and lit one myself. "What's been happening?" he said lighting his.

"I'm just hiding from my old man."

"I heard he lost some money last night."

"I don't know about that." I shot him a look he should have seen.

"I heard it was about five hundred," he smirked as he said it.

I smiled. Rocky had a bad habit of multiplying things by ten but there was no need to say anything. Besides, I didn't know for sure. An eighteen wheeler growled past about then, the driver shifting gears about every hundred feet or so and I thought of April and Lester. Then I remembered something else. "Say, Rocky, wasn't you the one that was talking about the wheat harvest a couple of days ago?"

He grinned, "sure was."

"You said you knew someone that has the equipment to do that kind of work?"

"Sure do. An old boy out to Frederick. He goes on the harvest every year."

"And you got a job waiting?"

"Sure do. Soon as I get out there," he grinned again.

I nodded, half believing him, half not. "Reckon he'd put me to work?"

"Why, I imagine so, if you was with me that is."

I studied him carefully and did some quick thinking. I'd never driven a truck before but I learned fast. Besides, it couldn't be all that hard if April had driven an eighteen wheeler and Kathy Dean could do it. Kathy was kinda cute but she really wasn't all that bright. And it was away from Crane. I studied Rocky again, wondering, "Rocky, you want to leave in the morning?"

He squinted his narrow eyes. "I don't know why not. Yeah, that'll be fine. I was just waiting for someone to go with me. We'll leave in the morning and hitchhike out to Frederick."

"Hitchhike?" My voice squeaked.

He grinned real cocky like. "How did you reckon we was gonna get there, fly?" Then he laughed.

I was having some second thoughts about this little deal but then I thought, I can always come home. "I thought maybe we could get a car somewhere."

"Can't take no car on the harvest. You got to drive the trucks when they move." He smiled at me knowing he knew something I didn't.

And he was right, I didn't know. "What do you mean, 'when they move?'"

He laughed now. "Don't you know nothing?" He laughed again, "Why, this old boy goes plumb to Canada every year."

"Canada!" I almost yelled it.

"Why, hell, yes. He cuts wheat all the way there. What's wrong, you chicken?"

For a second I was stunned. Here it was. My ticket out of Crane. I still had another year of school, but that was no problem. I could come home for that and then, go back. I looked up the practically deserted street, a devil of dust swirled in the hot wind and danced down the street; something pulled at me from the inside. "No, I ain't chicken," I said hard. "We leave in the morning, right?"

"Right," he avoided my eyes.

"Dad will give us a ride out of town if we leave early enough."

Rocky nodded. "I heard he was a flag man on the Madill road now."

"That's right," I said hard, "you want to make something of it?"

"Na, na," he held his hands out toward me, palm out. "I just heard he was."

I stared at him hard. "Then we leave in the morning, right? About seven-thirty."

"Right. Early in the morning."

I stood, excitement and anticipation growing in me as I pictured myself driving a truck. "You be ready, Dad will not want to be late for work."

"I'll be ready. Say, give me another cigarette."

I shook him out one, then lit one for myself watching an old bitch dog trot down the middle of the street. Her dugs were distended and swinging and she smiled at me as she passed. Rocky walked on up the street and I was alone again but the whole situation had changed. I was leaving in the morning, going maybe to Canada. The important thing was, I was leaving. A sudden tremor of excitement passed through me, I was finally going to be free of Crane Oklahoma. Another tremor shook my whole body. I felt if I didn't tell someone, I'd burst. Sara. The café was practically empty now. I flipped the cigarette away and walked across the street.

The jukebox was wailing a sad country song. The troopers were gone. Sara was sitting in her booth, the paper open in front of her. She smiled hesitantly as I slid in the booth. "You look like the cat that ate the canary. What? Someone die and leave you some money?"

"Almost as good," I blurted nervously. "I'm leaving in the morning."

She grinned, "leaving? Okay, where you going?"

"Out West, to cut wheat."

"What!" Her eyes widened and her freckles stood out.

I nodded, "Me and Rocky Cobb. He knows the guy that cuts wheat--"

"Rocky Cobb!!" She almost shouted.

"Yeah, he knows this guy---"

"Dave! You're smarter than that!"

"Will you shut up and listen? He knows this guy that cuts wheat. He goes all the way to Canada every year."

"He lies, Dave! He's a thief and a liar!"

"I know that Sara, but---"

"You'll wind up in jail somewhere."

"He might, but I won't. I don't do that and you know it."

"It doesn't matter. If you're with him, you're both guilty. Besides," she smiled slyly, "they eat little boys like you out there."

I felt myself blush. "I can handle myself."

"She laughed. "You never been more than ten miles away from your family in your whole life. How do you know you can handle yourself?"

"I just know I can. I hang out at LeRoy's all the time."

"And that don't mean nothing. There ain't never serious trouble in LeRoy's. You ain't never seen a real fight in your life. And you want to go on the wheat harvest? Alone? Damn Dave, you better think on this real hard."

"I have thought about it and I'm going. In the morning, with Rocky Cobb. Sara, I have to do something or I'm going to go crazy."

"Have you talked it over with your mom and dad? They might have something to say about you running off like that,"

I stiffened, "No, I haven't told them yet. But it don't matter. I'm going."

"Dammit Dave," her eyes filled with worry. She put her hand on mine. "What do you think you're going to accomplish out there?"

"There's work there. I can make enough money to buy me a car. Besides, it'll get me away from Crane."

She shook her head then rested it against her hands. "Well, is sounds like you're bound to go and all my talking won't make a bit of difference. At least talk it over with your mom and dad."

A scene flashed in my mind, Mom crying, her hands to her cheek. Dad mad, cussing and ranting shaking his finger in my face. Me standing tall, resolute, determined. Then the tearful goodbye, Mom still crying, Dad shaking my hand, just a hint of a tear in his eye, but me, still standing tall as I walked away into the sunset. Then the scene changed. I drive up in a brand new Corvette and thousands of dollars in my pockets. Dad shaking my hand, saying how proud he is of me as I give him money to pay all the bills. Mom crying again because I've grown so much. Now I tower over her, at least six-foot-three, and later Gayle, naked and pressing against me.

"There ain't nothing to talk about, Sara," I said firmly. "I'm going, and that's that!"

She smiled and shrugged. "Okay, but for God's sake be careful. You have the phone number here and mine at home. If you get into anything you can't handle, call me. I'll come and try to help. I promise." The tone of her voice was worried and so were her eyes as she looked deep into mine.

The last scene in my mind changed suddenly. Now it was Sara pressed hot against me, her green eyes flashing as I stroked and rubbed her naked body.

Mom walked out of the kitchen just then and the dream popped. I cocked an eyebrow at Sara and shook my head. She nodded. Mom might start crying and hug my neck or something if I told her now.

"What are you doing in town?" Mom sat next to me.

"I just walked in after we got through with the tree."

"You and your father have a fight?" Her tone and eyes were worried.

"No, not really anyway. He wouldn't let me have the car though."

"He was feeling pretty bad today."

"I figured that out real quick but he didn't have to take it out on me."

Mom flushed suddenly. "He didn't really mean it Davie. He was really taking it out on himself."

"And I got caught."

"That's the way it is. I know it's not right but that's the way it is." She smiled then. "Why don't you go on home now?"

It was five-thirty by the big clock over the jukebox. "Yeah, I might as well. *Walt Disney* will be on at six, and then *Cheyenne* comes on. Yeah, I'll probably go on home." I gave Sara a look that said, 'keep your mouth shut,' Mom stood and I slid out of the booth. My mind was racing so much I didn't even remember the walk home.

Disneyland was just coming on when I walked in. Dad was asleep in his chair. The show this week was from *Adventure Land,* but it was a re-run and I'd already seen it. But, we only got two channels and there was nothing on the other one so I watched it anyway. After a while I got restless and went outside.

The moon was almost full and low in the east, just rising over the trees bathing the earth in its pale light that was almost bright as day. The tree frogs were calling for rain and the whippoorwills were just calling. From far away I heard the lonely call of a mourning dove. A big bull frog barrumped from the tank across the road and a coyote yapped from the woods. The west wind brought the dry, dusty smell of cured grass and for the first time this week, I thought of Early Dean. Well, he could just keep his old job and give it to whomever he pleased. I had work now, or at least the promise of some, and travel and adventure. And that was the best of all, adventure! I did hate loosing the car though but I figured I'd make enough to buy me a nice one now. At least I could hope, now that I had work.

The mosquitoes found me and began droning around my ear, almost drowning out all the other noises and, after I got bit twice, I went back in. *Disneyland* was off now, but I'd seen *Cheyenne* too, so I got a book and tried to read but I couldn't keep my mind on it. Then I figured out what was bothering me. How was I going to tell Mom and Dad about me leaving? There wasn't any good way and I knew it would start a fight I really didn't want.

I stared at the book a while longer before I realized that I wasn't reading, only looking at it so I went to the kitchen for a drink, came back in the living room picked up my book and tried to read again, got up, walked outside, came back in and sat down.

"What's wrong with you?" Dad asked. "You're as nervous as a whore in church."

"I don't know," I said too fast, too hard. "Just jumpy. I think I'll go on to town to get Mom."

"Okay, just don't burn up all my gas dragging Main Street."

"Alright," I took the keys he held out and walked out to the car. A few minutes later I was going down the big hill towards Main Street.

No one was in town so I only dragged Main Street twice then stopped at the café. It was empty too, except for Mom and Sara. Sara was still working the crossword puzzle. I went behind the counter, got me a drink out of the cooler, marked it down then walked over and sat beside Sara. She smelled musky, sort of a mixture of sweat and perfume and the flash I'd had before of her naked in my arms came to my mind again.

I let go of that picture, picked up the paper from Oklahoma City and automatically turned to the auto sales page then closed it, thinking, I'll make enough this summer to afford a good car for sure.

Mom got up saying, "I've got work to do in the kitchen," and she walked to the back.

Sara cocked an eyebrow at me. "You still leaving in the morning?"

"Yeah, I guess so," I mumbled, not wanting to get her started again.

"Your bound to go, aren't you? Damn and double-damn, Dave, be careful." Then she shrugged, resigned to the fact that I was going, no matter what. "I'll worry about you," she said low, "You know that?"

"I know, Sara," I put my hand over hers, squeezing it lightly. "I know you will and I'm glad you will. It makes me feel good, knowing you'll worry."

"Well, I don't know if you're worth it or not, stupid little shit." Then she smiled and squeezed my arm. "Yeah, you're worth it. Now, get up and let me do my work."

She smiled at me again, squeezing my arm even harder. I moved and she got up, brushing me as she passed. I could smell her even more now and, as I watched her walk to the cash register. The image of her naked came to me again. I couldn't help wonder if she really did have freckles all over her body like she had on her face and arms and I felt myself growing hard.

She started totaling out the cash register as if I didn't exist, so I went to work too. Pretty soon we were finished and walked outside. Sara locked the front door then turned and whispered, "Dave, please be careful."

She glanced at Mom who was getting in the car, then she raised up fast and kissed me. It was just a peck on the lips, gone before I could react but it meant more than anything that had ever happened to me before. Then she was gone, walking to her car. I watched her a second. Then I got in our car and drove away.

I didn't talk on the way home, trying to figure out how I was going to tell them I was leaving. When I pulled up in the driveway I still had no answer. Mom went on in the house but I hung back for a while, trying to gather courage. Then, knowing there was no easy way, I just walked in and said, "I'm leaving in the morning."

They both looked shocked.

"Just where do you think you're going?" Mom asked.

"Out West, to cut wheat. Me and Rocky Cobb are leaving tomorrow morning. We're going to hitchhike out to Frederick. Rocky knows a guy out there that owns a cutting rig. He has work for both of us."

Dad stood up, looked at me and I thought, here it comes."

"Well," he said. "I guess that will be alright."

And I was shocked.

"You don't plan on finishing school?" Mom asked.

"Oh, yeah," I stammered out. "I'll be back in time for school."

Mom said, "well, we'll need to pack you a suitcase then."

Now I really couldn't believe it. Neither one of them was going to yell at me. I was all primed, ready for a good hollering fight but they acted like they didn't even care.

"I won't need a suitcase, Mom. I'm just going to take a couple of changes of clothes."

"You'll take a suitcase," she snapped. "And you'll take more than two changes of clothes. I'm not sending you off into the world with nothing. You'll take what I pack!"

I didn't argue.

I watched her pack the old battered suitcase for me: Blue jeans, tee shirts, shorts, socks. Then she took down an old pink quilt. "Mom," I gasped. "I can't take that!"

"You'll take it," she said. "It might get cold at night out West," and she closed the suitcase. I was packed, ready to leave, but I still couldn't believe it.

She left the bedroom for a second then stepped back in with a carton of cigarettes in her hand. "I almost forgot these," she put them in the suitcase. Then she handed me a ten-dollar bill. "You'll need some money to eat."

I didn't want to take it, but her look said, 'don't argue,' so I put it in my billfold. Dad came in then and handed me a piece of paper. "Put this in there too," he said. I looked at it. He had printed out. *In case of sickness or accident, contact Mister and Missus Robert White, RR 1, Crane Oklahoma.'*

He had our phone number and the phone number at the café.

He really does care, I thought. He just doesn't want me to know but he really does care. I said, "Thanks Dad," and put it in my billfold. I had one already in there but I didn't tell him. I just put it away.

"You'll be wanting a ride out of town in the morning," he said.

"Yeah, I thought we might go by and pick Rocky up too."

He nodded. "That will be alright, if he's ready. Well, we better get to bed, tomorrow's going to be another day and it's going to be hot."

"Yeah, I guess so," I said, still not believing what had happened.

"Okay," Dad said. "I'll wake you up in the morning so you can get an early start." And they turned and walked out of the bedroom.

"Okay, Dad," I said, and shut the door. I stood there a second, then I got real excited. I was really leaving in the morning. I was all packed and ready and whether I stayed a day, a week or the rest of the summer didn't matter. I was really going.

I undressed, turned out the light and lay down, shivering with excitement. I went over in my mind everything I knew about the western lands, the panhandles of Oklahoma and Texas, Kansas, Nebraska, Colorado, Wyoming, the Dakotas, Montana.

The names rang in my mind like bells of the Old West. I knew absolutely nothing about wheat but the picture on the wall shone vaguely in the half-light of the moon. The snowcapped peaks gleamed, calling to me and I shivered again. Then, through the open window, I heard Mom say, "do you think he'll be alright?"

"He'll be alright," Dad answered.

"Maybe we shouldn't let him go."

"Now, just how are we going to stop him?"

"I don't know. There should be some way."

Dad laughed, "he won't be gone two days."

"I'm not so sure of that. He might get a job and go on north with the harvest."

"Well, if he does, that will be alright too. He's a good kid and he makes a good hand but he needs some growing up. This just might be where he gets it."

"I'm worried about him going off like this."

"Hell, Mary Bell, I went off to work and so did everyone of your brothers, mine too. He's tough and pretty smart. He learns fast. He'll be alright."

"Things was different back then. There wasn't the meanness in the world like there is now. He's only seventeen."

"Dammit, he'll be alright. Like I said, he won't be gone more than two days. Now, let's get some sleep."

"Okay, but I'm still worried."

Mixed emotions spread over me. Two days huh, I thought, and I was suddenly mad. He don't think I can make it out there. Two days. I'll show him. But then I realized Dad was only hoping. He was worried too but he just didn't know how to say it. They were both worried and Sara too. A warm feeling spread over me thinking about them being worried. Especially Sara and my mind went back to the kiss.

I smiled as I thought of Sara.

The next thing I knew, Dad was hollering at me from the door. At first I wondered why he was hollering at me in the middle of the night. Then I realized it was morning and I had been asleep. I lay there just a second wondering what all I had to do today, then remember. It was today. I was leaving today, and I jumped out of bed. I dressed quickly and walked to the kitchen expecting a big lecture on what to do and what not to do while I was gone. I was wrong. They acted like it was just a normal day.

Dad looked at the clock after we ate breakfast and said, "well, we better get to getting. It's getting late and we got Mister Cobb to pick up."

I went to my bedroom to get my suitcase, looked around the room a second, then walked out. Mom met me at the door and hugged me. "You write or call to let us know you're alright and you be home in time to enroll in school." She hugged me again and as I walked to the door she said, "be careful and be sure to write."

"Okay, Mom. I'll see you when I get back." I walked on out to the car and got in. Somehow it hadn't gone exactly like I had it pictured.

Dad got in and we drove to town in silence. He knew where Rocky lived. He knew where just about everyone in the county lived. He'd been born here in 1909, and grew up here. And, with the exception of about four years we lived in New Mexico and California when I was real small, he'd lived his whole life in Crane, never wanting anything else. The only reason we had ever left was because of the depression and there was really no work or money back here. But he had come back as soon as he could. That was in 1948. I just barely remembered the trip.

Dad honked the car horn when we pulled up to Rocky's house. He came out carrying a big, blue suitcase and got in the car. "Good morning, Robert," he said.

Dad just grunted and drove off.

About a mile west, out of Crane, the highway forked. The west road went to Ardmore, the other fork, south, to Madill. Dad pulled over to the shoulder. I opened the door to get out and he gave me the only piece of advice I'd heard from him.

"You call home for money, you better use it to come home on. I'll not send money twice because we just don't have it. Now be careful and write to your mother."

I started to say something but it choked in my throat so I just got out and watched him drive away, never looking back. A hollow, lost, empty feeling came over me as I watched the disappearing car.

I knew how he felt. I just hoped he knew what I couldn't say either.

Rocky yawned sleepily and blinked then sat on his suitcase. A tremor of excitement went through me, but I contained it. "Well, here we are."

"Yeah," Rocky said. "With a long way to go. Say, you got a cigarette?"

I gave him one and got out the road map. "I figure we'll stay on Highway 70, to Davidson, then cut north to Frederick. That sound alright?"

"Yeah. I reckon that'll be fine."

I folded the map and stuck it in my pocket, then sat down. Then I remembered, in all the excitement I hadn't let Gayle know I was leaving. The thought stunned me but there was nothing I could do about it now. I'll write her the first chance I get, I thought. That won't be good enough for her but it's the best I can do. I'll write her a good, long letter, first chance I get.

Just then I saw a car coming. We got up and I stuck out my thumb like I'd been doing it all my life. The car slowed, then crossed the center line and speeded up as it passed. Well, I thought, there will be other cars and I sat back down. The second car stopped for us and as we got in the back seat, I recognized Linda Bradford, a girl in my class in school.

"Why, David White and Rocky Cobb," Linda said. "Where are you two going?"

"We're going out West, to the wheat harvest" I said. "How far are y'all going?"

"Why, we're going over to Ardmore to do some shopping," Linda said. "The wheat harvest. That sounds exciting."

I said, "I just hope to find work."

Mrs. Bradford looked at me in the rear-view mirror. "Do your folks know you're leaving?"

"Yes Ma'am," I said. "Dad brought us this far this morning."

"Well, I just thought I'd check." She looked back at the road.

Linda was all bubbly over it though, if you can imagine a six-foot-tall, red haired girl, bubbly. She was real nice though. We'd started the first grade together so she was more like a cousin than anything. "Aren't you real excited?" she asked. "It makes me excited, just thinking about it. Hitchhiking all that way, then working all summer."

Sure, I was excited, real excited, but I didn't let on like I was. "Na," I said. "I just hope to find work. God knows there isn't any around here."

"Well, I'd be excited," Linda said. "I wish I could go with you."

"Linda!" her mother barked. "Young ladies don't say things like that."

It was real hard for me to imagine anyone calling Linda Bradford a young lady. Up until two years ago she could whip any boy in the class. She proved it quite often too.

I winked at her though and she winked back then cut her eyes over to her mother and stuck out her tongue. It was all I could do to keep from laughing out loud.

I sat back to enjoy the ride now, trying to imagine how it would be when we got there. Trying to figure out how I was going to get work when I'd never driven a truck and never even seen a combine. But soon the passing countryside commanded my attention and the thought passed like the wooded hills we were passing through.

Just east of Ardmore, we entered an area of huge houses set way back from the road and the old, lonesome, jealous rage came over me again as I watched them pass. Soon though, we hit the ring of salvage yards and cheap drive-inns that surrounded the city and the feeling faded, at least partly. I felt more at home here at least.

Mrs. Bradford took us all the way through Ardmore to where Highway 70 intersected with Highway 77 to let us off. As we got out, Linda said. "Have fun. Be careful but have fun. I sure wish I could go too."

She sounded as if she really meant it and was jealous of me going and somehow I felt sorry for her. My mind passed to Gayle, wishing she had felt the same and I wondered then why anyone wouldn't? How anyone could keep from wanting to go? I didn't know.

They drove away with Linda waving from the window. We walked away from the intersection a little way then sat down again. I had a sudden feeling of isolation, almost tearing inside me. I was gone now, really gone and on my own for the first time in my life. I thought about what Mom would be doing now and I stood, looking back east towards Ardmore and Crane and I almost started back. Then, in my mind, I heard Dad's voice, 'He won't be gone two days.'

And then the wildness, the wanderlust, that had been pulling me at me, calling me, whispered in my ear and I felt something move inside. I remembered the feeling I'd had watching Linda Bradford drive away and I felt a stretching, almost a tearing.

Now it snapped and I turned, looking west.

CHAPTER 5

The pickup was old but the man driving was ancient. He wore bib overalls and a cotton shirt, buttoned at the sleeves and collar in spite of the heat. A few scraggly gray hairs protruded from around a battered straw hat that looked to be as old as he was. When he talked or smiled, he displayed gums completely smooth. I really couldn't believe he was alive, much less driving, but here we were, burning up the road at twenty-five miles an hour.

"Yep Son," he was saying. "I found this piece of land I'm living on now, in 1910. Bought two thousand acres for fifteen hundred dollars, lock, stock, and windmill. I been here ever since. Had a man offer to buy me out the other day. Said he'd give me forty thousand dollars for her but I told him, 'not today, Young Feller.' I got to do a sight more working on that land before I'll sell her."

"That's a lot of money to turn down," I said, wishing I was in the back with Rocky. The old man had so much junk in the pickup cab, there was only room for me.

"Yep," he said with a smooth grin, "That's a lot of money alright but when you get as old as I am, money don't mean much to you."

I thought, when you get as old as he is, don't nothing mean much except waking up the next day. I'd tuned the old man out a while back and now I was just listening to the drone of his voice. But something was bothering me, something I had heard somewhere. I remembered then.

It was Dad that had said it, but how did it go? Then I remembered. He had said, *"Listen to everyone, to everything they have to say. Study it, learn from it what you can, because everyone is different and everyone learns different things in a different way. Remember what you learn and you'll be a better man than you were."*

I started listening again. Maybe the old man had something to say after all.

"Six sons I had," he was saying. "Six sons and one daughter. I killed three wives getting seven kids, three by the first, two by the second and two by the last. My two oldest boys was both killed in the Great War. The next one went off to find work during the Depression. I never heard from him again. I had one drank hisself to death-- somewhere down in Mexico. The next was a bomber pilot during World's War Two. He come up missing in action. I never heard anything else. My last boy got hisself gored by a wild cow, out to the ranch. He's buried out there, next to his mother. He's the only one that I know where he's buried. My daughter was the youngest. She took up with a bootlegger and runned off. Last I heard she was up to the City, living fancy. I keep hoping she'll come home someday to settle down, maybe have me some grandkids around the house."

He paused for a second. "It sure gets lonesome out there by myself."

I nodded silently, wishing now I hadn't listened. The old man might have a big ranch worth forty thousand dollars and more but he really didn't have anything. I thought back to Easter when my whole clan congregated at home. There must've been fifty of us. Everyone cutting up, having a good time, drinking and raising hell. We might not have much, but there sure was a bunch of us. And when we all got together, we sure had a good time.

The old man was slowing now, pulling to the side of the road. "Well Son, this is where I turn off." He pointed to a road running off into a pasture. "If you boys want to, I'll try to find you something around the ranch to do. Couldn't pay you much, but I'll board and sleep you."

I felt the tear in me again. Here was work, not far from home, not too far anyway. I could probably work the whole summer here and buy a car with the money I'd make and be able to go home on weekends. I thought real hard on it for a minute or two, but just then, an eighteen-wheeler roared past and I heard the whining song its tires made on the highway. And I heard it calling me. Then I remembered how the geese sounded flying over in the spring, honking to each other, calling me to go with them. I couldn't stop now. I'd come this far. Now I was hooked. I had to go on. Where? I didn't know and I didn't really care. I looked west. The highway ran for about a mile then disappeared over a hill. I just had to go. I had to see what was on the other side of that hill.

"Mister, I appreciate the offer. I really wish I could stay, but I've got some wild oats to sow and I might never have another chance. I sure hope you understand."

"Yeah Son," he nodded. "I understand, probably even better than you know. Just be careful out there. It's a big old mean world out there with lots of mean people in it. You can get yourself in a lot of trouble if you ain't careful."

He sighed deeply and a far away look came to his eyes. "Moving, is like a drug, Son. It gets in your blood. A man can waste his whole life right there on that highway just moving from place to place. And Son, that ain't no good life. A man needs to root somewhere." He smiled then, "Now, you go on and have your lark and if you come back this way, why stop in and holler at an old man."

"I sure will," I said as I got out of the pickup, knowing full well I'd never see the old man again but I looked back at him. "You know, you might try to get ahold of your daughter. She just might want to come home if you let her know you really want her to."

"Now, you know, I might just do that. I never really thought about it like that before." He smiled, displaying his naked gums. "I just believe I'll try that, maybe tonight." Then he drove off across the pasture.

I felt an empty sadness watching him go and fought the urge to run after him. Just then another eighteen wheeler roared past in a sudden gust of wind and dust that stung me and I watched it disappear over the next hill.

I picked up my suitcase and started after it.

"Hey, White," Rocky said as he followed. "You got a cigarette?"

"Yeah, Rocky, here you go." I shook one out to him, looking at the country as I sat on my suitcase, wondering what was over that hill.

We sat there an hour waiting for the next ride to stop. I didn't mind all that much. I was busy in my mind just looking, thinking. The land had changed. The rolling, wooded hills around Crane and east of Ardmore had given way to a flatter, more treeless land. I knew we were on the very edge of what had been called, *The Great American Desert.* What Coronado had called the, *Sea of Grass,* when he passed through just north of here back in the early fifteen hundreds. Farther west it was called the, *Llano Estacado,* the Staked Plains, because the land had no distinguishing features. After that it was called, *The Dust Bowl,* when the land had all blown away back in the big drought of the Thirties. This all passed through my mind and for the first time, I noticed the wind. The sun was hot but there was a good breeze blowing, really a strong wind. I lit a cigarette, looking at Rocky and wondered about the job.

He was leaning back on his suitcase and I suddenly wondered just how much of what he had told me was true. I started to ask him when another pickup topped the last hill. We stood up, stuck out our thumbs and watched the driver as he slowed to a stop right beside us. "Where you boys going?"

"Out to Frederick, Sir," I said.

"Well, get in. I'll take you a piece. I'm going out past Randlett."

We threw our suitcases in the back, both of us getting in the front this time. The man was neither young or old, dressed in blue jeans, a western shirt, and a big cowboy style, straw hat. When the pickup leveled off at ninety, I smiled, thinking about the old man driving twenty-five. At this speed, we'd be to Frederick by noon.

"What you boys got going out to Frederick?" the man asked.

"We're going on the wheat harvest to find work," I said.

"Wheaties! I should have known!" He had an edge to his voice.

"What's that you said, Mister?" I asked.

"Wheaties! Wheaties. That's what we call the wheat tramps. The harvest people," he said hard, glaring at both of us.

It hit me wrong, not what he said, but how he said it. "Sounds to me like you called me a son of a bitch, Mister." I said back.

He nodded, "means about the same. Maybe nigger."

He smiled then, but his eyes stayed hard. "Yeah, 'bout the same."

"Now look here, Mister," I said. "You can just stop this pickup and let us out. We don't want to put you out none."

He laughed, then smiled sarcastically, "Ahhh hell, I guess it'll be alright. You boys don't smell too bad."

Now I was mad. "Mister, I'd really appreciate it if you was to stop. I really want out. The smell of cow shit in here is about to get to me."

He laughed again, longer and louder. "Don't get so huffy Boy. I didn't mean it personal. It's just that most of you Wheaties don't bath too often. Besides, you probably smelled cow shit before."

"Yes I have, but I never stood by and let a man tell me I stink before."

"What's so bad about the harvest people?" Rocky asked.

"Scum of the earth," he said. "They're just scum, most of them. Not the equipment owners, most of them's good people. It's the workers that's bad. Most of them's drunks or bums that can't get a job or find work nowhere else. Else why do they go wandering all over the country like the dust in the wind."

"Maybe they're like us. Ain't no work where we came from." Rocky said.

He nodded, "Well, maybe so, but I sure don't want my sister bringing one home. They're just here today and gone tomorrow and they cause trouble everywhere they go."

"What kind of trouble?" I asked.

He shrugged and said, "Ah, getting drunk and getting thrown in jail. Just not like ordinary people."

I said, "don't ordinary people get drunk and throwed in jail?"

"Yeah, I reckon," he nodded. "But it just seems like the wheaties do it the most. They're all the time causing trouble, getting into fights and bothering the women. Was I you boys, I'd think twice about going on. Y'all don't want to be no wheaties."

"Mister," Rocky said. "We're just looking for work, that's all. We got jobs waiting for us out to Frederick."

We passed a road sign that I barely caught: Randlett, ten miles. That's good I thought. Then we'll be rid of this guy.

"He laughed. "Y'all ain't got no jobs waiting for you in Frederick. Not on the harvest anyway. The harvest is gone from there. It was over the early part of last week. They done moved on."

"Well, I know an old boy that goes every year and we'll catch him somewhere," Rocky said.

The man laughed again, "where was he going next?"

"Well now, I just don't know," Rocky said.

I felt a sinking in the pit of my stomach when the man laughed really hard and said, "then you got the whole southwest to look for him in. If it was me, I'd try Texas first, it's closest." He laughed some more then smiled as he looked at me. "Don't worry Son. Y'all won't have no trouble finding work. Them wheat crews are always needing hands. It ain't nothing for half a crew to get drunk and throwed in jail. The owners don't care because they's always a bunch being let out so they just hire them and move on."

I saw the Randlett turn off coming up so I felt pretty safe. "Mister, it sounds to me like you got some first-hand experience with all of this. It sounds to me like you either been there or you are there, a wheatie I mean."

He grinned at me then. "You got me Boy. Yep, I been there and boys, it ain't no picnic. I thought maybe I could scare you enough to make you turn back. Maybe enough to make you want to go home. It sure ain't no life for a man, much less a kid. How old are you boys anyway?"

"We're both seventeen," Rocky said.

He shook his head. "Well, you're too young anyway. You got to be eighteen to drive a truck and neither one of you've ever seen a combine."

"I reckon we can lie," I said. "Besides, if they're needing help as bad as you say, we shouldn't have any trouble getting work."

"You can lie to the operator. He don't care. You can't lie to the State Police because he'll want to see your license." He slowed, pulling to the side of the road. "Why don't you boys just cross the highway and go on home. Y'all would be a whole lot better off."

I looked him square in the eye, "no Sir. I reckon not. We've come this far, and I reckon we'll just go on a little farther. There ain't nothing where we come from to go back to. No work of any kind."

"You're bound and determined to go on then, are you?" he asked as we got out of the pickup.

We both nodded.

"Alright, I'll tell you what," he checked his watch, then glanced at the sun. "It's twelve-thirty now, y'all will be in Frederick in, oh, say, an hour, hour and a half. You look for your man out there and if he's already gone, which he is, y'all start north to Clinton. I'll be headed that way early in the morning. If I see you on the road, I'll pick you up. Okay?"

"That's sounds alright," I said, not really believing him.

Rocky nodded.

He grinned again, "If I don't see you again, y'all be careful now, you hear?"

"Okay Mister," we said in unison. He drove off, turning south into Texas.

I looked at Rocky, "you think he was telling us the truth?"

"I don't really know," he said.

"What do you mean, you don't know? You're the one that knows the man. Didn't you ever talk to him about this?"

"Yes, I talked to him about it. He told me all about it. I just didn't want to scare you none because then you wouldn't have come."

The sinking feeling hit me in the pit of my stomach again and I thought. He's lying. The sucker is lying and has been all along. I felt cold and bumpy all over and the hair on my arms stood up. Dad would have said, *'A goose stepped on my grave.'*

I felt better, just thinking about Dad and a calmness came over me. I stared back at Rocky but he avoided my eyes. But if he's lying, I thought, why did he come? How does he know so much about the harvest? I couldn't answer either question so I lit a cigarette without offering him one and sat down. Maybe he wasn't lying. Maybe, just maybe, he did know someone out in Frederick. If so, we could find where he'd gone and catch him without too much trouble. But the sick feeling wouldn't leave me.

"Hey, White, you got a cigarette?" Rocky said.

"Yeah, Rocky, I got a cigarette."

He glanced over at me but still avoided my eyes. The dust whipped by the hot wind had coated his greasy black hair making it a sickly gray color.

"You gonna give me one?" he asked, almost apologetically.

"Yeah Rocky, I'm gonna give you one and that's all. You buy you some the next chance you get."

"I will, Dave. I sure will. I just forgot this morning."

"There's a lot of things you forgot Rocky. Like telling me this old boy was probably already gone. " I shook out a cigarette and handed it to him.

"I didn't know that. Besides, he probably ain't. We ain't there yet."

"Yeah, you may be right. We ain't there yet," but the sinking feeling still wouldn't leave me and now, I was afraid.

Suddenly, I felt hot and sticky. I was thirsty, hungry too, tired and not too happy with myself and I remembered what Linda Bradford had said when they let us out in Ardmore about this being so exciting and I had to smile. Boy, sitting here on this hot dusty, road with no shade was sure exciting. It reminded me of something I had read somewhere about adventure being mostly just that, going dirty and being scared.

CHAPTER 6

Rocky was real quiet after that, almost subdued. And I settled down some after I realized that even if he was lying I still might be able to find work. At least that's what that guy had said and he seemed to know what he was talking about.

But then, so did Rocky.

I thought about it a little while and decided I was only about a hundred miles from home. I'd made it this far. If worse came to worse, I could always go home or back to work with the old man. I wasn't going to worry about it. I was going to enjoy myself and see as much as possible.

A man and a woman stopped about then, taking us out past Grandfield. I watched the countryside unrolling as we rode, letting Rocky carry on the conversation with them. The land had turned brown. Brown dirt and tawny brown grass lay cut in the fields windrowed and ready to bale but it didn't look like any hay I'd ever seen. It wasn't until they let us out that I realized it was cut wheat. These were wheat fields we were passing through. Oh, I'd seen the giant storage elevators back in Waurika. I knew what they were from pictures in my textbooks but I'd never seen wheat growing before. I walked out into the field and picked up some of the straw and husk, knowing it was called chaff, but I had never seen it before.

The land had changed completely now even the rolling hills were gone, well, not gone but so gentle now the land appeared flat. The horizon seemed to go on forever but the land seemed to raise out there in the far distance making it seemed as if I was standing in the bottom of a shallow bowl. The sky changed colors from pale blue at the edge of the world, growing darker as the eye traveled upward until, straight up, it reached the deepest, purest blue I had ever seen. I turned in a slow circle, just looking. Except for the highway reaching out to, what seemed, forever in two directions, the land was the same, the view the same. The sun hung directly overhead, a ball of molten brass in the sky and only south had meaning. The wind came from the south and there was no escaping the wind and no sound other than the wind.

I felt the wind pulling at me, calling to me, whispering then shrieking in my ears. I felt alone and looking around, I was alone in the terrible emptiness of the prairie.

The wind whispered to me, told me to come go with it, to wander free across the face of the earth, to go nowhere but touch everything, to be all things, to be nothing. And I felt myself answering the calling wind.

"Have you gone crazy? You're just out there standing in one place turning in circles." Rocky's voice came crashing through the silence, breaking the spell, causing me to sit down, shaken. I'd heard the wind and I had listened to its sirens song. Then I had answered the wind. I'd felt it reach down into the core of me and now, I was afraid.

My hands were shaking when I tried to light a cigarette, remembering stories of people that, for no reason, just started walking out across the prairie and walked until they died. Now I knew why. I knew the secret of the wind.

"I thought you had gone crazy. You was just standing there, turning around and around with a wild look to you. You was just looking off into nowhere. I thought you was going to start walking off any minute. You scared me. Dammit, talk to me!" Rocky pleaded.

"Just a second and I'll be alright. I was just looking, turning and looking. I guess I got dizzy." I said, grateful to him and at the same time hating him for breaking the spell. I looked at the ground, at the road, then picked up a dead weed and began drawing in the dirt. I was afraid to look up now, afraid of the terrible empty distances, afraid of the wind.

A car came by. Rocky stood up to thumb it down. I still sat looking at the ground. Then something Dad had told me once, came back to me. It had been long ago when I had been afraid to go outside at night, afraid of the dark.

"Davie," he had said. *"There's nothing to be afraid of out there in the dark. It's just what you think is out there that you're afraid of, but really, it's all inside you. There ain't no real monsters so a man makes his own, in his mind. There ain't nothing out there at night, that ain't there in the day. The only difference is, you just can't see as far."*

I thought about that for a while, then looked up. The only difference here was I could see farther. The wind blew at home. It was over. I wasn't afraid anymore. The wind didn't talk to me anymore. I stood up and threw the weed away. A car was coming. We stuck out our thumbs, watching it slow then stop right beside us.

"Where you boys going?" came the call from inside the car.

"Frederick," we said in unison.

"Well, y'all are in luck because that's where we're going."

We piled in, Rocky in the front me and the suitcases in the back seat. And as the car pulled away, I looked back at the demon I'd left behind.

The man driving asked the same questions. We gave him the same answers. It had become a drudge now, but grateful for the ride, we felt obligated to talk to him.

We went thirty miles at forty miles an hour, less in the small towns we passed through. We turned north at Davidson, then eleven more miles and we pulled into Frederick, a dusty little southwestern town that could have gone by twenty other names.

"Do you have any idea where this guy lives?" I asked Rocky.

"No, but we'll find him. Don't worry."

"I ain't worried. Right now, I'm hungry. Let's go over there to that café and get a bite."

The old man had let us off at the town square. The café was just across the street. We walked over and went in. A fan stirred the hot air making it a little cooler but not much. A radio was blaring an old song, *'Hearts Made of Stone.'* The place smelled of burned grease and soggy vegetables. A fat girl in a grease-spotted apron smiled as she sat two glasses of water on the table. "Y'all just passing through?" she asked as if she didn't really care.

"Yeah," Rocky said. "We're with the harvest."

She smiled again, "Is that right? I figured all of y'all had done left town."

"Well, we been working down in Texas and we're just now going on north." Rocky said.

"Is that right?" she smiled now. She had cavities between her front teeth. "Are y'all going to eat?"

"Yeah, we might," I said.

She said, "Okay, just call me when you're ready to order. I'll be right over there," she pointed to the back booth.

"Okay," I said, picking up a plastic covered menu but then I noticed a menu printed on the wall behind the counter. A hamburger was thirty-five cents, all cold drinks a dime. I folded the menu, never looking at it. "Ma'am," I said loud enough to be heard over the radio. "I believe I'll just have a hamburger and a Coke."

Rocky ordered the same.

The girl got up grudgingly and walked to the back. A few seconds later the greasy smell of frying hamburger meat overpowered the other smells, making me feel even hungrier and lonesome as it reminded me of the café, Mom, and Sara.

"You reckon you should ask here if they know this old boy we're looking for?" I asked.

"Yeah, I reckon I could but they probably don't," Rocky said.

"Maybe so, maybe not, but it wouldn't hurt to ask." *Peggy Sue,* by Buddy Holly was playing when the girl came out with the hamburgers and set them on the table. I drew back. I had never seen a hamburger so small, just about the size of the palm of my hand. I opened the bun to salt and pepper it and got another shock. That's all the thing was, meat and bread. Back home we got hamburgers twice that size with lettuce, tomato, pickle, and onion for a quarter. I looked up to say something to the girl, but she was busy. Two glasses of ice stood on the counter in front of her and she was dividing a single ten-ounce Coke between them. I looked at Rocky saying, "you believe this?"

"I'm seeing it, but I don't believe it," he said.

"I wonder if this is all of it?"

"I reckon it is because here she comes with them Cokes."

She set the Cokes down, turned away without a word, walked to the back booth and sat down again. There was nothing to do but eat and never in my life had I eaten anything as bad. The bun was stale, dry and hard. What meat there was, was burned dry. Dad told me once that I could digest a rusty nail, now I believed him. I choked the mess down, drank half my Coke and the glass of water. I flipped open the menu, waiting for Rocky to finish and couldn't believe my eyes. On the inside of the menu, where the prices were, was a strip of masking tape, the paper kind. Written on the tape was a whole new set of prices. Quickly I ran down the list; hamburger seventy-five cents, drinks twenty-five, water a dime, no refills.

I said, "Rocky, you better chew that thing slow because you'll break your teeth if you ain't careful." I flipped the menu over for him to read. "The damn thing's made of pure gold."

He looked down and read the menu as he chewed. Suddenly he swallowed, choked, coughed and spat the entire mouthful of food all over me.

I brushed the food off my shirt. "That's about thirty cents you just spit out, Rocky. Really, you ought to be more careful with your money."

He was still choking but at least now he was coughing in his hand. When he finally got his breath, he said, "man, I'm sorry. I just couldn't help it."

"I know you couldn't. If I had seen it when I was eating, I would have probably done the same thing."

"You going to pay her that much for this mess?"

"I reckon I will, and I reckon you will too." I said. The radio seemed even louder as I looked over his shoulder at the man that had just come out of the back. He wasn't the biggest man I had ever seen. He wasn't even as big as LeRoy. But he was big enough.

He glared at me as he walked to the booth the girl was sitting in and sat down. He leaned an arm, that looked like a branch off that old elm tree, over the back of the booth and scooted his back against the wall so he could see us and the girl. I took a word from the wise. "Let's get out of here."

"Yeah. Before I loose my head, get hungry again and order something else."

"Ma'am," I said getting up, "We're ready to pay now."

She got up, figuring something on her pad, then walked to the front. "That'll be a dollar-thirty each." She didn't smile as she said it.

"A dollar-thirty!" I yelled. I just couldn't help it.

She did smile now, a mean, wolfish smile, "Yep, seventy-five-cents for the burger, a quarter for the drink, that's a dollar. A dime for the water, fifteen-cent tip and a nickel tax. A dollar-thirty each, or do you want to argue about it?"

I could see the man in the mirror behind her. He was glaring at us with a bored, yet poised and ready look, like if we gave her any trouble at all, he'd come over and break both of us in half. My heart pounded in my ears, even drowned out the screaming radio as we each paid the dollar-thirty. But as she turned to walk away, I asked it. I had to.

"Ma'am," I said, "What's the menu up there for?" I pointed to the one on the wall.

She smiled her wolfish smile and said, "Oh, that's for our regular customers."

I didn't say a word as I turned to walk out. Then I heard her say, not mumble, but out loud. "I just hate a damn Wheatie!"

I felt myself go cold and glanced at Rocky.

He'd heard it too. I could see his jaw twitch as we walked away from the café.

I was about to cry. "I reckon," I mumbled. "This is how the colored folks feel when we call them nigger."

His jaw was still twitching. "Yeah, I reckon so," he said low.

"I don't know about you," I felt dirty and degraded. "But I don't think I'll be doing that again, now that I know how it feels."

"No, I don't reckon I will either," he said low, staring straight ahead as we walked down the street towards the square.

"Say Rocky, why don't you check in here," I pointed toward the courthouse. "We got to find that old boy pretty fast because at these prices, I ain't going to be eating long without I find work."

"Well, I reckon I can," he said as we walked onto the courthouse lawn. "Why don't you just sit down. I'll go in and check."

I don't know why I did it, maybe it was the shade trees there, maybe it was the day catching up with me, but I sat down on the grass and didn't go in the courthouse with him. I guess I should have, but I didn't.

He was gone ten, maybe fifteen minutes. The shade was cool and the grass smelled good after the hot, dusty road. My feelings were still hurting from the café so I lay back on the grass and was just dozing off when he came back.

"They said he's already left this part of the country," he said looking down at me. "And they said they didn't have any idea where he was going next." He shook his head in disgust. "And we done come all this way. Ain't that just our luck. I guess we should have called him or something, told him we was coming."

I went even colder than before and everything balled up in my mind. A dog was barking somewhere close. A pretty girl drove by in a convertible. I felt he'd been lying before but now I was sure. I got up, brushing off the seat of my pants and stood in front of him, relaxed and ready and said, "Rocky, you're a damn liar! You been lying to me from the start. You never knew anyone out here. You just lied! Now tell me you lied and maybe I won't beat the hell out of you."

He looked me straight in the eye. "Now Dave, I wasn't lying to you. I did know this guy. He's got all kinds of equipment, trucks combines and such. You don't really think I was lying to you?"

"I damn sure do and I'm going to kick your ass right now." I grabbed him by the shirt front with my left hand and had just started to pull him forward, ready to hit him, when I heard the voice.

"What the hell's going on here?" It roared.

I made a quick brushing motion on Rocky's chest then turned around. He was a big man but he looked even bigger with the badge on his chest and the gun at his hip.

"Why, there ain't nothing going on here, Sir," I said. "My friend just had something on the front of his shirt that I was just brushing off."

He looked amused. "Looked to me like you was going to hit him."

He rolled a toothpick in his mouth, glancing from Rocky to me, to the suitcases. "Looked like you boys was going to fight. I don't allow no fighting in my town."

"Oh, no, Sir," we both said. The dog was still barking

"No, Sir," I repeated. "We've come a long way together. There wasn't going to be no fight."

He glanced at the suitcases, then at me, "you boys just passing through?"

"Yes Sir," I said. "We just got into town and we're looking for work."

His eyes narrowed, "what kind of work?"

"Harvest work, Sir," Rocky said. "We're going on the harvest."

"Dammed wheat tramps," he hawked and spat. "I should have known. I thought I was done with you damn scum for this year." An expression of disgust came over his face as he looked around, trying to locate the barking dog. Then he glared at Rocky, cut his eyes at me, threw the toothpick away and roared, "what the hell are y'all doing on my grass?"

"Why, we was just resting, Sir." I tried to keep my voice from trembling. "We've come a long way today. We was tired and was resting a little."

"Scum don't walk on my grass," he hissed low. "And scum damn sure don't rest on my grass. Say, you boys got a place to stay?"

I said. "No Sir, we don't. Like I said, we just got to town and we're looking for work."

"Well, there ain't no work here," he growled. "Not for the likes of y'all. Y'all are done too late to find any work around here." He looked at his watch. "It's four-thirty now. You boys either get yourselves a room to stay in or get your asses out of town before six o'clock, you hear? If I see either one of you outside after six o'clock, I'll arrest you for vagrants. That's three days in jail, you hear?"

"Yes, Sir," we said together.

"We'll be moving on," I added. "We don't want no trouble."

"Well, trouble is what you got unless you do like I say. And by the way, I don't allow no hitchhiking in my town neither." Then he laughed.

I picked up my suitcase. "If it's alright with you, Sir, we'll be moving on now." Try as I may, I couldn't keep the wavering tremble out of my voice.

"There's the road Boy," he pointed with his eyes and a nod. "I ain't stopping you."

Rocky glanced at me then the sheriff. He picked up his suitcase and we started walking in the direction of the nod. I guess we'd gone two blocks before I began to breathe again but then I glanced over my shoulder. He was right behind us in his car. At first I thought he was going to pass us, but no, he just hung there, idling along behind, matching our speed. I whispered, "Don't look back, Rocky, but he's--dammit I told you not to---."

"He's right behind us!" Rocky hissed.

"I know. I told you not to look--" I gasped.

"That bastard is laughing at us," Rocky said.

"Well what the hell did you expect?"

"He's just following us."

"And I bet he does it all the way out of this piss hole." I glanced back. He had all the windows rolled up so the air conditioner was on for sure. And he was still laughing.

My suitcase hadn't seemed heavy this morning but now it hung like a rock from my arm, gaining weight all the time and banging my leg with every step. I switched arms and it was better for a while. Soon, I was switching arms every ten steps or so. Suddenly, he blew his siren, causing people to look at us. Some pointed, laughing as we passed, honking as they passed in their cars. I felt like a fool, not being able to keep from looking at them, looking at us. But there was nothing to do except keep walking.

The business district gave way to small stores and gas stations, which finally gave way to houses but it was no better here. He blew the siren again causing dogs to bark at us from the yards. Kids ran to the yard fences, shrieking and cat-calling. People came out of their houses to look, to point and laugh.

The houses finally got farther and farther apart but we were back out on the prairie, maybe a mile and a half from downtown, before we crossed the city limits.

He honked then, and turned around, driving back toward town. We let him get almost out of sight, then we both gave him the finger.

I sat on my suitcase and looked around, still mad, still burning with humiliation but too hot and tired to do anything about it. The dryness in my throat made me wish I'd paid that extra dime for another glass of water.

"What are we going to do now?" Rocky asked.

"I don't know," I said. The sun was beginning to settle pretty fast, "It's about six. I reckon we'll spend the night out here somewhere."

Looking back toward town and into the wind, I could see the water tower and the grain elevator. Unconsciously we had headed north. I got out the map and checked it. Highway 183 to Clinton, the next major town on the map. I remembered what that guy had said earlier, *'Y'all head north to Clinton and I'll pick you up. I'll be headed that way early,'* Maybe, just maybe, he would.

We sat there for over an hour without anyone coming by before I said, "to hell with this," picked up my suitcase and started walking up the road.

"Where you going?" Rocky said.

"Maybe they'll be a house or a pond or something up the road. I'm thirsty and I'm going to try to find something to drink."

After about a mile we topped a small rise and saw the house. It was still over a quarter mile away but it was just off the highway. It was just coming dark when we walked up in the driveway.

The house was old, tattered and run down. It was surrounded by pieces of machinery, some with grass growing up through it. A battered GMC pickup sat in the driveway. The yard fence was falling down in places and the yard was a clutter of automobile and machinery parts, bottles, beer cans and bailing wire. We walked on the sagging porch amidst a pack of barking dogs and I knocked on the door. A woman appeared. I stepped back when she opened the screen.

"What can I do for you boys? she said.

She could've been anywhere from thirty to sixty, barefooted and dressed in a faded print dress with one sleeve missing. At one time it had buttoned up the front, but now about six inches of her stomach was showing through a gap where a safety pin held it almost together. She had three teeth missing in front and wore no bra. Her breasts hung almost to her waist. A little girl about six peeked out from behind the woman's dress. The term, *'poor white trash',* came to my mind as I said, "Ma'am, we're traveling and real thirsty. Do you think we could have a drink of water?"

"Why shore," she smiled, unmindful of her missing teeth. "It'll be no problem. Y'all just sit yourselves down there on the porch and I'll fetch you one." She turned quickly, almost knocking the little girl down, saying. "Ellen, get outta the way," and disappeared into the house.

I looked at Rocky. He was grinning, about to break out and laugh.

"Man, I'm thirsty and a drink is a drink," I said.

She was gone awhile, five or ten minutes. When she came back she had a large pitcher of strawberry Koolaid, and four bologna and cheese sandwiches. "I figured you boys might just be hungry too," she said.

The little girl was following with two large glasses of ice.

Mentally, I called myself a son of a bitch, as I took one of the glasses from the little girl who was looking at her bare feet, just peeking up every now and then. I took two of the sandwiches from the woman. The bread was soft and fresh so was the meat and cheese. Feeling worse about what I had thought, I said, "Ma'am, we didn't mean to put you out none. You really shouldn't have done this."

"Why, it wasn't no bother," she sat on the edge of the porch, tucking her dress under her legs and smiling again. "No bother at all. We got plenty and like I said, you boys looked hungry."

"Yes Ma'am," I said. "We was, but we didn't want to beg."

She just nodded and smiled again as we ate.

We finished the sandwiches, the whole pitcher of Koolaid, and got up to leave. "Ma'am," I said, "We sure appreciate the food and drink." I reached for my billfold and took out two dollars I couldn't afford to give. "Here, I'd like to pay you."

"I just won't hear of it," she said as she stood. "You keep your money, but I appreciate the offer."

I said, "Well look, if you won't take the money for yourself, take it to buy the little girl something the next time you're to town."

She smiled broadly, again showing the world her missing teeth. "Well now, I hadn't thought about that, but two dollars is just 'way too much for sandwiches and Koolaid."

"It's not for the food Ma'am," I said, "It's for the thinking about us."

She smiled again. "Okay Mister, I'll take the money." She took it from my hand. "I'll use it to buy Ellen something nice."

"I'll bet she'll like that," I turned, still embarrassed about my thoughts, and we walked out of the cluttered yard to the highway. We'd walked about another hundred yards up the highway when Rocky started laughing.

"What's so funny?" I said

"I was just thinking," he laughed some more. "About what else we could've got from that old gal for them two dollars you gave away."

I didn't say a word as I set my suitcase down, turned around and hit him in the mouth and he hit the ground. I don't know if I knocked him down or if he was just off balance and fell down, but he was down.

"What did you do that for?" he whined, touching his lip. "I didn't do nothing."

"I just didn't want you making light of that lady back there." I was bouncing, ready for him to get up.

"Lady! She wasn't no lady! Did you see her dress open, them teeth missing? Didn't you see the way she was living? She wasn't no damn lady!"

I almost kicked him for that, but instead I said, "she fed us. She gave us something to drink. She didn't ask for that money. She didn't even want to take it. She fed us because she wanted to and she probably couldn't afford to give it. And you'll not make light of that---or her! You hear me?" I was screaming by this point, mad clear through. The whole day had caught up with me I guess, Rocky's lying, hitchhiking out here, the bad scene at the café, the sheriff and now, this.

He started to get up. "Don't do it, Rocky," I hissed. "Not yet. Don't get up or I'll hurt you!" Gradually I was calming down and finally I turned, picked up my suitcase and walked away. I walked another half-mile before I was calm again and stopped. Rocky was tagging along about fifty yards back. I sat down on my suitcase and lit a cigarette waiting for him to catch up, thinking, this has been a bitch of a day.

"What do you think?" I said as he sat beside me. It was almost dark now and the huge moon rising from the flat prairie gave a silvery, ghostly look to the land.

"I don't know," he said low. "I don't know what to think." He looked at my cigarette, but he didn't ask.

I looked around, "I think this is as good a spot as any to spend the night. Out here, it don't make much difference but I'm tired and this has not been a good day." I walked about fifty yards into the field and opened the old suitcase, mentally thanking Mom for insisting I bring along that old quilt, thinking at the same time she could have picked one that wasn't pink. I took out the quilt and a pair of blue jeans, doubled the quilt longways so I could lie on half and cover with half and spread it on the ground, then lay down using the rolled up jeans for a pillow. I looked up at the stars, dim in the bright moonlight.

"What are you going to do tomorrow?" Rocky said, making his own bed.

I didn't even have to think about what I said, "I'm going on north until I catch the harvest and try to get a job. That's what I came out here for, so that's what I'll do. Why, what you got in mind?"

"I don't know, I thought maybe you was ready to go back."

"Go back! We just left this morning. I came out here to find work and I'll not go back empty handed after just one day. Besides, they'd laugh us out of town if we went back now."

"Yeah, I guess you're right. But I'm just about ready to anyway."

"Why don't we get some sleep and we'll talk about it in the morning." I said, just about to doze off. I hadn't realized I was so tired until I lay down.

The last thing I remember was Rocky saying, "Yeah, I guess we'll talk about it tomorrow."

*　　*　　*

I woke with a start, wondering where I was, raised up and looked around, then remembered. The sun was just barely above the horizon.

Guessing it to be about six-thirty, I decided to go ahead and get up. I was a little stiff from sleeping on the ground and my hand was swollen across the knuckles. Rocky was still asleep. His lips were swollen too. I didn't feel bad at all. He deserved it.

I heard a motor and looked down the road, unable at first to tell what it was. Then I realized it was something on the back of a truck. As it got closer, I could tell it was three of them in a line, headed north, looking for all the world like some ugly monsters perched on the back of something too small to carry them. The sun glinted on the paddle thing sticking out over the cab of the truck and protruding out on both sides, taking up the whole road, but high enough for cars to pass underneath. About now I decided these were combines.

Apprehension that was mostly fear went through me as I wondered if I was man enough to drive one of those things or a truck hauling one. A sudden homesickness passed over me but then I thought about the car I could buy, maybe. If I could find work and if I could handle it once I found it.

I woke Rocky up after they had passed, hating to. I was sick of him and his bullshit. He grunted, groaned, sat up, blinked and looked around, bewildered.

"Good morning," I said.

He just grunted again and touched his mouth, rubbing it gently, exposing the cut on the inside of his upper lip where it had mashed against his teeth. He stood up walked a few steps away, pissed and walked back, running his fingers through his hair. "Damn, I feel groady."

I did too but there was no need to bitch about it.

He sat down by me. "Well, what are you going to do?"

Knowing full well what he meant, I said. "What do you mean, what am I going to do?"

"Are you going back home today."

I'd made my mind up last night when it all seemed so simple, but now? A wave of homesickness washed over me but then I heard myself say, "I'm going to sit right here and wait for that guy from yesterday. Maybe he knows someone that will put us to work." It sounded weak, even to me.

"He might not come by." Rocky sounded hopeful.

"He'll be by. He said he would and he had no reason to lie. Most people don't lie without having a good reason." My voice had more conviction now.

"I don't know. I'm about ready to head back home. I'm hungry."

"Rocky," I looked at him hard. "I really don't care what you do. You can come along or go back, but even if that guy don't come, I'm still going on."

This time he knew I meant it and didn't say anything else.

We walked back to the highway and sat for what seemed to be a couple of hours. The sun was well up now and it was hot, despite the wind. There was not a cloud in sight, a tree either for that matter. I thought about Mom and Dad. Dad would be on the road by now, Mom cleaning the house. I'll bet she was worried about me, wondering where I was and how I had spent the night. My stomach growled. I had to do something so I picked up my suitcase and started walking.

"Where are you going?" Rocky said.

"I don't know. I just have to do something." I said.

He got up and followed me.

We walked north, the ever-present wind pushing us along. I hadn't even thought about the wind after that occurrence yesterday. It was just there, constantly blowing. We were still walking when I heard a car behind us and turned around to hitch it down. I smiled. It was the man from yesterday.

He was laughing when he pulled over and stopped. "Well, how do you boys like the wheat harvest now?" he asked from the pickup.

"Not worth a damn," I said, leaning through the open window.

"Why it's just fine," Rocky said.

"Where did y'all spend the night?"

"Right out there." I pointed to the side of the road. "About a quarter mile back."

"Nice place ain't it?" he was still laughing.

"I've stayed in better places but when you're tired and don't have better, the ground is alright." I grinned.

"Yeah," Rocky said. "We got a ride this far, but the old boy was turning off so we got out and got stranded here. We couldn't catch another ride. That's the only reason we stayed here."

The man looked at me then cut his eyes over to Rocky, then back at me. "I'm glad I caught you boys. I got a truck and a combine waiting for me in Clinton but I got no driver for the truck so I can put one of you to work tomorrow. The other is welcome to ride there if he wants. Now, either of you ever drove a truck before?" He was looking at me.

I looked him square in the eyes and said, "No Sir, I haven't, but I can sure learn. I learn real fast," my voice trembled a little as I spoke.

"I drove a truck before, all last summer," Rocky cut in. "Yes, Sir, the man I worked for said I was about the best truck driver he'd ever seen. I'm real good so with my experience, you ought to hire me."

The man looked at Rocky then back at me. All of the fear I had just felt was replaced with rage. I knew Rocky was just like me. He'd never been inside a truck cab before.

The man nodded and said. "I'll tell you boys what, you settle it between you right now as to who gets the job and who don't. Flip a coin or whatever but I only need one of you." He grinned, looking back and forth between us.

We settled it or rather I settled it. I didn't need to flip a coin either. I just hit Rocky in the mouth again, hard. The tap I'd given him last night was just that, I hadn't been set right. This time my left foot was planted hard and just a little forward as I pivoted at the waist, aiming for a point about where the back of his head would be, and bam! My full weight was behind the swing. I felt a crunch and my hand went numb to the elbow but Rocky went down and this time there was no question. I knocked him down.

I turned to the man in the pickup, shaking my hand in the air; the feeling was back. Wow, was it back! And damn, it hurt. "Mister," I said. "Like I said, I've never driven a truck before and neither has he, but I can learn."

He just looked at me and laughed. "Well, it looks like you won the flip. How's your friend over there?"

Rocky had raised up on one elbow and was holding his mouth with his free hand.

"You alright?" I said.

He nodded. His mouth was bleeding, but not bad.

"Rocky, if you wasn't such a damn liar you wouldn't spend so much time on your ass. You lied to get me out here. You lied yesterday about the fella you said you knew. You been whining all last night and this morning about going home. Then when we get a job offer, you lie to try to weed me out. You deserved to be hit in the mouth." I picked up my suitcase and put it in the back of the pickup.

"Ask him if he wants a ride to Clinton?" the man said.

"Do you want a ride?"

He shook his head. "No, I'm going back home, right now," he mumbled through his mashed lips.

I felt myself stiffen. "Rocky, you go on home but when you get there, you tell them what happened and how it happened. Don't lie about me because I'll hear it when I get back. If you lie, I'll look you up and when I find you, I'll kick your ass worse than you have ever had it kicked before. You hear me?"

He just nodded, glaring at me. I felt a tremor of fear go up my back. I'd just made a dangerous enemy. Rocky was real sneaky and one to back jump a guy. I'd have to watch him from now on because he held a grudge and he never forgot. I got in the pickup and slammed the door. "He said he didn't want a ride."

"Is he hurt."

I shook my head, not really caring, "Not too bad. He'll be alright, I reckon."

The man stepped out of the pickup, "You going to be alright Boy?"

"Yeah, I'll be okay," Rocky mumbled, getting up and brushing himself off.

"Okay, you take care now, you hear?" The man got back in, put the pickup in gear and we drove off leaving Rocky on the side of the road. And a good feeling came over me.

I did feel bad about going off and leaving him there, but he had lied once too often. I didn't feel bad about hitting him but my hand was on fire with pain and the knuckle on my ring finger was all flat like it had been smashed.

The man leveled the pickup off at eighty, looked at me, then at my hand. "We'll get some ice to pack it in up here a ways," he said.

"Yeah, that would be nice. It sure does hurt."

"You popped him pretty good."

"He deserved it," I said hard, but I couldn't keep from feeling sorry for him. Then I thought, piss on the lying bastard.

CHAPTER 7

My name's Frank Turner," he said reaching across the pickup seat. I started to meet his shake with my right hand, thought about it, then grabbed his hand with my left. "Dave White. Excuse the left handshake, my other one hurts."

"No problem. You say you never drove a truck before?"

I shook my head, "Mister, I've never driven a standard shift car before. We only got one at home and it's an automatic."

He cut his eyes over to me, slumped his shoulders and shook his head like he couldn't believe what he was hearing. He drove on a few miles without saying anything, then pulled to the side of the road, stopped and looked at me. "Dave, I like you. I liked you yesterday or I wouldn't have bothered with you today. You say you learn fast? Well get over here and we'll see." He pulled the emergency brake on and bumped the gear shift into neutral.

I walked around the pickup and got in under the wheel.

"Do you know the gears?" he asked.

"Yeah, sort of. Low, second, high and reverse." I pushed in the clutch and went through the gears.

"That's right. Now, put it in low."

I did what he said.

"Let off the brake," he added.

I did.

"Now, give her a little gas and let out on the clutch."

I did.

The motor revved, the tires screamed, the pickup jumped forward about twenty feet like a crazed animal, bucked and died. Frank bumped his head on the back window then banged his shoulder on the dash. His hat flew out the window and blew down the road. He glared at me a second, got out, chased down the hat, came back, kicked the front tire, stood there a second glaring at me, turned around and took a piss, then got back in, slamming the door and yelled. "Let the damn clutch out slow!" bracing himself this time.

I did a little better, it only jumped six feet this time.

"Stop and try it again."

I did it almost right this time, at least we were moving.

"Try again! I thought you said you learned fast!" he yelled.

"Most things I do," I yelled back, hitting it perfect this time. The pickup pulled smoothly away onto the road.

"Do it again."

After I had pulled off smoothly three times in a row, he said, "Alright, let off the gas and shift into second. I did, barely remembering to push in the clutch. The motor wound tight, and I shifted into high without being told.

"That's not too bad. Now, stop and do it again."

After about three or four times of going through the gears, he said. "Okay now, we're going to learn something else. It's called double-clutching. When you shift gears, you push in the clutch, pull it into neutral, let out on the clutch, push the clutch in, and finish shifting gears. Okay?"

I pulled over to stop, remembering to push in the clutch. The damn thing was a nuisance. I pulled away smoothly, went through the entire procedure without a problem.

"Again."

I did it again.

"Again."

I did it again.

"Let's quit farting around and get on down the road," he said.

I was ready.

I leveled the pickup off at sixty. Not being too familiar with it, I didn't want to drive too fast.

After a while Frank asked, "ain't you curious as to what you're going to be doing?"

"Sure I am. Why?" I grinned nervously

"You haven't asked any questions. Half the kids your age would be full of questions."

"I don't know anything about harvest work so I really don't know what to ask. I figure I'll learn when the time comes."

He nodded, "I like that Kid. I hate someone that has to talk just to hear his head rattle. And you're right, you don't know what to ask. Dave, me and you is going to get along."

A few miles on, just outside of Snyder, Frank spotted a roadside café. "Why don't you stop here."

I pulled into the parking lot and forgot to push in the clutch. The pickup died in a bucking fit.

He laughed saying, "you'll get use to it."

He seemed sure, but I wasn't.

We walked to the café and sat at a booth by the window so we could watch the pickup. A dumpy looking, middle-aged woman came with water an menus, "Y'all going to eat," she asked.

I told her I was, Frank just ordered coffee. This time I checked the wall menu, then opened the one in front of me. The prices were the same. I went down the list until I came to the cheapest breakfast. A short stack, plain, sixty cents. When she came back with the coffee, I ordered.

"You don't want no meat with that?"

I said, "no Ma'am, just the pancakes and coffee." I knew it wasn't enough but I was running low on money.

Frank had been watching me all this time. "You getting low on money?"

"Yeah, I got a little. About six dollars and seventy cents."

He shrugged his shoulders, "you're right. That ain't much. When did you leave home?"

"Yesterday. We'd been on the road a couple of hours when you picked us up."

"What was that all about back there when you hit that kid, Rocky? I get the feeling there was more to that than what I saw."

"There was. A lot more." And I told him about Rocky lying to me.

He laughed when I finished. "I knew he was lying yesterday. That was another reason I tried to get you to go home."

Then I told him about the incident in the café.

"It's a bad deal," he said. "But it happens. Usually just like it did. A couple of hands by themselves, like you two boys, walk in and it's easy. Usually, if a whole crew comes in, they get treated right. Wheat crews have been known to take a place apart when they get cheated. What the people do is have two or three menus made up special. They just saw you coming and figured you for just what you was, easy."

I told him then about the woman at the house feeding us, without being asked.

"You'll find," he said. "That holds true wherever you are. If you're broke and in need of help, go to the poor. They don't have much, but they'll share what they do have. They know what it's like, being down and out, because nine times out of ten, they been there themselves. The ones that can really afford to give, or to help, don't care."

The waitress brought my food: three plate-sized pancakes drenched in butter and a pitcher of syrup. She refilled the coffee cups and left without saying anything. I ate like a starved kid, having some trouble with my hand. It was swollen from my wrist to the first joint of my fingers now.

Frank leaned back, lit a cigarette and laughed. "You act like that is going to be your last meal."

"No," I answered between bites. "Its just the first in a while." I finished off the pancakes, still hungry, but we sat there a few more minutes and drank another cup of coffee before we got up to leave. Everything came to eighty-five cents so I let the woman keep the fifteen cents change for a tip and went on out to the pickup. I wasn't sure whether or not I was going to drive so I just stood by the fender and waited for Frank.

He came out a second later carrying something. "I'll drive," he handed me a plastic bread sack full of crushed ice. "Put that on your hand. It'll help the swelling."

I put my hand on my leg and covered it with the ice, wincing from the weight, but I knew it would help. I kept it there.

Frank pulled away smoothly and was soon leveled off at eighty. "You hit that kid too hard back there," he glanced at me.

"Yeah, I know I did." My voice was tight with pain.

"The next time you got a guy like that to take care of, pick up something to hit him with. You only got two hands Boy. Protect them. You ain't ever going to get anymore if you mess them up. Let me see that hand."

I held it out across the pickup seat. He took it and gently probed the back of it with his thumb. "Feels like you smashed that ring knuckle but there ain't nothing a doctor can do. It's going to be stiff for a couple of days, but if you keep that ice on it, it will be okay, I think."

He held up his own right hand. "You see them two knuckles there? The ring and middle finger?"

"Yeah."

"Smashed them in Prescott, Arizona, back, let's see, must have been eight, no, nine years ago. I was rodeoing then, just a young fart about your age paying my way through college. Got in a fight over a gal one night in a bar. I swung at this old boy but he ducked at the last minute. I hit the concrete wall behind him. It hurt like hell too but what hurt the worse was the gal left with another guy while we were fighting," he laughed.

I laughed with him, thinking about the story. One thing stuck out in my mind. "You say you was in college then?"

"Yeah, I got in a couple of years before I got drafted. I went to Korea for a couple of years, come back and finished up on the GI bill. I still rodeoed in the summers to help pay for it."

"If you got that much college, how come you talk like you do? I mean, you don't talk any better than I do?"

Frank grinned, glancing at me, "oh, I can speak proper English when it pleases me. It has a lot to do with where I am at the time, and to whom I'm speaking. By and large, the people I come into contact with don't really trust a person that speaks properly. So, I talk like they do. This makes for a better relationship and it's also a helluve lot easier to talk like this."

He went silent for a long time after that but I was content to just sit there watching the passing landscape. We were back in brushy, rolling hills now, country that was familiar yet, at the same time, different from what I was used to. I'd seen some mountains, or what had looked like mountains, off in the distance. But when we got close they turned out to be huge piles of granite boulders. I wondered about that, then I realized these were the Wichita mountains.

Really, they were what was left of a mountain range that had been eroded over the centuries to just what I saw; a pile of boulders. They were the very core of what had been a mountain range at one time so long ago there was hardly anything left.

Frank lit a cigarette then he bent down over the steering wheel groping for something under the seat. He brought out a pint of Jim Beam, took a long pull, shook his head, coughed and blew like a horse, and put the bottle on the seat beside him. He looked over my way, "where you from Boy?"

"Crane Oklahoma."

"Crane, Crane? I've heard that name, but it don't seem to be a town. Crane? Lester Crane? Yeah, Lester and April Crane. He's a rodeo rider or he was, seemed like he lived in a town by the same name." He looked at me again.

"Yeah, I know them. And they live in Crane or at least their folks do. I talked to Lester just last week. April too."

He grinned, "pretty girl, April. Just about one of the best looking women I've ever seen. How well do you know her?"

"Pretty well. I'm best friends with her little brother."

"You ever see that sword she carries?"

I laughed, "yeah, I've seen it."

"I seen an old boy pat her on the butt one night in a bar. She had that knife out and up his nose before he could blink." He laughed again. "Then, she said, real polite like, *'please don't do that again.'* Old boy just about swallowed his tongue. Real nice people, April and Lester. Helluva rodeo rider too. He still on the circuit?"

"Yeah, he's still at it. He said he was doing real good this year."

"Crane? Where the hell is Crane?"

"It's a little old bitty place, back east of Ardmore."

"Oh yeah, I never been back down in that country myself. Been to Ardmore though. That's where I was coming from yesterday when I picked you two up. Say, you reckon your buddy will get home okay?"

I shrugged, "if he don't, that's his problem. I don't reckon there is a thing that he can get into that he can't lie his way out of. I'm glad to be rid of him."

"His eyes was too close together," Frank said, over the rush of the passing wind.

"What?"

"I said, his eyes was too close together. Reminded me of a horse I drew twice in the rodeo. Crazy sucker. Try to drag you off in the corral and if that didn't work, he'd fall down and try to roll on you. Never did ride that horse."

Come to think of it, Rocky's eyes were awfully close together.

Frank said, "What did you say your name was again."

"Dave, Dave White."

He picked up the bottle again, took another long drink, coughed twice and laid it back on the seat. "Well, Dave White, that part I told you about me going to college, if I want anyone else to know that, I'll tell them. You hear?" He had a timbre in his voice I didn't like.

"Mister," I said flatly. "I figure your business is your business. One thing my old daddy always told me was not to have diarrhea of the mouth about other people's business."

He'd hurt my feelings saying that, almost making it sound like I couldn't be trusted. I had really liked him up until then, now, I didn't know. I looked him over real close. He wasn't much taller than me, just about five-nine but he must have outweighed me fifty pounds. He had broad shoulders and big bones, evident in his arms and hands, a narrow waist with a belly just starting to protrude. He was dressed the same as yesterday, western shirt, blue jeans, straw hat and cowboy boots.

He felt for the bottle and took another drink. It went down smooth this time and I noticed the tiny broken veins on his cheeks bones and the sides of his nose, the puffiness around his eyes. This might be his first bottle of the day but it sure wouldn't be his last, I thought, looking at the half-empty bottle. He still held the pickup at eighty, no weaving, or wobbling. He was a real drinker for sure.

"Dave," he said, startling me. "I didn't mean to sound so sharp a while ago. It's just that there're people you are going to meet that I'd just as soon not know about that part of my life. It's really no big deal. Just something personal."

I felt better immediately, "like I said, what's your business is your business. I ain't telling nobody, nothing about you. Okay?"

He nodded and grinned, "that's a pretty good deal Kid. Me and you are going to get along."

We were passing through Cordell when I saw a road sign, Clinton - fifteen miles. "Say, just what are we going to do in Clinton?"

"First off, meet the boss, Bob Teemer is his name. I guess then, we'll find a place to spend the night, if they have already loaded that is."

"Loaded?"

"Yeah, they should've finished cutting there late yesterday and loaded today. We're leaving in the morning for Straford, Texas. We have a thousand acres of wheat to start on as soon as we get there."

"A thousand acres, all in one field?"

He grinned, "Yeah, sounds like a lot, don't it?"

"One man plants all of that?"

"Up in Wyoming, we cut one old boy that farms fifteen sections."

"Fifteen sections!" I said, mentally doing the math, six-hundred-forty acres to the section times fifteen--- "Now, that's a lot of land. That's more land than any one man should own."

"That's the way it goes, Kid. The rich get richer, the poor get kids. Besides, that's just what he farms. He runs sheep on ten more sections and angora goats on another ten. Even he don't know how rich he is."

I thought about Davis and his big house as we hit the outskirts of Clinton, not me. That's a trap I won't fall into. I want more from life than shack and a bunch of kids.

Frank turned off the main road, made a couple of more turns through a residential area and stopped in front of a white frame house. "Here we are."

We walked up to the house. A man came out the front door to meet us. "Dave White," Frank said, "Meet the boss. This here is Bob Teemer."

"Howdy Frank," he boomed out. "Good to see you back. Dave White, you say?" They shook hands then Bob reached out his hand to me.

I stuck out my right hand without thinking and almost passed out when he took it in his. The man had the grip of an ape.

Frank must have noticed my grimace because he said, "Boy's got a bad hand there Bob. Nothing that will interfere with his driving though."

"Oh yeah?" he boomed out again. "Let's see it." He took my hand and looked it over carefully. The swelling had gone down some but it still looked bad. "Better take him on in the house and let the Missus look at that. She's the doctor in the family," he yelled out.

I glanced at Frank. He was grinning. "No," I said, in a normal tone. "It'll be okay. I might get some ice off you, if you don't mind."

"What's that you said? Speak up boy, don't be mumbling around me." He looked at Frank. "I hate people that mumble."

I raised my voice to almost a yell. "I'll get some ice to put on it." About now I had figured out this old boy was just about deaf but thought he was normal and everyone else just talked low.

He nodded this time, "yeah, we'll get some ice to put on it. The wife will see to that." He grinned at me. "Truck driver are you?"

I nodded, I liked the sound of that and I immediately liked Bob. He was shorter than my five-eight, but he weighed probably two-hundred-pounds, maybe two-twenty-five. His arms were short and stubby but power seemed to pour from him.

"We're all loaded," Bob said. "So there's no need standing out here in the heat. Let's go in the house, cooler in there." He turned to walk in, Frank and I followed. I was careful to kick the sand from my boots before I went in, Bob and Frank didn't take the trouble.

"All loaded up?" Frank asked as he sat down.

"Yep, finished about a half-hour ago. You timed it just right." Bob took off his baseball cap. He had a ring of gray hair about an inch wide over his ears but the rest of his head was completely bald. What the cap covered was totally white, but the rest of his face was sunburned a deep, reddish brown, causing me to think of Phil Stone, which caused me to think of Gayle and a sudden wave of homesickness washed over me.

"Doris! Doris, come here a minute," Bob yelled through the house. A woman walked in, Frank stood up so I did too. She was Bob's exact opposite. Tiny, that's the only description, about four-ten, and maybe eighty-five pounds. She had dark hair just beginning to gray, and ivory skin that never saw the sun.

"Have a look at that boy's hand." Bob boomed out. "Be careful though, it's hurt. Oh by the way, that there is Dave White, the new truck driver."

She walked to me. I was still standing, but Frank had set back down. He and Bob were talking about something to do with the upcoming trip. Doris took my outreached hand.

"Really ma'am, it's alright. It's just swollen some. I just need some ice to put on it."

She turned the hand over slowly, probing the mashed knuckle. Her hand was cool, light to the touch. "You really shouldn't have hit him so hard," she said in a refined lilting voice. "What could he have done that was so bad to make you want to hit him that hard?" She looked up into my eyes.

"He lied. That was enough."

She studied me a second. "Well if you think so, I guess then you're right." She looked back at my hand. "I'll be just a second." She walked out of the room. I sat back down.

"Dammit, Bob," Frank was saying. "Can we cut that field in a week?"

"Sure, no problem. We'll get out there tomorrow, get unloaded and get in the field at first light the next morning. We can do it."

Frank shrugged. "If we don't, then we will be late at Cheyenne Wells. A heavy dew will hold us up, you know that. Give Stratford ten days. It'll be no problem in ten days."

"Ten days!" Bob yelled. "With you and me and George cutting you know good and well we can cut more than a lousy hundred acres a day."

"Sure we can," Frank said. "Say, you got a beer?" Bob got up, Frank kept talking, "Like I said, sure we can and that'll make both of them happy."

Bob returned with three beers, handing one to me just like I belonged. It made me feel real good.

"You see," Frank continued. "Old man Bonner will be happy because we finished early,"

Doris came back in with an elastic bandage.

"Old man Dougal will be happy because we get to Cheyenne Wells early. We won't be rushed and everybody will be happy."

Doris had started wrapping my hand with the bandage, "Now, this may be too tight to wear all day and night so if it starts hurting, take it off and wrap it back up a little looser but be sure to keep it wrapped. And be sure to keep it packed in ice."

I felt like part of the family.

"Maybe you're right," Bob was saying. It was the first time I'd heard him speak in a normal tone of voice. "By God, you are right," he boomed back up to full volume. "I guess that's the only reason I put up with you Frank. You bring all these strange men into my house, drinking all my beer and making goo-goo eyes at my wife. But you sure got some good ideas." He looked at me and laughed.

I blushed. I felt it, my face felt like it was on fire. Bob and Frank both laughed. So did Doris, and that made me blush even more.

"Bob," Doris said. "Quit tormenting the boy."

He just laughed harder. Frank was no help either when he stood up, still laughing. "That's how he hurt his hand Bob, defending a lady's honor. You better watch him."

If it was possible, I blushed even more.

"Well," Frank stood. "We better go now, lover boy, before you get yourself in trouble with the boss." He was still laughing, even harder now. I was ready to leave. Frank started to the door. I followed. Him laughing, me blushing.

"She sure is pretty, isn't she?" he said, pulling away.

"Yeah, she sure is. Awfully nice too."

"Yeah, and she's a good woman, and that's a rare thing. Well, all that's left is to find us a place to stay. How much money you got left?"

"Five dollars and seventy cents."

"That ain't much."

"No, it sure ain't. I reckon I'll sleep in the pickup tonight, because I plan on eating tomorrow. And after eating today, I won't have any left."

"Don't worry. You're a working man now. You'll make ten dollars tomorrow."

That sounded good. "How's that?"

"Driving this pickup to Texas. Bob pays a dollar and a half, head-time, and a dollar road-time."

I took a drink of my beer. "That don't tell me nothing."

He laughed, "I forget you're still human and haven't learned the lingo yet. You draw a dollar an hour when we move, driving on the road like we will tomorrow. When we work, when the combines are running you get a dollar and a half an hour. He's got a big tent we live in. Saves on the motel charges but you have to eat on your own, except when we move. Then he furnishes sandwiches."

He pulled into a liquor store. "You got all that?"

I nodded.

"Okay. I'll be back in a minute." He went in the liquor store and came back out a few minutes later with a fifth and a pint. One for tonight and just in case, one to get him through tomorrow, I thought.

He drove a few blocks farther and pulled into a motel driveway. It was a shoddy, almost rundown place on the highway. Across the road were shiny three trucks, loaded with huge, red combines.

"Those are ours," Frank said, pointing to the rigs. "Law says we can only travel during the daylight hours with them combines loaded. They're too wide to haul at night. The first one has a fourteen-foot header. The other two have twelve-footers. The big one is mine.

I just nodded making a mental note to go over after awhile to look the things over. Frank must have been reading my mind. "We'll go over in a minute to check you out in one of the trucks. Right now, we need to get checked in." He looked at me, "Now, we can both get a single room or we can save a dollar by doubling up. What do you think?"

"I think I'd rather save the dollar, if it's alright with you."

"Dave, if it hadn't of been alright, I would have never mentioned it," he said as we walked to the motel office and checked in.

The room was down a little from the office so when Frank pitched me the keys I knew I was to bring the pickup around. I did with no problem, finally getting used to the clutch.

We walked into the room. That's all it was, a room. Two half-beds, a small dresser with a chair and a bathroom with a shower.

"It ain't much, but it beats where you slept last night, don't it?" Frank said jokingly.

"Yeah, that it does, especially the shower I can use that."

He laughed. "You'll get use to it. The going dirty, I mean. Sometimes we work around the clock when the cutting is good. You work about twenty hours straight, all you want is a bed when you get in. Sometimes, you will be too tired even to eat."

Now I couldn't imagine me ever being too tired to clean up some or to eat but I didn't say anything, thinking he's been there. I haven't, so I'll not dispute his word.

I bounced on one of the beds. It was harder than mine at home, but so was the ground. I thought I'd done pretty good today, I'd met a friend, one I could learn a lot from. And I had a job, making money tomorrow. I liked the boss and tomorrow I was going to get to see some of the world, even if it was just Texas. I had relatives in North Texas that we went to see occasionally but I'd never been in this part of the state and I was curious as to what it looked like.

Suddenly, I felt real good, real excited, things were working out real good. Then I thought about Rocky and that wasn't so good. I was over my mad at him. I never could hold a grudge like he did. I wished it had never happened. But I was glad now that I'd left home with him. Even if it was a lie, I had done alright. I still couldn't help wonder about him though, where he was, if he was alright. I hoped he'd get home okay.

Frank came out of the bathroom. "Now, let's have a little slug from the wonderful jug," he said, opening the fifth. "And then, we'll go have a look at them rigs before it gets too late." He took a good pull on the bottle, brought it down with an explosive, "Ahhh. How do they make it so good, and sell it so cheap?"

He nodded then and grinned, "let's go look at them rigs."

The good feeling I had was gone as we walked across the highway. Now I was scared. Those trucks sure looked big but as we got closer, I paid more attention to the combines. They were bright red machines with a huge paddle thing stuck out over the cab of the truck. The front tires looked to be five feet tall but the back tires were only about the size of a car tire. The combine itself was big bodied and clumsy-looking with an open seat for the driver, an oversized steering wheel and a big four-bladed fan sticking down at the rear.

"Quite a machine," Frank was saying. "Quire a machine. All the paddle-wheel does is bring the wheat into the scythe or sickle. That's this blade here," he pointed to a row of triangular, saw-toothed, blades that fit inside a bar with pointed prongs. This was at the very front of the scooped shaped trough behind the paddle.

"The prongs guide the wheat to the sickle that slides back and forth cutting the stalks," he continued. "The auger, this drill bit looking thing in the trough, pulls the wheat and chaff into the mouth, a hole in the trough, and then the whole mess goes through the thresher and sifter. That's inside so you can't see it." We climbed up the ladder to the driver's seat.

"The wheat comes in here," he pointed to a large bin with about a bucket of wheat kernels in the bottom. "The straw and chaff are worked through here," he lifted a panel on top of the machine. From the driver's seat, I looked in and could see wheat straw inside. "Then, all the straw and chaff go out the back, hit the spreader and fall to the ground. Like I said, quite a machine. What do you think?"

"I think I don't want to mess with the thing. I don't know a whole lot more about it than I did."

"Okay," he said. "Short lesson, that thing up there is called a header," he pointed to the paddle. "These are the drive wheels and the little ones in back and the steering wheels."

"You mean the back wheels steer the thing?"

"Yeah, the drive wheels are too big to turn."

I was amazed, "the steering wheel turns backwards then?"

"No," he shook his head. "It works just like a car."

"Well, I'll be dipped." I said in wonderment.

"Now, let's look at the truck." We climbed down from the combine and got into the truck cab, me under the wheel. "The gear shift usually is marked with the shifting pattern, " he said.

I looked at the knob on the top of the shifting rod. Sure enough it was marked, 1-2-3-4-R. The numbers were in the shape of an 'H', the R was nearest to me and up.

"All trucks have the same shifting pattern exept the position of reverse which can be at any of the four corners of the pattern. You'll have to find it in each truck. Now, you see that button there?" He pointed to a flat red button on the side of the shifting rod.

I nodded.

"That's called a 'two-speed,' but--. I'll tell you what, I'll ride with you the first couple of trips and show you how it works. It's a helluve lot easier than trying to explain it. Okay?"

"Okay." I felt grateful to him. I mean if help was as easy to find as he'd said. He could've hired someone that knew all of this already.

"Okay," he handed me the key ring, "Start it up."

I found the right key and started the truck. It sounded just like the pickup.

"Remember," he said. "Whenever you have a load, always start in first gear."

I moved the gear shift to one. The transmission scraped some but I felt it pass into gear.

"Always start off with the button down," he pointed to the two-speed, "Okay?"

I nodded.

"Now, check your emergency brake and make sure it's off, then pull it up a few feet."

I did, not jerking it too bad.

"Back it up."

I did a little better.

"Pull it forward." Real smooth this time.

"Back it up." No problem at all.

"I feel like I'm jacking the thing off," I laughed.

He laughed. "Okay, that's enough. I just wanted you to get the feel of the thing loaded. Let's go back to the room. I'm about ready for another drink."

I was ready for a bath and some food.

Back in the room, Frank got his bottle while I took a shower. I stayed in there quite a while watching the dirt and grime melt from me. Two days on the road and sleeping in the dirt makes an old boy appreciate a shower.

I finally came out when Frank started banging on the door hollering "You going to set up camp in there?"

He took a shower while I got dressed and re-wrapped my hand then he came out of the bathroom still naked. I couldn't help noticing two things. With the exception of his face and hands, his body was completely white, never touched by the sun. And the scars. He had several, some long and jagged, three round and deeply dimpled.

He turned noticing me looking and said simply, "Korea," took another drink and began to get dressed. I noticed the bottle was down a full three inches now.

After he had dressed he said, "let's go get something to eat."

I was ready. Those pancakes I'd had for breakfast had left a long time ago.

The small café was about fifty yards from the motel and as we walked in I heard someone holler at Frank. I looked over to see two men sitting in a booth. Frank walked that way so I followed.

"Dave White," Frank said, "Meet Slim." He motioned to a fellow in the booth that fit the name in one way. "And this here is George. Boy's, Dave is our new truck driver."

"Howdy Dave," George said.

"Glad to meet you," Slim commented, then scooted over so I could sit down. I noticed right off that he was two or three inches shorter than me. It was real hard to tell with him sitting down but I would have bet he wasn't a bit over five-four. George on the other hand was a good-sized man, from what I could tell.

"What happened to your hand Dave?" George asked.

"Ah, he knocked hell out of an old boy today," Frank said before I could answer.

George said, "all we need around here is another hot head. You ain't touchy about anything are you Boy?" George asked.

Frank started laughing, Slim got a kind of sheepish look about him. I didn't know what to say.

"Old Slim here," George pointed, grinning, "Is kind of touchy. You can call him about anything and it don't bother him. But God made him so close to the ground that he don't like to be reminded of it. Do you Shorty?"

All my life I had heard of looks that could kill, staring daggers, evil eyes, looks of the devil. I thought I had seen a couple in my life, but I was wrong. Slims eyes seemed to sink back in his head, growing hard and icy. His face lost all expression as his upper lip pulled back exposing his teeth, changing his entire appearance into something totally unrecognizable, something primeval and predatory. Suddenly he became a being that had once walked the earth but had gone extinct, years ago, eons ago. A chill passed through me and I felt the hair on the back of my neck stand up. Reaction set in and I began to move to get out of his way, moving to keep from getting hurt, to keep from dying. But as soon as it came, it passed. He was looking embarrassed now, almost sheepish again.

George and Frank were laughing but it was a nervous laugh, they'd seen it too, and they laughed to prove to themselves they weren't afraid of the thing this man had changed into. I sat back down, laughing too while the only words that came to my mind to describe what I had seen were, *'Stone Killer.'*

It was a term I had heard my dad say describing a couple we saw on TV, Charles Starkweather and Carol Ann Fugate, that had gone on a killing rampage a few years back. I don't remember how many people they killed.

I do remember they started with her grandparents.

Charles was twenty-one, Carol was thirteen. She lived with her grandparents who wouldn't allow her to date him. So they killed them. Charles and Carol stayed in the house with the bodies for three or four days before they went on their spree. They didn't seem to be crazy or anything but, for the most part, there was no reason for what they had done. The people they killed were just at the wrong place, at the wrong time.

And I made a mental note to never, never call this man Short, or to cross him in any manner.

The waitress brought mine and Franks food. The food was good, I guess, I ate it too fast to really taste it.

"You never did tell us how you hurt your hand," Slim said, after I had finished eating.

I told the whole story, playing down the hitting or at least trying to.

Frank wouldn't have it though. "He hit that old boy as hard as I've ever seen anyone hit," he said. "Lifted him off the ground and laid him out. When I saw the kid go down, I thought he was dead with a broke neck. Dave here, gets in the pickup, rubbing his hand, I ask him why he did it and all he says is, *'he lied.'* But he ain't so tough either though, just watch this."

He hollered across the café. "Hey Joan, come here a minute."

The waitress came walking across the café with that special hip swing all good looking waitresses have, knowing when they walk they're the complete center of attention. I had no idea what was about to happen but I had an idea I wasn't going to like it.

She grinned at Frank, as she approached the table and cocked a hip out saying, "you need something serious, Honey?"

"Na," he said. "Us boys just want a professional opinion as to this boy here. George says he's just a kid, Slim thinks he's alright. I think he's kind of cute. What do you think?"

Picking up on it, she moved over toward me and rubbed my face. "Well, he might be all three. He is cute, but he's picked just a little green for my taste. I like my men well-grown and full-seasoned." Then she grinned and bent down and kissed me on the nose.

That did it. I didn't just blush, I turned purple. George would have fallen out of the booth if Frank hadn't been there. Slim was laughing so hard he was choking. Frank was howling and pounding the table. Joan had to sit down and put her head on the table. I was miserable. They made such a racket, the cook came out to see what was so funny. One look at me and she started laughing.

"Knocked an old boy, bigger than him, plumb ass over tea kettle just this morning and look at him now. Scared to death of a little slip of a thing like Joan. What do you think about him now?" Frank gasped.

"I think if it was me," Slim was trying to say between laughing and choking, "If it was me, I'd hurt you Frank. Anybody," he was settling down some now. "Anybody that can take this without going off the deep end is alright." He slapped me on the shoulder.

George just nodded, still laughing. I guess I was returning to normal. At least my face wasn't so hot now, that is until Joan, settling down some, came over and kissed me on the cheek saying, "Honey, don't let these old big boys upset you so. Just come on home with me and I won't let them tease you anymore."

I don't know how it could have been, but this time was worse. And the whole spastic fit started all over again. This time I guess I turned black. Sara was right, they did eat little boys out here. If I was going to make it, I was going to have to grow up some.

After about ten minutes everyone calmed down enough to leave. They were still laughing about it in the parking lot as we walked back to the motel, that is until I flipped that cigarette butt away. It was something I'd done a thousand times and never thought about, until now.

Frank was on me in a flash. He grabbed me by the shoulder, spun me around, glared at me hard, and for a just a second I thought he was going to hit me. He turned me loose, picked up the cigarette butt and brought it back.

George looked disgusted. Slim had already gotten his old smoky look to him.

Frank stuck the cigarette butt in my face. The smoke curled up my nose.

"Don't you ever, not ever, let me see you do that again!" he growled. "Boy, I've seen ten thousand acres of wheat on fire with nothing but God to put it out. I've seen men die in wheat fires. You don't throw away lit cigarettes. Not in the fields, not here, not anywhere. It's a habit that will kill all of us."

He tore a slit in the butt, dropped the hot coal and tobacco on the ground, rubbing it back and forth with his foot. When he moved his foot, there was nothing left. He rolled the paper into a small ball and dropped it, then he scuffed some dirt and buried that. He looked at me wildly and began jabbing me in the shoulder with a stiff forefinger. "That is the way to put out a cigarette!" he yelled. "I swear, if I ever see you do that again, you're gone, through, fired on the spot. I don't care where we are, in town, or on the road, or in the fields. You're fired and I hope you understand me Boy, because when I fire someone, I just naturally kick their ass at the same time. It saves trouble later."

I figured the best thing for me to do was nothing, so I just nodded and looked sorry. He settled down some and then and only then, did I speak. "I just wasn't thinking, Frank. It won't happen again."

"It had damn sure better not," he said, not quite as loud as before. Then he looked at Slim and George and said, "Ah, what the hell. Y'all want to play some poker tonight?"

They both nodded. Slim said, "Yeah, might as well." He looked at his watch. "It's almost six o'clock. What time we leaving in the morning?"

"Leaving at first light," Frank said.

Slim said, "that means we'll be up at four-thirty, to eat and pack. Yeah, I'll play a couple of hours."

"You going to play, Boy?" George asked me.

I nodded saying, "yeah, I'll lose what I have. That ain't much though." I was glad to be asked after the dressing down I had just gone through.

All four of us walked to our room. There were only two chairs so we sat on the floor. Frank took a drink of whiskey and offered the bottle around. Both George and Slim took a drink.

Frank looked at me, then set the bottle beside him without offering, dug in his suitcase and brought out a deck of cards, shuffled and began to deal. "You ever play poker before?" he asked me.

"Some, but not much." My feelings were smarting from the snub.

"We play straight poker," Frank said. "One joker, wild with aces, straights and flushes. Nickel ante, quarter limit with three raises. We don't go in for any of that kid stuff, Dr. Pepper, or Mexican Sweat, just poker. Okay?"

"Okay." I looked at the five cards I had been dealt. "What's the game?"

"Up and back, jacks or better to open. No one opens, it goes too low," Frank said. "You know what I'm talking about?"

I had to smile. I'd heard it said that I cut my teeth on a pair of dice. And I had been playing poker as long as I could remember. Nothing fancy, no card tricks, no cheating. I couldn't tell if a deck was stacked, nor stack one in a basket, but I could play poker. And, yes, I knew what he was talking about. I had the first open and a pair of queens, so I said, "I'll open for a dime."

I held the queens and threw the other three away.

"Big operator over there," Slim said. "I'm in."

George and Frank both stayed. I had eighty cents left and nothing to lose. Frank dealt. I got another queen. I waited until all the cards were dealt then I said, "Bet's a quarter."

"Kid thinks he's a poker player," Slim said throwing out a quarter. George just grunted and folded his hand.

"I'm in," Frank said, pitching out his money.

I turned over the three queens and drug the pot. The deal passed to Slim. He dealt out three cards down. "Seven card stud, roll your own." he said.

Without comment I picked up my hand, three spades and I turned over the lowest one, a four.

"We got us a ringer here," Slim said. "This boy has played poker before."

"That right Dave?" George asked.

"Yeah, I've played some," I said, thinking of the hundreds of games I had watched at home and the thousands I had played with my family.

I filled my flush on the sixth card and raised the bet to a quarter. Everyone folded except Frank. "I'll call and raise you a quarter," he said. "I don't think you got it."

One thing Dad had always said was, *You got no friends in a poker game. Don't even think about who you're playing with, just play the hand as it lays.*

So I raised him back a quarter without looking at my hand. He looked at his hold cards, studied a minute, then called me. The last card came face down, three down, four up. Using the best five out of the seven, I had a king high, spade flush with only three spades showing. Frank had a pair of kings showing, a possible full house but I doubted it, most likely three of a kind. I bet another quarter without looking at my hand.

"I don't know what the kid has but he's sure proud of it." Slim said.

"He knows what he has," George commented. "He ain't looked at that hand for the last two cards."

"Piss on it," Frank said as he threw in his hand "What you got?"

I turned my cards face down, put them in the discards and drug my pot.

"Ain't you going to show me what you had?" Frank asked with an edge to his voice.

"Nope," I said, "You pay to see my cards."

George's eyes narrowed and Slim sucked in a deep breath. Frank had reached for the discards but he stopped suddenly. His hand quivered in the air. There was no spoken comment but suddenly I knew I had made a serious mistake, now two in one hour. The cards were still there, untouched. No one but me would turn them over, those are the rules when the big boys play. George was the next dealer. As he reached for the discards, I reached in front of him, turning over my hand and spreading them out. "I had a little spade flush," I said, low. "Nothing to brag about."

Slim let out the breath he had been holding. George grinned as he picked up the cards. Frank grunted, "Beat the hell out of three kings." And took a drink. "Here," he said, handing me the bottle.

I took a drink and passed my acceptance test.

CHAPTER 8

The poker game broke up after about two hours with me the big winner of about ten dollars, which after the first few rounds of hands, didn't surprise me at all. George only bet when he thought he had the pot won. Slim was shifty-eyed and gave away everything he had. Frank was erratic and bluffed a lot but I learned to read him early on too. I'd had a good teacher, even though Dad had been losing a lot here lately. And, I was playing for my life. I needed that money.

George quit first with a yawn and a look at his watch, then Slim folded. Frank nodded, "yeah, it's about time," and took another drink, passing the bottle around.

George and Slim took a drink, but I passed saying, "I think I'll walk over to the café and get me something cold to drink."

"Kid wants to be a wheatie and don't even drink." Frank snorted.

George and Slim laughed but I said. "I just don't drink it straight."

"You will," George said getting up heavily.

Slim said, "stick with this bunch and you will." And started out the door. "You said about four-thirty Frank?"

Frank said, "yeah, four-thirty, we'll meet at the café. Sun's up about six. We can leave then."

"Sounds early to me," Slim said as we walked out. They went to their rooms. I went on over to the café, bought two drinks and talked Joan out of some more ice for my hand. She was still laughing about my blushing so. On the way out I noticed a postcard rack with some of the cards already stamped. I bought four and walked back to the room. An eighteen-wheeler roared out of the darkness just as I opened the door. I smiled as he passed and went on in. Frank was already in bed, but still sitting up, smoking a cigarette. "What do you think Dave?" he asked.

"About what?"

"About all of this?" He waved his hand in a simi-circle.

"I haven't been here long enough to think about it. I still don't even know what questions to ask."

"Where did you learn to play poker like that?"

"My dad. He's a lot better than me though," I poured one of the drinks in a glass and added a little whiskey.

"I'd hate to sit across from him in a real game then," Frank said. "By the way, you better go easy on that stuff. We have a long way to drive tomorrow. You got any questions about the rigs or the trucks?"

"Like I just said, I don't know enough to ask anything. I think I can handle the pickup okay tomorrow."

"It's no problem. Really just common sense. And once you get the clutch down, the truck will be no problem. You'll do alright."

"Say, you got a pencil?"

"There's a ball point in my shirt pocket. Why?" He pointed to the shirt.

"I have to write a postcard. I got the pen and sat at the dresser.
Dear Mom,
I am fine. Hope this finds you and Dad the same.
I am in Clinton now and have a job. We are leaving
for Stratford Texas, in the morning. I have met a real
nice guy named Frank. He is going to Texas too.
Rocky started back this morning, as far as I know, so look
for him home soon. That's all the room on this card.
Your loving son, Dave. I will write or call when I can.

It wasn't much but it would let them know I was still alive at least. There was no telling what Rocky would say when he got back.

"Your mother?" Frank said.

"Huh? Yeah, Mom. She made me promise to write. I would have anyway though."

He grinned, "Yeah, mothers have a way of worrying some. I'll just bet yours is standing on her head about now. You plan on going back?"

"Back? Going back? What do you mean?" I shook my head, wondering.

"Going home. You ain't out of school yet are you?"

"No, I have one more year before I graduate."

"You going back to school?"

"I'm not sure."

He snorted and said, "you're a fool if you don't. School is about the most important thing a man can have. Oh, you can be a wheat tramp all of your life, or there are other things you can do, but without an education, you ain't nothing."

I shook my head, wondering about that. "You got college. I heard you talk about it. What the are you doing here?"

"Boy," he kind of growled. "I'm here because I want to be, not because I have to. Why are you here anyway?"

"Just like I said yesterday. There ain't no work where I'm from."

"And you come looking, just like that?"

"Just like that? Yeah, just like that."

"Not having any idea where you would be going or what you would do when you got there. Have you ever been away from home before?"

"No, but that's one of the reasons I left too. I thought I might get to see some of the country while I was working."

"You are some kind of a kid, and you have some kind of a mother. Not many would let a seventeen-year-old-kid go off like that."

I had to laugh. "She wasn't all that happy about it. But she knows I can take care of myself. That's why I'm writing though. She'll be worried."

"I know what you mean. And she's right to worry and you're stupid to think you can take care of yourself. You have no idea what's out here or who's going to pick you up next. And any time you work around machinery, you can die or get messed up pretty quick. I've seen men die, lose hands, arms, legs. Good men, so fast they didn't know what happened.

Anything can happen and you have no more control over that than you had over those cards we were playing tonight."

He drained his bottle and looked at it sadly, then grinned. "Another dead soldier." His voice hollow sounding and far away. His eyes grew hard then too and he said, "it's like that in a war too. Luck of the draw. A sniper has three men to choose from and he picks one. Suddenly, that one is dead and the other two are hidden. But why that one?"

He shrugged, still looking at the bottle. "Why him--and not me? An artillery round falls in a group of soldiers. Three are killed, two are maimed, and one is barely scratched. Why?"

He glanced as if I might have the answer but I looked in his eyes and knew he wasn't looking at me. He was looking at something only he could see. Something that wasn't in the motel room. Something that was inside his head.

I looked back at the postcard I had written, deciding it wasn't much, but then deciding like I had thought, it'll let them know I'm alive and well. And that's really all that mattered.

"Lester Crane knows about the luck of the draw," Frank said, low and from far away. "He was over there, taken prisoner. They treated that boy bad. We got drunk one night, me and him, and he started talking about the war." Frank laughed without mirth. "He was going to win it too. Just like me. I guess everyone over there was going to win the war. Lester was worse than most when he came back though. He spent a year in a mental hospital. He was really messed up in the head. I think maybe it would have done us all good to spend some time in a hospital instead of just being kicked back out in the world. Sometimes--- it all comes back."

He laughed after that, a hard, bitter laugh. "It don't have to come back. It's always there. Just under the surface. This used to help." He held up the bottle. Then he shook his head and looked at me, this time he really looked at me. "And that's enough of that. What's the country like down at Crane?"

I said, "rolling hills, lots of woods, oak mostly, some pecan, hickory, walnut, elm. The cedar is about to take over in a lot of places. No work, unless your folks own a place. Then that's all you do is work, but no pay."

He smiled his hard smile, the one where his eyes stayed icy. "It's like that most places. Eisenhower was supposed to stop all of that, like Hoover was. Eisenhower did end the war though," his smile was even harder. "He did do that. At least we signed a treaty. At least the fighting was over, and we came home."

We talked a little more, mostly me talking about Crane. Frank was still preoccupied, almost as if he was lost in his mind again. I noticed when I finished telling a story that seemed real funny to me, he never changed expressions. It was almost as if I wasn't even there, like he had gone somewhere else. Somewhere he couldn't be reached. I realized then he was back in Korea, still fighting the war that had no real ending. The lost war. Some called it the forgotten war. The only one we never really won. The only one they signed an agreement and just stopped fighting.

I sat quietly when I realized that, and soon his eyelids began to droop. Then they closed. I sat there a while longer, just looking at him. I barely knew the man but I felt drawn to him. Something told me I could learn from him, all of the things I couldn't ask Dad, or even Bill, my older brother, because neither of them really knew the things I wanted to learn. They hadn't done the things Frank had. The things I wanted to do, but didn't know how. But there was nothing to do or say now, so I undressed and went to bed.

*   *   *

Four o'clock came just as early as I thought it would but I felt good, excited, really. I was a working man today and today I was going to see the country I had only read about.

Frank looked like he felt as good as a man that had drunk most of a fifth could but he was up and that was something. We were dressed, packed and walking to the café by five o'clock.

Bob was already having coffee when we walked in, "where's Slim and George?" he boomed out as we walked to him.

"They're up and will be along," Frank said.

"Morning, Bob," I said as we sat down. He nodded, grinning.

The waitress brought menus and water without being asked and left. I drank my whole glass of water and was still dry. Bob noticed my empty glass and pushed his over. "Rough night?" he boomed.

I winced at the sudden sound.

Frank jerked, "Bob, he's only three feet from you. You don't have to yell so damn loud!"

"I didn't yell," Bob said in a mock whisper.

Frank growled, "you damn sure did! That settles it. I'm buying you a damn hearing aid, first chance I get. You old deaf bastard!"

"Ain't nothing wrong with my hearing," he boomed back to Frank.

"Just sit there and don't talk Bob, not right now. I really can't handle it right now. We'll talk later, okay?" Frank was holding his head between his hands.

Bob must have taken the hint because George and Slim walked in about that time and he just nodded their good mornings. The waitress came back over with their menus. Slim and Frank just ordered coffee. Bob and George had regular breakfasts. I had a short stack with three fried eggs and a double order of sausage mentally thanking someone for the ten dollars I had won last night. I also remembered what Dad had said: *"Eat when there is food and eat your fill. You never know how long it will be until your next meal."*

I figured it would be at least noon before we stopped to eat. That was six hours from now. Dad had worked out away from home a little but he never talked about it much, not even when I asked him about it. I never really knew why. And I had never asked.

We sat in silence after I finished eating, drinking our coffee, waiting for the sun to come up. Frank was in worse shape than I had thought. He just sat there, staring off into his own private world, drinking coffee the way he'd been drinking whiskey the night before.

Finally he glanced up and stood. "It's light enough, let's go. Bob will lead out with his pickup and trailer. Slim, you're next. George will follow you. Dave, you get my pickup and follow George. I'll be the rear guard. Everyone keep at least three telephone poles apart and watch the man behind you. Especially you George. Bob will set the pace, no falling back or tailgating."

He looked around at us. "Everyone clear."

Everyone nodded.

"Okay, Slim and George, y'all check the chains and boomers before you pull out." He looked around again and nodded. "Let's get at it. We got a long drive."

As we stood to leave he added, "if you get into trouble, flash your headlights. Other than that, just keep them on all the time." He acted like he sure felt rough, but, most men would still be paralyzed after drinking that much.

I walked to the pickup, dropping the postcard to Mom in the mailbox. All the rest went across the road to the trucks. It was light enough for me to see them checking out the equipment, kicking tires, shaking chains, and checking the motors of the trucks. I started the pickup and waited for George to pull onto the road. Two days ago I had left home, just about this same time. A little tremor of excitement ran up my back. I was nervous, excited and scared all at the same time.

Bob pulled out in his pickup. George eased his truck out on the highway. The top heavy combine caused the truck to raise and fall as he crossed the shallow ditch. Slim's truck did the same. I started forward slowly. The pickup bucked and jumped for about fifteen feet, then leveled out. I looked in the side mirrors, watching Frank, slowly pulling into line, finishing the convoy and we were on the road.

We headed north again on the same highway. The moaning wind was at our backs, pushing us along. The excitement I had felt soon wore off as the sun and the heat climbed. The higher they got, the less excited I felt and soon it was hotter than a bygod and boring. The land was flat with an occasional rolling hill, several shades of brown with an occasional patch of dark green but mostly flat, and unchanging.

Four hours later we were still driving having stopped only once to piss since we had left Clinton. I just topped a hill and could see over George's combine ahead of me. The road stretched out like in one of those *'Road Runner,' cartoons*, over a hill and down a valley, over the next hill and down the next hill.

We were in Texas now and had been for about an hour when I passed a sign: Pampa, fifteen miles. We had been driving through some pretty rough country that was about the driest I'd ever seen. It was mostly rock, thin brown grass, some thorny looking brush and an occasional cow. I couldn't help wondering what they found to eat out there, or drink.

We pulled a long winding hill and all of a sudden, the earth went flat. I thought it had been flat back in Oklahoma, but this looked as if it had been ironed. As far as I could see, there was nothing, not a hill, not a tree, nothing but golden ripe wheat, stretching out for miles. It was all the same height about eighteen inches to two feet, waving in the constant, shrieking wind making it seem as if the earth had been transformed into a swaying, tawny ocean. The highway was the only break in the wheat and the highway reached to the horizon as straight as man could draw a line on the curved surface of the earth. There was no ditch in most places and the wheat grew to the edge of the highway, waving and undulating in the wind. And it seemed as if I was lost, alone in a land where time and distance had no meaning.

I realized now we had entered the Llano Estacado, the Staked Plains of the panhandles of Texas, Oklahoma, Kansas, Colorado, and New Mexico, thrown in. I had read about this country. I had read that no one really knew where that name had come from but there were stories from the Comanche and Kiowa tribes about Coronado crossing here, back in the early 1500's. The legends said he had driven stakes in the ground to find his way back. He had to come back the same way he went because of the scarcity of water. Now I believed the tales. There was no focal point in sight, nothing to guide a man on horseback through. It was a land of distances, terrible distances that reached out as far as one could see to nothing. It was all the same, only the golden wheat, waving in the wind. Nothing else. I thought again about Coronado. He'd crossed this area looking for the Seven Cities of Cibloa, the fabled cities of gold, never finding them. When all the time he had been riding over land that grew gold.

An hour later the view was the same. We were traveling at forty-five to fifty miles an hour and I couldn't really tell we had moved. Oh there had been side roads going off into the distances and once in a great while a splash of green, man-planted trees around a house, or where one had been in the past. But other than that, there was wheat. I had no idea there would be so much wheat in the world. Then I remembered that this reached all the way to Canada, another thousand miles or more. It was mind boggling.

I saw Bob pulling over now into what seemed to be a roadside park. Really it was just a turnout with nothing else, but it was a place to get off the road. George followed, pulling in behind him. I lined up behind him and took a welcome piss. Frank was checking his chains when I walked up. "Well, Wheatie, what do you think about driving now?" He laughed as he asked.

"Thinking about it is a helluve a lot more exciting than doing it." I said.

Frank laughed again. "You'll find that to be true about most things in life, Dave," he looked around the and nodded. "Yeah, this is the rough part, but it could be worse. Bob could have us working."

I wondered just what he meant but I didn't ask. He did look like he was feeling some better.

"You like the view around here Dave?" Frank asked then grinned and waved his hand in a semi-circle.

I shook my head. "Why do you ask that? There ain't no view around here. It's just flat, and wheat."

"Get use to it Wheatie, because that's about all your going to see for about the next three months. You'll get so you can see wheat when you close your eyes. Standing wheat or cut wheat. That's the only difference from now on."

I was terribly disappointed for a second but then I thought, he's just saying that. "It is kind of pretty though, with the wind blowing it almost looks like a brown ocean."

"Yeah, it's hypnotic, almost like looking into a fire. It changes all the time but it never really changes. Almost like people."

"Let's eat," Bob hollered in his normal tone and we walked to the house trailer. On a small table, he had pressed ham, bologna and liverwurst meat, cheese, mustard and mayonnaise, lettuce, pickles, onion, potato chips, corn chips and two big cans of pork and beans. A case of Coke rested in an ice chest to wash it all down with.

I made two sandwiches to start with using a piece of each meat and cheese, a good portion of lettuce, pickles and onion on the side, and dished out a solid helping of beans, then added a good helping of corn chips just to round things out. I opened a Coke and sat cross-legged on the ground. Just as I sat the wind blew a hat full of dust across my plate. It didn't even slow me down.

I finished off that helping, made another sandwich in the same manner and dished out some more beans. They were getting low so I minded my manners and didn't take as much as I wanted, settling for another handful of corn chips.

I ate that, finished my Coke, opened another and lay back on my elbow, relaxing. I heard Slim and George laughing and looked up. Bob was just standing there looking shocked. Frank was grinning.

Slim was saying, "can't no one that skinny eat that much. He like to have made me sick this morning and now this." He shook his head

"Bob, it's a damn good thing you ain't paying board, because he'd eat up all your profit plumb up," George said between laughs.

I could have eaten another sandwich. I was just being nice.

About fifteen minutes later Frank stood up, nervous like. He started picking up rocks from the road bed and throwing them. Finally he said, "let's get on the road."

We got up, put away the rest of the food and everyone started back to their truck. I got in the pickup before I noticed all the rest had their hoods up. Feeling like a fool, I got out and checked the oil too. I was learning, not fast, but learning.

For the next hour and a half we rolled through the wheat. Frank had been right about the view, it didn't change much. We were headed north on Highway 87 now, having passed through Dumas about ten miles back when I saw a sign that read, Stratford, 14, and I was glad the trip was almost through. I was ready to stop although I had no idea what would happen then. Occasionally now I'd see a crew working the fields and we met several loaded trucks going back into Dumas. But other than that, it was just miles and miles of nothing but miles and miles of ripe golden wheat, rippling in the wind.

I thought, no wonder Frank had dressed me down so for throwing that cigarette butt away. Ripe wheat is nothing but dead grass. And the grass fires we had at home came to my mind, how hard they were to catch and to put out. Compared to this, those would be as easy as blowing out a match. It was a scary thought.

It was still almost ten miles into Stratford but I could see the water tower and the grain elevator looming out of the wheat fields from here. I didn't expect much of the town. I wasn't disappointed or surprised when we pulled on through. It was just another dusty little town, baking in the afternoon sun, being tossed by the never-ceasing wind.

A few miles farther on I saw Bob turn off the highway onto a section line. He drove for two miles then turned onto another road, drove for about a half-mile and we were there. It was a sprawling, old, wood-frame house, painted white, a large porch with a swing and a fenced yard. The small area of green grass and trees looked out of place in the ocean of brown but the place sure looked like a home.

CHAPTER 9

$$\sim$$

Bob stopped out in the road that circled in front of the house but George pulled on in by the barn. Not really knowing what to do, I stopped behind Bob. Frank and Slim pulled on in behind George. I saw Bob get out so I did too.

Bob walked up to the house. I went around behind the barn. Frank, George and Slim were all pissing on the side of the barn, so I joined them. After he finished, Frank sat down in the shade. The rest of us followed suit. Looking over at me, Frank said, "Dave, why don't you go get us a Coke?"

I walked back to the trailer and using my head, brought the whole ice chest back. I got out four then sat on the ice chest, leaning back against the barn. Bob came back about that time with three generations of Bonners. One man about sixty, one about thirty and one about three. I stood up and got out three more Cokes and opened them before handing them out.

"Boys," Bob boomed out. "Want y'all to meet the Bonners, George, George, and over there," he pointed at the kid who had run over to Frank's truck and was checking out the tires, "is George."

"George and George," Bob boomed out again, "Y'all know Frank there." Frank raised his Coke. "This here's our George, Slim and Dave."

George and Slim got up, so did I. We shook hands all around then Frank stood and said, "good to see you again, Mister Bonner and Sons," shaking their hands. Then he hitched up his pants and said, "let's get at it boys. We got work to do and time's wasting."

Frank backed his truck up to a dirt ramp built up to the height of a truck bed. George loosened the chains holding the combine while Slim started to back it off the truck. The combine sat on three two by twelve boards as wide as the tires which were wider than the truck bed. When Slim would back off of one board George would move it to behind the tire. When the combine cleared truck bed Slim moved down the dirt ramp. Frank pulled away and Bob backed another truck in. Frank told me to start putting the side-boards on the truck bed and within an hour we were completely rigged and ready to cut wheat.

Bob, Frank and the three George's walked out into the field stopping occasionally to strip a wheat head. I walked to the edge of the field and pulled a few heads myself. I rubbed them between my hands to rid the kernels of the chaff which left me with a couple dozen wheat kernels. Each kernel was about a quarter-inch long and by itself weighed nothing. But I figured a thousand acres would make a pretty good pile when it was all cut.

They started back toward me, all smiling and I could hear Bob yelling in his normal tone. "No sir, it couldn't be better. This here is the exact right time. The grain's still heavy, but dry, and the stalks is just dry enough. The stuff will cut like butter. She's perfect."

"Let's go Wheatie," Frank said as he passed. "We got work to do."

I fell into step beside him. "What's that?"

"Got to get to town and get the tent set up right now. Then," he looked up at the sun, then at his watch. "Then, I'm not sure."

Slim and George were both sitting in the shade by the barn and both got up as we passed.

"Yes sir," Bob boomed, "Yessirree, y'all just go on into the house and let us get to work and just don't worry, we'll get your wheat cut. We'll be gone just about an hour and start when we get back, you hear?" Everyone with in a half- mile heard.

The Bonners nodded and went in the house. Slim got in the pickup with Bob. George and I got in with Frank. I remembered the ice chest out behind the barn and told Frank about it. He pulled the pickup around and as George got out and put it in the back of the pickup.

"Okay, Wheatie," Frank said as we drove away. "You mind this road well because we're going to start tonight. Now don't worry, I'll go with you the first couple of runs just to get you settled but after that, you're on your own, hear?"

"Yes sir," I replied, causing George to snicker.

"Frank," George said over the seventy mile an hour wind noise. "Just when did you become a *'Sir'?*"

"Boy's got manners, that's all. It shows he's had the hell knocked out of him a time or two."

George laughed a second at that, then said. "What's got into Bob, wanting to start cutting tonight?"

"Ah, old man Bonner got a hair up his butt. He watched the weather report on TV last night. Said it might rain later on in the week."

Being dumb, I asked. "What's wrong with rain? It might cool things off a little."

"It will cool things off alright," Frank said. "It will cool things off a bunch. Can't cut no wet wheat Boy. The ground gets wet, them combines get stuck. The wheat gets wet, it'll rot in storage if not in the fields first. A poor-assed farmer prays for rain all year except for one week and that week is now. A rain will kill us. A heavy dew is bad right now, but we sure don't want rain."

When we pulled onto the highway Frank stopped suddenly, saying, "look for you a landmark so you'll know where to turn on the way back. There's one," he pointed. "That old crooked telephone pole there."

I saw the pole. Sure enough, about four feet from the top of the pole was a dog-leg crook, easy enough to see and remember. "Okay," I said. "I got it."

Frank pulled away. It was about seven miles back into Stratford but the grain elevator and water tower were plainly visible.

As we came into town Frank pointed to a drive-in, hamburger joint just ahead. He slowed as we came to it, then said, "this drive-in is your landmark for the elevator, Dave." He didn't turn as we drove past a tiny little ramshackled building with an awning out front, a dirt parking lot and a girl sitting outside on a bench.

"The elevator is right down to the end of that road. Fact is, the road ends at the elevator, so you can't miss it. When you get there just do what the man tells you, okay?"

"Okay." I was checking out the girl on the bench. She was pretty, so I made a mental note to stop and check her out further when I could. We stopped just then at a motel, café, service station combination.

"This is it," Frank said pointing at a vacant lot behind the station. "We buy all our fuel at the station and eat our meals at the café so they let us camp here. The station has a shower in back they let us use and we get to use the rest rooms. It saves us almost five bucks a day so it's worth it."

I said, "at those prices I'd be sleeping in one of the trucks."

Bob and Slim were unhitching the trailer, getting it set up. The rest of us got the tent out of Bob's pickup and set it up. It was a nice tent with plastic screened windows inside so we could roll up the canvas walls and plenty of room for four cots, even with a table and chairs sitting in the middle.

We were through in less than a half-hour so we all piled in Bob's pickup, Bob, Frank and George in the cab, me and Slim in the back and headed back to the field. We passed a row of combines, still on trucks and I noticed a large sign on one of them, *'FOR HIRE'*. Just to make conversation, I asked Slim what it meant.

"Them's independents," he said. "We're custom cutters. We work the same fields every year. Bob's got contracts to go from South Texas plumb into Canada, cutting all the way. Most operators do now days so them old boys there just pick up what's left, kinda scabby like. They're a dying breed, the independents, because all the good fields are already contracted. The other fields, some of them is in bad shape, rough, not level, or too small to make any good money on. Like I said, they're a dying breed. But every now and then a custom cutter can't make his contract because of breakdowns, rain, and what-have-you. Then, they get hired. So then they come into a good field. But it don't happen often."

I noticed their equipment wasn't as nice as Bob's, faded old trucks and combines looking somewhat run down. But I didn't really care, I had other things on my mind right now and started paying attention to where we were going, knowing I would have to drive it soon. But sure enough, there was the dog-legged telephone pole. I could see it from almost a half-mile away.

We turned off the highway and were at the Bonners in a quick couple of minutes. Bob pulled right up to Frank's combine, real close. He stopped and looking at me yelled, "check the fuel on them rigs."

I was willing but I didn't know anything about the rigs so I looked at Slim.

"I'll show you how," he said as he climbed out of the pickup. "You never done any of this sort of work before?"

"No, sure haven't."

He grinned. "Well kinda stick by me right now and I'll show you the ropes. And don't worry about it. They was a time when none of us knew anything about this kind of work. We all learned. So will you."

"Okay." I liked Slim. I liked the whole crew. They all treated me like a retarded little brother but that was okay. I was learning.

It took over an hour to get all the rigs ready then we went to work on the trucks. Just fuel, check the oil and kick the tires for them and we were ready. I had missed the rest of the bunch when Slim and I started working on the rigs. Now I saw them way out in the field, walking back toward us. "What have they been doing?" I asked Slim.

Slim said, "They just been checking the field for rocks and holes and such. Rocks plays hell with them rigs and if the fields got holes, you can dig that header in the dirt. That raises hell too. They spend a little time now and save a lot of money later."

Frank walked up about then and hollered, "let's cut wheat!" He climbed on his combine, looked at me standing there. "Come on Wheatie," he yelled, "Ride with me," as he fired up the rig and pulled off.

I ran to catch him and jumped on the ladder. He put the header in gear just before we entered the wheat, and lowered it until it was inches off the ground. The paddle wheel started rotating, slapping the wheat heads, pulling the stalks into the scythe that was clattering back and forth, cutting. The auger pulled the whole mess into the mouth of the beast that appeared to be eating the cut straw. Almost immediately wheat kernels began popping into the hopper from a spout. I reached out, grabbed a handful, tiny insignificant things made out pure gold. It felt great. I felt great. I was finally working.

We turned a corner. Frank was sweeping wide, keeping the fourteen-foot header buried in the standing wheat. I looked back. Bob was coming, cutting a swath almost as wide as Frank's. George followed Bob at about the same distance, missing the outside edge of the wheat by an inch or so. Sweeping around the square corner, they left a triangular patch standing to be cut later. Got to keep the header buried and don't waste time. Time is money, wheat is money. We got to get it cut.

The sun was setting. The continual wind moaning, rippling the wheat over the entire field, causing it to glint and glitter in the fading sunlight like a blanket of spun gold. We turned again, this time going with the wind and we were completely enveloped in a cutting, choking, suffocating, cloud of dust, straw, chaff and insects. The cloud blocked out everything and whipped by the strong wind, hit me like a thousand needles, stinging and scouring every square inch of exposed skin. My shirt had been wet with sweat. The dust turned it to mud. In an instant my eyes, nose and throat were filled. Panic gripped me. I couldn't see. I couldn't breath. I wanted to run, but there was no escape, no place to hide. There was nothing but the all encompassing, choking, cloud.

For what seemed like hours we rolled in the cloud of dust, then we turned and it was gone as fast as it had come, blown away by the same wind that brought it. Frank was completely covered with dust, his eyes glaring red, watering, smarting. He hawked and spat then closing each nostril with a finger, blew a gob of mud from his nose. He looked at me and laughing, yelled over the noise of the rig, "Well Wheatie, how did you like that?"

I yelled back. "You knew that was coming. Why didn't you warn me?"

"I figured I would break you in right. Damn, you are nasty. Don't you ever bathe and change your clothes? That's all you Wheaties are, just nasty, just the scum of the earth," he laughed again.

I couldn't see me, but if there was any comparing with Frank, he was right. Damn he was nasty.

We were coming down the outside edge now almost to where we had first entered the wheat. Frank stood, piercing my ears with a shrill whistle made by blowing across his lower lip. Slim started toward us in a truck and pulled parallel to the still-moving combine. When Slim had the speed and distance constant, Frank pushed down a lever and the wheat began pouring from a spout on the side of the rig into the bed of the truck. Within minutes the hopper emptied. Frank closed the lever and honked. Slim stopped, letting Frank go on then waited to pick up Bob and repeated the events as smoothly and naturally as a ballet I had seen once in a picture show.

"Am I going to have to do that?" I yelled over the noise of the machine.

"Yeah, but later, after you get used to the truck. You can do it. It ain't hard so don't worry about it, okay?"

I just shook my head, thinking, I would sure have to go some before I could do that.

We started another circle of the field, and looking down I could see all kinds of movement in the wheat. A covey of quail flushed. A turtle climbed ponderously out of the way of the rig. Now, a jackrabbit went bounding away, deeper into the wheat, where before long there would be no safety. The waving rippling blanket would soon be gone, cut down and turned under to rise again next year, only to be cut down again by this monstrous beast man had created to feed himself.

It was almost impossible to talk above the clatter and roar of the machine so I just looked. Far off in the horizon a plume of dust was rising in the late afternoon. Cutting wheat. Out on the road, miles away another crew was moving in. Soon, I guessed, this whole area would be a beehive of combines and trucks and I was part of it. The harvest.

I hadn't really thought about it before now, but what we were doing was important. We were feeding the nation, the whole world, right here. There was no telling where this wheat we were cutting would wind up or what form the flour would eventually take. Bread, cookies, cake or whatever, someone would be eating what I was helping cut, right here. But then the hay I had hauled with Early Dean, back home, went to feed cows and was turned into milk and meat. So I had done this before. It just seemed different now, more important. This was people food I was harvesting.

I had come a long way, but I had a lot farther to go. I was ready, because this, just this, made the whole trip seem worth it. It had only been three days since I had left home but it seemed like a year. I had trouble remembering what I had done yesterday for wanting tomorrow to get here to see what it would bring. For the first time in my life, I really felt important, needed, something, someone.

We made the third turn again, the dust catching us and obscuring the world again. But this time I was expecting it and knew it would pass. Maybe I even welcomed it because surrounded by the dust, I could become the field. I was the wheat. I was the harvest.

CHAPTER 10

As we cleared the dust, Frank grinned, his teeth sparkling against the dirt covering his face. This time when we went down the outside edge he pulled out of the wheat and stopped. Slim pulled under the spout and got out of the truck, looking puzzled. "Something wrong, Frank?"

"No, me and Dave are going to take that load to town," Frank yelled over the noise of the clattering drill like agure

"Gonna show him how it's done huh? Okay."

Bob came clattering up, stopping in the wheat. "What's wrong Frank?" he yelled.

"I'm going to check this boy out on that two-speed. He ain't never drove one before," Frank yelled back.

Bob shook his head, making a motion near his ear with his hand signifying he couldn't hear.

"Go tell the old deef bastard we're going to go to town with this load," Frank told me.

"Okay," I yelled jumping free of the rig, running over to Bob's combine, climbing the side. "Frank said he's going to go with me on this load to show me how to work the two-speed," I yelled in Bob's ear. He was just as grime covered as we were.

"Okay," he yelled back. "I just thought he had broken down or something." His yelling hurt my ears even over the sounds of the running machine.

Frank had shut off his rig and was climbing down when I got back. "I don't know as how I want to go to town with you," he laughed. "You are nasty. Don't you ever take a bath?"

"No worse than you," I laughed back as we walked over to the truck and climbed in.

"Put her in first gear and push the button down," he said when I started the truck. "Let out on the clutch and give her a little gas. Not much now or you'll bust the drive shaft."

I was scared but did like he said, listening to the roar of the engine wrapping up real fast as we pulled away. The torque of the engine causing the truck to lurch. "Okay now, pull the button up, push in on the clutch and let off the gas at the same time, then let the clutch back out and give her the gas."

I did, feeling the transmission shift and hearing the engine change at the same time. The torque was still causing the whole truck to lurch and jerk. "Don't worry about that," he said, almost reading my mind. "You'll learn how to do it smoother."

"Okay," he yelled over the racket of the engine and the lurching whine of the transmission. "Shift to second, but just before you let out on the clutch, push the button back down."

I did, grinding the gears but managing it.

He shook his head, "You didn't double-clutch it like I told you. Always double-clutch it." The motor was wrapping up again, but this time the lurching wasn't as bad. "Pull up on the button and single clutch it."

I was better now, trying to remember the sequence, and felt the truck shift again. This time it took longer for the engine to wrap.

"Just hold her right about there till you get out of the field," he yelled. "It ain't really necessary to use the clutch with the two-speed, but I was taught that way, so you do it too."

I drove around the barn and out into the road. Frank nodded his head. "I'll make a truck driver out of you yet. You're doing fine."

I felt my whole body swell up. God, I was proud.

The gravel road wasn't a problem, I just had to shift the gears but I was getting use to that by now. When we came to the first turn, Frank said, "now we're going to learn down-shifting. It's just the opposite of up-shifting but you use the gears and the engine compression to slow the truck. Saves the brakes that way, especially when you're loaded."

I was in fourth gear and as we approached the corner, Frank said, "don't worry about the two-speed, that's for going forward, slow down just a little then double-clutch it back into third but don't give it any gas when you let out on the clutch."

I did and the motor revved real loud but the truck slowed almost immediately. As the engine sound died away and we slowed even more, he told me to go to second. I did and then applied the brake to make the corner, then speeded back up.

"That was real good," he said as I shifted back into third. As we approached the highway I went through the whole sequence without being told, then stopped. I pulled onto the highway smoothly, and turned on the headlights. It was just turning dark. I up-shifted through the range and leveled off at about forty-five. Frank was silent again, with that old faraway look on his face. I wondered what he was thinking but I didn't ask.

We passed a house, all lit up, and through the open window I could see the people setting around the TV. A woman was standing like she'd just come in from another room, probably the kitchen.

"I hate this time of the day," Frank said, breaking the silence. "No matter where you are, you can't help but think of home at this time of the day."

"Yeah, I know." I swerved to miss a rabbit in the road, causing the truck to lean and sway. I hated to kill anything unnecessarily.

"You want to be careful doing that." Frank said hard. "This ain't no Volkswagen you're driving. One of these things can get out of control before you know it. And then, you have a mess to clean up."

"Okay." I hit another rabbit, shuddering at the crunch it made under the wheels. We passed another house, then more, closer together then we pulled into the outskirts of Stratford. I began looking for the drive-in land mark which reminded me I hadn't eaten in a long time. Suddenly I was starved.

"Turn here! Turn right, right here!" Frank yelled suddenly. I slammed on the brakes, almost going into the ditch as I barely made the turn.

I yelled, "what did you do that for? The turn ain't here, it's up a little. You almost caused me to wreck the truck! You gone---"

"Stop it! Stop the truck! Here!"

I stopped, sliding the tires almost going sideways, forgetting to push in the clutch, causing the truck to lurch and die. "Frank! What is wrong--"

He was gone. He had just jumped out of the truck and was gone. First I was shaken, wondering what had happened then I was mad. He'd almost caused me to wreck the truck. That feeling soon turned to fear as I stepped out wondering why, where he had gone. I looked up and down the road. There was nothing except a few ramshackle houses, no one but me. A dog barking caused a chill to pass over me. It was like something unreal, almost as if he had never been. I got back in the truck, real scared, shaking, feeling lost, alone. I knew he had come with me but where had he gone---The door flew open, I yelled and jumped.

"Let's go!" he yelled as he climbed back in. "Get the hell out of here! Go, dammit!" he yelled again.

I started the truck, forgot to shift it back into first and killed it trying to take off. I started it again, and pulled away not knowing whether to be mad, scared or happy.

"Turn here!" he yelled.

I turned and started down a torturously narrow road. Up ahead a car was parked. I inched my way past, then yelled at him. "Where did you go?"

Then I saw the paper sack and heard the *'chink'* of full glass on full glass. I saw him reach into the sack, pull out a pint bottle and tilting back his head, take a long gurgling drink.

A bootlegger, I thought. He had made me almost wreck the truck twice so he could stop at a bootlegger's.

I wanted to say something. I wanted to yell, to scream at him. But I didn't. I knew instinctively that anything I said now, I'd be sorry for later. But I wanted to hurt him. I wanted to tell him how I felt, how he had made me feel. But I didn't. I just drove the truck.

A minute or so later I came to an intersection and knew to turn right. A few minutes later I saw the back of a truck with more trucks in front of him and growing out of the deepening gloom, I could see the elevator ahead. I pulled up smoothly and stopped behind the truck but Frank didn't notice. He was having another go at the bottle. I shut off the engine and sat in silence.

Frank coughed twice and took another drink, gave an explosive, "Ahhhh," and handed me the bottle. "'Cheap rot gut. But it'll sure do the job."

I was still mad, seething mad, churning inside. I hadn't ever been this mad before, not even when I had hit Rocky.

"Here," he said, shaking the bottle. "Have a drink. Come on, have one. Say, I'm sorry about that back there. I had almost forgotten where that old boy lived. I didn't mean to scare you. Come on, take a drink, it'll help."

I grabbed the bottle and took a big drink. I coughed, spluttered, blew, coughed again, not able to get my breath. The whiskey was like liquid fire, burning, searing my mouth and throat, hitting my empty stomach like an exploding bomb. Quickly I opened the door, hung my head out and vomited. It was worse coming back up.

Frank laughed, threw back his head and laughed, "I knew you was a pansy," he howled. "I knew you wore lace panties. You can't hold your liquor. How are you ever going to make a Wheatie if you can't hold your liquor?"

I still had the bottle so I took another drink, a small one this time. I sloshed it around in my mouth and spat, almost vomiting again then took a very small drink. I held it in my mouth a second then swallowed. God it burned all the way down. I swallowed three more times to keep it down. Frank laughed even more this time. I heard a honk and looked up. The truck in front of me had pulled up about sixty feet. I started the truck put it into first and pulled up smoothly.

"You'll do," he said. "Almost wrecked us back there but you pulled it out real good. I couldn't have done better. Yep, you'll do." He took another drink.

I didn't know if he meant all of that or not but it sounded good, real good. And it made me feel a whole lot better. And the more I thought about it the better I felt. My mad was gone now, I was alright again. I reached over, took the bottle from him and had another, very short drink. The stuff still burned but it went down a little better this time. I only had to swallow this drink twice.

I pulled up again, this time to the large platform scales just outside the elevator door. "You weigh in, then dump," Frank said. "Then you weigh out. They'll give you a ticket with your weight on it. The man will ask who you're driving for. Remember his name?"

"Yeah, George Bonner."

"That's right. You tell him that and when he gives you the ticket, check it. It should have Bonners name, the weight in, the weight out, and the balance on it. Always check the tickets and hang on to them. The ticket is the only proof we have of this load. You got all of that?"

"Yeah. I got it."

"Okay, pull up. Make sure you're on the scales."

I did, looking in the mirrors to see the back wheels. A voice came over the speaker. "Who are you?"

"George Bonner."

"Okay, pull up."

I let the clutch out too fast. The truck jumped and died. I started it again and pulled into the huge door of the elevator. Two boys about my age were standing by the door, one on either side, both had scoop shovels. I'd seen them work on the last truck. The dump gate was in the middle of the bed and when the dump bed was raised, they would scoop out wheat caught in the corners of the bed. It looked like hard, back-breaking, work to me. The boys were even dirtier than we were. Only their eyes and teeth were clean. The boy on my side blew his nose as we passed. It was just a gob of mud as it hit the inch thick dust and rolled into a ball, crossing the floor. I had never read Dante's, *Inferno,* but I had heard about it. A man's trip to hell. Well, I thought, these boys were just about as close to hell as a man could get and not be there.

One of them hollered. I stopped the truck and looked at Frank.

"Okay, those two knobs there," he said pointing at the black and red knobs protruding through the dash. "Push in the clutch and pull out the red knob."

I did, feeling it grinding into gear.

"That's the power take off, now, pull out the black knob, that's the hydraulic line, and let out the clutch."

I did and with a whine the truck bed started to rise. By the time it was all the way up, one of the boys hollered again.

Frank said, "Push in the clutch, push in both knobs and let's go."

I did, watching the bed start back down even as I was driving off.

"Real good," Frank said. "That was real good. I won't even have to come back with you again. You're doing fine. Now, let's pull back across the scales."

I stopped on the scales again.

"Who are you with?" The disembodied voice came over the speaker again.

"George Bonner."

"Pull on up and come in," the voice said tiredly.

I pulled up, stopped the truck and walked to the scale house. There wasn't much to it, just a shack with a man at the desk, the huge clock like dial of the scales on the wall in front of him and a pad of paper before him. He had a black lunch bucket and a red insulated jug handy. An empty cup and a full ashtray sat on the edge of the desk. "Here you go," he said. "You're with Bonner, right?"

"Right." I answered, watching the dial move as another truck pulled onto the scales.

"This is your first load of the season, right?"

"Right. We just started this afternoon. There'll be more."

He nodded, tore off the top sheet of the pad and handed it to me. "Don't loose that paper," he cautioned. "You loose that paper, you loose that load." Then he turned back to the speaker, "who you with?"

A different kind of hell, I thought. He's in a different kind of hell, but he's in hell just the same. And I felt sorry for him as I walked back to the truck.

I pulled away smoothly, noticing the difference between a loaded and empty truck. This was a lot easier, smoother, not that much different that the pick up. We passed the drive-in this time but the whiskey had killed my appetite at least for the time being. I was getting the feel of the truck by now and felt pretty confidant. I kicked it up to sixty on the way back. It was full dark by now and a sudden thought hit me. I couldn't see my land mark, the crooked telephone pole. "Frank, how am I going to find the right road in the dark?"

He laughed, "I've been wondering when you were going to think about that. I'll show you this time. But from now on make a note of your speedometer mileage on the way in then come back out the same distance, okay?"

"Why, sure, I should have thought of that myself."

"Well, you just learned something else then. Before you get back home you'll be nothing but a storehouse of knowledge."

I thought about that and he was right. Looking back at all the things I had learned already made me wish for tomorrow even more, yearning for the things I would learn then. I glanced at Frank but he was silent again, lost somewhere in his own world. But I thought about all the things he knew, all the knowledge he had and the things he'd seen. And I wished I knew just half as much, but I had time. I would learn.

"Turn at the next section line," he said, breaking the silence.

"Okay," I said, wondering how he knew.

Slim was gone with a load when we got back to the field. The third truck was sitting parallel with the cut wheat, almost loaded. "You need me to go back with you?" Frank asked, concern in his voice.

"No, at least I don't think so."

"Make up your mind. I will if you want me to."

"I can make it. I think," I said nervously.

"You think! You better be sure Boy." Caution dripped from his words.

"Okay, I can make it. I'm sure I can make it." I said, confidence growing in me.

"Okay, you got it. Good luck, you hear?" And he walked away.

"Yeah, I hear you. And I appreciate it," I was glad he was worried, but even more glad he was confident enough to let me go it alone.

He climbed back on his combine and was gone in a roaring clatter and cloud of dust. I got out of the truck, watching him go. The combine looking for all the world like some primeval beast moving through the night, its eyes shining, penetrating the darkness, its paddle, pulling it along through the wheat. Looking around I could count seven more combines working in the night. The road was busy with trucks. The harvest that hadn't been here yesterday was now in full swing.

Bob and George made the last turn about then so I moved the truck closer to the edge of the wheat and stopped it. Bob looked at me curiously as he stopped so I climbed on his rig and said. "I don't think I want to learn to catch on the go in the dark."

"Good idea," he yelled. "You need to learn a little more about the trucks before you try that."

I nodded and climbed down and moved the truck for George, when he dumped. I pulled the empty truck close to the uncut wheat and headed back toward town I was scared stupid and all hunched up, knowing I was going to wreck the truck or tear it up somehow. I made it out of the field alright and that bolstered my courage and by the time I'd reached the highway, I was feeling pretty good about myself. The trip in still seemed like it took me hours longer than the one with Frank but when I pulled up to the elevator, I felt ten-feet-tall.

The same disembodied voice came over the speaker and the same boys were scooping out the truck beds. Everything was the same except me. I felt I had really done something, an accomplishment of some kind. And I guess I had crossed a bridge of a sort, because this was the first time I'd ever done work for someone, other than Dad, all by myself. It was the first time anyone had ever trusted me this much. And it felt good, even taller than ten-feet.

I hauled that load and one more that night before Bob hollered, "quit." No one commented on my accomplishment so I didn't say anything either. I realized then, I'd only done what had been expected of me when I signed on. And that these guys had been doing things like this so long they'd forgotten what it was like to do it the first time. It was second nature to them, no more complicated than putting on a shirt in the morning. I also realized that no one was going to blow my horn or pat me on the back for doing my job. I was working with men now. And men did what was expected of them without a lot of fanfare or congratulations. And when I realized that, I was finally part the way across that bridge on my way to being a man.

*   *   *

The trip back to town didn't take long but it sure seemed that way. Someone had mentioned eating before we left and my stomach told me it was ready. All the excitement during the trip with Frank, then being scared half out of my mind on the next two trips by myself, had made me forget that I hadn't eaten in a long time. By the time we got to that café that hamburger I had back in Frederick would have tasted good.

We just unloaded and walked in the café, all five of us, nasty, dirty and sifting dust when we walked. I guess they were used to it here. At least they didn't say anything. Sara wouldn't have let us in the door of the café back home.

We all piled into one booth. George grabbed a chair and pulled it close to the end of the table. The waitress, young, pretty and with that special hip swing, came over to the table. After she had taken our orders Bob said, "boys, this one is on me. Y'all worked real good today. We made good time getting here and got a lot of wheat cut. I'm buying supper."

We all nodded our appreciation, thanking him. I would have thanked him more if he would have said it before I ordered. But it was a lot more than most would have done, and still alright. I only had eight dollars and ten cents left and I knew now from experience that wouldn't last long.

She brought our meal in two trips, swinging away both times giving us the real show. I wondered why the morning waitress is usually some tired-looking old woman while the night waitress is usually young and pretty. It just works that way I guess. But besides being pretty this little girl knew her business, probably knew how to cold-cock an old boy that got too friendly too.

I'd never been around a bunch a men kidding a waitress before. Back in Crane or the whole of Notashota county for that matter, everybody knew everybody else so we were careful of what we said or did because it would surely get home before we could. Here it was different. Here we were just a bunch of rowdy old boys away from home. Here we didn't care. Home was a long way away.

"Ain't she just about the prettiest thing you ever saw?" George commented.

"Man, I reckon." Slim threw in.

"Never seen one carry a glass of water quite that nice," Frank said.

"Wonder if she would like to learn how to drive a truck?" Slim said. The girl wasn't far away, taking all of this in with a bored expression on her face as if she had heard it before.

"Hey Darlin'," Frank asked. "You want to learn how to drive a truck?"

"No, not today," she said.

"Well then, how about a combine?" Frank laughed as he said it.

"I reckon not," she said. "I don't care for things like that. Besides, I got my career right here, hopping these tables."

"Well," Frank said. "Alright for now but should you decide to, I'll be back."

"You can come back till doomsday and I don't care," she said loud. "Because I don't have no truck with no Wheaties. Especially not none as nasty as you boys." Her voice was hard, the tone sharp. Then she laughed but not a friendly, joking laugh, a sharp, hard laugh, like her voice.

We all went quiet after that. There was really nothing to say after that. But the word, Wheatie, went through me like a knife. I thought, we were just having fun. There was no need for her to act like that, like we were a disease or something. Sure, we were nasty and sifting dust. We'd been working all day and half the night and if we had stopped to clean up, the café would have been closed.

I looked at Frank, looking for something, some kind of reason or explanation.

All he said was, "I told you so." And he grinned.

I guess it was alright, but it still hurt.

"Boys, we done some good work today," Bob boomed, like nothing had happened. Everyone in the café turned to look. "We keep this up, we'll be though here in a week, then on to Colorado."

On to Colorado. That had a ring to it that I liked and I smiled in spite of the put-down from the girl. I couldn't wait to see the mountains and I got real excited, just thinking about them. I was so excited I forgot to try to look down the girl's uniform top when she brought the check over to Bob.

The café was closing when we got up to leave. Bob walked over to pay the check. The rest of us each, left the girl a quarter tip. She would remember that. She damn sure didn't deserve it, but she would remember it.

I looked at the clock on the way out. It was just after eleven and all of a sudden I was tired, real tired. I had been up nineteen hours and working most of it. It had been a long day, in a lot of ways.

Back at the tent, everyone got their cleanup gear and went over to the gas station. The shower was just a pipe with a valve on it coming through the wall and cold water. But it sure felt good, even if I did almost freeze.

Walking back to the tent, I wondered what I would wear after tomorrow. I only had one change of clothes left. Frank was sitting on his cot when I walked in. He had emptied his pants pockets beside him. George and slim had already gone to bed.

"What do you think about it now Dave?" Frank asked.

"I really don't know," I said. Then added, "Why do you think that girl said that?" My feelings were still hurting over the put-down.

Frank said, "she knew she could get away with it is why. We have no other place to go and we have to eat."

"Yeah, but there wasn't any call for that. We were just kidding her."

"You have to remember where you are, Boy. Who you are. It's like you're a foreigner now, something different. You're a migrant worker now, a transient. They don't care about you or your feelings. Just as long as you spend your money and keep your mouth shut, you're okay. But you have to remember your place. And stay in your place. And your place is to spend your money and keep your mouth shut."

He laughed then, a hard, brittle laugh. "Don't worry about it though, and don't dwell on it. That wasn't the first time you've heard it, and it sure won't be the last time either."

I thought about that for a little while. I wasn't no foreigner. This was Texas. I had kin-folks living in Texas. Besides, we were just doing a job of work that these people couldn't or didn't want to do, and it was really helping them out. It was just too much for me right now. I still had my laundry to think about. "Say Frank," I said. "Are we going to work this late every night?"

"Probably not. Everyone is pretty tired. We'll probably knock off early tomorrow, around six, I imagine. Why, you got a date?"

I had to laugh at that. "No, I have laundry to do."

"Yeah, I imagine we'll knock off pretty early tomorrow. I'll talk to Bob about it."

I sat down on my bunk, completely exhausted. Frank turned up his bottle, taking a long gurgling drink, then he handed the bottle to me. I took a short one, causing me to cough and my eyes to water. When I handed him back the bottle, I saw the knife on the bunk beside him. A knife like I had never seen before.

I reached over and picked it up. It was beautiful. A folding knife but it had only one blade. It opened real smooth, silky like, but when it was full open it clicked. I tried to close it but it had gone completely rigid. I tried harder but it wouldn't close.

"Here," Frank said. "Don't break it. You have to press this release here." He pressed part of the handle-heel in an indention of the handle. The blade dropped almost half-way closed. He handed it back to me saying, "close it."

It was an old superstition that I knew, never close a knife someone else has opened or you'll cut yourself the next time you use it. And if it was a friend that opened it, you'll cut the friendship. I opened it full again. The blade was a full four-inches-long in a hollow ground, Bowie style. I tried it on my arm and shaved hair from my elbow to my wrist. The handle was made of some type of dark redwood, sweat-stained black on one side. Both sides were inlayed to precisely fit the brass body of the handle. The blade was engraved, 'Handmade, Germany'.

"That's a helluva knife," my voice went thick as I said it.

"Thanks, I like it. Here, let me see it."

I closed the knife and handed it over to him. He turned it in his hand and holding the blade with his thumb and index finger, flipped his wrist downward. The knife popped open in his hand with a distinct click,. The weight of the handle traveling down with the wrist flick had done it.

I wanted that knife. My God, how I wanted that knife. He closed it, handing it to me saying, "try it."

I did. It sprang open like something alive in my hand. I wanted it so bad it almost made me sick but I closed it and handed it back to Frank without saying a word.

He must have seen it in my face or read my mind because he said, "I couldn't ever part with my baby here. We've been through too much together." And with that, put it in his pants he had laid out for tomorrow.

George raised up about then saying, "y'all going to bullshit all night? It's twelve o'clock and five comes pretty early you know!"

I took the hint and laid down. Frank took another pull on the bottle and turned off the gas lantern then laid down too. With in minutes, he was snoring. A few minutes later George started helping him, then Slim started talking. I lay awake, listening to the crescendo, thinking about the knife. The last thing I remember was turning over and thinking, I need to write to Gayle.

CHAPTER 11

George was right, five o'clock did come early. We were awakened by Bob's cheerful bellow, "y'all gonna sleep all day? We got wheat to cut."

Frank mumbled something about cutting his throat if he didn't shut up. Slim rolled out of his bed and came up in a fighting crouch in one easy, fluid, motion. He looked around wildly for danger and finding none, grinned and began dressing. That was scary that a man can come full awake from a dead sleep and be as ready as he was.

George raised up, sat on the edge of his bed and yawned. He stretched, scratched his ribs, ran his fingers through his hair, dug in his eyes with his knuckles then stood up, scratched his balls, cut loose with a tremendous fart and began dressing.

Frank dug under his bunk, found his bottle and took a good pull. He shuddered, sat up and took another, coughed, blew and began dressing. I sat up, discovered I had a hard on and the insides of my underwear were all sticky, so I pulled my pants halfway up while I was sitting down. I turned my back to them, embarrassed, to pull them the rest of the way up.

After all of that and a line up trip to the bathroom, we were ready for another day.

I was right, the good-looking, hip-swinging, quick-talking, girl had been replaced by a dinosaur. Old, ugly, no hips, but who cares at five-thirty? No one. Maybe that's why the young, pretty ones always work at night. In the morning you're to sleepy too care but at night, after a hard days work, you need something to appreciate even if it was just to look at.

Bob was already seated at the same booth we had had the night before. I ordered the same breakfast I had back in Clinton. Bob and George had breakfasts. Frank and Slim ordered coffee.

I felt real good, despite the small amount of sleep I'd had in the last couple of days. I was almost bright and cheerful and ready to go. Full of piss and vinegar is what Dad had said back home. But looking at the rest of the bunch, I was quiet about it. A look from Frank would scare a grizzly bear. The coffee cup shook in his hand. George was placid enough, but not talking. Bob sat and stared. Slim had gone back to sleep.

The old woman brought my breakfast in two plates. Frank turned pale and looked away. Slim woke up, shuddered and closed his eyes again. George looked at his breakfast, then at mine, shaking his head. But Bob let everyone in the place know what he thought, "You gonna eat all that?" he hollered.

Frank jumped like he had been shot. Slim and George winced. I ate.

"By the way," Bob boomed out.

"Bob," Frank yelled. "Just lower the volume a little, please?"

"By the way," Bob started again, this time in a normal tone. "Y'all had better order lunches today and I made a deal with the café owner so we can just sign for our meals and pay when we get ready to leave. That okay with everyone? Now it will cost you an extra ten percent to do it." He looked around, questioningly.

"Yeah sure," George mumbled.

Frank just nodded, so did I, I had my mouth full.

Slim opened his eyes long enough to say, "yeah, okay with me."

The waitress came back with the coffeepot about then, filled our cups and took the empty plates. I thanked her but she didn't even grunt. We all ordered lunches to go while she cleared the table. I didn't know how that would work out but I thought I'd try it once at least.

By this time Frank was getting twitchy again so we drank the last cup and left. It was a cold ride out to the field in the back of the pickup making me wish I had brought a jacket. But thinking on it, I had no where to carry one. So I just huddled against the pickup cab and made the best of it without complaining. Slim wasn't complaining and he was dressed the same as me.

Bob and Frank walked out into the wheat while the rest of us serviced the equipment. I must have had a puzzled look on my face watching them walk out because George said, "they're seeing if the wheat is dry enough to cut. The elevator won't accept it if it's got too much moisture in it. Dew falls at night, so we check it every morning."

I guessed it was alright because when they walked back they were smiling, even Frank who got a grease gun and greased the sickles on all three combines.

Frank, Bob and George climbed on their rigs, starting them all at the same time. The din was deafening. One at a time they pulled into a line burying their headers in the wheat. Slim and I checked and fueled the trucks then sat in the sun watching for them to come back around.

It was warming up now, the sun sat just over the horizon and with the sun came the heat. And with the heat came the wind. Oh, it had never really stopped blowing, just lessened during the night but with the heat it came back gusty at first but then settling into the constant rush of the past days. Moaning slightly at times as it did gust, rustling the dry wheat stalks making a brushing, tinkling sound.

The heat yesterday hadn't been so bad. We were moving all the time except during the unloading. Today I would be driving most of the time, I hoped. It was going to be a scorcher. I felt a little tremor go through me. Today, I was a truck driver.

I looked across the field at the combines almost a half-mile away. They had spread the distance between them now to about a hundred yards so the one behind wouldn't have to eat the others dust so bad. Each of them was traveling at the maximum speed possible and still cut all the wheat but they seemed to be moving in slow motion from here. I couldn't hear the clattering roar of the combines because of the distance and the wind blowing the sound away from me, and that made them appear even more unreal. The only sound was the constant moaning sigh of the wind.

"Where you from Dave?" Slim said, breaking the silence, causing me to jump.

"I'm from Crane, Oklahoma," I replied, almost glad for the conversation.

"That's right down there on the lake ain't it?"

"Yeah. Pretty close."

"You do much fishing?"

"Not a whole lot. We don't have a boat and I don't get down to the lake too often. I do quite a bit of pond fishing though." I thought about the big pond across the road and how I went down there almost every day for something.

"I'd druther fish a pond myself," Slim said. "Lake is too big but a pond, now that's alright. You know where the fish are in a pond."

I didn't answer. The combines were getting close and I was getting nervous, anticipating the drive to the elevator, hoping I wouldn't have any trouble. I'd done alright last night, sure, but this was today.

"You want the first load?" Slim asked, noticing I was nervous.

"Yeah, if you don't mind."

"You never drove a truck before?"

I shook my head, "not before last night."

"Ain't nothing to it really. I been driving since I was twelve. Drove an eighteen-wheeler about five years."

"Oh yeah?" I could hear the singing tires in my mind, feel the whoosh of the wind as one passed me and see the tail lights, disappearing in the darkness.

"Yeah, ain't nothing to them either. Just a little longer is all. Bends in the middle too and you got to watch that, but it ain't no trouble."

"What did you haul?" I asked, thinking about the open road, and just going.

"Bulls for a rodeo. Big, mean ones. Riding bulls. You had to watch them too because they'd try to kill you, you wasn't careful."

I started to say something about Frank being in the rodeo but I thought about it and didn't. Maybe he didn't want that to be told either. "I know a guy that rides bulls in the rodeo." I said, "A guy from back home."

"Oh yeah," he said excited, "Who's that?"

"Lester Crane, he rides horses too."

Slim grinned broadly, "sure, I know Lester, I seen him just about six months ago out to Lampasas. He's got the prettiest little wife I believe I ever saw. He's a helluve a rider too. Indian boy, but he's got them blue eyes. That's real strange when he looks at you."

"That's him. Yeah, I know his wife too," and April's face swam before my eyes. Then I had a flash, completely forgotten, of more than Aprils face.

She'd been about thirteen then. It was just before the trouble. I had spent the night with Tommy and we had gone to bed. April and Tommy slept in the same bed in the main room of their house. They only had two rooms. April had sat up late, doing her homework. I was almost asleep when I turned over and saw her standing naked, washing herself with a bucket of water she had heated on the stove. It was the only time in my life I had seen a totally naked woman. And even at thirteen, April was something to see. It was the only time in my life I had seen a naked woman. I got an instant hard on, because even then April was a woman, swelling tits, pink nipples, blond pubic hair, and all.

I'd had hard on's before but that was the first time I realized why I got hard. I was farm raised and had watched animals having sex for as long as I could remember. But then, in a flash, it suddenly all made sense. And even now I had an instant hard on, just thinking about her standing there washing her body.

*   *   *

"No one else had ever ridden the rusty, old son of a bitch," Slim was saying. "But old Lester climbed on, and eight seconds later he was still stuck like a tick on that bull's back. That was four years ago, up in Miles City, Montana."

"Why did you quit driving the big trucks?" I asked, not really caring.

"I killed an old boy in a fight," he said as calm as if he had said 'good morning' and a chill passed through me cleaning the image of April's naked body from my brain.

Slim studied me carefully. "I spent the last three years in Huntsville prison for it too and it wasn't even my fault. The law said the old boy provoked the fight, but then the Judge said I shouldn't have stomped him so long when he was down. He gave me five years for manslaughter. I'm out on parole now."

I didn't say anything. I couldn't, not knowing what to say.

Then Slim said, "you won't get a full load from this go around, have to wait until they come back around."

The way he said it, his tone of voice, his expression was the same as when he had said, 'I killed a guy in a fight.' Nothing. No emotion, no guilt, just a calm statement. I moved slightly away from him. Something about him was terribly frightening now.

Frank was coming down the line then and I stood, walking to my truck. Frank pulled alongside my truck and stopped then started to unload. I went to the combine and climbed the ladder to watch. The wheat poured from the spout in a steady stream, splashing in the bed of the truck. "How's it going?" I asked, noticing my voice was unnaturally shrill.

"Pretty fair," he looked around, pulled out his bottle and took a short drink. The bottle was two thirds full. The auger in the bottom of the hopper started rattling, Frank pulled up a lever, stopping it. "Well, got to go. We got wheat to cut." He put the header in gear and pulled away.

I jumped to the ground got in the truck and pulled it close to the standing wheat. Bob stopped and unloaded and drove off with a rattling roar and a wave. I pulled up again to let George unload then killed the truck. Slim came walking to me and I felt a shudder of fear pass though my body. I was afraid of him now.

Slim said, "you need to learn to catch on the go Davie, waste too much time like this." Then he sat down on the running board next to me.

"I ain't quite ready for that yet," I said, trying to keep my voice calm. "Maybe tomorrow."

He nodded, watching me carefully. "I reckon it does take some getting used too." He was silent a long time. "I reckon now, I take some getting used too-- now." He looked across the long distances, shook his head slightly. "I don't remember too much about it. I woke up in jail with my hands all swollen and blood all over my boots."

He went silent again and the wind moaned low around the truck. "But I'm a free man now. Done my time and paid my debt. Parole Officer let me come on the harvest when Frank signed for me." His voice rang with pride, then dropped low, "boy, did I pay. That Huntsville prison is a bad place, Davie."

I felt a little better about it now. At least I was calmer but still, all I could do was nod at him.

"I was drunk," he said. "Dead drunk on my feet. But still, that ain't no excuse. I'm sorry for what I done, but I ain't ashamed of myself. They was two of them boys that seen the fight, stood up for me. Said that old boy had been pushing me all night. I guess he pushed a little too hard. I really don't remember. They said I had to pay and I did. 'Course that don't mean much to him. He's still dead. I am sorry for that," he paused a second. "But I still ain't ashamed of it."

I glanced over at him. His thin shoulders were hunched and drawn making him look even smaller than he was. I didn't know what to do or even what to say. So I just did nothing and said nothing.

Neither did he.

The combines were coming back by now so I climbed up on the truck standing almost knee deep in the wheat. Franks hopper filled my bed enough and he hollered, "take it on in."

I nodded, climbed back down and got in the truck. Slim was walking away. His head was hanging and his shoulders were still slumped as I drove away. God, he looked dejected and small, almost as if he was in pain. And I guess he was.

I let it pass from my mind and paid attention to what I was doing until I reached the highway. After that it was just driving and if I was doing anything wrong I didn't know it. Slim came back to me then, how small and drawn he had looked as he was telling me. Then later as he was walking to his truck, head down and slumped. And I felt bad. I knew I'd handled the whole situation badly. But my God, this was the first killer I'd ever been close too. I thought about it then, long and hard and then I said, "to hell with it. I don't care what he's done. He's helping me, teaching me what I need to know. And I can learn from him, and from this. It don't matter who he was. All that matters is who he is now."

And I thought Slim was a really nice guy. I nodded my head and drove on.

The rest of the trip was fairly smooth. The same disembodied voice came over the speaker when I weighed in and the same boys were scooping the wheat out of the corners of the truck beds. They were a little hard to recognize now though, they were still fairly clean. I dumped my load and returned to the field, meeting Slim coming with a load on his way out. We honked and waved and that the only way I got to see him the rest of the day.

We never broke for dinner that day, not together anyway. Just each one of us eating his own sandwich at his own time. I guess I ate mine early because I got hungry before we quit, also the one sandwich wasn't much. It was a good sandwich all right, ham, thick-sliced with cheese and lettuce. But there just wasn't enough of it. So along about two or three o'clock, I stopped at the drive in where we turned off. I screwed up again and ordered a drink and a hamburger without checking the prices. The total came to a dollar-fifteen. It was a good hamburger though, but it still wasn't worth a dollar-fifteen. The good looking girl paid no more attention to me than she would have a bug on the driveway.

I noticed the wind shifted on the way back to the field. For four days it had blown steadily from the south, now it coming from the west-southwest. It was gusting too, not the constant blow it had been. It was almost cool and had a tingly feeling, and if I had been back home I would've said a storm was coming. I cleared town about then and looked west and, sure enough, the thunderheads were building. I hadn't been able to see them in town because of the houses.

When Frank pulled to my truck to unload, I climbed up on his combine and said, "storm's coming."

He nodded, "been expecting it. Bonner said he heard on the news it was going to get here tonight. Maybe it won't hurt us much. I got to go. Got to cut as much as we can before it gets here." And with a wave he pulled away.

I was driving the third truck this time. Frank's hopper made me a load so I pulled my empty truck up near the standing wheat and left.

All five of the Bonners were standing in the yard watching the clouds build as I passed. I'd seen it before, back home. A storm causes some people to run to their holes, cellars built especially for that purpose, so they can hide when nature runs rampant and the twisting whirlwind causes havoc in the country. The Bonners had a cellar. The door stood open but they chose to stand and watch the clouds as if daring God to ruin their crops and their lives.

The storm grew. The massive thunderheads piled and crashed into one another until there was only one, but it was a monster that blocked the sun. It was shining white and bulging on the sides but flat on top and streaming out in the shape of an anvil, black and roiling on the bottom from where the rain fell in sheets so dark, the cloud seemed to touch the ground. I stopped to cover the tiny grains of gold with a tarp rolled up at the front of the truck bed just in case. Wet wheat means rotted wheat.

By the time I got to town the whole sky was black but the air had a greenish tinge. Dust filled the shrieking wind and distant thunder muttered threateningly. I pulled into the elevator just as the first fat drops of rain began to freckle the dusty, dry ground.

I tore the road up getting back to the field and got there just as all three combines were dumping into the waiting truck. I was able to get it covered before the intermittent, gusty, rain hit.

"Take it to the elevator and bring the truck back to the tent," Frank hollered and I pulled away, shifting gears like I had done it all my life.

Tarped down tight, the rain couldn't get to the wheat, maybe. When I hit the scales the man came out and reached under the tarp to feel of the wheat and waved me on to dump. As I drove through the elevator doors a giant sheet of lighting ripped the sky followed immediately by a tremendous clap of rumbling, booming, crashing, thunder, followed by a torrential downpour. I threw back my head and laughed. I had won the race.

CHAPTER 12

I drove the truck to the tent and gathered the all important dump tickets. I stuck them in my pants, bent over and ran through the driving rain. In the tent I said, "boy, Frank, when you say you'll see to it that we get off early, you really mean it." They all broke up, even Bob who had the most to lose.

"I reckon you don't have to go to the laundry now Dave," George said. "Just hang your clothes outside, they'll wash."

"I think as nasty as they are it will take more than pure water to get them clean." I said, taking off my shirt and wringing mud from it.

"Just like a Wheatie, nasty as a hog," Frank laughed.

Someone hollered. "Let's go eat.

I was ready. but Frank had an even better idea. "Let's get cleaned up first, then go eat," he said. It split the group. I went with Frank; the rest went to eat. We ran through the driving rain to the station.

The shower was still cold but it still felt good, and I learned the trick to taking a cold water shower from Frank. You jump in, get wet all over as long as you can stand it then get out to warm up and hurry with the soap while you're still wet. You jump back in to rinse off then if you're not frozen or real, real dirty, repeat the whole process. Cold water livens up a shower some.

Covered by my last set of clean clothes, Frank and I set off to the café, running through the rain. The rest were still there and Frank said, "would you just look at the scum they let in the doors here?" While we sat at a different table.

Picking up on his statement I said, "yeah, you would think a body would wash some before he goes to eat."

"Well, no one ever accused a Wheatie of being human," Frank said. "They're a race unto themselves. Of course, they look almost human, but it ends there." And we all laughed.

The waitress was a different hip-swinging girl from last night, younger and prettier. I noticed she was smiling at what Frank had said so I grinned at her when she walked over. As soon as she saw me grinning, she went cold. Her face turned to an expressionless mask and, when she laid the menus on the table, she looked through me as if I wasn't even there. It went into me like a knife.

I must have blushed because as she walked away, Frank said, "Dave, you have to quit letting this bother you. It's going to be a long summer and if you let it bother you this bad, you're going to have problems." He laughed, "Son, it's not personal."

"Just tell me how to get used to being treated like dirt." I snapped.

"Every man has his own defense. Me? I've been doing this so long-- I guess I don't think about it anymore. I tried to warn you. Watch her with that bunch that just came in."

I looked over. They seemed just like a bunch of guys to me but to her, they were Wheaties. And she knew what they were and she treated them just as cold and emotionless as she did us.

"Boy, this is nothing new." Frank said. "This has been going on for centuries. You see Dave, this is just the first time it has happened to you. Back in Crane, think hard. Do they even let the colored in the cafés?"

I didn't have to think. "No, they have a table back in the storage room for the colored. And come to think of it. They have a balcony in the picture show for them. They're not allowed in the main seating area."

"And you have never thought anything about it. Have you? You never tried to stop it. Never even let it cross your mind, did you?"

I had to shake my head. I was embarrassed now.

"You see," he said. "It was happening to someone else. And because of that, you paid no attention. You never let it bother you. It bothers them but that's their problem." He grinned. "From now on it'll bother you when you see it though. Maybe everyone needs a little taste of prejudice. Maybe then it would stop. Just get used to it and learn from it."

I shook my head trying to think. In my mind I went back to the café in Frederick, *'Now I know how the colored feel when we call them nigger,'* flashed in my mind. I'd said that to Rocky. Then I thought back to the café in Crane where they had a little table in the back. The balcony in the picture show, we even called it *'Nigger Heaven,'* and I knew Frank was right. I didn't care. At least I hadn't cared. And now, I knew I was just as wrong as the girl. Just as bad.

The girl brought our food and set it on the table without comment. This time I noticed her movements while she worked. She did everything at arms length, acting as if she was afraid to touch either of us, even get close to us, as if we had a disease or something. Frank noticed me watching her and laughed as she walked away.

I said, "What's so damn funny?"

"Just the way you were looking at her."

"Well, she's acting like she would catch something if she rubbed up against me."

He shook his head. "That's not what she's afraid of Dave. Think about it Son. Look at her and think about it."

I shrugged and looked at her. "So what am I supposed to see?"

He shook his head and looked at me like I was retarded or something. "She's what, sixteen, maybe seventeen?"

"Yeah, something like that."

He nodded. "She was probably friendly as a pup when she first went to work here. But now, just how many men do you think pinched her on the tits or rubbed her on the butt or just made a crude remark to her while she was trying to make a living? Think about it. These old boys are a long way from home and most of them are just like you, first timers. And they don't care. They're going to be down the road tomorrow so they grab a feel now and then. The girl needs the work or she wouldn't be here. But that gets old, really fast, and she doesn't like it so she's careful not to come on to anyone in anyway or to even get within grabbing range. That is called self-defense. It's not just you, it's all of us and we made her what she is. She's afraid of us. And with good reason. One smile, one wink and she would have that whole table over there," he pointed with his head at the other crew, laughing, and now that I noticed them, talking rough. One was openly staring at the girl and his face was an open book. He had only one thought in his mind and even I could see it wasn't a good thought.

"On her," Frank continued, "like bees on honey. She doesn't want that. She doesn't want to be looked at like that or thought about like that. But she has to endure it so she fights back with the only weapon she has. And yes, she hates us, but with damn good reason. We've made her hate us through our own actions and our own words." He began to eat.

And I began to think. And he was right. Not only was he right but we'd done the same thing the night before with the other waitress. And now, I was embarrassed.

We finished eating in silence. I was lost in my own thoughts and I guess Frank was too. He had that dreamy, faraway look about him like he got sometimes. I was trying to sort it all out and make some sense of it all. Finally, he came out of it and we signed for our meal and walked back to the tent, neither of us saying much.

I gathered my clothes and started to the Laundromat that I had seen a couple of blocks down the way. I was almost there before I noticed the rain had stopped. It had been blown on east by the same wind that had brought it.

I knew we wouldn't work tomorrow but because the rain had blown through pretty fast and hadn't been that bad, we could probably be able to get into the fields the next day. It was then I realized I had no idea what day this was, or even how long I had been gone.

I found the Laundromat and as I loaded my clothes in the machine I counted back. I had been gone five days now. This must be Friday. When I got change from the woman at the counter, I could see a calendar on the wall behind her. Sure enough, it was Friday night. Gayle would be expecting me over tonight to pick her up. Well, I couldn't help that, but I sure wouldn't be there.

I got change for the soap machine on the wall and when I bought soap, I noticed it also had dry bleach. Remembering my television training and how bleach gets clothes brighter and cleaner, I bought two big packs and dumped the whole mess in the machine. The machine started automatically so I sat back, picked up a magazine and started to read. A while later the washer quit and I took the clothes out and stuffed them in a dryer without looking at them.

When I took them out of the dryer, I couldn't believe my eyes. They were all splotched with white, the colors had all mixed and run and the whole mess was a total ruin. But they were all I had. I would have to wear them. I folded everything as neatly as I knew how, trying to choke back the tears, which almost made me miss the big poster on the wall of a man on a bucking horse. I hadn't seen it before, but now I read, *'RCA Rodeo, Guymon Oklahoma, Friday, Saturday and Sunday.'* It made me feel some better. I figured Frank would want to go and it gave me something to tell them, other than I had ruined all my clothes.

Frank was alone when I got back. He was stretched out on his cot, reading a book. His bottle was close by.

"Did you get your clothes clean?" He asked without looking as I came in.

"Sure did," I said hating what was coming when I laid them out on my cot to put them back in the suitcase. He took one look and started snickering. That soon turned to a giggle, which finally erupted into a full-fledged belly laugh so hard that tears were coming from his eyes.

At first I was hurt and mad all over again but it passed. It's hard to stay mad at someone you like, even if he's laughing at you. Besides, it really was stupid of me to bleach all those clothes.

After he calmed down some he said, "Boy, I didn't mean to carry on so about those clothes but they bring back a lot of memories. I done the same thing the first time I went to wash and my wife done the same thing her first time by herself. It cost me almost five hundred dollars that time. She ruined every stitch we owned."

I felt better about it after that.

He said, "It's them commercials on the TV that done it, I'll bet," he was still laughing.

"Yeah," I said shaking my head. "That's what did it. Someone ought to do something about them." I was alright now, the hurt and mad both gone then I remembered the poster. "Say, we ain't going to work tomorrow, are we?"

"No, the wheat will be too wet to cut tomorrow, maybe the next day."

"I saw a poster at the laundry. It said there is a rodeo over at Guymon, today, tomorrow, and Sunday. Reckon we might go?"

"Don't see why not. It's been a while since I've seen one." He laughed then, "I might just enter the thing and pick me up some extra money. Sure, what say we tell the rest about it, then we'll get up early and make a whole day of it over there?"

"That sounds good to me," I said all excited.

Bob's pickup drove up about then and Slim and George came in smelling of beer and carrying two six-packs each. They had been up to Texoma, on the Oklahoma border to have a few. This was a dry county.

"Here Boy," Slim hollered throwing me a beer. I caught it, opened it with the opener he pitched at me and took a big drink, grinning at him.

He nodded and grinned back.

"Say," Frank said. "Me and Dave is going to run over to Guymon tomorrow for the rodeo. Y'all want to come?"

Both nodded. "Why sure."

"Who knows?" Slim said. "We just might scare us up some women folk."

"Old Dave here could use a good woman," Frank laughed. "Look here." He held up a pair of my blue jeans, all white splotched and faded and all four of us cracked up laughing.

"I done it once myself," George said when he got his breath back. "Damn bleach commercials on the radio."

"They're worse on the TV," I said. "You can see them women holding up all them pretty clothes on the TV."

About then Bob came in hollering, "what's all the racket about?"

George threw him a beer and pointed to my pants. "I told him to just hang his clothes out in the rain, but no, he wanted to get them clean."

"Looks like he got them clean all right," Bob boomed as he laughed.

"Say, Bob," Frank hollered loud, mocking him. "We're all going over to Guymon tomorrow for the rodeo. You want to come?"

"Damn, you talk loud," Bob hollered. "No, you young bucks go on. I got to work on my books and get my beauty sleep. "Y'all have a good time though, you hear?" They heard him at the café.

Someone suggested poker about then, so Frank dug out the cards. I cleaned off the table and dragged a cot over for me to sit on and the game was on again.

We played for about three hours. Frank was the same, a poor winner and a worse loser. George was just placid George, never taking a chance only betting when he was sure he had the hand won, easy to bluff unless he had a dynamite hand. Slim was still shifty-eyed, giving away each good hand he drew with the expression in his eyes.

"Always look at their eyes," Dad had said. *"Look them deep in the eye and nine times out of ten they'll tell you what you want to know."*

But Bob had taken lessons from Dad too. He was a tough player, completely unreadable. I had the advantage though, I was playing with their money and really didn't have anything to lose.

Bu the end of the game I had won over twelve dollars, most of it Bob's. It seemed like every hand he and I wound up head to head. I bluffed him a couple of times. Most times, I didn't have too. I was drawing some good hands.

When the game broke up, George suggested everyone ante five dollars for one last game of five-card-stud. I kicked in and won it with two pair, caught on the last card. I remembered my manners though and just drug my money with no whooping and hollering. I just folded my money, over thirty dollars and put it in my billfold. I'm not saying I didn't want to dance, yell and holler. I'm just saying I didn't do it.

George and Slim went on to bed. Frank and I had another beer as we sat quietly in the dark. I looked him over close, thinking back on the night, about the girl in the café. It just wasn't right, none of it. But I knew there'd been truth in his words, on both parts. If she had given those guys, or us for that matter, any encouragement they would have been all over her with their crude suggestions. And we would have too, knowing it wasn't right, but doing it anyway. But to me, that didn't seem as bad as what she had done. But to her, I didn't know? I wasn't her. Maybe what we were doing was just as bad or worse to her. And all she was doing was defending herself. It was a quandary that had no easy answer because both sides thought they were right. I had to laugh at that thought because things like that starts wars.

Finally, Frank's words came back to me and I thought he had summed it up pretty well when he said *and that's the way it is.* Because that's the way it was, and things like that didn't change.

I finished my beer, laid down and was soon asleep, dreaming about a truck chasing me. It was being driven by the girl in the café and she was trying her best to run me down. Finally, just as she was closing in on me and I was too tired to run anymore, I jerked and came awake, terrified. She'd been laughing as she tried to kill me. I lay there a while, finally deciding it had only been a dream and I was relieved and saddened at the same time. Relieved because it had only been a dream and saddened because, that's the way things were.

I got up and needing to piss, stepped outside. The night was dark, but clear, and ten million stars twinkled and blinked some of them looking close enough to touch. A carload of laughing kids drove by making me think of home and Gayle, and a horrible wave of homesickness washed over me. I sat on the running board of the truck and I went there, in my mind, to Gayle and what would be happening about now.

We would probably be on the way to her house, stopped somewhere, necking. I closed my eyes and could see her in the moonlight, lying back across me, her breasts naked and lovely. She had the most beautiful breast I had ever seen, not overly large, but well-formed and work-hardened. Her nipples were just darker than her skin, a pale shade of pink that reminded me of the sun shining through the clouds at sunset. They were small and pointy and they wrinkled as I touched them and hardened when I kissed them. My mind traveled down her flat, hard, stomach to her blue jeans with the top two buttons open and the top of her panties showing.

A tremor went up my back as that goose stepped on my grave again.

CHAPTER 13

We slept real late the next morning, getting up around nine or so, had breakfast and just lay around for a while before we left. The trip to Guymon only took about thirty minutes with Frank at the wheel. I was glad Bob hadn't come. That would have put me in the back. As it was we all four got in the cab. It was a big cab so it wasn't real crowded.

We pulled into Guymon, just before twelve. It was a nice-sized town, strung out along the highway, lost in an ocean of wheat. Slim and George got out at the first bar we came to. Slim saying it looked like a good place to start and George, just to get well. I stayed with Frank.

He drove straight to the rodeo arena. He didn't have any rigging so he had to find someone to borrow from, and he had to register for the two events he'd planned to enter. He wasn't that wild about riding now that he was sober but he'd made his brag and I guess he felt like he had to back it up.

As we pulled up to a small shack, I noticed a whole knot of men standing around waiting. "They're waiting for the draw," Frank explained. "They put the man's registration number in a box, the horses' and bulls' number in a different box. Then, they draw them out, one at a time. Horse's number, man's number, bull's number to keep it honest. Everyone wants the worst bucking bull or horse because both the man and the animal are judged and if they can ride him, they get more points. The most points wins and that's what they're here for."

I knew without being told these were the riders. They all looked alike, young, slim-hipped, broad shouldered, a certain look they all had in their eyes flatly stating, 'I ain't scared of nothing.' One had his arm in a cast, but he was going to ride anyway. A reckless lot, all of them. But when you think about it, a man that makes his living riding wild horses and bulls has got to be a little wild and reckless, and crazy.

Frank knew a few of the older ones out of the twenty or so riders. He introduced me to them but I didn't remember the names. They all looked like all the rest anyway, just a little older, a little stiffer, a little harder and more cautious. I looked for Lester, but Frank just laughed and said, "Lester rides the big rodeos for the big money. This one is just small potatoes."

It was alright and really I was glad he wasn't here. After last night I don't think I would have been able to see April Rose. I think I would've had to go home if I had seen her. And I wasn't ready for that yet. Because now, in the glaring light of the day, standing here in the moaning wind, I knew I had some more country to see before I went back. The ache was still there. The homesickness, still pulling at me. But the wind pulled me too, in a different direction and that's where I would go.

Frank had no trouble finding a saddle, spurs and a bucking strap for the bareback bronc riding and we settled down to wait for the drawing. He finally got his numbers and we walked down by the chutes to get everything ready. He'd asked for the last ride because he had to borrow equipment. No one minded and I was glad. That way I got to see most of the show without having to worry about him.

I had been to several rodeos, the small ones that came to Crane, smaller even than this one. But I had never been able to stand in the arena and watch or to go behind the chutes to watch the riders ready themselves.

It was a different world back there, smelling of dung, sweat, urine, noisy with the whinnies and blowing of the horses and the bellering of the bulls. Each rider had his own little ritual to go through before his ride. Some were standing, talking, some setting stretching their leg muscles. Most were silent, staring inward, psyching themselves up for the eight seconds of fury that was coming.

All knew what they had on the line: their futures and their very lives, because sometimes that eight seconds was the last they had to live, still in one piece, or to live, period. It didn't happen often, but it did happen. And my mind went back to Denver's leg, crushed by a bull so bad it didn't work anymore.

The pros were mixed in with the local contestants and a young one was riding now. I watched as the horse sunfished and turned in the air, screaming, fighting to rid himself of the predator on his back. He jumped then and began a series of kicking bucks that should have dislodged the man. But they didn't and he easily slid to the ground after the buzzer sounded. He picked up his hat and slapped it against his thigh, then, grinning broadly, waved to the crowd.

Frank nodded, "that's the ride to beat."

He said it just before the announcer said the same words, then added, "fokes that's the ride to beat, That ride totaled ninety-four points and that's the high score from the man who won yesterday's go-round. Boys, you got your work cut out for you."

This was only the second ride.

The announcer had been a rider himself in days past. He knew all the old pros and was making the most of his knowledge by calling the names of the contestants, where they were from and how much they had won this year. I could feel Frank growing tighter and tighter as the rides continued then the call came. "Turner, you're up next."

A muscle in Frank's jaw was twitching as he climbed the side of the chute and lowered himself onto the horse. He had drawn a little dun mare that looked friendly enough, but something told me she wasn't nearly as friendly as she looked. She couldn't be broke to ride or she wouldn't be here. Even small rodeos didn't have plain riding horses but at least they didn't have the real killer horses of the big rodeos.

Frank sat loose, holding the bucking strap which was tight around the horse's withers, in his left hand.

"And now ladies and gentlemen," the announcer bellowed out over the loud speaker. "A, not-forgotten, top hand on the bucking circuit a few years back, Frank Turner, coming out of chute number two on, Brown Lady."

Frank grinned, nodded and hollered, "let her out!"

The chute gate swung open and the horse jumped half way across the arena before she landed hard on all four feet and went straight up. She screamed and came down hard again then immediately began to buck and spin. On the third spin, Frank left the horse's back in a spread-eagle dive and came up spitting dirt. It had taken about three seconds.

The announcer didn't comment on Franks ride as he stood and started back to the chutes, knocking the dirt out of his pants. Then the loudspeaker crackled and the winner of the go-round was announced. The young guy, not much older than me, with three years on the circuit rode to the center of the arena from another gate. He waved his hat to the applauding audience then rode back, stopping by Frank. "Too bad, Mister Turner," he said loud enough for most to hear. "My dad said you were one of the best--- back when."

A chill when up my back as Frank's eyes went flat and cold. The kid turned his horse, riding back to the gate he'd come out of and I walked out to meet Frank.

"Let it go Frank," I said. "He didn't mean nothing."

"I'll whip his young ass and show him, 'back when'," Frank growled, brushing past me.

I followed him saying, "and it won't prove a damn thing Frank. Let it go! You ain't lost nothing yet."

He stopped and turned. "What do you mean, 'yet'?"

"What is that kid, nineteen, maybe twenty? Sure you can whip him and what will that prove? That you're man enough to beat a kid?"

A puzzled look crossed his face and I could see his anger fading. Then his jaw locked. "He ain't no damn kid or he wouldn't be here shooting off his face."

I said quickly, "he is a kid and that's the reason he shot off his face! Think about it! Would one of the real pro's have said that? He's a show-off who happens to be a pretty good rider in a small potatoes rodeo. He'll never be the rider you were and he knows it or he never would have said that."

He studied me a second, then I said, "come on, Frank." I slapped his shoulder. "What say we go up in the stands and watch the rest. I don't think I can stand another one of those."

He looked at me hard, searching my face, wanting to find something there, a grin, a mocking look, disappointment, something he could fight. He didn't find any of it.

Suddenly he grinned, "now Davie, that ain't a bad idea you have there." Then he laughed. "I don't think a big man could whip me and make me get up on that saddle bronc. I've already made a big enough fool of myself here today. Let's go." He slapped me on the back and we walked away from the chutes.

We entered the stands and found seats way up high where we could see better. I slipped his pint out from under my shirt and handed it to him.

He grinned and said, "to all the old, damn fools of the world," and he took a drink but the far away look in his eyes said more than he had, so I didn't answer, not even when he said it again, softer this time, shaking his head. "To all the old, damn fools of the world."

He was silent a long time, staring at the arena but I knew what he was seeing and I was silent too. After a while though, he began to talk, pointing out the small details of the rodeo, how this one rode and why that one was disqualified. But I could feel that something had gone out of him and I knew what it was. He'd realized it had been a dream. He had thought he would, maybe not win, but at least place in the riding. At the very least, finish the ride. And he'd just realized that someone else had taken his place now. And now he knew he was a has-been. And it hurts to be a has-been.

The rodeo only lasted an hour or so longer. We walked back to the pickup when it was over. I guess the whole countryside had turned out for it. They did at home anyway. As we drove back down through town, I wondered aloud about Slim and George. "They should have been to the rodeo," I said.

"Most likely they found something a lot softer and better smelling to ride," Frank chuckled. "Which shows they're a lot smarter than I am."

I laughed too. The town did have quite a few single women walking around, most of them pretty, at a distance anyway.

"We'll start looking in the bars but don't worry, we'll find them somewhere." Frank said as he pulled into a parking space. "There's another rodeo tonight and a dance after that so they'll be at that even if we don't find them sooner."

He'd stopped at a different bar from where we had let them off, but that one was just up the street. The jukebox was thumping, '*White Lighting*,' by George Jones as we walked in. Frank motioned to an empty booth and went to the bar. I walked over and sat down.

The place was shabby and run down. It smelled of stale cigarette smoke, spilled beer, and cheap perfume. The jukebox changed and Marty Robbins started singing about, '*El Paso*'. Several people, men and women sat in the booths and at the tables. Some on the stools that lined the bar. Two men were playing shuffleboard. A man and a pretty woman took up the pool table. Frank came back with the beer and sat down.

"They haven't been in here," Frank said. "But we'll have a couple before we go looking again," he watched me closely as I took a drink. "You ever been in a place like this before?"

I nodded, "Sure, lots of times."

He shrugged and growled. "You damn sure don't act like it." Then he laughed, "hell no you don't act like it. You've been them bars back home where you know everyone and they all know your daddy, right?"

I just nodded, wondering what I had done wrong.

Frank said, "Well, this is a whole new world out here Boy. They don't know your daddy here and they don't care whether you live or die." He never took his eyes off mine as he said, "who's the most likely to start trouble in here. Real trouble?"

I looked around quickly. Everyone seemed to be having a good time, no problems, no one popping off, no trouble. I looked back at Frank and realized he expected an answer. "Those two guys playing shuffleboard." I said.

He never looked, again, he never took his eyes off mine. "Those boys are just having a good time. They'll fight anyone in here at the drop of a hat but they're not likely to cause any trouble. Now, when I tell you, and not until, you, very carefully, glance at the old boy at the end of the bar. Don't stare at him. Don't even let him know you're looking at him. Just a quick glance. Now."

I quickly glanced and that's all it took. He sat there tearing at the label on his beer bottle, looking morose, cold and very hard. Sitting there alone and quiet, he made me think of a coiled spring, a tightly coiled spring, ready to uncoil in a fury, at any second, with anyone that he even thought had crossed him.

I suddenly felt a cold chill pass over me as something came to my mind. A Walt Disney film I had seen about lions in Africa, hunting lions, ready to pounce on a herd of antelope. One lion in particular, a large female, was laying in the grass, stalking, waiting for the slightest opening. Only the tip of her tail twitched. Her head was frozen, eyes fixed on the herd. I blinked and glanced back, I hadn't been wrong. He was just as fixed and ready as that lion.

"You see what I mean?" Frank said softly.

"Yeah, I see what you mean," and even I heard the tremble in my voice.

Frank said. "You never even saw him before, did you?"

"No, he's so quiet, I didn't notice him."

"Learn to look, Dave!" he said intensely. "As you walk in the door, you look at everyone in the room. Start with the ones closest to you. They're the worse threat at that time. Once you've checked them out, move to the next layer, the ones just out of your reach, then on to the rest, but look at everyone in the place. Don't stare. Don't even let on that you are looking. They're looking too. They're checking you out. When you sit down, try to get a place next to the wall. Let it protect your back, then look them all over again, one at a time." He tensed, "Here, watch the ones in the bar. Don't look at the door."

A drunk cowboy and a girl were coming in the door. I looked around the room; the laughing, drinking, and cutting up continued unabated, but Frank had been right, everyone in that bar had looked at the door. Just a quick glance, but that old boy had been checked out and classified as trouble or not.

"See what I mean?" he said.

I nodded, taking a drink of beer.

He continued. "Stay ready to move and stay on edge. You don't get drunk in a place like this, not alone anyway. If there are more than two of you and you trust the ones you're with, have your fun but still be careful. You can get your hat mashed pretty quick in a place like this."

I grinned at that and finished my beer. The juke box changed about then and a real old Hank Williams song about a wooden Indian came on. I could see the girl behind the bar singing along with the record.

But Frank wasn't through. "Now, if it does happen," he said, just as intently. "If there is trouble you should be ready. You should have the place pretty well fixed in your mind. Know where all the doors are and plan a way out. If you stumble over anything and you fall, you're down, and in here, if your down, you're stomped. Mind now, these boys play for keeps, they don't fight just for fun."

The place was filling pretty fast now as the rodeo crowd came in, getting primed for the next go-round, but Frank wasn't finished. His voice had dropped to a low growl now, his face was tight. "The most important thing to remember is, if something does happen, stay out of it! What happens to your fellow man is no concern of yours. If he can't take care of himself, he don't have no business in here and the same goes for you. Don't ever expect any help in here or anyplace like this, not even from your friends."

"I can take care of myself," I said hard.

He laughed, then his voice went flat and cold. "Boy, I could take you apart while you were getting ready to fight. Before you even knew what was happening. You've been fighting kids." He whistled and held up two fingers.

The girl behind the bar nodded and came our way, carrying two beers. She was dressed in a hat, boots, and blue jeans that she had been poured into and then they shrank and was still singing along with the jukebox as she dancingly dodged her way through the crowd. I noticed her looking me over real close and remembered the legal drinking age in Oklahoma was twenty-one.

She stopped singing as she sat the beer down and said, "That'll be fifty cents."

I handed her a dollar and said, "Keep the change, Darlin'." And grinned.

She grinned back, took the dollar and turned, walking away, singing with the jukebox and giving us a display of how to really swing hips. The front of her wasn't bad to look at either.

Frank laughed, "that was pretty smooth. If you hadn't tipped her, she would have checked your ID."

"I figured as much."

"You're learning, Wheatie," he laughed. "You're learning. You stick with me and I'll make a man out of you yet. Now, drink your beer and let's get out of here. The crowd is making that old boy at the bar real nervous. Besides, we still have to find Slim and George."

We finished our beer and went to the bathroom, which was a horror all unto itself, smelling of years old urine that the piney smelling soap couldn't even come close to covering. Then we walked back out into the bright sunlight that, as we neared the pickup, turned suddenly cold. Because now I could see George sitting in the cab, all scrunched down. But Slim was nowhere around.

"Something's bad wrong," Frank hissed, opening the pickup door. "George, where is Slim?"

George turned to look at us, grinned stupidly and said, "he's gone."

"Gone?" Frank almost shouted. "Gone where?"

George just shook his head. "I don't know. He's just gone. He stold a car and he's gone." Then he stared at my eyes and mumbled something.

Frank said, "What the hell are you talking about George? What the hell happened?"

George smiled again, shaking his head, "Damnedest thing---I ever saw."

"What? Dammit? What?" Frank yelled, "Where!"

"In that bar, where you let us out. It happened there." George smiled again almost dreamily and motioned toward the bar with his head.

Frank dragged him out of the pickup and threw him up against it, hard. George's head bounced off the cab top. He closed his eyes and shook his head. "You hurt me," he almost whined.

Frank hissed. "That ain't nothing to what I'm going to do if you don't start talking."

George blinked a couple of times as a cop car drove by going fast his red light was on, but not the siren. "We was in that bar," he said. "We was drinking and Slim was trying to pick up this girl. Doing good too. Boy, she was pretty too. He was doing real good, when this great big bastard came in."

George's eyes almost clouded over, as if he were seeing it happen all over again. "Big old boy. Must have stood six-four or six-five. He bumped old Slim. Slim turns around and kinda looked at the guy. He must have weighed two hundred and fifty pounds, maybe more. And the guy says, 'What you looking at Sonny?'"

George laughed, "old Slim started to burn at that, but I told him 'What the hell Slim, he didn't mean nothing.' And Slim nodded and went back to the girl. Then the sucker bumped Slim again." He went silent.

"Get on with the story, George!" Frank said.

I could feel the anticipation growing in me and that cold finger of fear was back, going up and down my spine. I really didn't know if I wanted to hear the rest. But I felt like I was in the fable of the bird and the snake, I couldn't not hear it. I was rooted there.

George nodded, "I was just thinking, getting it all straight in my head."

He smiled vaguely again. "Yeah, Slim got really mad that time. I could tell he was really getting hot, but then the big guy, starts in on the girl. 'What you doing honey, picking on kids today?' he says, then he says, 'Why don't you come on with a real man?' And old Slim starts to get that ole smoky look in his eyes. He's really hot now. So I walked over to stop the fight. I gets in between them and the big guy looks at me, sizing me up, then he leans over and says to Slim, 'Well Shorty, looks like you got a man to do your fighting.'"

"Frank shook his head exclaiming low, "Oh my God!"

I felt my heart flutter. A sudden flash of Slim back at the café in Clinton came to me and I went cold all over and started to sweat at the same time.

"Yeah," George, said nodding wildly, his eyes going even wilder. "Yeah, old Slim goes crazy about then. He comes around me like a flash and climbs that boy like a squirrel. He gets a hammer lock on his head with one arm and takes his thumb."

He stopped, and looked at his own thumb and a shudder shook his whole body. "He takes his thumb---and popped that ole boy's eye--- right out of his head."

Frank's mouth dropped open, "Oh my God!" he almost whispered.

I felt my stomach flop and a strange, brassy taste came to my throat.

"Yeah!" George shouted, "It fell plumb down on his cheek. And it got real quiet in the bar, everyone shut up, except for one woman and she screamed. But it seemed like everything slowed way down, kind of like in the movies."

George smiled vaguely again. Then he giggled. "That ole boys eye was big as a hen's egg, just laying there on his cheek." And he went silent as he stared into nothing.

Frank was very calm when he said, "Finish it George."

"I was going to." George said. "I just got to get it straight in my head." He nodded then said. "Yeah, his eye fell plumb down on his cheek, right about here." He touched his own cheek. "It was big as a hen's egg, and just dangled there for a long time, seemed like. Everything is real quiet now, except for that woman screaming and the jukebox, and then, even it stopped. And then old Slim screams, 'What's it look like to you now, asshole!'" And he grabbed that eye in his hand and---popped it like you would a grape."

George looked at Frank, but I could see the horror in his eyes as he said, "and, then, Slim starts for his other eye."

Frank's eyes closed and he shuddered. I felt my stomach give a double flop and the sweat started pouring out of me.

"What happened then George?" Frank said low.

George shook his head and smiled again. "Well, the big guy is fighting like a panther now, trying to get Slim off of him. He's screaming and yelling for someone to help him. I grabbed Slim and drug him off the guy and out the back door. I can hear the cops coming, so I hang onto Slim till he calms down some. Then we ducked down an alley into a parking lot. Slim is okay by now but he's bad scared. 'I ain't going back to Huntsville,' he screams and starts looking in all of the cars. He finds one with the keys in it and he drives off. 'Tell Bob I'm sorry,' he yells out the window and he's gone." George shrugged then and stared back off into space.

I could feel the gorge rising in my throat just thinking about that eye lying on the guys cheek. I swallowed hard, but it hit bottom and bounced back, almost choking me.

"The stupid, hot-headed, little bastard," Frank hissed looking around. "The stupid, crazy, little son of a bitch. Damn him and his temper!"

"I was right there, when it happened," George said faintly. "That old boy's eye was big as an egg. Big as a dammed egg." He grinned then, then almost laughed. "When it fell down his cheek, I remember thinking, he can see the floor with that eye." He did laugh then, while I gagged. My stomach was turning handsprings inside me now.

"I heard it pop," George said low. "Popped-- like you'd pop a leaf on your hand." Then he wiped his cheek and stared blankly at his hand. "Some of the stuff---squished on me."

That did it! I ran to the back of the pickup puking my guts out.

"We ain't got time for that dammit!" Frank yelled. "How long ago did all of this happen, George?"

Between my retching I heard him say, "Bout a half-hour, maybe less."

Frank yelled, "Dave, get in the damn pickup and let's get the hell out of here before someone recognizes George for being there."

I retched once more then forced what hadn't come up, back down, turned and started to the pickup door. George and Frank were already in, and I almost made it before what I'd swallowed hit bottom and bounced. One more good heave, cleaned that out though. Then I got in.

Frank drove out of town in the wrong direction then doubled back. George was sitting in the middle, all scrunched down to make himself look smaller. We were expecting to be pulled over any minute, but we drove back through town without anyone even batting an eye.

There was a crowd, still at the bar, and I guess every cop in that part of the state was there. It was so bad one of them was in the street, directing traffic, but we drove right past without so much as a wave.

Once out of town, Frank kicked the pickup out and was soon doing ninety. He took his bottle out of his pants and took a drink then handed it to George. He took a long swallow and handed it back to Frank. The hot whiskey seemed to bring George back around. He coughed and blew and coughed again. Then he took the bottle back and took another drink. The wind was screaming in the window but I hung my head out, it helped. George took another drink and handed me the bottle. I rinsed my mouth out a little, spat, then took a real short drink. It went down like liquid fire and brought tears to my eyes. But it stayed down.

I handed the bottle back to George. He killed what was left and handed the empty back to me. I threw it in the roadside ditch. Frank stopped at a liquor store in Texoma before we crossed back into Texas and bought two fifths and a pint.

George chuckled weirdly as Frank got back in. "I ain't never seen nothing like that in my life," he said. "It all happened so fast there wasn't nothing no one could do. Slim just popped that old boy's eye out and squashed it like you would a tomato, or maybe cracking a pecan, just squished it. Damn! I reckon that old boy won't be going around picking on people no more. Old Slim done showed him the err of his ways and read to him from the book. And he damn sure learned him to pick on someone his own size."

I felt my stomach flop around a little again but it wasn't as bad this time. Now I could at least think about it without getting sick. And I thought about something else, how fast it really must have happened and in a bar exactly like the one Frank and I had just left.

I hadn't paid a whole lot a attention to everything Frank had said back there. At the time I really didn't think I'd ever need any of it. Well, some, but not all of it. At home, things were different and what he had been saying really reminded me of some of the stuff Dad tried to cram down my throat at times. But now, I went back over all of it I could remember because something else had just occurred to me. Some of those things Dad had crammed down my throat had come in pretty handy. That, and the fact that I remembered I was in a man's world now, and I was expected to act like a man in that world, whether I knew how or not.

The trouble was, in spite of all my bluster and bravado. I really didn't know how.

CHAPTER 14

George had finally shut up and I was better by the time we reached Stratford but as I walked in the tent, I knew something else was wrong. All of Slim's stuff was gone. So was the old cardboard box he used as a suitcase. There was a note on his bed. I picked it up and read,

I shor hate to leve but I cant go back to prizen It wood kil
me to go back I hate to leve you short handid Bob but I cant
help it You was reel good to me Bob and Franc I will miss all of you.
                                                              Slim.

The script was painful, drawn more than printed, like a little kid would do or someone that couldn't write. I read it twice before I could really make out what it said.

Frank, stowing his whiskey under his bunk, asked, "what you got there?"

I handed it to him, "Slim's gone, took his stuff and he's gone."

"What!" Frank yelled. "Let me see that." He grabbed the note, reading it out loud. "Well, Jesus Christ!" he yelled, "The little bastard ought to know they couldn't find him here. Hell, they wouldn't look for him here. They probably won't even look for him at all. Damn!"

I said, "he stold a car Frank. They would look for him."

"Where are they going to look!" He glared at me hard. "We could've ditched that damn car and buried it. Hell, drove it a hundred miles away and burned it. They would never know where to look. Or who for."

I said, "Yeah Frank, you could have. Maybe even I could have, but Slim don't think that fast. All he wanted was to get away from this whole area. He's on parole for manslaughter and they'd send him back for sure. He knew it. He had to run," I hollered back.

Frank settled down some, uncapped a bottle and took a long drink then offered it around. Both me and George had one.

"Well," Frank said quietly as he took the bottle back from me, "I, for one, am going to miss the sawed-off, little, hot-head. He made a damn good hand. " His voice was deep and tone serious.

I heard the words I'd heard before but now I suddenly realized *'making a damn good hand,'* was about the best compliment a man a working man could ever hope for. All I could do was nod and say, "Yeah, I liked Slim. He was a good man."

"Me too," George said, reaching for the bottle.

Bob came in about then and hollered. "Well, did y'all have a good time?"

No one answered. I thought about it a second. No, I hadn't had a good time.

Bob sat on Slim's bunk listening to Frank tell the story.

"That's just too bad, just too bad," he said in a normal tone after Frank had finished. "Just popped that old boy's eye out and mashed it." He shrugged, "well, old Slim was a mean one alright but he was a damn good hand. I'm going to miss him."

There it was again, Dad had told me those same words when I'd left, *'you made them a hand'*. I smiled, then watching the three of them.

Then, I thought about the other guy. The one that had lost an eye. No one seemed concerned about him or even bothered that he was half-blinded for life. It bothered me. It almost made me sick again. But then I remembered what Frank had said about what happened to my fellow man, not being any business of mine. And the chill I felt shook my whole body because I just realized, that's what the people in that bar had thought about me. I went back over everything Frank had said there, remembering most of it, remembering mostly, *'There is no such thing as fighting fair. You fight to win, and that's all. You fight to keep from getting hurt, by hurting the other guy first. These boys play for keeps and there ain't no giveaways in here'.*

And I thought, you just learned another cheap lesson Davie, a real cheap lesson. Remember it.

As it was, we were a pretty somber bunch even after we had toasted to Slim several times. I held back on the drinking. My stomach wasn't really in all that good shape still and it still flopped every time I thought about the unknown man. But it was tough, not drinking, listening to stories about Slim, before I had joined the crew. And each one, Frank, Bob, and George had several. They laughed as they told them. I laughed with them but my heart really wasn't in to it. Nether was my mind. My mind was with Slim, running for his life. I wondered where he was by now, out on the highway somewhere running scared, running from the law. That would be a hard way to go. I lay back on my bunk and just thought of it.

As far as I knew, Slim didn't have anywhere to go. At least he'd never talked of a home or a family. It was a sad, lonesome thought and made me think of home. Home made me think of Gayle. This was Saturday night and late now. She would have already given me up by now and might have talked Phil into taking her into town. She was sure going to be hurt when she found out I was gone. I knew what I would do. I would just sit down and write her, tomorrow night when I was sober and not hurting so bad.

Suddenly I was lonesome and I felt very small in a world I never knew existed. Suddenly I was very frightened and I wished I were home.

*   *   *

It was ten o'clock before we got to the fields the next day. Sunday doesn't mean a thing when there's wheat to cut. And the only reason we were so late was we all had hangovers. I seemed to feel the best of all, not having drunk as much, but I kept my mouth shut about it.

Bob was pretty quite for once. Frank was like a bear with a sore tooth and all of us stayed out of his way. George felt pretty good and was his old self again for the most part. He'd scared me yesterday. I thought he'd lost his mind but I guess it had been the shock of being there, seeing it all happen. He still felt bad about Slim this morning, having said several times last night that he should have seen it coming and done something to stop him from blinding the guy.

Frank had laughed about that, and growled, "the bastard got exactly what he deserved." His tone of voice and the expression on his face when he said that scared me.

George helped me service the rigs while Bob checked the field for dryness. Frank went into town to try to find another driver. Like he said, it didn't take long. He was back within an hour with a tall, lanky, kid, about my age. "Boys," Frank said. "This is Gus Henderson, from Colorado. He's our new driver."

I shook his hand, "my name's Dave White, from Oklahoma."

He took my hand, "glad to meet you."

I felt like he really meant it. He looked hungry.

Frank introduced him to the rest of the crew quickly, then looked at Bob, "Wheat ready to cut?"

"Maybe an hour or so more," Bob said in his normal bellow, making Gus jump.

"We got time to service the equipment?"

"Close enough, or we can wait. Whatever you want." Bob hollered.

Gus looked at me, his eyes wide and a questioning look on his face as he cocked his head toward Bob.

I mouthed the word, "later."

He nodded.

Frank yelled, "we might not have time later. Let's do it. Dave, you and Gus get a grease gun and start greasing them trucks. Change the oil too. We'll do our own combines. Let's do it!"

Gus came with me over to Bob's pickup. I handed him a grease gun and, hoping against hope, said, "you ever grease a truck before?"

He nodded quickly. "Sure, my old man runs a service station back in Colorado. I worked there half my life. No sweat."

He sounded funny, his voice that is. He had an almost clipped way of speaking. But after living in Oklahoma all my life and having half my relatives from Texas, any person without a drawl sounded funny.

"That's good. I haven't ever done it before. I'd appreciate you showing me how."

"Sure, let's go. Say, why does that man yell all the time?"

"He's about deaf, and he can't hear himself talk, so he yells."

Gus shrugged, "I was just wondering. I thought maybe he was mad."

"Na, he does it all the time. You'll get used to it."

Gus said, "you never worked on trucks before?"

"Man, I ain't never been near a truck before this week."

"Well, don't worry about it. I've worked on them all my life. I'll show you how." He started to one of the trucks. I followed. "I'll show you on this one. Then we'll do one apiece and I'll check yours when you're through." With that, we crawled under one of Bob's trucks.

"You say you're from Colorado?" I asked, watching him wipe off a dirt covered grease zerk.

"Yeah, born and raised there." He fitted the gun tip on the zerk and began pumping grease.

"You live in the mountains?"

"Almost. You can see them from Cloud Chief. That's my hometown. You can see Pike's Peak, real good from there."

A sad longing came over me. "I'll bet they're pretty."

"Yeah," he fitted the gun to another zerk. "What's it like in Oklahoma?"

"A lot of it is like this, but where I'm from is mostly wooded hills. You got a car at home?"

"Yeah, a '49 Chevy. I've got it fixed up pretty nice though."

He crawled over to another zerk. I was trying to fix their location in my mind. "All these trucks got zerk's in the same places?" I asked as he steadily worked.

"Pretty much the same. These aren't hard to see. These trucks get serviced real regular I'll bet. You got a car at home?"

"No, I hope to make enough money to buy me one when I get back there though."

He nodded, "maybe you can. If you stick it out that is. These guys custom cutters or independents?"

"Custom," I mentally thanked Slim for that lesson. "Bob has contracts that go all the way up into Canada."

Gus grinned, "that's good. That means steady work and clean fields. We're ready to change the oil now and check the rear end and transmission." He pulled a wrench out of his pocket and started unscrewing a plug on the transmission. "You got a girl back home?"

"Yeah, her name is Gayle."

"Mine's named Janet. I sure do miss her sometimes."

"Me too. If you got a car and had a job, why did you leave? I mean, what are you doing here?"

He stopped working a second and looked at me. "I'm really not sure." He unscrewed the plug in the transmission until a drop of heavy, black oil ran out. "That's good, as long as you can see the oil run out, it's fine. Let's move back to the rear end. You check it the same way." We crawled back to the rear of the truck.

"I guess," Gus said. "I was bored with Cloud Chief. There's not much there and I wanted to see a little of the country. This seemed like a good way," he laughed. "And it was until I got drunk and got throwed in jail for a week for contempt of court down in Etter. And they were right, I did have contempt of that court. In the first place, I wasn't that drunk and I had just got paid. I had almost two hundred dollars in my billfold until that fat cop asked for my ID. I told the judge that and that's when he said I was in contempt of the court and fined me fifty dollars or a week in jail. 'Course, I didn't have any money so I spent that week picking up trash in the town."

I told him about my run-in with the law down in Frederick while I checked the rear end of the truck.

He said, "at least you got out of town that day and not a week later. Well, that's it under here. I'll pull the oil drain-plug and the filter and you fill it up and we'll be through with this one."

I crawled out from under the truck and got the oil. By the time I got back Gus said, "fill it up, anytime."

I hollered, "Okay," and started pouring the oil in. When I got through, I said, "That's it."

"Okay, start it up and I'll check for leaks."

I started the truck and let it run a second until he yelled, "that's good."

He crawled out from under the truck with the pan full of used oil and poured it into a barrel in the back of Bob's pickup. Then he turned to me. "Okay, you start on one while I do the other, then I'll check what you've done."

"Okay," I said and started on Frank's truck.

Gus was through with his in about twenty minutes but I worked on mine for almost an hour before he helped me finish. I was still learning, slowly, but I was learning.

Frank came over about then, stopping by his pickup for some hair of the dog. He took a good drink then he said, "y'all about finished?"

"Yeah, all through," I said.

Frank looked at me questioningly, then at Gus. "This boy said he knows about trucks. Does he?"

"A whole lot more about them than me. He'll do," I said.

"That ain't much," Frank snapped. "But if you say he'll do, he'll be okay." And he walked off hollering, "let's cut wheat!"

The combines roared back to life in a clattering, shaking, banging, rattling, cloud of dust, straw and chaff and began their ponderous ever decreasing circles around the field. The excitement was gone now, only the dirty, sweaty, sun-blistering, mind-rendering, work remained.

That day and another passed with out incident. Gus turned out to be a top hand and easy to be around which, as close as we worked and lived, was good. He was a good driver too, a lot better than me even after all this time, but I was pulling my weight now. At least no one complained about my work and in this world someone that didn't pull his weight, didn't last long.

The days had settled into a routine now, almost like the land, endlessly the same. I pretty much knew what I was doing and I guess the lack of something to expect made time pass slower. But this afternoon seemed to drag on for some reason. I wasn't sure why. It was the same as the last day we had worked. I sat in the shade of a truck, waiting to load, then after driving to the elevator, sat in the shade of the truck, waiting to unload, so I could drive back to the field and wait to load.

I didn't even notice the wind now. It was just always there. An occasional dust devil would whirl across the field sucking up dust, straw and chaff, carrying it high into the air. Some of them traveled a quarter of a mile or more before they blew themselves out.

I had begun to notice the sky more. I guess that was because it was the only thing that changed. Some days it would be completely clear and so blue it hurt to look at it. But some days, like today, giant puff-ball clouds were everywhere, forming weird configurations that constantly changed with the wind. They were peaceful to watch, almost like looking into a fire or looking at the stars.

I guess they were too peaceful to watch for long because I was almost asleep when I heard Frank whistle. I jumped in the truck and drove to him. He stopped his combine to unload so I got the water jug and climbed up with him.

"How is it going?" He poured himself a drink.

"Pretty good. I was almost asleep when you whistled."

"I figured as much. How is Gus working out?"

"He'll do. He knows his trucks. I'd say he's as good as Slim."

Frank rinsed out his mouth, spat and nodded. "Go on in with this load. You're not quite full but you can't hold another hopper." The unloading auger began to rattle so he pulled up one lever and pushed down another. The header started turning.

I jumped down and he was gone in a cloud of dust. I pulled the third truck close to the standing wheat then started to town in the full one. I met Gus coming from the elevator. We honked and waved and drove on.

The trip in was just as uneventful as the fifty or so before but, on the way back, I knew something was wrong as soon as I pulled onto the highway. Up ahead a couple of miles was a huge wedge-shaped, black and gray cloud that seemed to touch the ground. At first I thought it was a really big dust devil. But about then I figured out it was smoke, a lot of smoke.

The road was straight, heading due north. The omnipresent wind was from the due south. The smoke was rising from near the highway but it seemed to be coming up from the west side. Our field was about two miles east of the highway. I breathed a sigh of relief when I realized we were safe.

But then, something hit me. Most of the smoke was black. It should have been white or at the most, whitish-gray, like a grass fire. But this smoke was a boiling, ugly, greasy-black, rising in billows almost as if it were being spurted into the sky by a giant machine.

I was still a mile away when I could see the highway patrol cars with their flashing blue lights, blocking the highway, and all the frenzied activity around the smoking wreck. The wheat field west of the wreck was black and now a pall of gray smoke had separated from the plume of black smoke and was being fed by the wheat fire that had been blown out of sight by the moaning wind. The traffic had stopped on both sides of the highway but now they were waving the ones on my side on, to open the road.

I drove on, very slowly, watching the people put out the fire, seeing now it was the result of a wheat truck that had hit a small, concrete bridge abutment, head on.

The trooper motioned frantically for me to move on so I sped up some then slowed again as I came near what was left of the truck just as they lifted the driver out, or at least what was left of the driver. He looked for all the world like a blackened log except he still had arms and legs, and a grinning head. The sight sickened me but I was mesmerized, unable to look away.

The trooper yelled at me to go on, jarring me back to reality. I sped up a little but not fast enough, not before the smell hit me full force, the sickening, sweetish, stench of burned flesh that I would carry with me to my grave. Time stopped and I believe the world stopped moving. Everything went into slow motion as I was seemingly caught in a time-warp. I wanted nothing more than to get away, to leave the gut-turning stench but it seemed as if I couldn't move. I couldn't tear my eyes away from the charred corpse and the smell of it permeated my whole body. And even as I passed, and the grinning, cinderized, specter of what had been a man passed from my view, I looked back in the side mirror of the truck for a finial horrific view.

My turn-off was less than a mile ahead. I made it there before I had to stop. My stomach was churning and my hands shook so bad I couldn't light a cigarette. I don't know how long I sat there, seeing and smelling him in my mind before the most horrible thought came over me. It might be Gus.

I didn't know. The truck was crashed and bad burned and I didn't look at it that close. I went back over the whole scene but nothing except the burned man came clearly to focus in my mind. I simply didn't know. I forced myself to calm down and drove on to the field as fast as I could. I met Frank coming out in the pickup, just at the edge of the field.

He slid to a stop and jumped out, yelling, "what's all that smoke?"

I killed the truck and got out, running to him, yelling, "truck wreck and a wheat fire. Frank! Where's Gus?"

"Gone to the elevator," he said questioningly. "Why?"

"The driver's dead, burned up in the fire."

He paled then went rigid, "Gus?"

I shook my head. "I don't know. I can't be sure."

He started back to the pickup and I ran to get in as he took off spinning the tires and sliding sideways when we pulled out on the road. The pickup engine was screaming as he shifted into high. "How do you know the driver's dead?" he yelled over the noise, and the rush of the wind.

"I seen him, all burned up." My stomach began churning again.

Frank just nodded and mashed the accelerator harder, squalling the tires as he speed shifted into second and fishtailed onto the highway. The engine began screaming again and he dropped it into high, hitting seventy. In no time he pulled off the road as close as we could get to the wreck and we ran the rest of the way. We got there just as the ambulance went wailing into town causing me to wonder what their hurry was. The load they carried wasn't hurting any and they sure weren't going to bring him back to life.

The truck was a mess. The front end was smashed and buckled and the tires and sideboards had been burned away. It had been carrying a full load of wheat which, partially burned, had fallen to the road when the sideboards had given way. I stopped at the back but Frank walked around it, then looked at me, shaking his head, "I can't tell," he said. "Not for sure."

I didn't want to but I walked to the front, or at least almost. I walked to the smell of the cab then ran back and this time I couldn't hold it. I grabbed hold of the truck bed to keep from falling and puked my guts out. There were several people still hanging around, most of them grown men. No one laughed.

Frank brought me a drink of water from somewhere and while I rinsed my mouth out, he said, "I'm not positive but I don't think it's one of ours."

I nodded, afraid to say anything but that did make me feel better. The trooper came up then, telling us to clear the road. Frank nodded uneasily, looking at me. I rinsed my mouth again and spat. Then we walked back to the pickup and started toward town.

Frank's jaw was twitching as he drove and I could feel him making a concerted effort to hold down his speed. We didn't talk. We met several trucks in the four or five miles, but not Gus. The line of trucks waiting to unload almost reached the drive-in where we turned off the highway and the driver's looked at us curiously and we drove slowly past them. Still no Gus.

Frank hit the steering wheel with an explosive, "damn!" And I felt empty as we reached the scales. Frank circled the scale house and stopped. Still no Gus. "Well, I guess that's that," he said and seemed to deflate.

I felt it too. It was as if something had been ripped out of me. "He might have stopped to get a drink or something." I said weakly.

"Not loaded. And he hasn't had time to unload and leave," he said hard. Then he yelled, "look there!"

I turned, following Franks finger and saw Gus pulling back onto the scales.

"Well damn," I said low, breathing again. "He must have been in the elevator, unloading when we drove up."

Frank laughed, "The only place we didn't look. I'll be dammed."

"You want to tell him anything, Frank?"

He laughed again, "na, let's go on back. It might make him feel good if he knew we was worried about him." He pulled away before Gus saw us and we headed back. But instead of going directly to the field, we chased the fire.

We caught it after several miles and turned down a section line to get a close look. It had already burned several square miles of standing wheat and jumped the road in several places igniting other fields before we caught it. There wasn't anything we could do but watch the twenty-foot wall of flame roll across the field like an evil presence, roaring and shrieking, moving even faster than the howling wind. There was nothing anyone could do. The fire was like a glowing red beast, consuming everything in its path. The flames would spin now and then into tornadic like vortexes, raising high into the startling blue sky, howling as if they were live things in pain, crackling like a thousand rifles going off in a constant roar that hurt my ears even from a distance. I sat enthralled, watching the most magnificent, and at the same time, the most frightening thing I had ever seen.

"Something else isn't it Wheatie?" Frank said.

All I could do was nod, totally mesmerized by the wildness, the fury of the fire.

He laughed, then said, "now you know why I climbed you so hard back in Clinton when you threw away that cigarette butt."

"Yeah," I croaked out, my voice cracking. "How are they going to put it out?" I asked, knowing the answer even before I spoke.

Frank just shook his head. "In this wind? They won't put it out. There ain't nothing no one can do. It'll burn like this until it hits an open spot or a field that's already been cut. Other than that--- it'll just burn."

The noise was gone now with the fire, blown by the moaning wind, away from us across the field. Only the blackened field remained and the clumps of the bodies of small animals, that never had a chance to get away, lay on the smoking, scorched earth. The pall of grayish white, boiling, smoke was visible now, still racing northwards at an incredible rate of speed, faster than I could have ever imagined. It rose almost out of sight and spread into the sky to cover the whole northern horizon. Frank just shook his head and headed back to our field.

Gus was all excited about the wreck when we got back. We were just glad to see him again. The third truck sat, full and ready to go in. Frank looked me over closely. "You okay Wheatie?" His voice was full of concern.

I nodded. "I think so."

"The best medicine is to get back in there and do it now. The longer you wait, the more you're going to think about it and the worse it will be." His voice was stern, flat and hard.

"I know that. It might just take me a little longer to get there and to get back though." I couldn't look at Frank, him knowing I was about to mess my pants.

He slapped me on the shoulder. "Don't worry about it Dave. Just get in that truck and do it." He grinned then, "You'll be okay, and take as long as it takes."

I climbed in the truck and drove away, my whole body quivering like an exposed nerve. But the farther I went, the better it got and by the time I pulled out onto the highway, I was in pretty good shape. I shuddered, thinking about passing the wreck but when I got there only the burned spot, the pile of wheat and the chunk gone out of the bridge-rail, remained. And the memory.

*   *   *

We broke late that night, around ten, barely making it to the café to eat before it closed. I didn't have much to say and tuned the rest out too. The happenings of the afternoon were bearing heavily on me.

I saw a newspaper the next morning about the boy being killed in the wreck. No one knew him, not even the man he worked for. Joe, was his name and the only identification they knew of had been burned with him in the fire. There was no last name, no town, no nothing. Just Joe.

That bothered me a lot. The paper said a boy named Joe died in a firey wreck and a local farmer lost his wheat in the fire. The farmer said he'd been hurt but he'd recover next year. There was a picture of him, standing in his burned field. He was crying in the picture, crying for his wheat. No one would cry for Joe: no one that cared even knew he was dead, and probably would never know where he'd been buried. It weighed on me all day, just how fast it could happen. One minute you're driving down the road, the next minute, you're dead. And no one knows your name. And no one even cares.

"What's your problem?" Frank asked me that night at the tent. "You've been walking around half dead all day. You look like you're about to step on your bottom lip."

I shrugged, "I don't know just feel bad I guess."

"Act like someone bigger than you, kicked your dog."

I had to grin at that one, but only for a second. "I been thinking about that boy in the truck yesterday, I guess."

"Don't worry about it. He's dead. He ain't hurting none."

"I know that. I was just wondering about his folks. They'll never know what happened to him or where he's laying." And the old man back in Oklahoma came to my mind. *"Six sons," he'd said. "Six sons and I only know where one of them is buried."*

"You worry about stuff like that, you'll go crazy as I am." Frank scoffed. "Try not to let it bother you," but then he softened. "Dave, it happens all the time. I know it ain't no good deal, but it happens. Boys get killed with no identification on them, or like him, all burned up. Man, don't dwell on it or it'll eat you up."

He dug under his bunk then and came out with his bottle, taking a long drink.

"Over in Korea," he shook his head. "I don't know how many there was, all blown to pieces, no way to identify them. Sometimes, after a big battle, we would find bodies that had been stripped by the North Koreans, with nothing left and no way to identify them either. We would just stack them up and ship them out and then count heads of all us that were left. Sometimes---most of the time, someone we knew would be missing. And then--."

He shrugged then, as if it didn't matter but I had heard the crack in his voice.

"Shit happens!" He said hard. "And if you dwell on it, it'll eat on you like maggots till you got nothing left. The thing to learn here is don't let it happen to you. You can't help that boy but you can help yourself." He took another long drink and his eyes clouded over as if he had gone somewhere.

I thought about it a long time, lying on my cot, staring at the peak of the tent. Then I took the paper with my name and address Dad had written, the night before I left, out of my billfold and put it in my suitcase. Just in case.

I felt better the next day, almost back to normal. Good enough to eat my regular breakfast and noticing the pile Gus put away, I was glad he was around. It gave them someone else to laugh at.

By noon, I was over it. The whole incident seemed like something that'd happened a long time ago, or maybe in a dream. And except for when I drove past the burn, almost as if it had never happened. But somehow, that made the empty sadness I had felt before seem even worse.

The next afternoon we moved to the other field. It was a simple process drive across the road and open the gate. Except the problem as I could see it was the gate was only twelve feet wide. How does a man drive a vehicle fourteen feet wide through a gate only twelve feet wide? Frank did it with no problem. He drove alongside the fence until he had just cleared the gate then turned hard. The body of the combine was almost against the gatepost while the header cleared the other side with some, not much, but some to spare.

Other than that there really wasn't much difference. Turn right instead of left. Everything else was the same.

The view had changed some, most of the wheat was cut now, and now and then I would meet a crew on the road moving north with the ever-present, moaning, sometimes shrieking wind. They seemed to be restless people, like the restless wind always moving, blown north by the hot south wind. Then back south by the cold north wind to wherever they called home.

I tried to understand why they moved. The money couldn't be all that good, not to be on the road for half a year. And to put up with the town people, which I imagined were about all alike. I wondered how they could stand it, year after year, never having a real place to call home.

Maybe they were like me, I thought. Maybe it beat what they had at home. Maybe the geese and the singing truck tires called to them too. I didn't ask. Maybe I was afraid to find out the real answer. And I knew that, more than likely, they couldn't tell me why they did it. Maybe I was better off not knowing. I did know that it was getting in my blood now, even more than before. I was lonely here but I'd lonely at home too. I know I felt different but I couldn't explain, even to me, why or how I was different. I just was.

*   *   *

We quit early that night. Bob had called ahead and the wheat in the next field wasn't ready yet so there was no need to hurry. I was sitting on my cot when Frank came in and flopped on his, then looked at me. "What do you think now Wheatie?" he grinned as he asked.

I just shrugged, "this is just about as much fun as burying a dead cow."

He laughed, then sat up. "Tell you what. Let's go up to Texoma and see if we can't get our wicks wet."

I laughed excited, quickly saying, "let's go!" I would have gone to hell on a shingle about then, just to break the monotony.

We asked the others. Gus was broke, but I loaned him five dollars. Bob and George stayed back. Bob said he was tired. I really think George was afraid to go. He hadn't completely gotten over the last time he was in a bar. So Gus, Frank and I loaded up in the pickup and fifteen minutes later pulled up to a bar.

I was disappointed from the start. The place was a dingy hole in the wall that smelled of stale cigarettes, beer and urine. There were a half-dozen stools at the bar. Another half-dozen booths lined one wall. Four tables took up the middle. Farther back two grimy pool tables stood sad looking and unoccupied. A jukebox took up one corner and was thumping out a song about unrequited love.

I checked out what crowd there was and with the exception of two old men, they looked like wheat crews. Frank was easy and relaxed as we sat at a table. The waitress gave us no trouble when Frank ordered three beers. She was the only woman in the place and looked like she had crawled out from under the floor after it had been built a while. Almost like the cockroach I saw crawling up the bar right now.

"Pickings is slim in here," Frank said smiling.

I nodded, "Yeah, I don't think I would take it, even if she offered."

Gus laughed, Frank smiled, tipping his hat back. He leaned back in his chair and ordered another beer by holding up his empty bottle. I paid for it when the crone came and gave her fifty cents for the now silent jukebox. She went immediately to it and the haunting voice of Patsy Cline, singing, *Sweet Dreams of You,* filled the bar.

Gus and I shot one game of eight ball, which I lost almost immediately. Gus was good. Then he and Frank played a game. Gus beat him by four balls. Another guy that had been watching put a quarter on the table. Frank and I sat watching. The jukebox had run dry again so I waved the crone over and gave her some more money. She played the same songs she had before and went back to behind the bar, singing with the music. I looked over at Frank. "Is it always like this in these places?"

He smiled knowingly, "usually, during the week."

"I expected there to be more going on."

He laughed. "Is there more going on where you are from?"

I thought about that a second and shook my head. "No, not really. There are more kids to do things with though."

"That's because you belong there and you know where to go. Here, you're just a stranger and in a strange land."

I watched Gus make a good shot that won the game. The other guy handed him a dollar and began to rack the balls. Frank was slowly tearing his bottle label to shreds with his thumbnail, staring vacantly off into space. A sad song by Johnny Cash came on the jukebox.

The crash of the pool balls breaking rack caused me to think of the pool hall back home. Home made me think of Gayle. That thought and the sad music caused me to go away in my mind, back to the dark country roads and music on the radio and Gayle, half-naked in my arms.

Frank moved slightly and I suddenly realized I'd broken the cardinal rule in a bar. I wasn't paying attention to what was going on. I turned slowly just in time to see the guy playing pool, hand Gus a five and start racking the balls again. And I felt Frank began to tense. He made no outward sign or movement. I just felt it as he watched the game, intently now.

Gus broke the rack and made two balls after that. Then the other guy shot, making three of his before he missed. Gus shot again, making two more balls, then missed a shot, I could have made. His miss left the other guy set up and he ran the table easily. Gus laughed, handed him back his five and put his cue stick back in the rack. The other guy smiled, then went to sit back down. The tension drained out of Frank immediately as Gus sat back down. The other guy and three more drank their beer and walked out.

Frank nodded to Gus. "That was a cool move."

Gus said, "yeah, he was getting pissed. I still won two dollars off him though. I didn't think he'd mind that much."

Frank grinned. "If you had won that last game, we would've had a fight."

"I know," Gus said quietly. "That's why I didn't win."

And I just learned another real cheap lesson without even realizing what was going on.

I guess we stayed there another half-hour or so, drinking and listening to the jukebox when Frank killed his beer and said, "let's get one to go and head back. We got wheat to cut tomorrow."

I looked around the bar. For some reason I had expected more.

*   *   *

After that night, the days blended together like mixed paint. One look's at it and he can see the difference. Stir it some more and it's all the same. The days were like that, and time for times sake, ceased to exist. Only daylight and dark had meaning. We were into the fields before the sun and out after dark and by now, I could shift the truck in my sleep. There was nothing else to learn, only the same over and over and over, until I couldn't remember if today was yesterday or tomorrow. It was always the same. The same day. The same road. The same tent. The same wind, always the wind, always the same.

Then it was over. This field was finished, done, through, finally all cut. Thank what Gods there may be, we were loading today and moving on. The harvest was over, here at least. We'd been here ten and a half days but I felt as if I'd been born here.

I hauled the last load in that day. The same disembodied voice came over the speaker. The same boys scooped out my truck bed. I dumped the load with a long sigh of relief. A promised ten-day-cut, a delivered nine-day-cut. I didn't count the day we'd lost because of the rain. I didn't even count the loss of Slim. Gus had turned out to be a top hand and now, thanks to him, Slim and the rest, so was I. I still didn't know it all but I had sure come a long way. And it felt good.

We finished loading after I came back from the elevator but it was too late to leave. The next stop was Cheyenne Wells, Colorado, almost two hundred miles north. We would leave in the morning.

Gus was excited about that. Cheyenne Wells was only about a hundred miles from his hometown, Cloud Chief. He'd been gone over a month now, three weeks working and a week in jail but he'd called home just recently and after that, he said something that got me real excited.

"Look," he said. "If my figuring is right, we're going to get to Cheyenne Wells early. The wheat won't be ready by almost a week. Me and you might beg off and go over to Cloud Chief, see my folks and run around a little. Maybe just pick up some girls."

Now that sounded good to me. Real good! I hadn't realized how much I had missed being around kids my own age until Gus had come. I knew I missed Gayle, but that was different. Gus had made it a lot easier just by being there and talking to him had helped the homesickness and creeping loneliness that ate on me at times. We were completely different, he and I, but at the same time we were alike. Both of us were filled with a restless longing for something neither of us could describe. Like the other restless people, we had an emptiness within, a calling, that drove us away from home but at the same time, called us back. But torn between the longing and the homesickness, the longing in me won and I promised myself I'd tough it out. I would stay with the harvest until the new school semester began and I'd go north to wherever the wind went. Then and only then would I go home.

At least it sounded good.

*   *   *

The loading had gone as smoothly as the unloading, sideboards and tailgate off, combine on. Put the chains in place, boom her down tight and wire the handle of the boomers down to keep them in place. We don't want no slips. Slips means a lost combine. A lost combine means a lot of trouble and a lot of money lost. Boom her down tight, boy's, then tighter.

We drove back to town and Bob met us at the tent with our pay. A buck and a half an hour times a hundred and ten hours comes to a hundred and sixty-five dollars! Add to that, the twenty I still had left from the poker games and I was rich!

We all marched over to the café to pay our tabs. Mine came to twenty-five dollars and some cents, not as bad as I thought it would be. The second thing I did was buy a money order at the post office. I kept a hundred and sent the rest home. I didn't have anything to say to Mom and Dad so I just sent the money order. They'd know by that I was alright.

Frank was reading a book when I walked back to the tent. The rest had gone to town for one thing or another. I sat down on my cot and said, "Man, I'm glad we are leaving here. I thought we would never finish that field."

Frank closed his book, took a drink, then handed the bottle to me. "Yeah, I know. It ain't going to be any better when we get to Cheyenne Wells, though. We got twice as much to cut there."

"Two thousand acres?" I took a small drink and handed him back the bottle.

"Yep."

"All in the same place?"

"Yep, one field."

"I like to went crazy here."

"This is your first field. The others will be better. You know more about what to expect. You should read more. It gives you something to do when your bored. You think back on the books and then it ain't so bad. I have several here if you want to read them." He held up the one he was reading, 'The Wayward Bus,' by John Steinbeck. "This is a good book. I've read it, I don't know, half a dozen times. It gets better each time. Good books do that."

"I might later," I said. "I might have to. I need something on my mind. I've been thinking a lot about home."

"Dave, you ain't been gone two weeks."

"I know. That's about the only reason I haven't gone back. I'm afraid they'd all laugh at me." The old lonesome feeling washed over me again.

"I wouldn't worry about that. Let the bastards think what they will on their way to hell." He sounded hard.

"That sounds good, but it bothers me, what people think."

He smiled then, "sometimes I wished it bothered me. Maybe I wouldn't be such a sorry bastard then. I might even sober up and amount to something if I worried about what people thought. Trouble is, it just don't bother me. I know what I am and I don't care where I'm going."

He opened his bottle again, took a short pull, lay back down and covered his eyes with his arm. Soon he began to snore softly so I got up and walked out, wishing now I'd gone to town with the rest but at the same time, glad I hadn't.

The sun was just sinking below the horizon but the heat outside the tent was like a blow from a hammer, even this late in the day. I walked over to the café for a cup of hot coffee, which didn't make a lot of sense, but I had to do something.

The same girl was waiting tables but we hadn't spoken since the night when she'd hurt my feelings and she seemed to have no desire to talk tonight, so I didn't speak either. I wished I could talk to her though, maybe even joke and kid with her a little. She sure was pretty. And I sure was lonesome.

Sitting there, watching her, reminded me of home so bad it was probably good she didn't speak. I was ready to go back but I wanted to go on. I really didn't know what I wanted. I finished my coffee and went back to the tent.

Tomorrow we'd be leaving, going on up the road.

Maybe tomorrow would be better.

CHAPTER 15

⎯⎯⎯

I don't know how long I sat there, away in my mind, but it was dark when I went back to the tent. Frank was still asleep, Gus and George still gone so I climbed up on the pickup hood, leaned back on the windshield and looked at the stars. A carload of kids, radio blaring, straight-pipes blubbering, drove by laughing and the homesickness washed over me even more.

Gus and George came in a little while later waking Frank up. He cussed them some then came outside and pissed on the pickup tire. I moved slightly causing him to jump and yell. "You like to scared the fire out of me."

I laughed.

"Dammit Dave, what are you doing out here anyway? You're supposed to be in bed."

I laughed again, "just couldn't sleep, I guess."

"Still homesick?"

"Yeah, pretty bad."

"Don't you know why it's worse now?"

"No."

I could see him smile in the darkness. "We're leaving in the morning. Think about it," he waved his hand at the tent. "That's been home for over a week now."

"It seems like a year."

"And now, we're leaving."

The kids drove back by. I could hear a girl laughing over the radio. He was right and I told him so.

"It's like the field, Dave. This is your first one. The others will get better. We'll have the tent set up in Cheyenne Wells tomorrow afternoon and you won't even know we've moved."

"It would be a lot simpler for me to just go home."

He shook his head. "For you maybe, but I can't afford that. I need you to drive tomorrow. Look, if you feel the same when we get to Cheyenne Wells, you can leave. But now Son, I need you."

I had no argument to counter that and it was real good to hear. I smiled, sliding off the pickup. "If I got all that way to drive, I had best get some sleep then."

Frank put his hand on my shoulder and we walked in the tent.

I still couldn't sleep for thinking about home, of Gayle, of the hot summer nights, parking down at out special place in dad's old Ford. Of holding her in the drive-in movie outside of town and the parties at the houses of friends. I even missed Rocky a little and that said something.

The kids in the car drove back by. I knew it was them by the sound of the straight pipes but that's all I heard. He's taken the rest home and now that's where he is headed, home. I thought, staring at the peak of the tent. Home, that word again, that hurt so bad to think about. But Frank had said he needed me. Needed. That was a good word. I drifted off to sleep, feeling good.

The next morning wasn't any different, but it was. Bob hollered in the tent at five-thirty, as usual. Everybody went through their own waking up routine, as usual. But there was a tinge of excitement in the air, a sense of something different, like the night before Christmas or the night before I had left home.

The sky was just a faint lighting in the east, a vague grayness just lighter than the black above as we walked to the café. We ate with a feeling of urgency. Everyone talked louder than normal and nervous laughter seemed to affect us all. I thought about what all had happened to, and around, me here and it seemed unreal, like I had read it all in a book.

I thought about the pretty waitress on the night shift and laughed to myself because now I knew she'd done what she had, partly out of fear. We were the movers and she had to stay. Maybe, she wanted to stay. But we would know what was out there beyond her world, things she was afraid to learn. And she was afraid of us because we would know.

Frank looked up then and said, "light enough, Boys. Let's drink up and get on the road. We got some miles to burn today."

We all finished our coffee in a gulp and walked out. The tent was still standing but everything else had been loaded. Fifteen minutes later we were pulling away.

A few wispy clouds hung low in the east just enough to gather and reflect the morning sunlight into streaks of gold behind a fleece of pink. The rest of the sky was clear, promising a scorching day. I was still driving the pickup, which was alright by me. Gus had driven a truck loaded with a combine before. I still had that to do but I could wait. I could wait a long time for that.

Northwest we headed, up Highway 287, toward Boise City, crossing the panhandle of Oklahoma, known, not so long ago, as No Man's Land. Back in the days gone by, the panhandle had been a territory that had gotten left out when the maps had been drawn. It was a strip of land thirty-six miles wide but over one-hundred-sixty miles long, that was claimed by Texas, Oklahoma and Kansas. And parts of it claimed by Colorado and the New Mexico Territory, all at the same time, but owned by no one. It had been a lawless haven for thugs, outlaws and ne're-do-wells in general, policed only by Federal Marshals out of Ft. Smith, Arkansas, over three hundred miles away. That was until 1890 when congress settled the dispute and gave the strip to Oklahoma Territory.

Then the maps were re-drawn and farmers and their wives came. The women insisted on real law. Churches and schools replaced the saloons and whore houses, telephones replaced the telegraph. Cars and pickups replaced the horse, for the most part. By then the West, as it had been, was gone and a whole era slipped into history.

I was sorry that I'd missed it.

We turned due north on Highway 287/385 and headed toward Lamar,

Colorado, crossing the Comanche National Grasslands, the ever-present wind at our backs now pushing us farther and farther north.

The land changed again to the rolling hills of the true prairie, each successive hill was a little higher as we climbed all the time into the high plains. This was buffalo country of years past, beaver country, which had been ruled and fought over by the Comanche, Kiowa, Southern Cheyenne, and Arapaho for eons past. They had been fierce people but ones that had lived in harmony with nature and according to natural laws.

But then, the trappers came and caught the beaver for hats to decorate the heads of Europe. And the hunters came to kill the buffalo from a half-mile, taking only the hides for a leather-hungry world and leaving the rest to rot. And the Indians starved until they were no longer fierce. Then what was left of them and the pitifully small herds of buffalo were herded onto reservations and the land was tamed. It was broken by the plows and planted until what had been was no more, and would never be again.

And man called this progress and called it good.

I watched the rolling hills unfold, exposing land that was now ruled by the hawks that hunted, wheeling and soaring through the startling blue of the sky. Or they rested, perching magnificently on the man-made trees that lined the roadside, reminding me that the barren country was still alive under the high grasses. And I wondered, just how good was it? And again, I felt sad for the missing of the times.

The farther north we drove, the more I looked to the west across the rolling, grass-covered prairie, totally deserted with the exception of an occasional windmill or the remains of a crumbling shack. The shacks stood alone, weathered silver and staring with vacant, dead-looking eyes, telling stories, at the same time, of better days and worse.

I was looking for the mountains I'd only heard about and seen in pictures, thinking any minute now I'll see them out there at the edge of the world, rising out of the undulating prairie, clawing at the sky, big-shouldered and snow-mantled. The anticipation made me tremble.

We turned east at Lamar and a few miles further on I saw Bob pulling into a roadside park. I stopped behind Gus, walked to Frank's truck and tested the chains holding the combine for him. They were all still tight with no problems.

"What do you think Wheatie?" he said climbing down.

"I missed the mountains somewhere back there."

Laughing, he said, "No you didn't. You remember what I told you back in Texas about enjoying the view?"

"Yeah, I remember."

He laughed again, "well, enjoy it Boy, because this is it." He swung his hand in a semi-circle over the empty, arid landscape, shimmering in the heat.

"You mean we won't even see any mountains?"

"Not unless you go about fifty, sixty, miles west, you won't."

"I never thought about Colorado being flat like this," I said as Gus walked up.

"Yeah man," Gus said. "This is the flat part. West of here you get into the mountains but almost half the state looks just like this."

"Well hell!" I said. "I could've stayed in Oklahoma and seen this. What did we come here for anyway?"

"To cut old man Dougal's wheat, that's what for. You ain't on vacation Boy," Frank said with a grin. "Act like tourist or something."

"Let's eat," Bob boomed at normal volume.

I was sure disappointed but it didn't hurt my appetite any. Gus's either. We both hung back till the rest had finished then the race was on. I don't know who won but Bob paid Frank on the bet. Laughing Frank said, "Bob, you lose one more hand, you're going to go broke feeding us."

Bob just shook his head. George mumbled something about a couple of human garbage disposals and opened another Coke.

We stayed there over an hour eating in the shade of the trucks, talking about nothing. Frank was drinking less now and didn't get twitchy so bad but after a while, he walked over to his truck, pissed on the tire and raised the hood. We all did likewise.

Back on the road and turn north at Granada. The land stretched out again. It wasn't as flat as it had been in Texas but not as rolling as before. The land was several shades of brown and gray melting sometimes into the silver of the bearded grasses. These colors were broken only by an occasional creek or stock pond that glistened green with watered trees and plants that looked like an oasis in a desert of grass. The highway was a black line that disappeared into a shimmering, reflecting pool of a mirage, glistening in the heat. The wind was at our backs again blowing us farther and farther north.

We finally reached Cheyenne Wells and drove on through. It looked like a hundred other towns we'd gone through, strung out along the highway, baking in the sun. The only thing moving was the dust in the wind. It reminded me of Crane.

I saw a few other crews that had beaten us but not many. We'd come a long way north leaving most of them picking up behind us. We drove on out of town for a few miles then down a section line to the farm.

The house was rock and, from the looks of it, had been there for some time. From the looks of Dougal, he might have built it. The man had to be ninety years old, but out here on the prairie the constant sun and wind seem to suck the juice out of a man, leaving only leather. Which is what Dougal reminded me of, old leather.

Frank had told me about the old man and in doing so he told me about life on the prairie. He talked about how during the Depression when Dougal was broke, he had gathered wheat, lost from the hauling wagons, from the roadside to plant. And how one bad winter, he had killed his prized riding horse to eat, keeping the plow horses to work.

"I don't blame him a bit for that," Frank had said. "To hook a good riding horse up to a plow would be worse than killing him for food.

Frank had told me that Dougal had no idea how much money he had now, with two thousand acres of wheat, two thousand of corn and another five thousand for soybeans and five thousand more for horses, cattle and sheep. And he had earned every square inch of it, two hundred and eighteen sections, with blood, sweat and tears. The graveyard out back testified to the tears, two women and four kids. I saw the headstones. None of the kids lived past the age of three. He had two more kids living, one helping him on the place, the other gone, no one knew where. He also had a wife and from the looks of her, she was at least thirty years younger than him but that didn't say much either. Like I said, he looked to be ninety. That is until you saw his eyes. They reminded me of pure, case-hardened, blue steel and quick.

We had automatically started the off-loading of the rigs. Bob had gone to talk to Dougal. The unloading went just like clockwork, everyone knowing just where to be and what to do. In an hour and a half we were ready to cut wheat.

Bob and Dougal came out to the field, Frank and George had already checked it though. Both had come back shaking their heads.

"What do you think Frank?" Bob boomed out.

Dougal just looked at Bob then shook his head.

"Green still, three days at least--- maybe a week. Too damn green," Frank growled.

"That's what Dougal said, a week," Bob said.

I looked at Gus and grinned. He grinned back. Maybe, just maybe.

"No," Frank said, "Three, four days will get it. It'll still be heavy but it'll pass."

"You sure?" Bob boomed out.

"Hell, no, I'm not sure!" Frank snapped. "It could come a cold front or rain or anything. Three, four days of sun and hot wind, yeah maybe. But I'm not sure."

Bob looked at Dougal and said, "What's the rest of the crop around here like?"

"No you don't Teemer!" Dougal said. "No you don't. You're contracted to cut my wheat and it's my wheat you will cut when it comes to ready. You'll not go running off over half the county looking for work and get tied up, causing me to lose half a crop. " His voice was deep and resonate. It reminded me of a preacher I had heard back home.

"Well, we can't just sit here on our asses whilst your crop comes to ready. I got hands to pay," Bob yelled louder than normal.

"Don't you raise your voice to me, Teemer!" Dougal snapped back. "I got two thousand acres on level ground here. I can get me another wheat tramp you know."

"Oh you can, can ye?" Bob really yelled, "Can ye this year? Or will you let some mangy independent in here? You got two thousand acres alright. I can cut it in fifteen days. Some independent will take at least three weeks, maybe more, allowing for breakdowns and you'll loose at least a third of your crop anyway." Bob's face grew vivid and his neck muscles bulged with anger.

"I'll tell you what," Bob said, calmer now. "You feed my crew, pay them ten dollars a day. Not me, them, and I'll wait till hell freezes over. Without that, I'll find another field to cut. You hear?" Anything within a half-mile heard.

Dougal said. "Now, let me get this straight. You guarantee me a fifteen day cut when you start?" The old mans hard, blue eyes were twinkling now. His cheek twitched in what passed for a grin.

Bob stared him into the ground. "Yes," he said. "I guarantee a fifteen day cut, once we get started."

"Done!" Dougal yelled. "This your whole crew, four of them?"

"Yes." Bob said, but some of the conviction had gone out of his voice.

"You cut my wheat in fifteen days and I'll pay the waiting time. You don't, you pay the same wages." Dougal almost cackled.

I heard Frank hiss, just before Bob boomed out, "Done! Fifteen days from the start, right?"

"From the start." The old man grinned. "Now, Teemer, how much faith you got in this crew?"

Bob just nodded, "all the faith in the world!"

"Then you won't mind if we double the bet?" Dougal asked slyly.

Bob never blinked. "I don't mind."

"Done!" Dougal yelled almost as loud as Bob. And he almost smiled.

I looked at Frank. He was about to pop but holding it in. Rapidly I thought, we worked our butts off back in Stratford to cut a thousand acres in ten days. Now we got two thousand to cut in fifteen. Wow, it's going to be close.

Dougal walked away chuckling to himself.

"Bob!" Frank yelled. "You're a double-dammed, ring-tailed fool to let that old man do that to you. You know good and well we can't cut this field in fifteen days."

Bob just shrugged and said, "we'll give her hell though, won't we?"

"Yep," Frank answered, shaking his head and grinning. "That we will." He looked at the rest of us. "What do you say boys?"

"We'll give her hell!" I said. The others nodded and we loaded in the pickup and headed for Cheyenne Wells.

Bob had the same deal worked out here, tent space and bathroom, for buying fuel and meals. Gus and I were real excited about maybe going to his home I told him I'd ask Frank later.

The filling station was shabby around the edges, like the old man in grimy coveralls that met us. The paint was scabby and peeling. The gas pumps and driveway were greasy, covered with dust and three wrecked cars sat rusting out back. The bathroom smelled of antiseptic soap that didn't quite cover the smell of stale urine. The café was small but clean. A gray-haired, heavy woman, that brightened the world with four gold teeth when she smiled, was behind the counter. A dark-haired, cross-eyed, girl about seventeen waited on us when we piled into one booth. She was pretty in a homely sort of a way, other than the eyes.

After we ate, we sat up the tent and cots then just sat around looking at each other. Frank was hitting the jug, still mad about the bet, so I didn't know. He took another drink then offered me the bottle. I took a good slug, thinking I'd need the Dutch courage. It went down smooth. I only had to cough twice. And figuring there was no time like the present, I said, "say Dad, can I have the car tonight?"

Frank looked at me almost startled, then boomed out laughing. "Well Son," he said. "I don't know, just where was you planning on going?"

Gus and I both laughed, then I said, "oh, we figured it's going to be at least three days before the wheat's ready and we're going to be working twenty-four hours a day when it is. We figured we might run over to Gus's hometown for a day or so, if you don't mind."

Franks brow furrowed and he said, "well I don't know about that. Just how far is Gus's hometown from here?"

"About a hundred miles, that's all," Gus said.

"When was you planning on leaving?" Frank said.

"Right now," I said, hoping against hope. It was about 1:30 now.

"When are you planning on coming back?"

"We'll call you in two days and every day after that just to make sure," I said. "Call you at the café at six o'clock every evening or we'll come back for sure the night of the third day. Come on, Frank."

A truck roared by on the highway. A woman coming from the café laughed. Frank took a drink then grinned. "I got to talk to Bob about Gus. He's working for him."

"Okay," I said, real excited, and pleading at the same time. "But talk to him now, okay?"

"Okay," Frank said. "Keep your damn shirt tail in. I'll go talk to him now." He got up to leave, taking another drink first.

The tension was unbearable until he got back. He took another drink, then looked at Gus. "You ain't going to run out on us are you Boy? Get home and see your momma then go play doctor with your girlfriend and want to stay home, are you?"

"Oh no Sir," Gus said. "I'll come back when you say. I sure will."

Frank just looked at him long and hard. "We're depending on you Gus, you hear? I won't have time to hire and maybe train a new hand. This is going to be bad enough with what we have."

"Hell Frank," Gus said evenly. "I can leave any time I please. Right now included, so when I say I'll be back, I mean it."

Frank studied on that a second. "I guess you're right. You can leave, like you said, anytime. It'd cost you an ass-kicking, but you're right, you can go whenever."

He reached in his pocket and handed me the keys to his pickup. "Fill her up out of the big tank and call me the day after tomorrow evening at six o'clock sharp. Get the number from the café before you leave and be careful. Have yourselves a good time but, dammit, be careful."

Gus and I just looked at each other, not really believing we were going to get to go. Suddenly, both of us were in motion, grabbing our suitcases and running to throw them in the back of the pickup. We were followed by Frank's and George's laughter as we piled in the pickup. I pulled it next to Bob's to fill it from the big fuel tank he carried for filling the rigs.

"You check the oil, and I'll fuel it up." I said hurriedly. "Then when you get through, go get the phone number and by then I should be through." Excitement made my voice shaky.

Fifteen minutes later we were clear of Cheyenne Wells and on the road, headed west at a howling eighty-five miles an hour, fighting the wind that now hit us broadside.

Gus was saying, "I figure we'll stop at my house and clean up a bit, then I'll call Janet and tell her we're coming and to have you a date fixed up. All right?" His voice shook with excitement.

"Sounds real good to me," I said thinking about Gayle. I hadn't dated anyone else since I had been going out with her but she was a long way away, and this was here and now. I'll write to her when we get back, I thought to myself. I sure will, I'll write to her.

We'd come about twenty-five miles and were just pulling into Kit Carson when I figured out what it was. I had been thinking it was a low cloud on the horizon for a while but now I knew from pictures in my history book. It was Pike's Peak, rising up out of the prairie, broad shouldered and snow-capped, getting bigger and prettier ever minute. By God, I'd seen a mountain now and I knew in reason I'd see more of it before we were through. I thought back and the old lonely feeling tingled through my body as the mountain called to me.

Just about then Gus said, "there's your mountain Dave, right there in front of us. Pretty ain't it?"

"Yeah, it sure is, Pike's Peak ain't it?"

"Yeah, that's it alright. Still over a hundred miles away."

"You're crazy. That mountain ain't even close to a hundred miles from here."

"Sure is, or close to it," he said indignantly.

I didn't say anything, thinking, let him rave on, we'd be on top of the thing in another twenty-five or thirty miles. Just to make sure, I checked the speedometer. About sixty miles further on we passed through Limon but the mountain wasn't a bit closer or at least it didn't seem to be. About another twenty miles farther we pulled into Cloud Chief, another dusty little prairie town. I could see the whole mountain from here, some closer, but not much, still another forty or fifty miles away. And I remembered

202

now about reading of the early explorers that could see this same mountain for days, sometimes weeks before they ever got to it.

"Stop here," Gus said, pointing to a gas station, café. The place had been there awhile, that was evident, but it was well kept now. The paint was clean if not fresh, the driveway clear and swept. Neat racks of oil cans and tires lined the sides and the surrounding grass was a well-watered, neatly-clipped green.

I stopped. We walked in the café.

The café was clean and well arranged with checkered tablecloths on the wooden tables in the center of the room and in the booths that lined one wall. It was just after three-thirty and a few people were entering. The supper rush would be coming soon. A warm, homey, dinner-time, assortment of smells came from the kitchen and I heard someone holler, "Gus! Hey, Gus is home!"

A tall, lanky woman in a white uniform dress and a splattered apron came out of the kitchen. She left no question about who Gus looked like as she ran around the counter, grabbed him, hugging and kissing him.

"Mom, quit it," he said blushing. "Quit. I ain't been gone that long."

I thought it was real nice, but it would have embarrassed me too, especially in front of one of my friends.

About then a man, dressed in stained, but clean coveralls, and a shorter version of Gus came in the café. The boy ran to Gus and wrapped himself around his leg. The man, short, thick-bodied, with a beet-red face, and thinning sandy hair, came over saying, "glad to see you Son. It's good that you're home."

Gus pushed his mother away, shook hands with the man and as he picked up his brother, turned to me saying, "hey, I want you to meet a friend of mine, Dave White, from Oklahoma."

The man walked over to me, extended his hand and said, "glad to meet you Dave. Glad you're here." His grip was firm, his hand callused and hard, and he said it like he meant it. The woman walked to me and extended her hand. I had never shaken hands with a woman in my life, but I did then.

"We are real glad to have you Dave," she said, turning to Gus. "You're home for good now, aren't you?" she said to him.

"No Mom, just a couple of days then we have to go back."

"Go back! Gus, I wish you wouldn't go back." Her voice almost broke at the end.

Gus said firmly. "I got to Mom. I gave my word."

"That's good enough for me!" his father said. "You gave your word, you're going back alright. I won't have a son of mine breaking his word."

Now I liked that man. He reminded me some of Dad.

"By the way Dave, this little twerp here is Mark," Gus said bouncing his brother.

"Hi Mark," I said shaking his hand, then hearing a squeal behind me, I moved quickly away from them. It was a good thing I did because a middle-sized, female version of Gus, also dressed in a white uniform dress, launched herself from across the room at him, almost knocking him down when she grabbed him around the neck.

That would be Terry, his sister, I thought, wishing suddenly I hadn't come. There was something here I hadn't seen in a while. A real family. Love.

"Dammit Terry, get off of me," Gus was hollering. Between her and Mark, they almost had him down, each one trying to get closer to him than the other. Finally he got Mark set down, peeled Terry off and held her away for a second, but she twisted out of his hands and hugged him again. "Dave," he said, "This crazy girl is my sister, Terry. Terry, this is Dave White, from Oklahoma."

She turned to me saying, "hi Dave, Glad to meet you." But she was only interested in her brother.

I felt completely out of place, like I had intruded on something personal, so I moved off to one side and sat at the counter. A big truck rumbled past on the highway outside. A slow, lonely song, '*Only You,*' by the Platters came on the jukebox. The waitress came over. I ordered a cup of coffee and watched the reunion, trying not to cry.

They had Gus completely surrounded now, all five of them asking questions at the same time. Every now and then Mark would reach out to touch him or Terry would put her head on his shoulder or hug him. I sat at the counter, alone, lost in my own thoughts of home.

After about an hour or so, the place began to fill up and Gus remembered what we'd really come for. He made a phone call and I could hear him talking about me, telling Janet to bring a friend.

CHAPTER 16

We left the pickup at Gus's, taking his old Chevy and picked the girls up at Janet's house, twenty or so miles away. Janet was a bouncy, cheerleader type, short with big tits, cute as a bug but no brains, the exact opposite of my date.

Her name was Mary Ann and she was lovely. She was wearing boy's blue jeans and a western style, boys shirt, the kind with snaps instead of buttons. But no boy ever filled them out like she did. Gus had already told me she was seventeen. I could see the rest. She was about five-feet four, slender and willowy, but with enough bulges in the right places to grace the pages of *Playboy Magazine*. She had dark hair and dark eyes so deep a man could drown in them. Her voice had a musical huskiness that could only be described as sexy but she used good English, like Frank when he was drinking heavily or had something important to say. I would have considered it a put-down from anyone else but, like Frank, she did it so comfortably that it seemed natural. She also had that funny, clipped way of talking even worse than Gus. He'd picked up some drawl from the wheat crews. Her accent was pure and I loved it.

We said our, "howdee do's" to Janet's mother. Her dad was a truck driver, gone on the road somewhere up in Oregon. I wished he'd been there. I would have liked to talk to him. Janet's mother was tall, with dark hair and for some reason she reminded me of Mary Ann but it was only a vague resemblance. She acted just like Janet, bouncy and bubbly. The house was a rambling wood frame, shabbily comfortable but open and warm. I felt completely at ease there, almost as if I belonged, but we said our good bye's as soon as we could and left.

Gus and Janet got in the front seat. Mary Ann and I got in the back. I was at a loss, wondering what to do, how to act. I'd never dated a girl I didn't know, or know of, before. Being raised in a small town has that advantage, which now was a disadvantage. But when I started passing beer out, Mary Ann said she'd have one and I felt a lot better. I did notice my hands shook when I opened them though.

We drove around for an hour or so, just drinking beer, talking and singing along with the radio. Gus and Janet were practically making out while he was driving but Mary Ann and I stayed pretty much on our separate sides of the car. Oh, she was friendly enough and we talked some but mostly she was cool and aloof. I think she was scared. I know I was. But we were driving through some rough county, not mountains by any means but ragged and rugged enough to be pretty. Every now and then we would come to a place high enough to give me a view. And there they were, the whole eastern face of the Rocky Mountains, stretching out north and south for miles, still far away, but looking close enough to reach out and touch. I was mesmerized by them and unable to look at anything else. They were beautiful in their aloofness, snow-capped and ruggedly remote, friendly and unforgiving at the same time. I guess I paid more attention to the mountains than I did Mary Ann but she really didn't seem to mind.

She only really looked at me once the whole afternoon I think. That was when the road came out of a stand of pine trees and I could see the sun setting behind the mountains. The mountains were black dark on our side and stood out in a stark, saw-toothed, bias-relief against the blaze orange of the sunset. There were just enough clouds above to be set on fire and glow with orange, corals, salmons, and violets to make me hiss as my breath was taken away.

"Are you alright?" Mary Ann asked.

I could only nod and point to the dying sweep of beauty. "I've never seen anything so beautiful," I finally said, and felt like a fool because my voice croaked with emotion.

I glanced at Mary Ann to see if she had noticed. She was watching me, a funny little sad smile, completely different from the seemingly forced one she had worn before, was touching her mouth and her deep, lonely eyes. I tried to say something else, something funny, maybe smart, but my eyes moved involuntarily back to the rapidly fading splash of changing light and color and I was gripped with the beauty, unable to tear myself away. I felt stupid, making so much out of a sunset, and I could feel myself blushing because of it. But I couldn't stop looking until we passed through some more trees and it was gone.

When I looked back at Mary Ann, she said, "it was a beautiful sunset."

I could only nod, hoping the dark hid my firey face.

After a while I mentioned we were getting low on beer, so Gus stopped. He grinned at me when we walked in the little roadside store and said, "I'm going to find us a place to stop pretty soon. What do you think?"

I said, "sure, that'd be fine."

"How are you doing in the back seat?"

"Not great, but we're getting acquainted. It's okay."

"It's rough, I know. I've been there. Maybe it will be better after we stop."

"Who knows?" But I was thinking my chances were better at getting struck by lighting from the black, star-covered sky.

The fat man behind the counter grinned around an evil looking cigar when Gus set the case of beer on the counter neat the cash register. "That'll be eight dollars, boys," he said, getting out of his chair with an effort. "Or do you want me to check your ID's?"

We both laughed nervously and put up a five each. It was about two dollars too much and about the same deal LeRoy gave back home.

The fat man blew out a cloud of smoke and grudgingly laid the change on the worn counter but then I grabbed a couple bags of chips and he grinned again, keeping both of the dollars. We smiled and left quickly.

Janet giggled as we walked to the car and when we got in. I noticed Mary Ann had scooted over closer to my side of the car. I also noticed she was glaring at Janet, who was still giggling in her hand. I smiled at Mary

Ann as Gus drove off. Mary Ann smiled back but it seemed forced again. I couldn't help thinking, she wants to be with me almost as much as I want to be set on fire.

And I felt miserable.

We sat inches, but miles apart, silent while Gus drove and he and Janet went back to what they had been doing. There was a heavy, half-moon out now and I tried to watch the countryside that was becoming increasingly rugged. But now, I couldn't keep my eyes off Mary Ann. After twenty or so long minutes, Gus turned off the highway, going back into some really rough country. Then after about ten miles, he stopped and killed the engine, but left the radio playing a fast, guitar twanging song by the Ventures called, *Walk, Don't Run*. He turned sideways in the seat and grinned at me. Janet giggled, scooted even closer, and wrapped herself around him. Then both of them slid beneath the back of the seat.

A few minutes later I looked at Mary Ann. She had her arms folded tightly across her breast and a look in her eye of abject fear that reminded me of a rabbit I'd caught once in a trap. I tried to smile but I couldn't, knowing what she was thinking, so I whispered, "look, don't worry about it."

She let out the breath she had been holding, nodded slightly and tried to smile, but the look in her eye didn't go away. I touched her hand, still whispering. "I'm almost as scared as you are, so please don't worry. I'm not going to try anything."

She squeezed my hand and relaxed some, smiling all the way now. "Thank you Dave," she whispered. "I was afraid."

"I know, and it makes me feel miserable." I turned in the seat, facing her. "I know you don't want to be here, but I'm glad you are. I'm glad both of us are."

She squeezed my hand again smiling. "Thank you," she whispered and the fear finally left her eyes. "And you're right. I was afraid, and I didn't want to be here."

I cut my eyes to the front seat. Some strange noises were beginning to come from up there and it was getting embarrassing. I looked back at Mary Ann and said, "let's, uh, do something. Maybe take a walk or something."

She dropped her eyes and nodded jerkily, and even in the dark. I could tell she was blushing. I got a six-pack and an opener as we got out and walked away, the gravel of the road crunching beneath our feet. I don't even think Gus and Janet noticed we'd gone. After a while I said, "I'm sorry, I just had to get out of that car."

She said, "I'd rather not talk about it if you don't mind."

"I don't mind. I just didn't know that was going to happen."

"I didn't either--- or I wouldn't be here." Her voice was hard.

I took her by the hand, stopping and turning her to face me. The moonlight played tricks with her face, enhancing her high cheek bones and full lower lip, forming shadows under her deep, dark eyes, making my heart pound. "I know that." I said. "So, even out here you don't have to worry about me trying anything."

She smiled but her eyes were worried. Then she blinked and looked away. "I was worried. I mean---after--well, I came with Janet and she---I thought you might think that I--"

"No," I said low. "I don't think that."

She smiled again. "Thank you. I appreciate that." A vagrant breeze teased a lock of her hair down over one eye and for a second my heart stopped. She brushed it away in an unconscious gesture and smiled again, really smiled.

I started walking again. The moonlight was bright enough to see the road without really looking. A cool, clean-smelling breeze was rustling the pine trees. And Mary Ann's hand was warm. For the first time since we'd arrived this afternoon, I was glad I had come.

We came to an outcropping of rock that made a good seat and a back rest and sat down. I opened two beers. She smiled again when I handed her one. "I was really sorry I drank that beer in the car," she said. "I sure needed it at the time, but when they started---. I said I wasn't going to talk about that, but I was sure you thought--- And then Janet laughed at me for sitting on my side of the car---"

I laughed. "That was the give-away. When I came back you were looking at Janet like you wanted to kill her."

She laughed. "I'm just so relieved I'm babbling. And you're right again.

I could have killed her. Do you know what she called me? A damn door hugger! And laughed at me!"

I had to laugh at that one. It was the same term we used back home.

"And now you're laughing at me," she said. "I've never been on a blind date in my life. I didn't know what to expect or what to do--"

I was laughing so hard now I couldn't talk.

She said, "And I was scared to death. And then, they started-- that. And you don't have to laugh quite so hard," but she was smiling all the way now.

When I got my breath, I told her why I was laughing so hard and we both laughed. After that, it got down to the normal first-date talk, mostly about school and movies and songs we liked. Then, after an hour or so, she looked at me and said, "what is it like being away from home, being on your own Dave?"

I started to give her a big spill about adventure and daring and excitement but it all soured in my mouth. And even though I heard my own voice, I couldn't believe I said, "it's scary, and it's terribly lonely. I thought I would get to see some of the country, but it all looks the same. The work isn't hard but it's boring and nasty. I miss my folks." My mind flashed to Gayle and a feeling of guilt washed over me.

Her expression changed to one of deep thought. "But there is something else," she touched my arm. "Something that's driving you, keeping you from going home because that would be simple. I mean, you could leave, go back, at any time. What else is there?"

I was silent a while, thinking about the calling geese, the wind talking to me, the singing of the truck tires. "I don't know," I said. "Maybe I feel like I'm growing out here, learning things." I shrugged. "I can't explain it. It's not the money. Oh, the pay is good enough but I could've had a job real close to home."

I looked deep into her eyes, seeing the moon reflected in them and I heard myself say, "I want to see where the wind goes."

My voice sounded hollow, and strange, even to me, and it seemed to come from deep within me, someplace I hadn't known existed. I turned away then and blushed at the corny sounding words.

But I felt her nod and I felt her squeeze my arm. I turned back and she was looking at me, silently looking inside me, as if she hadn't really seen me before.

Then she said low, "I understand. Sometimes I wish I was a boy, then I could do what you're doing. Sometimes I feel if I don't get away from home soon, I'll die. I don't care where I go, just away."

I took both her hands, holding them, squeezing them gently. "I'm glad you're not a boy."

She looked away, then back into my eyes. "You know what I meant," she whispered in that fantastic voice.

"Yes, I know."

She turned slightly and leaned back on my shoulder. Then she looked up at me again. "That rock hurts my back," her voice was low, husky.

I knew why she'd said it, but I didn't care that she felt she needed an excuse. I slipped my arm around her and held her hand, feeling more lost and alone than ever before. And we sat like that a long time, not talking, just looking at the stars, feeling the wind on our faces.

I felt her move slightly and came back from somewhere in my mind. I looked down at her. Her eyes fluttered, then opened and she said, "ummm---I think I've been aslee…."

Just then I kissed her, lightly, very softly.

There was no real acceptance but at the same time, she didn't push me away. I broke the kiss and looked into those wells she had for eyes. And suddenly I was scared again, not knowing what to do. I didn't want to come on like a sex maniac but at the same time I didn't want to seem like a know-nothing hick.

So I kissed her again, very softly, very gently, just barely more than a brushing of my lips against hers. And Gus honked the horn. She pulled away suddenly, almost embarrassed, as if we had been caught doing something really bad.

I said, "I guess they're ready to go," my voice was husky and sounded strange again.

She moved to her side of the rock and started to stand but then she relaxed. "Yes, really, it's getting late."

I sat there a minute. "I hate to leave."

She didn't say anything.

I glanced at her and hoping against hope said, "are you doing anything tomorrow?"

She looked away, then back. "No, not really. Why? What do you have in mind?"

I shrugged my shoulders. "I don't know. I'd like to see some of the country around here. I probably won't get another chance."

"You don't think you're ever coming back here?"

I shrugged again, "I don't know. I can't promise anything. I know I'd like to." I looked away. "But I can't really say."

"We'll talk about it later, okay?" She said as she smiled and hugged her knees. "Right now, we had better go."

I brushed off my pants, and helped her up, pulling her slightly to me. She came forward, putting her arms around me. I kissed her lightly again, just a peck on the lips. As we started crunching back to the car the horn honked again. We were almost there when I stopped her.

"Look," I said. "I'm scared to death I'm going to do something wrong with you. I like you a whole lot so I don't want to make you mad. I want to see you as much as I can while I'm here so if I'm doing something wrong, just tell me, okay? Then maybe we can work it out." The moonlight played with her face again and I felt myself trembling.

She smiled and took my hands. "I feel the same way Dave but I'm a little mixed up at the same time. So let's just play it cool, if that's alright."

It wasn't alright, but I said it was. I had never met anyone quite like her before and I was feeling things I'd never felt before. It was like I was crazy inside, like she'd said, *'All mixed up.'* All I could think about was holding her.

And Gayle was getting farther and farther away all the time.

We walked to the car after that and as we stepped through the ring of beer cans, I saw the gold dollar glinting in the moonlight. At least that's what we called the foil off of a condum back home. It didn't surprise me any, after what had been going on before we left, but I did step on it so Mary Ann wouldn't see.

I opened the back door for Mary Ann, but just then Gus got out saying, "me and Dave are going to walk down the road a little way. Why don't you girls honk when you're ready for us to come back."

Janet giggled but Mary Ann didn't get in. I was a little surprised. I'd been needing to piss for a while but I had never thought about her needing too. Gayle went down the road all the time and I never thought anything about it. But for Mary Ann? It just didn't seem ladylike.

I guess we'd walked about twenty yards before we stopped, then Gus grinned and asked, "how did you make out?"

"Not nearly as good as you. I saw your gold dollar back there."

"Just one?" he laughed.

"That's all I saw," I tried to keep the anger and disgust out of my voice. I wasn't one to brag about who I was having sex with or how many times.

He laughed again. "There's another one there somewhere. And I did make use of them. Thanks for going down the road."

I thought, I didn't have a helluve lot of choice but I said, "no problem." Then a thought came to me. "Say, do you know much about Mary Ann?"

He shook his head. "Not too much. She goes to school over at Castle Rock. Why do you ask?"

"I was just wondering. I asked her for a date tomorrow. She said we'd talk about it later."

"What did you have in mind tomorrow?"

"Nothing really. I'd like to come back up here and drive around a little. I'd like to see this country in the daylight."

"Like it up here huh? Well that's no problem. I had a repeat performance of tonight planned." He slapped me on the shoulder. "And you might just better pick you up some rubbers too. Who knows, you might have a chance to use them."

I felt the hair on the back of my neck stand up as the surge of rage came over me. I moved away from him, clenching my fist, mentally measuring the distance to his jaw, but the horn sounded just then and he turned, looking down the road.

"I guess they're ready for us to come back," he said and started toward the car but stopped a few feet away, looking back at me. "You ready?"

I stood a second longer, feeling the anger pass from me thinking, he didn't mean it bad toward her. He just wants me to have a good time. And I walked to the car beside him.

Mary Ann was on her side of the car when I got in and a tremor of fear ran up my spine as I thought that somehow I had screwed it all up and she was mad and I would never see her again. But when I reached for a beer, she handed me a ready one and slid over, touching me with her shoulder. I slipped my arm around her, feeling like I'd died and gone to heaven.

The trip back took at least a half-hour but it seemed like that many seconds. And I wasn't ready for it to be over when Gus pulled into Janet's driveway. Mary Ann held my hand as we walked to the house. Just before we entered the circle of the porch light, she turned to me. "I never thought I would say this tonight, but I had a wonderful time." She smiled at me. "And I'm glad you asked me to go tomorrow, instead of taking for granted that I would."

I slipped my hands around her waist, looking deep into those eyes. I started to speak but my throat closed up and it came out as a squawk.

She smiled, trying not to laugh.

Finally I got my throat working. "Then you-- you'll go--- tomorrow?" The *'tomorrow,'* ended in a squeak and she looked down and laughed again.

But then she leaned forward and kissed me long and slow and said, "I would love to go with you tomorrow, Dave."

I could hear my heart pounding in my ears, almost drowning out what she'd said, but then she kissed me again lightly and smiled, her eyes glinting in the moonlight. My hands started to shake so I dropped them from her waist, feeling like a fool, thinking, I've never acted like this with a girl before. That caused a wrench in my guts. When I was with Gayle, I was nothing but cool, usually in complete control, but with Mary Ann, I acted like a freshman. That caused me to blush and made the roaring in my ears even worse. Gus and Janet walked up just then, keeping me from making a complete idiot of myself. Mary Ann looked at me with concern in her eyes. I put my hands back on her hips and kissed her lightly saying,

"I'm real glad you're going tomorrow. And I had a really good time tonight too!"

Thank God! It all came out right.

She smiled at me but there was still just a touch of concern, maybe worry, in her face. Then she turned, her hand running down my arm to my hand. She squeezed my hand, ever so slightly, and walked into the light.

I felt my guts wrench again, watching her go. A sad, empty feeling came over me, making me feel alone, lost maybe. I took a step to follow her but stopped, feeling foolish again. She turned, looking at me a second and she smiled that funny, sad little smile that burned itself into my brain. Then she was gone.

Gus touched me on the shoulder and we walked to the car. We had almost a half case of beer left so we drank a couple on the way back to Cloud Chief. Gus drove slow, not talking. A slow song was playing on the radio. I didn't have much to say either.

After a little while, Gus said, "Dave, I'm sorry about that in the café this afternoon."

"What's that?" I had to ask, my mind had been on Mary Ann.

"I said, I was sorry about this afternoon, in the café."

I knew what he meant. "Don't be. They were just glad to see you is all."

"You kinda got left out."

"They got no reason to be glad to see me."

"Yeah, but---"

"But nothing," I said. "Hell, Man, you got a great family. You just got home and they didn't want to talk to me. It would be the same at my home, so don't worry about it, okay?"

"Sure, okay," he grinned. "They are quite a bunch."

"They're nice people, good people. They were just glad to see you. It made me kind of homesick."

"I know how you feel. It's going to be tough to go back."

"Gus," I said, and my voice turned hoarse again, "I got a feeling it's going to be tough for me to go back."

He glanced at me, "Mary Ann?"

"Yeah."

He chuckled, "I talked to Janet. I think you're in pretty good."

"Oh, yeah!" I almost yelled.

"Yeah, she said Mary Ann really likes you."

I felt myself smile in the darkness, savoring the words over the pounding in my ears. I looked at the moon, remembering what it had looked like reflecting in her eyes and my guts knotted so bad I couldn't breath.

"Did you hear me?" Gus said.

"I heard you. I was just thinking about her."

He laughed, throwing his beer can out the window. "Man, you got it bad." He laughed again as he pulled into his driveway. The house was dark and suddenly I was bashful.

"Look, Gus. I'll just sleep out here in the pickup."

"No you won't! Mom would skin both of us if you did. I have a big old bed in there, plenty of room."

"You sure your folks won't mind?"

"They'd mind it a whole lot more if you slept out here." His tone was final.

"Well, if you're sure."

"I'm sure."

We picked our way through the dark house. The walls and flat ceiling seemed strange after being in the tent so long, almost closed in like. Gus turned the light on in his room when we got to it. As we undressed, I said, "say, I have to buy some clothes tomorrow. I ruined all of mine back there in Stratford."

"Sure, we have a store here in Cloud Chief. They'll fix you right up."

"Okay." I got in bed, tired but trembling with anticipation of the coming day. Today had sure been a day. It had at that.

The bed felt strange after sleeping on the cot for so long. The walls so close were strange too. I don't sleep real good in a strange bed and tonight was no exception. I kept waking, dreaming I was falling off of Pike's Peak, jerking and waking up. Finally I grabbed one of the bed posts for something to hold on to. Then sleep came and a dream of Gayle.

She was out in a wheat field, with nothing around her for miles and miles, just standing there, alone.

CHAPTER 17

───

The Henderson family got up way before the crack of dawn. Mark jumped in the bed as soon as he came to life, scaring hell out of both of us. And then nothing else would do him except his brother getting out of bed for breakfast. So, feeling uneasy, I did too.

Walking through the rambling old house to the kitchen, I noticed it was four-thirty. We'd only been in bed about three hours but my stomach growled when I smelled the coffee brewing and the bacon frying. I could hear the buzz of conversation but couldn't make out the words, then Gus's father laughed loudly. Now I wished for sure I hadn't come because as we walked in the kitchen, I was alone again, an outsider, and this was a home.

Gus's dad smiled at us, his wrinkled, brick-red, face lighting up even more. He was dressed in green coveralls like he had been yesterday. They were clean but stained and faded almost white. He nodded to me and said, "you boys was out pretty late last night. You must have found you something."

Gus laughed. "Yeah, we did alright."

"How is Janet?" His mother said, as she loaded the table. She and Terry were wearing white waitresses uniforms.

"She's fine," Gus laughed. "Mary Ann Tremont went with us."

"Oh, she did?" His mother's tone carried a question and surprise at the same time.

"Did you have a good time?" Terry asked in a hateful, spite-filled voice.

Gus laughed out loud. "Yes, Terry, I had a good time."

Mark stuck out his lower lip. "I just don't see why you had to go running off with an old girl! You could have stayed and played with me."

Everyone laughed then and we all sat down to breakfast, hot on the table, fried eggs, bacon, oatmeal, biscuits drenched with butter, cream gravy, a huge pitcher of milk and coffee black and steaming. Everyone was laughing and talking at the same time, all but me.

I was home too, in my mind. Home, ten years ago, before they all left, my brother and sisters. They'd drifted away, one at a time, until there was only me. Poor Mark, I thought. He'd be the only one to know how I felt. He would know because he was the last one too. I sure felt sorry for him.

My mind slipped to the dream I had had of Gayle. I didn't need anyone to tell me what it had meant and a guilty feeling washed over me. Gayle was the only girl I had every really gone out with. Oh, I'd met others at the picture show, before I got my drivers license. But I had never sat and looked at the stars or watched the moon rise over the woods with them. I'd never held them half-naked and talked of the future. I'd never told them I loved them like I had with Gayle.

But even at that, there was something missing with her, something important. She didn't seem to understand me when I tried to talk about my feelings. She didn't seem to care. But Mary Ann did. In the space of less than eight hours, Mary Ann understood more about me than Gayle did after eight months. And I couldn't get past that. I couldn't get her out of my mind.

I came back to reality noticing I hadn't been missed and listened to the conversation, not really paying attention to what was being said. Most of it was family stuff, what Aunt Ida and Uncle Fred had done and how Cousin Hilda was, bringing Gus up to date on the family. I wasn't included and it was as if I wasn't even there. It was a cold, shut-out feeling, even worse than it had been at the café. So I went back in my mind.

Thinking of the café reminded me of Sara and I smiled as I thought of Sara. Sara was like the moon and stars and the new Corvette, down at the

Chevrolet house, something to dream about. But Gayle was my steady girl and I had been gone two weeks now. And I still hadn't written to her. I felt myself blush with shame and made a promise I'd do that really soon.

After we ate, the rest of Gus's family went to town to open the station and café. Gus and I went back to bed. He started snoring almost as soon as he lay back down, but I couldn't sleep. My mind kept bouncing back and forth between Gayle and Mary Ann. Then thinking, I'll be leaving in a day or two at the most. It won't hurt a thing to see Mary Ann again. And what Gayle don't know sure can't hurt her. Besides it wasn't like Mary Ann and I were going to do anything. The kissing we'd done wasn't much more than I gave my sister. I turned over and went to sleep.

I woke up again around eight and, knowing we had a full day ahead of us, woke Gus up. We laid around the house for about an hour then drove to town to do my shopping. I had almost a hundred dollars on me, more money than I had ever carried in my life. Cloud Chief had only one clothing store but the selection wasn't bad. Almost no one wore western shirts back in Crane but out here, everyone did. So I decided to join them. I bought three shirts with snaps instead of buttons and three pairs of blue jeans, a couple packs of tee shirts and a blue jeans jacket, thinking any one seeing me in my underwear wouldn't mind the off color. If they did, I'd just put my pants back on and go home.

We drove to the laundry next. This time I played it smart and gave the woman working there three dollars to wash and iron the jeans and shirts and do the rest of my laundry.

After that, we drove to the café for a cup of coffee while my clothes were being tended to and Gus made a phone call. The girls were ready, waiting for us, and when would we be there? As soon as my clothes were finished.

It was slack time, around ten o'clock, so the whole family and I sat at one table. They'd finally figured out I could talk and were asking me about Oklahoma. It was just passing time and I knew they really didn't care, but I told them all I knew about the oil wells, and hardwood forest. I talked about the rolling hills, and what we called mountains, the Arbuckles and the Kiamichi ranges. But they laughed and told me that out here on the flat prairie we were almost as high as the highest point in the whole state of Oklahoma and higher than any mountain in either of the ranges I had mentioned. And after they stopped laughing they started talking among themselves again. Deciding enough of this was enough, I said. "I think I'll walk on down to the laundry to check on my clothes."

"I'll drive you," Gus said.

"No, you stay here and visit. We ain't going to be here that much longer and you want to see your family."

"You sure you don't mind?"

I shook my head, "no problem. Y'all have your talk. I'll be back soon," and I walked out.

About halfway to the laundry was a nice little gazebo affair with a place to sit. I really didn't think the clothes were ready yet so I sat in the shade and looked at Gus's hometown.

Cloud Chief was a half-horse town with the one laundry, one bar, a small bank, three filling stations, two cafés, one with a small motel, two churches, a hardware store and one drive-in that advertised the biggest hamburger in Colorado. A few of the larger buildings were vacant. A weather-faded sign said one had been a Pontiac dealership. Another one had sold tractors. I could feel the town was dying in the glaring sunlight and I knew why; there was nothing here to keep the young adults, no work, no hope, and nothing to do when the work they had was finished. The kids that weren't born with money or property left as soon as they could get away, going to Denver, Colorado Springs, or even Castle Rock. Jobs, night life and fun weren't all that far away. I shook my head thinking Cloud Chief, was even worse than Crane, being stranded out here on the baking prairie, the wind constantly howling. But just look up and there it was, a snow-capped mountain calling you to come. That mountain was worse than listening to the trucks on the highway or even the geese that flew by in the night. It just stood there, hollering all the time, constantly reminding a person there was something else out there and not that far away. I could sure see why Gus had to leave.

I walked on down to the laundry. My clothes were ready, all starched, pressed neat and hung on hangers. I thanked the lady and went back to the café.

I put the clothes in Gus's car, and went on in. They were still talking but when Gus saw me he got up. "Well," he said. "I have to go. Me and Dave have a date and we're already late."

The rest of the bunch didn't seem to think too much of that, but they didn't say anything. Terry, his sister, didn't have too. She stared at me with a look in her eyes that would have put Slim to shame. Gus didn't see it and I didn't say anything, but it hurt. It hurt a lot.

We drove away with me wondering about spending another night in Gus's house. They were good people, some of the best, but it was a bad situation and sometimes, even good people do wrong things for all the right reasons. And I just didn't feel welcome. And Dad always said, *"I don't go where I don't feel welcome, not more than once anyway."*

About then Gus shifted gears. "I'm glad you left. I'm sorry about that back there, sorry you felt like you had to leave, but I'm glad you did."

"Hell, Man, it's alright--"

"No, it wasn't," he snapped. "We came as close to having a family fight as we ever have. They--- well, Mom and Terry and Mark, don't want me to go back to Cheyenne Wells."

I stiffened, "You gave you word to Frank."

He shifted gears again as we left the town and he began to pick up speed. "And that's the only reason I'm going back." A passing truck almost drowned out his last words.

"I'm glad to hear you say that. What was the problem anyway?"

His eyes flashed. "Look around!" he said hard waving his arm at the dry prairie. "That's the problem," then he softened. "We try to farm and run some cattle too. Between that and the station and the café, there's just not enough people to go around, without me. And they can't afford to hire help. I want out of here so bad I could die, but--" His voice died in a silent scream.

I looked him over close, knowing he was being torn apart. "You are going back?" My words came out more like a demand than a question.

He nodded, "I gave my word I would and Dad stuck with me." His voice dropped to almost a whimper. "But I'm not going on after Cheyenne Wells."

"I'm glad you're going back." Then I smiled. His Dad reminded me a lot of my own in a lot of ways and suddenly I missed Dad and the talks we had when we were alone at the house. He had a quiet strength about him that I had never realized how much I depended on. And I knew that if I gave my word, he would back me to the gates of hell.

That's when it hit me. I had given my word to Gayle. She had my class ring and all and we'd promised not to date or even flirt with other people. I felt like crawling under a wet rock. "Man," I said, "I can't go through with this---"

"With what?" Gus turned down the screaming radio.

"With this, I can't do this today. I got Gayle back home waiting for me."

"That's the secret. She's back home! You're here. If you don't tell her, how's she ever going to know?" He laughed. "I don't see a problem."

"It don't matter that she won't know. I'll know. I gave my word to her."

He laughed again, "That's different."

"What's different? My word is about all I got."

He scoffed. "It's just different. That's all. It's not like you're married or anything. Besides, you gave your word to Mary Ann last night. Now which one are you going to break? Gayle is back home. Mary Ann is here. Dave it ain't going to hurt a damn thing. All we're going to do is drive around some and then have a picnic. What's that going to hurt? All we're going to do is have fun."

"It don't matter, Gus. I said I wouldn't date anyone else, and I can't."

"You already have. What about last night? I seen you kiss her. Man, it ain't going to hurt a thing. What Gayle don't know will never hurt her. And if you don't tell her, how is she ever going to know?"

I did feel bad now but at the same time a vision of Mary Ann swam before my eyes and I felt myself weakening fast. I said, "no, I think I'll go on back. Right now."

"Go back!" Gus yelled. "Man, you can't do that! I was planning on having another good time tonight. If you go back, I'll have both of them on my hands and then where will I be? Hell, Dave, you gave your word to me too."

I did feel bad now. And I was caught between the devil and the gate post, wondering what to do. Finally I said, "Okay, I'll go with you, but I'm leaving tomorrow, in the morning for sure." As I said that I thought, I'll go, but just to see the country. I'll be with her, sure, but I won't have fun and that will be alright.

Gus smiled just as we pulled in his driveway. "That's great. That'll be alright. Now, come on in and we'll get cleaned up and leave."

I thought of something else just then, "Gus, I'll go today, like I said, but I don't feel right about staying in your house tonight."

He started to say something but I stopped him. "That's the way it has to be. Either I get me a motel room tonight or I leave right now."

A look of real pain crossed his face. "I wish you didn't feel that way,"

"I'm sorry Man. This is your family and I don't think they mind me being here but I feel like I'm in the way. I feel like they think I'm forcing you to go back."

He nodded sheepishly. "We're a pretty close bunch alright."

"Man," I said. "You have a great family."

He smiled, slapping me on the shoulder. "Let's go get those girls."

I felt like a traitor but I said,. "That's not a bad idea."

It was a different house as I walked inside in the daylight. I looked at the rump-sprung, shabby furniture. Without ever seeing them do it, I knew that Gus's dad sat in the black-vinyl recliner and his mother in the overstuffed easy chair at the other end of a battered, threadbare divan that Terry and Gus sprawled on, leaving Mark to play in the floor. The furniture was sitting in a semi-circle around a fairly new TV. An old record player stood across the room. The pictures on the walls were all of family, kids mostly, in all stages of growing up. A stubby, lever-action rifle, probably a .30.30, a rusty, old pump shotgun and a bolt action .22 hung in a rack over a small bookcase. A large, open Bible lay on a small podium under a picture of Jesus praying. And I knew I had made the right decision. I also knew that it wasn't just me. It would have been anyone who invaded this home.

We both took a shower. I dressed in a set of my new clothes, wishing I had some shoe polish, but I didn't ask. My old boots were in pretty bad shape, scuffed and worn, but they were all I had. I rolled up my dirty clothes in a tight roll, blue jeans to the outside, and put them in my suitcase. With everything I had brought there wasn't room for the quilt so I folded it. I gathered up everything and took it to the pickup in one trip. Gus watched me but didn't comment.

As I was loading, I said, "I think I'll take the pickup on in to town."

He shrugged. "Whatever you want."

I could see this was tearing him apart, and I felt bad about it. "It's not what I want, Gus, it's just the way it has to be."

He looked away then back at me, saying, "yeah, it's been rough on you. I know. I just hope you're not pissed at me."

"This is not your fault. It's not your families fault, man it's just the way things are. They don't want you to go back, and I feel like they're blaming me for you having too. You got a great family Gus. Good people. It's just a bad situation and this is the only solution I know."

He grinned then and slapped my shoulder. "I know Man, and I'm sorry, but let's have a good time today, okay?"

I grinned at him. "Sure we will," I said, not believing a word of it.

Ten minutes later we left the pickup behind the station. Almost as an after-thought I grabbed the old pink quilt, grimacing at the color, and piled in Gus's old Chevy. Three minutes after that we made a refueling, pit stop at a road house and, beer in hand with several more in an ice chest, headed west toward that terrible, screaming mountain.

CHAPTER 18

⁓

The girls were pissed. It had been around ten when Gus had called, now it was almost noon and they'd gone to a lot of trouble packing a big picnic lunch.

Mary Ann was wearing a pair of light blue shorts and a matching sleeveless, pullover top. Her arms and legs were deeply tanned and she looked like a dream come true. I didn't even notice Janet.

A phrase I had read somewhere came to my mind as she smiled and walked to me. *"The road to hell is paved with good intentions."*

She took my hand then, and all of my good intentions went somewhere, far away when she squeezed my arm as I helped her in the car.

"Where to?" Gus hollered as he and Janet piled in the car.

"Who cares?" I hollered back as Mary Ann scooted over to me. "I got all I need, right here."

Gus slammed the old Chevy in gear, pulling away. Mary Ann wiggled, snuggling even closer to me, whispering, "I missed you," in my ear and kissing me on the cheek.

I felt my guts knot and my hands started shaking again. My mind bounced to Gayle, then to Mary Ann, then back to Gayle. Then I looked into her eyes and saw that funny, sad, worried, little smile. Then, suddenly and without any warning, she leaned forward and just pecked me on the lips. Gayle, and all my good intentions, went even farther away.

We drove around for an hour or so through the rugged foothills around Castle Rock, probably the same country we had gone through last night. The difference was, last night I couldn't see. Today I could, and even Mary Ann had to take a back seat.

The country was fantastically rugged, covered with scrub oak, pine and aspen, with huge, outcroppings of rock jutting through, forming high, sheer-sided cliffs, that dropped into some good-sized canyons. Once we rounded a curve and saw a buck deer standing in the road not twenty yards away. He just stood there watching us, like we were watching him. Then Gus honked the horn and he was gone as if he'd never been.

Every now and then we passed a small stream. Once when it ran alongside the road I hollered, "stop."

I got out of the car and walked into the brush, hearing unknown birds twerping and at least three squirrels chattering. On the way back, I surprised a small rabbit and jumped back as it came bounding out of a tuft of grass at my feet.

I stopped at the stream, got down on my belly and took a drink. The water was so cold it made my teeth hurt, so pure it looked invisible, running over the rocky bottom. Then, I stood up and yelled, just for the hell of it, just because it felt good to yell. And the old Rebel yell, taught to me by my grandmother who'd heard it for real, echoed down the canyon and bounced back from the cliffs, reverberating from everywhere as it grew fainter and fainter. This is a man's country I thought, as the echoes washed over me.

"What the hell is wrong?" Gus hollered, concern in his voice.

"I love Colorado!" I yelled back. "I ain't never going home. I'm staying here! Right here!"

"You'll freeze your ass off come winter," he laughed. "Damn Flatlander's come up here in the summer and decide to stay. You ain't seen winter yet. Just wait till it's fifteen below and you're hip-deep in snow. You'll holler then I'll bet."

They'd all left the car when I yelled, wondering what had happened to me. I walked to Mary Ann, picked her up and swung her in a circle.

"Mary Ann will be here to keep me warm in the winter." I laughed, as I swung her. "She'll snuggle close and not let old man winter get me, won't you Darlin.'" I set her back down, kissing her before she could reply, then stood back and yelled again.

She came to me grabbing me around the ribs, hugging me tight. "I'll keep you warm, winter and summer." She laughed as she said it and I laughed with her until I looked at her face and I knew she'd meant what she said.

Gus hollered, "let's go!" just then, but it was fine. I'd seen the flicker of fear in her eyes as I felt a stab of fear in my guts. I think what we were both thinking just then, scared both of us. So we all piled back in the car and Gus drove away, driving slow so I wouldn't miss anything.

They had seen the country a hundred times before but I was making them see it for real. A stranger can bring out the best or the worse in a person and I was bringing out the best in them today. I was too enthralled to be embarrassed today, or maybe it was Mary Ann. I'm not sure. But every time I pointed to a colored cliff or a gnarling mass of roots that had been washed clean by the rain, anything out of the ordinary, she marveled too. And at times she pressed close to me, saying, "I've never see that before."

But I knew she had seen it. She'd just never looked at it before. Not like she was looking now, seeing it all again for the first time through my eyes. She was radiant, bubbling with excitement that, I guess, she absorbed from me. Her eyes were glowing, shining with it. I put my arm around her, pulling her close and was drowned in those eyes, those deep, brown eyes, glinting and shining, liquid eyes, glowing, laughing eyes but at the same time serious, hurting eyes.

I held her close, wanting her even closer. She smelled fresh, clean and pure, a piney smell, like the country. Suddenly all of the shyness, the shaking and the pounding in my ears was gone from me and I felt alive for, I think, the first time I could remember. I pulled her to me and kissed her, not just the brushing of our lips like last night but a real kiss that had meaning and deep feelings. And with Gayle far away but screaming at me in my mind, I said, ever so softly, "I love you."

She looked inside me her eyes questioning, searching, looking for the laughter that wasn't there. Then she smiled her funny, little smile, laid her head on my chest and gently, softly, her voice tinged with pain, said, "I love you too Dave."

It was a magical moment of promise, an achingly tender moment that caused time and distance to freeze, that caused Gus and Janet to disappear. We were alone together, transported somewhere and there was a oneness about us now, a sharing of thought, a blending and melding of us.

Then Gus hollered, "Hey back there, hand me a beer!"

I jumped. Mary Ann jerked away from me and I felt like hitting him as I was jolted back to reality. I felt her move even farther from me as if she were running from something---and I knew what we had had for a second, was ruined.

"Hey," Gus yelled again. "How about that beer, huh? You guys hoarding them back there? It's real quiet back there. Hey Dave, hold up your hands." He laughed again, "Come on now, you can get back to that later, but hand me a beer first."

I felt the fire in my face and knew I was blushing. It was almost as if Gus knew something had happened between Mary Ann and me. And I really wanted to hurt him for spoiling what had happened. But Mary Ann calmly handed him an open beer and came back. And when I looked into her eyes, I realized the moment had just begun.

Janet turned then, looked at us and giggled. Mary Ann blushed and now I was really getting mad. "This car needs a divider, right here." I said waving my hand over the top of the back of the front seat.

Janet really giggled then, and Mary Ann blushed even deeper. "What were you doing that you need privacy for?" Janet asked.

"Nothing!" Mary Ann snapped, " We weren't doing a thing!"

"Then why are you so red?" Janet giggled again.

"Maybe they're just planning on doing something," Gus threw in.

"We're just planning on having fun," I said. "Just plain old fun." Then, to change the subject, I hollered, "say, when are we going to eat anyway. I'm about to cave in."

Gus picked up on either my tone or what I was thinking because he said, "that's a good idea. Say Janet, where is that roadside park around here?"

"It's over on the highway," she said, turning back around. "Let's see," she went on. "Yeah, turn up here about a mile, then over to the highway and back about two miles."

Like I said, Janet wasn't all that bright, about one idea at a time was all she could handle.

Mary Ann was still blushing furiously, looking at her lap. I leaned over kissing her lightly, picking up her hand, squeezing it tightly. She squeezed back, looking over at me, smiling that sad, little smile, letting me know that nothing had been ruined and that I had been right. It had only just begun.

I felt my heart pounding as I kissed her again, not like before, just lightly this time, just brushing our lips. I felt hers quiver when I did. Gus had reached the highway and had speeded up and now the wind roared in my ears while it blew a tendril of hair across her face, causing her to smile again. I put my arm back around her and she snuggled close mumbling something in my chest that I didn't hear and didn't ask about.

Roy Orbison came on the radio just then, singing, *"Only the Lonely."* And my mind drifted away in the song. I looked down at Mary Ann, and felt her tremble like the leaves of the aspen trees that line the road, knowing she understood and she was away with me somewhere else, somewhere far away.

The car slowed then and Gus shifted gears as he turned into the park. "Would you look at this damn mess!" Gus shouted as he stopped suddenly for a bunch of kids playing in the road. The place was alive with people lying under the tall pine trees, eating, moving about and generally milling around. "Bunch of damn tourist," Gus yelled again as the swarm of small kids ran laughing out of the road. "Well, hell!" he turned to me. "Let's find someplace else. This place is full."

I started to reply but Janet said, "look, they have a bathroom here if nothing else. I don't mind going in the brush in the dark, but daylight is different."

Mary Ann blushed and nodded.

I shrugged my shoulders. "I don't care one way or another."

Janet said, "Well let's at least go pee, then we'll talk about it."

Mary Ann blushed again and turned her head.

Gus shrugged and drove on through the park. It was a lovely place or at least it would have been if it hadn't been so crowded. The pine trees shot up suddenly, their branches interlocking and almost blocking out the sun they fought for. A carpet of needles and scabby pine bark covered the otherwise bare earth. The glaring heat of the day suddenly changed into a cool, deep shade. The rushing wind of the prairie was tempered into a vagrant breeze that puffed teasingly, constantly shifting the spearing rays of sunlight that managed to penetrate the spiked, green canopy above.

The people smiled as we drove slowly past, some nodding at us, some waving. They ranged in age from a babe-in-arms to a dried-up, old man asleep in a lawn chair in spite of the blaring rock and roll music that came from everywhere. Every table was full and some had as many as three cars around them. Some had small fires burning. We passed another bunch of screaming kids and I saw an older bunch playing ball in a nearby meadow.

"Man," I said, unwillingly, "This place is full!"

"Damn bunch of tourist," Gus grunted. "It'll be like this till after Labor Day!" He turned to me, "I didn't expect this many this early though. Usually they don't hit in masses like this for a couple of more weeks."

"I don't blame them," I said. "This is about the prettiest place I've ever seen."

Mary Ann smiled. "Wait until we get to the back of the park."

"It can't be any better than this," I said.

She just smiled again.

"Look ahead Dave," Gus said.

I did, in amazement. The gentle slope we had been climbing suddenly turned into a steep mountainside out of which gushed a spring, about a third of the way up. The water bounced, chuckling and gurgling down the slope, occasionally catching a shaft of sunlight that reflected in the glistening droplets of spray causing them to shimmer and sparkle like precious jewels. Gus drove across a bridge, made of rough pine logs, that looked as natural as if it had grown there. Then he stopped beside the bathrooms that were built like old time log cabins.

"My God!" I finally choked out. "This is the most beautiful place I've ever seen. Look! We don't need a table. I have this quilt we can put on the ground. Let's stay here. There is a clear spot, right there. Come on Gus!"

He shrugged, then Janet said, "I'm for staying. I have to pee right now and I know I will later on too. She got out. "Mary Ann, are you coming?"

Mary Ann blushed again then got out on her side.

Gus looked disgusted. "Well hell!" he snapped then he shrugged again, "I guess it'll be alright." And he pulled the car off the road beside the stream that meandered through the park a little way then took off down the slope, turning suddenly, into a sun-warmed meadow where a dozen or so kids were splashing and laughing in the water. Gus and I got out of the car, me just shaking my head at the beauty of the place. Janet and Mary Ann came back from the bathroom. Janet looked at me and giggled. Mary Ann blushed.

Gus laughed. "You girls hang on before you start setting things up. We'll be back in a minute," and he headed for the bathroom. I followed.

Inside the bathroom, Gus looked at me and said. "You're doing alright in that back seat, but we just might change drivers later."

"No way, Man," I laughed. "I don't know where I'm going, remember?"

"Yeah, that's right. Too bad. Oh well, we'll have to find a place to stop later."

"Now that's not a bad idea, not a bad idea at all. Say, we're low on beer again."

He frowned. "We'll get some when we leave here. Janet drinks like a fish."

"She does put it away," I said laughing as we walked back to the car.

I don't know what the girls had talked about while we were gone but Mary Ann was blushing furiously again when we came back. Janet was giggling.

Every time Janet looked at me, she giggled, causing Mary Ann to blush even more.

Gus and I opened the trunk and took out the food. I spread the old quilt out for a ground sheet and the girls loaded it with fried chicken, deviled eggs, pickles, potato salad and chips. A real feast and plenty. Gus and I ate like there was no tomorrow. Janet and Mary Ann did pretty good too and there was hardly any food left when we finished. The girls began clearing up the mess while Gus and I leaned back against a tree, splitting our last beer. Gus said, "We'll leave as soon as they get the place cleaned up."

"I'm in no hurry," I patted my stomach. "In fact, I'm thinking about lying down a little while."

Gus grinned, "That wouldn't be too bad of an idea---without all of these damn tourist."

"They don't bother me that much."

"They bother me," he snapped. "I hate tourist. It's like this every summer. They come up here with their fat wives and squalling kids, clogging the parks and highways, driving the prices of everything up and throwing trash everywhere."

I studied him a second. "They're almost as bad as the Wheaties, aren't they," I said. "The next thing you know, they'll be wanting to date your sister." My voice was flat and cold, and it came out harder that I'd meant.

He threw a handful of pine needles in my lap. "It's not like that!"

"What's the difference Gus?" I said sharply.

"You make it sound like I was talking about the niggers or something."

I looked at him hard, not really believing what I was hearing. "I don't see the difference. I've been treated like dirt every since I left home and so have you. I'd think you would've learned something from it." I crushed the empty beer can in my hands. "I damn sure have."

Gus waved his hand around. "But this is different."

"I'm looking for work. These people are looking for fun. What's the difference? Except these people are in your yard."

"Maybe that's it. They are in my yard. Maybe that's the difference. Dammit Dave, I don't want this spoiled for my kids when I have some."

I laughed, "if you aren't careful, that'll be sooner than you think."

"You missed my point," he said disgustedly.

"No, I didn't miss your point. It's just that I never realized how much people hate other people. Just how much prejudice there really is in the world. I hate Yankees. You hate the tourist. The town people hate the Wheaties. Everyone hates the colored and they hate us back. And no one really knows why."

"You guys are sure deep into it," Janet said as she and Mary Ann sat beside us. "By the way, we're out of beer."

"You drink too much anyway," Gus said. "Well, are we leaving or not?"

I shook my head, slipping my arm around Mary Ann. "I don't want to, not just yet. I like this place, in spite of the damn tourist. Let's stay here a little while longer at least."

Gus stood, pulling Janet up, "What the hell," he said. "I don't really care but we're going to find some place a little more private." He kissed Janet lightly and grinned.

I kicked a bunch of pine needles into a pile then spread the quilt over them. "We'll be here when you come back." I said.

Gus shrugged and grinned, then took Janet by the hand and they walked away. I lay down on the quilt. Mary Ann sat beside me, stretching out her lovely, tan legs. She said, "I heard most of that, and Gus is wrong. And as much as I hate to admit it, I was wrong too because I cuss the tourist just as bad."

"It doesn't matter, who's right or wrong. We're not going to change anything."

She didn't even have to think about it. "We could--if everyone tried. We could change it then."

"That's the problem, Mary Ann," I sat up beside her. "Gus hates, and I don't care enough to stop him. I guess I hated before I was hated and learned what it was like. Gus didn't learn. He's home now and everything is peaches and cream again. Maybe it'll be the same when I go home. I don't think so. I think I've learned something this trip. But it's like Frank told me sometime back, what happens to my fellow man is his problem---and none of my business."

She cringed away from me, "that's a horrible attitude."

I pulled her back. "That's because you haven't been there. I've learned to keep my mouth shut and my feelings hidden, not because I want to, because I've had too." The wind shifted bringing the good smell of wood smoke.

She smiled sadly, "you don't do a very good job of hiding your feelings. Some of them at least"

"And now, my secret is out."

"It's no secret Dave," she said low. "It's just different. You're different. You see more. You hurt more. You--- feel things differently. Last night, when you said you wanted to see where the wind goes, I knew instantly what you meant and I wanted to go with you. I've felt this way for--I don't know how long, but I never could put it into words. But when you said, that---I knew, that was exactly how I feel. And you understand my feelings I've never been able to explain, without me even having to try to explain them to you. I've never told anyone I wasn't happy at home. That I feel like I'm being smothered by all the old rules." Her voice changed to a sing-song. "Be home by ten, Mary Ann. Clean your room Mary Ann"

I started laughing and she laughed with me then she said. "But that's not it either. I just feel empty. It's like I'm wandering somewhere, lost and alone. I'll graduate in a year, and I have no idea what happens then. It's real scary."

A kid screamed and a woman yelled. I looked around but nothing seemed to be wrong and the crowd was milling happily. I looked back at Mary Ann. "You'll go to college, then get married and start raising a flock of little Mary Ann's for you to yell at."

"You're probably right, but I don't want that." She sighed deeply. "I don't know what I want. But I do know it isn't that. The college maybe, but the other, I look at my mother and want to scream. She has done nothing with her life but be a housewife. I don't want that I want to something! But I don't know what. Or how." She sighed again. "I just feel so lost, so alone."

I touched her cheek then and reached into her soul. She looked at me and I knew how she felt. And never before in my life had I felt as close to another human being, and so in tune with another persons feelings.

Just then, Gus and Janet walked up. And I knew I would never again feel the loss of a moment-- like I did that moment.

"Hey Dave, come on," Gus said. "There's something over here I want to show you."

Mary Ann and I got up, I said, "what is it Bud? And it had better damn sure be good."

"No, you have to really see this." He took a drink out of a paper cup. Janet had one too.

Mary Ann pressed close to me and took my hand, squeezing it. I glanced at her and it was as if we had become a part of each other again. Even more so than before in the car. I smiled at her, then looked at Gus, "Okay," I said. "What the hell. Lead on." And we started walking to the other side of the park.

As we walked I began to notice that there were groups of people sitting, talking, laughing and drinking out of paper cups, like Gus and Janet had. It seemed odd. A man would leave a group then go to another, maybe across the road. The gang of kids ran screaming past us as a fat woman yelled at them.

Then Gus said, "There it is," and he pointed to a beer truck. A whole truck load of beer. Gus showed me the cup he had and said, "they're giving it away to anyone that wants it."

I said. "No one gives beer away."

He said, "just walk up there and see, if you don't believe me."

Mary Ann and I walked to the makeshift bar, a board across two beer kegs and I said, "I'll take two-- if you don't mind."

A big, broad-shouldered man with a grin that didn't quite make it to his steely, blue eyes said, "sure Buddy, here you go." And handed me two big paper cups full of draft beer.

I couldn't believe it but I handed one to Mary Ann and said, "Thank you Sir."

He just glanced at me, nodded and kept drawing beer.

"What's the deal?" I asked Gus on the way back.

"I don't know." He said, "I was just walking by and this guy hands me a beer. It's some kind of a party though or a reunion, or something going on. Everyone seems to know everyone else, all but us that is, and they're not tourist like I thought. All the cars have Colorado tags on them. But I don't care. I got a free beer and I know where there is another one."

"Who cares?" I said. "If they're giving it away, I'll sure drink it."

"Me too," Gus laughed. "And I'll see how much Janet can hold today." He laughed again. "I never had the chance before. I never had that much money."

We stayed there the rest of the afternoon, sitting in the shade, drinking, cussing and yelling at the kids that came past in droves. Janet could hold a bunch, we found out. Mary Ann just sipped her beer. I don't think she really liked it but drank just because the rest of us were.

Gus was driving and, Colorado being pretty tough on drunk drivers, especially underaged, drunk drivers, was taking it easy. I was taking it easy myself, not wanting to get drunk and pass out or puke and make a fool of myself. I was still planning on leaving early in the morning so now time, that had been so unimportant in the wheat fields, was extremely important to me now, important to the point that I hated for Mary Ann to be out of my sight, even to go to the bathroom.

By late afternoon Janet was drunk, not sloppy drunk, just pleasantly drunk. I poured her another cup from the gallon jug Gus had found in the trunk of his car. We had washed it clean and they had filled it up without question.

I still had the empty jug so I was elected to go fill it up again. I tried to get Mary Ann to do it, but she said she was afraid. She did go with me though. I don't think she wanted me out of her sight either.

I held her hand as we walked to the truck, noticing now that people looked at us oddly. The screaming mob of kids didn't though as they swarmed around us as if we weren't there. "I love this place," I said.

Mary Ann just squeezed my hand. "It's so much better when there aren't so many people here."

I just nodded. It would have been paradise if we'd been alone. There was more light now that the sun had changed its angle and the gleaming shafts came slanting to dapple and freckle the carpet of brown. The fire smoke gave the place a dream-like, misty look as it rose slowly swirling and drifting through the lower branches of the trees. I closed my mind to the mass of humanity, to the blaring radios and garbled conversation. And it was paradise. I pulled Mary Ann close, slipping my arm around her waist as we approached the makeshift bar.

The same steely-eyed guy filled the jug for me but this time when I thanked him, he didn't grin. He didn't even smile. I felt the hair on the back of my neck prickle for some unknown reason but I let it pass and thought no more about it, holding Mary Ann close as we slowly walked back through the fairyland of sunbeams slanting through the misty smoke.

We had just got back and I'd poured everyone a cupful when Gus said real low, "trouble on the way."

I knew what it was before I turned around. The guy at the bar, the steely-eyed one that didn't really smile, was coming.

He walked to us and squatted down near the quilt, looking hard and tough. "You kids have been hitting it pretty hard this afternoon," he said. "I just thought I'd check on you," his voice was flat, toneless and cold.

"We're alright Mister," I said. "We sure appreciate the beer."

He grinned but his eyes stayed hard. "Well," he said. "I really don't think you should get anymore. None of you is eighteen and it's illegal for you to drink."

I laughed. "We ain't going to tell anyone where we got it, even if we did get caught."

He looked at me funny, shocked like, then threw back his head and laughed out loud. "You don't have a clue do you?" He said after a minute and he grinned all the way this time, even his eyes. "You have no idea what this is, do you?"

I felt the cold finger go up my spine and glanced at Gus, he shrugged, his face a question mark. I turned to the man and said, "no Sir. I don't have any idea what this is." I put a cautious emphasis on the 'Sir'.

He laughed again, then said, "I didn't think so." Then he grinned again, an almost mischievous grin, like he was going to enjoy telling me. "Every year, about this time, we have a get-together, because the rest of the summer we're out chasing tourist. You see kids," he stood up, "this is the annual picnic of the Third Division, Colorado State Police. First off, we thought you belonged to someone here but, as it is, I really don't think you should come back for more beer, okay?"

My voice shook as I said a very cautious, "yes Sir. We do appreciate it and we'll leave right now---if that's alright."

He laughed again, "yeah Kid, that's not a bad idea. The State police patrols these parks pretty regular, and they're pretty tough on underaged drinkers, so it would really be best if you did leave." He turned then and walked away, still laughing.

We were loaded and on the way out before he got back to the beer truck. Gus honked at him. He waved. We all waved back and drove on out thanking what Gods there may be.

"Do you believe that!" I said as Gus pulled onto the highway. "We been drinking all day with half the highway patrol in the whole state."

"I don't believe it," Gus said, "But it's sure so." He speeded up.

"Unreal, totally unreal," Mary Ann said.

Janet just hiccuped and giggled. She was wiped out.

The bright sun was a shock after the dreamy, subdued light of the park. A few puff ball clouds had formed over the saw-toothed edge of the mountain range that the sun was just touching on its way to the other side of the world.

"That old boy was pretty nice about it all though," I said. "And from the looks of him, he ain't nice about to much of anything."

"Yeah," Gus said clicking on the radio. Linda Scott was singing, *I Told Every Little Star*. "But what else was he going to do?" Gus yelled over the music "I mean, it was their beer we been drinking all day. How do you think that would look in the newspaper?"

"That's true," Mary Ann said. "There wasn't much he could do but ask us to leave."

I said, "Well at least we all got about half drunk for free. That's not too bad of a deal."

Gus laughed, "I believe Janet got a little more than half."

Janet was singing along with the radio at the top of her voice, when she wasn't trying to climb in Gus's lap.

"Oh well," he added. "I'll know not to try that if I'm having to buy the beer. Did you see how much she soaked up? It made me think of Frank."

I didn't answer that. I liked Frank and what he did was his business. And I wouldn't talk about him behind his back anyway. I sure wished I could talk to him for a few minutes about Mary Ann. But he wasn't here. This was one I would have to figure out all by myself. And then, I'd have to live with it. I shuddered at the thought and felt myself pulling inward as we drove through the lonely time of the deepening afternoon.

My mind went to what Mary Ann had said about me feeling things differently, feeling things deeper and more. And I knew she'd been right. I didn't know why I did, but I had noticed it before. Things affected me that others just seemed to brush off. I'd learned not to make a big deal of it, and really, to keep my mouth shut. But she'd noticed it in me even in the short time we'd been together. Maybe, I thought, maybe that's why we were attracted to each other, because she felt the same. She was more intense than anyone I'd ever been around. I put my arm around her and held her close, more lonely now, than ever before.

The sun just touched the mountain top now, balancing there like a great, fiery ball for just a second, then slowly began to creep downward, lighting the clouds into streams and puffs of reddish gold. Long shadows played across the road and fairy glens opened through the trees. The mountain took on a strange half-light, half-dark as the snow pack glistened for a second and then, went suddenly dark. The air grew cold in the fading light and I rolled up my window, holding Mary Ann close, wishing the day would never end.

Gus pulled into a small town, found a drive-in and stopped. After hamburgers and a couple more cups of beer, I felt a little better. We also stopped at a filling station, filled up the car, went to the bathroom and we were ready to roll again.

The darkness cover the mountains now and the fairy glens were hidden in the shadows. A bulging moon grew brighter, as the sun went, and began to light the world with its ghostly glow. Janet was sobering up and the jug was empty so we made another pit stop, then headed silently towards home about forty miles away.

CHAPTER 19

Nothing had really changed. The radio still blared rock music, sometimes sad, sometimes fast, but with the darkness a silence fell over all of us. Even Janet was silent now as we drove through the night. And an empty, restlessness seemed to fill the car. And without anyone saying anything about it, a not-wanting-it-to-be-over, feeling seemed to affect all of us. So nothing was said when Gus pulled off onto a side road. And nothing was said when he pulled off of that road into a field, stopped and killed the car.

Janet giggled. Gus smiled. A sad song was playing on the radio as he pulled her to him and they slid beneath the seat. Mary Ann turned then and kissed my neck, nuzzling close to me and I felt the tears on her cheeks. "What's wrong?" I whispered, feeling like crying myself.

"I don't want this day to end," she said low. Her voice was husky, filled with pain and longing. I nodded in the dark and squeezed her even tighter, feeling even more miserable than before.

We began talking then, she and I. Gus and Janet were busy. It was really just conversation, talking about the day, remembering things we'd seen, things we'd said. Basically, we were trying to imprint the whole day on our memories, both of us knowing something important had happened to each of us today. Something that would be good to remember. And things were going good and we were happy, laughing and remembering when Gus raised up over the seat and said, "are you still leaving in the morning?"

"In the morning!" Mary Ann cried. "You're leaving in the morning?"

"Yes, I am," I said unconvincingly, "Early." I held her close now, wishing I could take back what all I'd said to Gus this morning when things had seemed a lot simpler. But there was a nagging thought in the back of my head. I really didn't have to go back. But I looked at her and knew, I really did have to leave.

All of this was going through my mind while Gus was saying, "I'll probably be along the next day." His voice told me that he was sorry he had brought it up. "I'll bring my car so I'll have a way back."

I said, "what ever you think."

"Why are you leaving in the morning?" Mary Ann cried. "Why didn't you tell me? You should have told me this morning."

"What difference does it make?" I said flatly.

"It makes a lot of difference," she said then leaning over whispered to me. "Let's get away from them."

I opened the door, grabbed the old quilt and a six-pack. "We'll be back in a little while," I told Gus.

He pushed Janet away long enough to smile.

We walked a while, aimlessly across the moonlit field. We were back on the prairie now but the wind was gentle and warm. Mary Ann wasn't talking and I knew that I'd hurt her but I didn't know what to say or do to help her so I didn't say anything.

"What were you going to do?" she finally said. "Just drive off without any goodbye, or warning at all?"

"No," I said low, "I was going to tell you later, when I took you home."

"Why wait until then? What was wrong with this morning when you came?" The wind rippled through her hair and that vagrant lock fell across her eye again and my breath left me again.

"I couldn't. Maybe I didn't want too. Maybe when I saw you, talked to you, I couldn't. Hell, I don't know. I've never felt like this towards any girl before. Maybe I didn't tell you because then you might feel sorry for me and I didn't want that."

She turned to me and looked inside my soul. "I told you how I feel about you this afternoon." She brushed her hair back then wiped at her eyes.

I spread out the quilt, opened a beer then lit a cigarette.

She sat beside me but looked away across the field. "Dave," her voice was thick. "Was it a lie? Did you just say that---today?"

A ragged cloud darkened the moon, then passed on. Elvis Presley singing, *Are You Lonesome Tonight?* Came low on the soft breeze. I could see the tears now, running down her cheeks. She wasn't sobbing but they were there. I pulled her close. She lay her head on my chest. I stroked that long, shining, hair. "Mary Ann, before I met you I didn't know what love was. Maybe it's because I'm so lonesome, so far from home. Maybe that's all. I really don't know. I do know I've never known anyone like you before. I've never felt what I feel for you before. Especially not tonight, not now."

She sat up and I saw the moonlight in her eyes. "You don't have to leave tomorrow. I heard you and Gus talking today. All you have to do tomorrow is call Frank." Then she smiled at me. "Please Dave."

I felt a tremor go through me watching the pleading in her eyes. "That's not why I have to leave." I looked away from her so I could finish. "Don't you know--why I have to leave?"

I looked back at her. She reached out, softly touching my face and the pounding in my ears came back. "I know Dave. You have to see where the wind goes," and she smiled that sad little smile.

I took her in my arms, rocking back and forth. "That's not the reason either." I could feel her breast, mashing into my chest, my voice caught in my throat and suddenly I couldn't breath. I felt my hands move to her hair, rubbing stroking. I felt them tremble. She looked at me and I kissed her, really for the first time. A long, slow, burning, kiss that I could feel traveling through my body like an electrical currant. I could feel her lips tremble and her heart beat.

She pulled away suddenly and moved back, away from me. I saw fear in her eyes. "Maybe it would be better if you did go back. If maybe--we went back to the car---" She looked away then and hugged her breast. "Or maybe---something!" Her voice was ragged now, almost pleading.

I was unable to speak. I'd felt it too, deep inside me, a hollow, longing feeling, aching and lonely, verging on pain, but accompanied by a great heat that spread through out me. A terrible wanting that I wasn't sure I knew how to deal with seemed to grow inside me. "We can't go back to the car." I said. "You know what they're doing back there." I tried to light a cigarette but my hands shook too bad.

She rasped out in a horse whisper. "Yes,---I know what they're doing---and that's what scares me so." And I saw her tremble.

I gave up on the cigarette, throwing it away into the moonlight and I touched her arm. "It scares me too," my voice quavered. She put her hand on mine. I took her in my arms, feeling her quivering against me and I kissed her.

I guess I shouldn't have, not right then but I did. I kissed her like before long and slow. She rotated her mouth and I felt her tongue barely brush mine, then pull back, then it was back again gently touching mine. She turned in my arms and I felt my hand move to her breast, almost as if it had a mind of its own. Then I felt it slide under her blouse, cupping her breast again, feeling the satiny bulge above her bra.

She broke the kiss then and looked deep inside me, then she whispered, "Dave, I'm afraid."

I was too, scared to death. But the empty longing I'd felt before filled me now. I tried to clear it from my mind but it wouldn't go. I tried harder. Then she closed her hand over mine and kissed me, a deep, yearning kiss, a lonely, lost kiss, a terrible wanting kiss. I felt my hand slide around and unhook her bra, then move back to the softness of her breast; the hard protrusion of her nipple. She moaned slightly and quivered against me. Something in my mind said, push her away and I tried. But I couldn't. She moaned again drowning out the roaring in my ears and the fear in my mind.

My hands trembled as I found the bottom of her pull-over top. She moved away slightly, raising her arms as I pulled it over her head. Her bra came off with the blouse. I sucked in a breath as I saw the whiteness of her breast gleaming against the tan of her shoulders.

She looked down and covered her breast with her arm, looked at me, then lowered her eyes. "I've never done anything like this before," her voice was full, almost hoarse.

"Neither have I," my voice quaked because it was the truth.

She looked up then, deep inside me, "I'm very frightened."

I touched her leg below her shorts, "I am too."

She smiled then and put her hand on mine. "I don't know what to do," she whispered. "I don't want to stop. I want to---but, I don't want to."

I nodded, feeling the same but I was unable to say it. I took off my shirt and lay back on the old pink quilt, holding out my arms. She came to me and we held each other close.

*　　*　　*

Later, I lay beside her, holding her, looking at the stars, wondering about what had happened. I knew I'd been clumsy and there had been an overall, guilty feeling that I was doing something wrong. And when I looked at her now, naked in my arms, a wave of guilt and shame for what had happened swept over me. I sat up, glancing down at her, my eyes drinking in the whiteness of her body where her bathing suit covered. Even in the moonlight I could see the pink of her nipples, just darker than her skin, and lower, the tangle of dark hair. She didn't seem to be feeling what I was, or to be embarrassed, but I felt she was uncomfortable. I covered her with my shirt.

She smiled and reached out touching my face, my shoulder. "I love you Dave," she said deep, meaningful.

And I felt like cutting my throat.

"I love you too. But I feel like a low down bastard." A shudder passed over me.

She sat up. The shirt fell away but she made no motion to cover herself. "Please don't," she said low. "I wanted it too." And I looked at the loveliness of her breast and I reached out and touched one, then pulled my hand away.

"I can't help it," I said. "I'm sorry, and I don't feel this way because of you. It's just because of what I did."

She touched my face. "You didn't do it all. You didn't force me. I---."

"I know all that," I said hard. "But I should have stopped."

A look of fear came to her face and she pulled the shirt up. "Is that it Dave? Or is it just that we did it---And now you don't want to touch me? Am I dirty now? Is that---"

I pulled her to me and kissed her. "My, God, no! I love you---more than anything."

She was stiff and unyielding in my arms, "Are you sure? I have to know for sure?" The questioning tone of her voice was like the cry of a frightened child.

I kissed her again, gently and tenderly, "I love you. I'll die for you or kill for you. I'll do anything you say."

She pulled away and looked deep into me for what seemed to be a long time. Then she came to me and held me kissing me and rubbing my back and shoulders. Suddenly she stiffened again and pulled back, hugging her knees to her breast.

She looked at me with pain in her eyes. "Do you have any of those---things?" Her voice was hard now, demanding an answer.

But I was taken by surprise. "What things?"

Her tone was cold now and very hard, "those rubber things. Those things, boys buy in filling stations. I've heard about them. Do you carry them, just in case?" Her body was rigid now, her face hard, eyes flashing. "Well! Do you!"

Her tone cut through me like jagged, broken, glass. "No," I said softly. "No, I don't carry them." I tried to look away from her but I couldn't.

She stared at me a second longer then a worried smile came to her and she shook her head. "Oh, Dave," she touched my arm and the shirt fell away again. "I just had this horrible thought. I had to know if---if you had planned all of this."

I reached for her and held her to me, the cool touch of her naked breast burned into my chest. "No, Mary Ann," I whispered. "I didn't plan it. You don't plan things like this--they just happen, like tonight."

She snuggled even closer to me and I felt her smile. "I'm glad it happened," she said low. "I'm glad. I didn't think about it at all, before. I've wondered sure, but I don't think about it. Last night I knew I liked you, a lot. But this?" She pulled back and looked me in the eyes. "This never entered my mind. Dave, I'm not a tramp, a whore. I don't even kiss on the first date. But you---you're different. Don't ask me why--or how. I can't describe it---It's just a feeling. I've felt it all day, last night. I don't know." She shook her head. "I don't know what happened." Then she kissed me. "But I'm glad, it did happen. I'm glad it was you," her voice was low pitched, husky and full.

And I felt as low and dirty as the cockroach I'd seen in that bar back in Oklahoma. I couldn't look at her. "I wish it hadn't happened. I wish I'd left this morning---when I had the chance." I looked at her now. "Now I don't know if I can leave."

The pale light shifting through the clouds played on her face causing hollows and shadows. The wind rippled through her hair. She was silent a second, then she smiled that sad, little smile that I loved so. "Yes. You can leave." Her voice was hollow, coming from far away. Her shoulders dropped and she smiled again, the same smile, then she said. "We would never make it."

She paused then, and a far-away look came to her. "I've seen it happen too many times before. Kids, like us, get married and live in a shack, then have a baby. Then they grow to hate each other because they missed out on so much life." She paused again. "And it's always the other one's fault. But really, it doesn't matter. Because now, they're trapped. And no matter what they do, they can't get out of the trap."

She shuddered as if she were cold, pulled the shirt up and around her and sat up. "I don't want that, Dave. I'm eighteen," she said. "I had plans for my life." But then her voice dropped and became soft and low. "I don't want to hate you. I want to have you forever---and when you leave--I'll have that. I'll remember us tonight. The way we are now, not screaming at each other---but the way we are, right now."

She looked inside me again and I felt a power in those eyes, a force almost emanating from her that went through me. "Do you understand what I mean?" she whispered.

I understood and deep down, I knew she was right. That didn't make it any easier though. Sometimes, being right can kill a fellow.

I reached for her then and held her to me, touching her, kissing her softly. Then I held her away from me, loving her with my eyes. I wanted her again, wanted it to be again. I pulled her to me but she knowingly, pulled away.

"No," she said so low I barely heard. "It wouldn't be the same and it would spoil what we have now." She looked at me and smiled. "I love you Dave, with all my heart." She dropped her eyes. "And if you want to--we will." She looked up again and there was a deep sadness in her eyes. "But it can never be like it was. Not ever. Not with you or anyone else. I'll never feel again--what we had." Her eyes changed now. They aged. Just her eyes, nothing else but as she looked at me now, her eyes were older than the mountains, older than time.

I pulled her to me again, kissing her softly, touching her satiny skin, loving her--hating her for being so damn right.

Gently I laid her down, leaned away and took the shirt from her. She didn't stop me and I looked at her as she lay in the moonlight. She smiled at me, making no motion to cover herself. Then I traced her body with my finger tips from her neck to her knee, memorizing the beauty before me. I leaned down to kiss her lips, her eyes, her throat, and her breast. Then I opened a beer, lit a cigarette and walked into the night.

I didn't go far or stay gone that long, but when I came back she was fully dressed, watching me. I stood before her as naked as she'd been. She studied my body and gently touched me. Then she turned away, her shoulders heaving with silent sobs as I began to get dressed. When I finished I sat beside her, kissing her cheek.

She leaned against me, holding me. "I love you," she said gently, softly, "I'll always love you."

"I love you," and kissed her softly before I stood. I reached down for her, helping her to stand. Then I shook out the old pink quilt. A strange feeling of joy and shame passed through me at the same time. The feeling of joy grew overwhelming the shame as I picked up the beer and we started back to the car. We hadn't walked twenty yards when the horn honked.

Gus got out of the car as we approached, walking off into the darkness. I followed. "How did you make out," he asked, as he urinated on the ground.

There had been three of the foil wrappers beside the car tonight but I lied without hesitation. "Not worth a damn." I said. "All we did was talk."

He grinned and laughed. "That's too bad, but I got an extra one for you tonight," and slapped me on the shoulder as we walked back, causing me to smile in the darkness.

We took Janet home first. They'd run out of beer and she was nearly sober. I said my goodbye, glad to have met you, as she and Gus got out. Janet turned and blew me a kiss then they walked to the house. Mary Ann and I moved to the front seat. It had been my idea. There was no need to cheapen how we felt about each other in the back seat.

"I hate her," Mary Ann hissed as they walked away. "I hate her! Gus will be coming back to her and I hate her for it. Besides, she's so cheap."

"Why do you run around with her then?"

"I don't," she said flatly. "She's my cousin on my mother's side. She called me yesterday afternoon wailing about Gus bringing some dammed Wheatie home and he needed a girl to keep him occupied."

I winced at the, *'dammed Wheatie.'*

Mary Ann smiled. "She said all I would have to do is be along to talk to him." She kissed me on the cheek and smiled. "Now for that, for talking me into coming last night, and believe me it took some talking! I love her."

Then her face went hard. "But for the way she acts and what she does, I hate her."

"Tell her I love her for it too. " I said, and kissed her just as Gus got back in. He didn't act surprised to see us in the front seat. But he didn't say anything about it either. It was abut fifteen miles to Mary Ann's house and we rode in silence. There were two beers left so I opened them and handed Gus one. He tried to make conversation on the way but we were silent. Mary Ann leaned against me and I held her hand. After a while he finally got the hint and shut up. I was glad.

A little while later Gus turned off the main highway onto a crushed rock driveway that wound up a small hill. He slowed at the high, chain-link fence and as we crossed the cattle guard, I could see the rose garden sprawling darkly and the bulk of the mansion lurking in the darkness.

Mary Ann and I got out of the car and walked up the steps of the porch that supported a tremendous chandelier. The house was even bigger than it had appeared. Massive columns supported a huge balcony. Tall, lighted windows stared coldly at me as if challenging my right to be there. Heavy double-doors, intricately carved, barred me from entering as the house as they dwarfed me, crushing what little of me I had left. I held her tight, torn between wanting to stay and having to go.

She held me close and we kissed, a gentle caring kiss that said more than either of us could have with words. Really, all of the words had been said, I thought. I held her to me and then even tighter, hating even the idea of letting her go. Then she pushed me back, looking deep into me with those huge, beautiful wells she had for eyes, and she said, "Dave, I lied to you." Her voice was thick, dripping with pain. She leaned forward and just brushed my lips again, and then she said, "I would have been happy in a shack---with you."

She kissed me again as I stood there stunned, not believing what I thought I'd heard. Then she walked to the door, turned and said, "I love you. I'll always love you. As long as I live, I'll always love you." And she was gone.

I still stood there in partial shock, wondering if I'd really heard what I thought I had. I looked around and the house seemed even bigger than before, menacing now, daring me to stay, to come back, laughing now at my worn boots, my stiff, new blue jeans.

The light in the house went off and there was nothing to do but leave.

CHAPTER 20

＊＊＊

"That is some kind of a place," Gus said as he turned back onto the highway. "I guess I should've warned you about that."

"It would've been nice," I mumbled as a big bug smacked against the windshield. Then I wondered if it would have made any difference.

"I thought about it last night when we picked them up," he tapped the steering wheel in time with a fast song on the radio. "But I didn't want to scare you off. Besides, you two are quite a bit alike, or at least I think so."

"You should have told me she was rich." My voice sounded hollow.

"I didn't think it would matter. I really didn't expect her to come tonight. She doesn't date much and, to tell you the truth, she always seemed to be stuck up, except today. I've never seen her like she was today. I expected her to be a wet blanket but I had a real good time today."

I had to smile. "So did I Gus. So did I."

"Well I'm glad. But I'm not surprised you didn't make out any. They call her *'The Virgin Queen,'* at school. She doesn't date that much and she don't put out to no one. Her great, great, grandfather was old Jed Tremont, an old mountain man that came here back in the 1830's and, after the beaver ran out, decided to go into ranching. At one time he claimed over one hundred thousand acres but the government broke most of that up. Her daddy's only got about twenty thousand acres now."

He looked at me. "You knew Janet and Mary Ann were cousins?"

"Yeah, she told me, on her mother's side."

"Yeah. Their mothers are sisters. Well, my mom went to school with them and she said they were dirt poor but Mary Ann's mom set her cap for the richest guy in the county, and got him. That's why she's so rich and Janet's not."

"I was wondering. Well, it don't matter none now anyway. I'll be leaving as soon as we get to the pickup."

He glanced at me. "I thought you were going to wait till in the morning."

"I was. But I'm not now. You should've told me about her before."

He was silent a second. "Yeah, I guess you're right, I should have. Well, I'm sorry you didn't have a good time. I was hoping you would."

I looked down the dark highway. "It's been a bitch of a trip."

He was still tapping the steering wheel in time with the music.

We drove the rest of the way in silence. I was glad, I didn't feel like talking. I didn't feel like listening. I didn't feel at all. The mansion house kept looming in my mind. And the way it'd made me feel. Gus had said it, dirt poor. I could've handled anything but that. That house rearing over me had been the final kick in the mouth. And I knew there was no need to even think about going back to see her tomorrow. I couldn't now, not even if I tried. I would've given anything to see her again but that door had shut as firmly as the one she'd walked through to go in that house.

We pulled into Cloud Chief and Gus stopped beside Frank's pickup. Gus said, "Man, I wished you would think about this. It's after midnight. I wish you'd wait till in the morning. Man, it will be alright for you to stay tonight."

I grabbed the old quilt and shook my head. "No!" I almost yelled. Then said softer, "no, Gus, I've got to get out of here. I have to leave. Tell your folks I appreciate them letting me stay and I'm sorry if I caused any trouble. I guess I'll see you in Cheyenne Wells, okay?" My voice had a dead sound, as if I didn't care. And just to tell the truth, I really didn't.

"Yeah. Tell Frank not to have a hemorrhage because I'll be back tomorrow or the next day. Just tell him I'll call him, like we planned."

"Okay," I said starting the pickup. "I'll tell him. He'll probably be mad, because you didn't come back with me, but he'll get over it."

"Well, I'll see you when I get back. Drive careful," he laughed as I pulled away into the night.

I drove automatically, like I did going to and from the elevator. My eyes and hands reacted but my mind was back in a field on the outskirts of Castle Rock. *'I love you,'* she said again, in my mind, *I'll always love you. We will have each other forever. No one will ever touch me there again. I'll never have what we had, again.'* All of these words and a thousand other things kept flashing through my brain as I saw her lying there, naked in the moonlight. And I knew them to be true.

I guess I was thirty miles down the road when I saw the lights of the bar. Not really knowing why, I stopped and went in. Pat Boon was singing, *Moody River,* from the juke box. Three men sat at a table. One woman in a low cut dress was at the bar. The place was empty other than them and the bartender,

I bellied up to the bar like I had been doing it all my life and ordered a shot of Jim Beam. I guess I looked like I needed a shot because the bartender looked at me closely, smiled and set it up. I tossed it down in the best John Wayne style I could muster and ordered another one. They came together this time, the bartender and the woman. He set up the drink. She smiled.

"Buy me a drink, Mister?" She cooed softly as she lit a cigarette and smiled again.

The men at the table laughed, "picking them kinda young tonight ain't you Hazel?" one of them said.

I let it pass and waved at the bartender to set her up. He brought her some kind of a mixed drink. I paid him and ordered another shot. "Hitting it pretty hard tonight ain't you?" the bartender said as he poured my drink.

I didn't answer. The jukebox changed to another sad country song about lost love and I looked at the woman, judging her. She was fortyish, thick-waisted and hard-eyed. Twenty years ago she would've been pretty, and in the dim light, she still was. But up close I could see the years of booze and, God only knows what else, had taken their toll and now she looked exactly like what she was, a whore in a dirty bar. "How much?" I said flatly.

"What are you talking about, Honey?" she cooed but her voice caught.

"How much you charge?" I said again, "I ain't got all night."

The men at the table snickered. I drank my drink, slid off the bar stool and walked out, knowing if I stayed any longer there'd be trouble. I wasn't afraid of the men and even welcomed the thought of a fight, but there were three of them and I knew I had no chance.

She followed me.

I got in the pickup. She walked up as I shut the door. "Look," I said. "I told you, I ain't got all night. Now, how much?"

"Ten dollars," she hissed out, hate pouring from her eyes.

I started the pickup, then looked at her, "I'll give you five. Take it or leave it. I don't really care."

She looked at me a second then looked at the ground, then she walked around the pickup, getting in beside me. And I thought, Sara would be proud of me. I'd finally grown up. I'd finally reached the pinnacle to where I could reduce a human being to the status of a piece of meat and the amount of a person's pride and self-worth, to five dollars. I almost cringed, knowing what Sara would've really thought.

But I was past that now. Compassion had been burned out of me. I'd grown up. Now I looked at the woman, "where to?"

She looked at me through the eyes of a person that had lost even what little self respect she'd had in the bar, hard eyes, eyes that dripped hatred for me and loathing for herself. "Right around the corner. The white house."

I drove away, hating myself for what I'd said and done, hating the men in the bar for laughing at her, and me. But most of all hating her for letting me do this, to both of us.

I drove to the house she pointed out. There was a light on in the rear. She went through a doorway then, just inside, into a bedroom and turned on the light. I followed.

Once inside, she turned to face me. She'd changed now. The hatred was gone from her eyes but a veil had fallen over them and everything else had gone too. Now there was nothing there. It was as if she'd closed a door in her mind and even she was no longer there.

"That will be in advance," she said. Even her voice came from a place far away, where she couldn't be touched.

I pulled out my billfold and handed her the money. She sat down on the sagging bed and began to undress without bothering to turn off the light. I could hear a baby crying somewhere in the house. Another woman was trying to hush it. A radio was playing somewhere, an old tune, *"Driftwood On The River."* I knew the song. It was pretty. The woman stood up, removed the rest of her clothing then she lay on the bed, raising up on one elbow. Her breasts sagged, one touching the bed, the other laying on that one. Her stomach sagged too, almost touching the bed, and her pubic hair was tinged with gray. "Come on Sugar," she said in a glaring hiss, "You paid for it."

*   *   *

Thirty minutes later I was screaming down the highway, headed east at an even one hundred miles an hour. I took another long, gurgling drink from the fifth of whiskey I'd known was under the seat. It'd been buried under some old wiping rags, covered with dust and lost from sight for some time. I took another long, long drink and tried to wipe the tears from my eyes.

It hadn't been any good with the woman. I'd wanted to hurt her, to lose some of the horrible frustration and pain I felt. But I couldn't hurt her. I couldn't even raise a hard on. She tried for a while, but then she laughed at me.

I saw a rabbit on the side of the road, blinded by the headlights. A big, jack rabbit, his beady eyes wide with fear, trapped in the glaring lights, not knowing what to do, which way to run. Gently, I turned the steering wheel and I smiled as he crunched under the tires of the pickup. At least it was something.

I took another long drink and passed a sign that read, *Cheyenne Wells, 60*. "I'll be there in forty minutes at this rate," I said, then I laughed over the screaming sound of the engine. I couldn't wait to get back. I couldn't wait to tell Frank I'd finally grown up. A thought came to me then, from far back in the dim recesses of my sodden brain. At this speed, as drunk as I was, I might not even make it back.

Well, I thought, that would be all right too.

But I did make it and I pulled into town drunker than I'd ever been. I found the tent. The light was still on although it was late, probably after three A.M. I pulled in slowly having a real problem now focusing my eyes and even keeping them open. I got out of the pickup and fell down. I tried to get up but I couldn't. So I just lay there, crying in the night.

I guess Frank heard or saw me pull in. Anyway, he came out and found me. I heard him say, "my, God, Dave, what the hell happened to you?"

I tried to answer but everything was spinning around and, to tell the truth, I wasn't really sure what had happened to me. I felt someone pick me up. I guess it was Frank but I wasn't sure. Then the light hit my eyes and I heard someone say, "Damn, I don't know how he made it. The kid is smashed."

I remembered the voice. It was George.

I tried to answer again but nothing worked anymore and I went away. And then there was nothing.

*   *   *

And then there was something, a pounding in my head as if someone were beating me. Every time my heart beat, someone hit me in the head with a baseball bat. I opened my eyes but the glaring light burned into my brain like white hot spears. I knew something was different but I wasn't sure what. I went back in my mind and the last thing I remembered was driving but now I wasn't driving and I wasn't sure why, or even where I was.

I heard someone say, "he's awake," and I thought, that's strange. That sounded like George. But George is in Cheyenne Wells. Then I remembered getting out of the pickup. And I remembered crying. Then

I remembered why I had been crying. And I wanted to cry again. I felt something cool and wet on my forehead and I opened my eyes. Frank was leaning over me.

He grinned and said, "welcome back."

I tried to smile but my stomach turned over. I lay very still but it was too late. I jumped off the cot and ran outside. I fell down beside the tent and began retching and vomiting. Someone lifted my head and poured something in my mouth. Whiskey. I vomited again and oh God, it burned. Then I vomited again, and again, until I was just retching, straining, long racking retching heaves with nothing coming out as my body tried to tear itself apart. They poured more whiskey in me but I just puked it back out. And my God it burned as it came out my nose. Then someone poured water in me, it was better. I puked it up too but it didn't burn so bad. They poured more and then more. Finally I was able to keep some of it down then I passed out again.

Something cool and wet was lying across my eyes when I woke again. I moved it, opening my eyes. Frank was leaning over me. "Just lay still," he said. "Just lay still, a minute. Don't try to get up." He looked haggard and worried.

I closed my eyes then opened them again. "I'm alright now, I think." I raised up on one elbow. I was light-headed, giddy and very weak but I swung my feet to the floor and sat up.

"Here," Frank said, "Drink this." And he handed me a small cup. It smelled like chicken broth. I took a small sip. My throat was raw and hurting. I drank some more and I could feel it entering, spreading through my body as my cells sucked it up. I finished the cup.

"Do you want some more?" he said.

I shook my head and the pounding started again. I quickly lay back down and it lessened. I raised back up, very slowly this time and looked around. George was snoring, it was dark outside. The lantern was on, but turned down low.

"What time is it?" I asked then wondered why I'd asked. What difference did it make?

Frank looked at his watch, "Two-thirty."

"Two-thirty? It was after midnight when I left Cloud Chief."

He smiled. "This is the next day, you've been out over twenty-four hours."

I looked down, all I had on was my underwear but I was clean. I remembered vomiting now, and falling in it. Someone had undressed me and bathed me. My stomach turned just thinking about it.

Frank smiled, worriedly, and said softly, "Dave, who the hell is Mary Ann? And what the hell happened to you? You weren't gone but a little over a day." His voice was ragged and he sounded as tired as he looked.

I lay back down very gently and told him the whole story. All of it. All of it that I could remember that is. The last part of the trip back was a blank.

He sat in silence while I talked, even when I had to search my mind for the right words to really tell him how I felt, how she said she'd felt. I even told him about her being a virgin. Then I told him about the woman and how I treated her. And how she treated me.

He was silent for a long time when I finally finished. Then he said, "you're lucky you're not dead. Don't ever drink that much that quick again or you probably will be. You had a rough go of it Son, but that's no reason to kill yourself. Now, to Mary Ann. That part was bad, but you did real good by leaving. I know you had it tough and you think now you'll never get over her, but you will. I know. I've been in love before too. It's just like everything else. The first time is always the worse, the hardest. But this will pass too. There was nothing else you could have done, except exactly what you did."

He smiled then. "And I'm very proud of you for doing it. That took a real man, thinking like a real man. And not many could have done as well."

"I love her Frank," I choked out, feeling my guts twist just thinking about her.

"I know you do, Son. But you still did the right thing for both of you."

Then a thought came screaming out of my mind. "Do you think she might be pregnant?"

He grinned, shaking his head. "It's not likely. It usually doesn't happen the first time. I don't know why. It just doesn't. Don't worry about it though. If she is, she'll get in touch with you. Her daddy will see to that, and I can just see him coming down to Oklahoma with his shotgun."

Just the thought of marrying her covered me like a warm blanket. "I hope so," I said. Then I thought of all the problems and embarrassment that would bring, "no, I really don't."

And then, for the first time, I completely realized that Frank and Mary Ann were right. We could never have made it. She'd said she would've been happy with me in a shack. But for how long? And even if she could be happy, could I? That huge mansion would always be there, crushing me, beating me down, making me remember what I'd taken her away from. And what could I give her in return? Nothing. I never had anything and more than likely never would. I could still see that mansion in my mind. You could loose my parents house in that thing and never find it for a week.

But she said it, my mind screamed. She said she could be happy with me, with what I had. And I knew she'd meant it. But the mansion would always be there for her too, and the fine clothes, and the new car for her graduation, and all the things that went with the mansion. Things that I couldn't even hope to be able to give her. But they would still be there and soon they'd be between us and then---

Frank had laid down when I started my story. Now he was beginning to snore softly. He said I'd been out for almost twenty-four hours. I guess he'd been awake, watching me taking care of me all that time. I appreciated it, knowing not many would have done it. I'd have to tell him in the morning.

I lay there a long time thinking about the last two days and marveling at how a person's life can be changed so completely, so totally, by a random series of seemingly unrelated occurrences. A lonely boy. A lovely girl. A beautiful sunset. A few words whispered in the dark by two kids.

I wished it'd never happened. I wished I could go back and change things to make it not happen. Then a thought began to form and grew in stature and substance. And I knew what I would do. I would get rich someday. Someday I'd pull up to that mansion house in my brand new

Eldorado Cadillac convertible. And I'd take Mary Ann to my mansion house that you could lose hers in and never find it for a week. I'd show them. I damn sure would. Just you wait and see!

The tears were coming faster now. Now, I couldn't control them at all. I turned over on my side, away from Frank, and I cried. Finally, I guess, I went to sleep, still crying.

*   *   *

I woke up sweating, God it was hot for some reason. I looked around, the tent was empty. I swung off the cot and carefully stood up. My headache was gone now and I almost felt human again. My suitcase was under the bunk. Someone, I guess Frank, had brought it in. I slipped on a pair of jeans, grabbed my clean up gear and walked over to the station for a shower. The cold water felt good, completely reviving me.

I dressed completely and walked back to the tent. It was still empty. I put my clean-up gear away and noticed for the first time the old quilt lying folded on the end of my bunk. I sat down, touching it gently. It was smooth and cool to the touch. I could feel the tears coming back but I blinked them back thinking, I'll not cry again, not ever again.

I heard someone outside, Frank and George walked in.

"Well," George said. "Lookee here who's come back to life. By God Frank, I believe he's going to live this time."

"About time too," Frank said grinning at me. "Welcome back. I guess you know you scared the fire out of me. Twice I threatened to take you to the hospital. But I just never could make myself do it."

"I'm glad you didn't." I said. "They would have called my folks and really scared them."

"Listen to him," Frank said. "Worried about his folks finding out he got drunk." He slapped me on the shoulder and laughed. "Don't worry Wheatie. I won't tell your momma on you. Say, I'll bet your hungry."

I could see the worry, still in his eyes. So I said, "I could eat a live cow, horn, hide, hair and all."

"We've already eaten, but I'll walk over there with you." Frank smiled.

260

"Sure. Glad to have you." He followed me out. We walked over to the café in silence and sat in a booth.

The place hadn't changed a bit. The old woman behind the counter still brightened the world with her shiny, golden smile. The girl that came to the table saying, "you gonna eat?" was different though, a big-hipped, blond.

I ordered a big hamburger and a drink. She swung away and I thought, no, things wouldn't have changed, it didn't happen to them and three days isn't enough to change anyone.

Three days echoed in my brain. It seemed like three years.

"You alright?" Frank's voice broke my thoughts.

"Yeah, I think so at least. I appreciate what you done, taking care of me and all."

"Don't worry about it. Wasn't any problem."

"Well I appreciate it."

"Are you alright now?" He had worry in his eyes, concern in his voice.

"Yeah, I'll be even better after I eat."

"How about the other? Mary Ann?"

I felt a ripping, deep inside me. A tearing that left a hole nothing could fill. "I just feel like something has been torn out of me. I just feel empty."

"I heard you crying last night. That's a good sign when you can cry."

I looked away, embarrassed. "Sign of a kid is all."

"No Dave, it's really not. It's a sign that you finally realize what's happened, that you know in yourself that it's over and done with."

"It will never be done with, Frank." My voice was shrill. "I'm going back."

"When?"

That one word completely deflated me. "I don't know. Someday. When I can I guess."

"We got wheat to cut Boy," his voice was gentle but his words said more than they meant. He was counting on me to be here when the wheat came in.

"We'll get it cut. By the way, how is the wheat?"

"Maybe tomorrow, if not, the next day for sure."

I was glad the conversation had changed and continued it. "Can we make it in fifteen days?"

"It'll be tough, but if nothing happens, we'll make it."

"I see Gus ain't back yet. Did he call?"

"He called. He'll be in this evening some time."

Suddenly I was cautious. "He don't know about Mary Ann, Frank. Don't say anything to him about her. Okay?"

He stiffened slightly and a hard look came to his eyes. "It's your business, Dave. I would've never said anything to him."

"I know," I said quickly. "It's just that he knows her. And I---just didn't want him to know---about me and her."

His eyes lost their hardness and he grinned slightly. "Like I said, that's between you and her. She must be one helluva girl, by the way."

I nodded and was taken back as a vision of her swam before my eyes. "She was Frank. She really was. I learned something there though. Don't ever take out a serious girl. I mean one that can think. They'll eat you alive." The waitress came over then with my food. It looked good and was.

"Yeah," Frank laughed. "You're all right. I can tell by the way you inhaled that hamburger."

I gave him the finger, called her back and ordered another one.

"You're right about the serious women too," he said. "They can be hard on a man." We both went silent at that statement. Both of us lost, somewhere in our minds.

The waitress came back then with my other hamburger.

Frank grinned as she turned. "Now you take an old gal like her," he said low, nodding toward her as she walked away, "Big tits, big ass, no brains, all an old boy needs. When you get through, you say, 'thankee ma'am,' pull up your pants and walk off. No sweat, no worry, no problems. Ten days later you won't even remember her name. But a girl like Mary Ann, they're real hard on a guy. The thing to remember too, is not to fall for a girl that lives six hundred miles from you. It's not real logical."

"So, how do you keep from falling for a girl?" I said around a mouthful of hamburger.

He laughed out loud. "Son, don't ask me that. God, don't ask me how to keep from falling for women. If I had that recipe, I'd bottle it and make a bunch of dollars. I will tell you one thing though, that little girl you had back there is one in a million. When she told you it would never be the same, she was right, Dave. You can't go back. You'll know more about that when you get home because you can't even go back there, not ever again. If you saw that girl today, you'd know what I mean. Things have already changed. They changed whenever you took her home to that big house. Now, they've changed even more. It's something I can't tell you, Boy. It's something you just have to learn. It's called growing up and you're the only one that can do that for you."

I just nodded, understanding part of it, mentally thanking whatever Gods there were for Frank. Just having him here, just being able to talk about it to someone helped. And Frank was the only person on the earth that I could talk to about this. He seemed to understand. At least he was worried about me. And he listened to me.

I thought back to Crane. That had been some of the problem there. There was no one to talk to, no one to listen to me. I could've never talked to Dad about things like this. Oh, he would listen alright, I guess. But I never would've brought it up. We just didn't talk about things like sex and women. But everyone needs someone to talk to. I was sure glad I had Frank.

We left the café and walked back to the tent. I was still pretty weak and still felt like I had been torn in half. And I would have given my right arm if I could sit down and talk to Mary Ann right then. Just to see her would have helped. Oh, I would go back alright. I didn't care what anyone said or did. I would go back. A big truck grumbled past just before we went in. He was shifting gears about every hundred feet, trying to build his speed back up. I wondered where he was going.

Gus came walking in the tent about an hour later with a case of beer under his arm, hollering, "howdy," to everyone. I was glad to see the beer. Gus himself, I wasn't so glad to see. He kinda rubbed salt into that sore of mine.

"I see you made it back," he said to me. "The way you left Cloud Chief, I wasn't sure you would. You must have been hitting a hundred before you got out of sight."

"Yeah," I said. " I made a pretty quick trip."

"He came in here so drunk we was scared he was going to die on us." George said. "This is the first time he's been out of bed since he got home. Had us all worried."

Gus reached in the beer case, pulling out four. He opened them and passed them around, looking at me surprised. "We didn't drink all that much," he said.

"I found Frank's stash in the pickup."

"Well, I was just wondering. You was all right when you pulled out. Oh, by the way, Mary Ann called that morning, real early, about six or so. She wanted to talk to you. She sounded like she'd been crying. I told her you had already left, and then she said something funny."

"What was it!" I almost yelled.

He shook his head and looked at me strangely. "She said, ' *tell Dave, I meant it when I said I lied'*. Now, what the hell does that mean?"

I felt something swell inside me. She'd meant it when she lied. She could've been happy with me in a shack. She just wanted me, not her big mansion house, just me.

I noticed Frank looking at me, concern written all over his face. I thought about what he'd said about not being able to go back I thought about the mansion house and I felt the swelling deflate. I'd have to think on it, think hard on it, but now, I knew I would go back.

"What did she mean Dave?" Gus asked again.

"It's just a joke," I said. "Just a private joke. You wouldn't understand." I took a long pull out of my beer and lay back on my cot, hearing them talk, but not listening. I was lost in my mind, thinking about a dark-haired, girl with eyes a man could drown in. A girl who said she'd lied to me.

CHAPTER 21

W e got to the field about nine-thirty the next morning. Frank wasn't
sure we could start but we came out anyway, just to check. Now,
Frank, Bob and Dougal were walking over the field. The rest of us were
sitting in the shade of a combine.

"And then," Gus was saying to George. "After we was there, drinking
all day, this old boy walks over and says, *'this here is a Colorado State Police
picnic, and you kids should leave.* Talk about chilling you out! I mean that'll
do it.

Even I had to smile some, remembering back on it. The problem was,
the day had only begun there. And I had to remember the rest of it too.
Gus didn't. I sure wished he would shut up.

George chuckled. "You talk about something that will chill you out.
You should've been there when Slim picked that old boy's eyeball out of
his head. Now that was something to see."

Gus laughed nervously and agreed, that would be something to see.
I had heard the story so many times now, it didn't bother me anymore.
About then, they walked up and the battle was raging.

Frank was hollering, "Yes!"

Bob was hollering "No!"

And Dougal was grinning.

Finally Frank looked at Dougal. "Risking a load is the only way to
know for sure. But if it's too green still, you'll lose the load."

Dougal stepped back, now the monkey was on his back and the average load of wheat was worth about a hundred dollars. "Why not?" he said. "I'm getting pretty tired of looking at that stuff. Besides, it's costing one of us eighty dollars a day for those boys to sit on their butts. Yeah," he nodded. "Cut a load and send it in. Even if it ain't ready, we'll know by how much and we can tell when to start from that."

Frank climbed on his combine and fired it up. I was tired of listening to Gus so I jumped on the side, riding with him.

"How's it going?" he asked, as he pulled into the wheat.

"Fair. It's getting better." I said over the clattering roar.

"It will, if you give it a chance." He reached under the seat, pulled out a bottle, took a drink, then handed it to me. I took a short one. It burned some but not too bad. I handed him back the bottle and looked back. George and Bob were falling in behind us, their headers buried in the wheat. We made it part way down one side and with the hopper almost full, Frank made a big circle out into the field.

"Hate to do this," he said. "It'll be hard to straighten up later, but we have to know." He circled around then, pulling back into the cut area and deadheading back to the truck. I looked back again, seeing Bob and George do the same thing except they kept their headers buried about half-way into the wheat, cutting on the way back. It wasn't hard to figure out, their combines had smaller headers than Frank's and cut less wheat.

All three hoppers only made about two-thirds of a load but we took it anyway. I drove. Frank went with me. A man came out of the doghouse when I pulled onto the scales. "Who you got?" he asked.

"Dougal."

"That's not a very good load," he said dubiously.

Frank got out and said, "it's a test load. We're not sure if it's dry enough yet."

"Okay." The man stepped back in the doghouse. He came back with a long, tube-like affair, sharp pointed on one end, a large, knob-handle on the other. Now, I got out to watch. He jammed the tube down into the wheat, turned the knob back and forth a couple of times, and took it inside the doghouse. He pulled the handle off the end of the tube and poured the wheat into a measuring cup. He raked off the excess, leaving exactly a cup full, which he sat on a small scale. I looked closer at the tube. It had several openings in it, each about four inches by two inches. Each had a little recessed door.

Okay, I thought, when he turns the handle, it opens the doors, catching the wheat at several levels in the truck bed. It was a pretty good idea. No one could bury a load of wet or green wheat that way.

He set the scales carefully, then checked a chart on the wall and turned around saying, "boy's she's still pretty green, but it'll pass. Go on and dump. I got your weight already."

Frank grinned, I hollered, "alright!" Ordinarily I would have been satisfied to draw my twenty dollars a day for nothing, but as it was, I was glad to get to work. Sitting around gave me too much time to think and right now, I didn't like to think.

We drove back to the field, happy but concerned. We had fifteen days to cut two thousand acres. Good luck. But we'd damn sure give it a try. We would give it hell. Everyone was happy when we got back.

Dougal looked at Bob with those ice blue eyes of his. He looked at the sun then checked his pocket watch and said, "okay Teemer, you got till noon, July fourteenth."

"Well then," Bob said, glaring back at him. "I guess we better get to cutting wheat boys." And he turned away, walking to his combine.

And the race had started.

I just thought we'd worked in Stratford. Nope, we were just playing games there. About four o'clock Bob gave Gus some money for sandwich material. Gus or I made them and passed them out for the rest to eat on the go. We never stopped moving after the combines had made the first complete circle of the field. Gus or I drove along, keeping up with the rigs, catching on the go when the hoppers filled, waiting for them to fill again.

No dew fell that night and we worked straight through, driving, loading, unloading, driving, loading, driving, unloading. The sun came up and we ate more sandwiches. I found a bottle of whiskey in the truck. We passed it around, sharing, stopping only for fuel and rig service, constantly moving.

About noon Bob pulled out of the wheat, got in his pickup and drove away. He was back in less than an hour and drove around the field to us, calling a halt. We serviced the rigs while he made sandwiches.

"Just grab a bite, a can of beer, an hours sleep, then back at it Boys. We got wheat to cut. We got a deadline to meet, a bet to win."

I pulled into the elevator for the millionth time. The man didn't even ask who I drove for. The whole country knew about the bet now and the odds were against us. The scoop boys had been working since five-thirty that morning, their eyes shining wetly through the caked dirt on their faces. Compared to me, they were clean.

We worked till midnight and Bob called Uncle. We drove to town, had another sandwich, a cold beer, a drink of whiskey, then a blessed four hour's sleep. We didn't clean up. I didn't even undress. I stripped the cot and lay on the bare canvas in my filth.

Frank smiled and mumbled, "don't say you weren't warned."

It was the last thing I heard until Bob came in two minutes later yelling, "let's hit it!" And that man could yell.

I rolled out of bed, took a long drink of whiskey to get started and was ready again. Gus and I had a giant breakfast to keep going on and then, back into the "*Inferno,*" back to hell.

Three days passed, then five, then I lost count. It didn't matter they were all the same and I was numb. Every fiber in my body had been screaming, "rest!" since yesterday, or was that two days ago? I had no idea when I'd slept last or even the last time I had eaten. Driving, loading, driving, unloading, driving, waiting, driving, driving, driving. My hands cramped in a cupped position from hanging onto the steering wheel. Daylight, dark, there's no difference except it was hot during the day, cool at night, light in the day, dark at night. Through it all we frantically worked. Driving, driving, while the field shrank.

"How long we been at it?" I asked, spitting water caught in my mouth from the shower.

"Ten days," someone answered. "Noon today, be ten days."

We had stopped long enough to clean up, change our dirt and salt-stiffened clothes, grab a hot meal, another drink of whiskey and six hours sleep.

I felt like a human again. I felt good.

Ten hours later it was as if it'd never happened, and I had forgotten again. I took another drink of whiskey and drove on. Driving awake, driving asleep. I began to see things in the road, houses, trees, elephants. For a while I believed they were real and stopped only to see them disappear. Then I figured out they didn't exist, that they were all in my mind and drove on. I wondered if I existed or if anyone existed. We all seemed to be shadows, shades of things past.

I could remember a girl. She had dark hair and deep, deep, eyes. A vision of her came to my mind, but I couldn't remember her name. I knew that she was important but I couldn't remember where I had met her. She was a shade too. And I wondered if she was real or just another vision in my brain.

We passed the bottle around again, each taking a long pull. It helped, now I could remember her. Now, I wished I could forget.

We serviced the rigs one at a time. Two would cut while one was stopped, saving time. The all-important goal was growing nearer and nearer. We had to get it done without wasting time but still, we weren't going to make it. There was too much wheat and not enough time. And no matter how hard or long we worked, there was not enough of us.

"What's today?" Someone asked.

"The twelfth," someone answered. "We got till noon, day after tomorrow." I took another drink of whiskey and drove on.

"What time is it now?"

"Noon, the fourteenth---We lost."

We missed it by three loads. Who cares? I do, some, but not much right now. We gave it hell trying. We did better than everyone expected but we didn't make it. We finished the field about two o'clock, loaded the rigs and came in.

It was about four o'clock in the afternoon, and hot, when we reached the tent. I fell on the cot, grime-caked, and stinking and went to sleep, stewing in my own juices. I slept till seven o'clock the next morning. Everyone else had done about the same.

We got up and took a very welcome shower. I changed into my last set of clean clothes and ate, then we just lay around awhile, wondering if it had really happened.

Bob paid us and suddenly I was rich. We had averaged twenty hours a day and my pay minus the eats and drinks, plus the waiting time, came to four hundred sixty-eight dollars. Adding that to what I had left, made over five hundred dollars.

Frank saw me counting it for the third time and I guess he read my mind. "That money will last about as long as a fart in a whirlwind," he said. "So don't even think about what you're thinking."

I glared at him, put my money away and took a drink of whiskey.

But he didn't stop. "Do you like what you're doing?" he hissed. "How you're living? Well, do you?" His voice and whole manner was hard, his eyes, burning blue chips of ice.

"Hell, no," I said. "But there are other jobs."

Now the fury he'd projected changed to pain and concern. "No, Dave, not really. You got no education, Son. You can't get a good job. You can work in a store, or drive a truck and slow starve to death. What the girl said was right. Whether she lied or not, she was right. Love makes a damn small turd when it's all you have to eat." His last words came out hard again.

"My daddy only has an eighth grade education and he done alright." I yelled at him.

"Did he?" Frank yelled back. "Then what the hell are you doing out here, busting your ass when you should be home playing and enjoying life?"

I started to stand up, ready to hit him.

"Dave!" He tensed for the attack. "I ain't running your daddy down but just think back on how his life has been."

I sat back down and relaxed, thinking of the times Dad had been out of work and the work he had to take because he had no education or real training. Mom too for all that matter.

Frank continued. "When your daddy quit school, the eighth grade was as far as most people went. When you graduate high school you'll have gone as far as most kids today, and it will be tough enough to make it on that. Your daddy's living proof."

I hated Frank right then. I knew he was right and I hated him for it. I looked at the whiskey bottle in my hand and took another long drink. It didn't ease the ache in me, but it helped.

Gus came in the tent and began packing his things, watching me oddly. I'd been avoiding him as best I could every since he had gotten back. He didn't know why and I couldn't tell him. I couldn't even talk to him, knowing he was going back there.

Frank looked at Gus and then at me. I took another drink, hoping it would ease the terrible loneliness that was tearing me apart. Gus picked up his things and walked out. I felt sorry for him, not knowing what was wrong, why I couldn't talk to him, why I was acting this way towards him. I really liked Gus. We'd been through a lot together. But he was leaving, going back to where I couldn't, at least not yet.

The car door slammed. The motor started he drove away. I felt my guts wrench and the emptiness grew inside me, driving out all other feelings, even the effects of the whiskey. I took another drink.

"You better go easy on that stuff," Frank said. "We have some traveling to do."

"I can handle it," I snapped.

"Didn't mean to piss you off," he snapped back. His voice was sharp as he stood. "But if you got any business to take care of, get it done. We're leaving in two hours." He walked out.

The emptiness in me suddenly grew sharper, different, as I watched Frank walk to the café. I wanted to go with him. Suddenly, I was tired of it, the moping, all the drinking here lately. Gus was gone, the last link broken. I had nothing now to remind me that she even existed, except me. And I had been doing a bunch of reminding the last couple of days. I remembered what she had said that night, *'This way, I'll have you forever. The way we are now, not hating each other'*.

I took one last pull from the bottle, almost gagging on it. I capped the bottle, threw it on my bunk and ran to catch Frank, falling in step alongside him.

He looked at me and grinned. "What do you say Wheatie?"

"I say, everybody stand up and piss, the world's on fire."

He laughed, reached out and slapped me on the back, and we walked to the café.

We sat in a booth, the day-waitress was on, still crossed-eyed and homely. "You look like a new man," Frank said. "What happened?"

"I reckon I just grew up." I said, "I don't know what happened. Gus left and that kind of done it."

"That quick?"

I shook my head and thought back over it all. "No, I still love her. I guess I always will. And I'm still going back." I looked up at him now. "But I don't know when. It's still not over. It's just better."

"Well, whatever," Frank said. "It's a damn good deal. One drunk in a crew is enough."

"Speaking of drunks, I've noticed you're drinking a lot less now."

He smiled. "I'm glad you noticed and glad you said something. Bob and George have been looking at me like I have two heads. I guess they've been afraid to say anything though."

"After what I've been through, I don't think I'll be afraid of anything anymore." I said forcefully.

"That's good and bad. A man should always be afraid of something."

"Why?"

"It keeps him honest. A man that's not afraid of anything starts getting cocky, and that'll get him hurt."

I shrugged. "I'll have to think on that one a little."

He stood. "Well think on it while we take down that tent. We got some miles to go today." He grinned at me as we paid the cross-eyed girl and walked out.

We took down the tent, folded and loaded it and everything else. George and the new hand, a short, big-nosed, pimpled faced kid with three cavities in his front teeth, named Bill, something-or-another, were nowhere around. "I told them to be here at eleven o'clock," Frank said disgustedly. "Wonder where they are?"

"What time is it now?" I asked.

"It's ten-thirty."

"That might have something to do with it. I've got some business to do, I'll be back at noon or before."

"Okay Son, " Frank said. "We won't leave without you."

"Well, I sure hope not." I said walking away.

I went to the bank an bought a money order for four hundred. That left me a hundred and twenty-five, more than enough, even though I knew how fast it went now. I put the money order in my billfold, figuring to write to Mom and Dad tonight. I might just write to Gayle, I thought. I hadn't really thought much about her in the past couple of days. I felt the scab lift as a vision of Mary Ann flooded through my brain and I remembered why I hadn't thought of Gayle.

I pushed Mary Ann back deeper in my mind, which was hard, but not as hard as it had been and I walked back. They were all there, ready to leave. We all loaded up and drove out the field where we'd left the trucks.

Dougal came out as we pulled up. "Well," he said." "See you boys next year and you done a damn good job. I haven't ever seen that field cut that fast. Made me think there for a while I had made a bad bet. But that's something I rarely do."

Bob was mad but he didn't show it. "Yeah, Dougal, we'll see you next year," he boomed out and drove away.

We all fell in behind him, me, in a truck this time. Frank said he didn't really trust the new kid. Bob had hired him and there wasn't much to pick from, which was pretty obvious. The top-heavy weight of the combine seemed weird for a while and the wind blew me around a little more than with just a truck but, I knew now, I could handle it and it didn't bother me. Like I had told Frank, I wasn't afraid of much anymore. By the time we reached the highway it was as if I'd been driving one all of my life.

We headed north again, straight up highway 385, with the wind at our back. It seemed as if we were one of the first to be leaving and everywhere I looked there was cutting going on causing the wind to be laden with dust and chaff, being blown north along with us. I looked back in my rear-view-mirrors at the elevator back at Cheyenne Wells, disappearing down into the prairie and a great sense of loss and loneliness came over me. I knew I was leaving a part of me there that I wasn't sure I'd ever get back. But then I thought, I hadn't left it in Cheyenne Wells. I'd left it a hundred or so miles west of there.

Now the vision of Mary Ann came flooding out of where I had tucked it away. And for the first time I wondered, really wondered, if I would ever see her again. And for the first time, I wasn't positive I would.

*   *   *

The trip to Holyoke took almost two hours of uneventful driving. The field was about two miles west of the highway this time. We pulled in and began the off-loading while Bob, Frank and a brick-faced farmer named Reynolds, checked the field. This wasn't one of the regular fields Bob and Frank contracted. Reynolds knew Dougal and had called, asking for a contractor. Bob had taken the field because it was so small, only three hundred acres.

But something was wrong. The wheat was thin and short, past ready and beginning to fall from the heads as they waved in the wind. Even I knew this field should have been cut two weeks ago. And, with a now practiced eye, I could see why it hadn't been. The land was terrible, rocky and not level.

George noticed it too and I heard him say, "man, this one is going to be a ring-tailed catiwampous to cut."

I started to say something but the yelling from the field stopped me. I couldn't make out the words but Frank's face looked like the wrath of God as they came walking back to the rigs. Bob's jaw was locked, telling me his feelings had been hurt. Reynolds looked like a whipped pup as he said, "but you have to start today, right now!"

Frank whirled, sticking a finger in Reynolds's face and yelled, "you say one more word and what we'll do is load up and leave."

"Boys," George hissed. "Let's hold up. We may not be unloading here after all." We all turned to watch.

"Now, Frank," Bob said glumly.

"Now Frank's ass!" Frank yelled, picking up a rock the size of his fist and throwing it into the wheat. "Why the hell did you take a field sight unseen anyway. Damn Bob, what was you thinking?"

"You have to start today," Reynolds said. "I'll lose fifty bushels by tomorrow."

"You'll lose fifty bushels if we start today or not," Frank said. "Those boys are tired, the equipment needs servicing and I'll be damned if we start without doing it."

He looked back over the field. "I've never seen a field this bad. We'll be lucky if we don't ruin some equipment here." He shook his head looking at Reynolds, "I don't see how you got it planted in the first place."

Reynolds started to say something but Frank cut him off with a glare. "Mister, you're pushing me. I told you already I can load up and leave and I damn sure will if you don't get the hell out of here. Now, we'll cut your wheat just because Bob said we'd cut your wheat, but if you keep pushing me--"

Reynolds's face turned even redder. The muscles on his neck stood out as he started raising his finger to Frank's face but then he turned away, stomping away to his pickup.

"That was uncalled for Frank," Bob said in a normal tone.

"Bob, I don't want to hear it." Frank growled. "You know better than to pull something like this."

"Yeah, you're right, but you was wrong to treat him like that. He's got money tied up in this field and he said he couldn't get anyone else to cut it."

"I don't doubt that a bit," Frank said. "And you yourself would've told him to shove it up his nose if you'd have looked at it first. Hell, we got money tied up in those rigs," he turned pointing, seeing all of us watching. "You guys on vacation?" he yelled. "Get them rigs unloaded and start servicing them and the trucks. Do it all, lube and oil and get them fueled.

We laughed as we went back to work.

Bob nodded, "We got a week to cut it, Frank. We can do it."

Frank turned back to Bob. "It will take a week to cut it if we're lucky and don't wreck a rig." He shook his head, "Just go on to town and find us a place to camp and if you see Reynolds, tell him to stay away from me."

Bob walked away as we unloaded the remaining combine. I showed Bill where the spare oil and grease-guns were kept and we started on the trucks as Frank and George worked on the combines. Two hours later when every piece of working equipment we had was totally serviced and ready to start at first light, we loaded in Frank's pickup and drove back to town. Frank was grinning again.

We located Bob's pickup and trailer at a café. He was sitting glumly drinking coffee when we went in. "What's the problem now?" Frank said immediately as we sat down.

Bob sort of grinned and cleared his throat. "It seems like they have an ordinance against camping in town."

Frank slapped the table with the flat of his hand. "Sure they do. It cuts into the motel business. Well, to hell with them. We'll camp in the damn field."

Nobody said anything but I wondered how we were going to eat and clean up. The waitress came over about then grinning while she chewed a wad of gum. "You boys going to eat?" she said.

"Yeah," Frank said, looking at all of us. "Yeah, let's eat then we'll go back to the field and set up." He had calmed down a little, making me feel some better too. I'd seen this side of him before and it always scared me a little.

After we ate, we drove around town until we located the elevator we were to dump. Then we found a welding shop that had fifty-five gallon drums for sale. Frank was laughing as he bought three and had one of them cut in half, long-wise.

"There's your bath tubs for the duration, boys," he said. "Now just as soon as we get away from here we can quit using them."

His laugh almost made my neck hair rise and no one had much to say as we cleaned and filled the other two barrels with water. He made one more stop at the liquor store before we headed to the field. I hated to see him do that but I kept my mouth shut.

The tent went up with no problems and in about a half-hour, I was home again, sitting on my cot. Frank was lying on his and had the biggest part of a pint of whiskey down but he was in a whole lot better mood. He took another gurgling drink and handed me the bottle. "Here you go, Wheatie."

I took a short drink and gave it back. Frank sat up grinning. "I guess I made a pretty good ass of myself today."

"You seemed like you were pretty excited."

"That Reynolds almost got his ass kicked. Told me I was going to start cutting today and he wanted the field finished by tomorrow night. Nobody tells me what I'm going to do. That's, by God, why I own my own combine." He grinned then his face went serious. "I wasn't kidding when I told Bob we'd be lucky to cut this mess in a week, not kidding at all, and that bastard said he wanted it cut---"

Just then Bob came in the tent booming, "Frank, back there---"

"Damn, Bob, quit yelling. I can hear you."

"I wasn't yelling," Bob said in a mock whisper, then back up to full volume. "Like I said, I called Doris today when I was in town. You're suppose to call your wife. Now it's nothing serious but you need to call as soon as you can."

"Nothing serious but call as soon as I can," Frank's face lost all expression as he repeated in a hollow sounding voice.

A sudden fear washed over me. I'd been gone over a month now and although I knew I was alright, I just realized, I knew nothing of the situation at home. Anything could have gone bad and they had no idea where I was.

Frank yelled, "dammit Bob, how in hell could you forget something like that? I mean, how many times has Debbie called me in the last four years?" He began pulling on his cowboy boots. "Hell yes, it's serious."

"Well, I don't know how I forgot," Bob mumbled apologetically. "But Doris said it wasn't serious. That's all I know."

Frank looked at me sharply. I said, "I'll go with you, if you don't mind."

He gave a short nod, "glad to have you."

And as we walked out, I heard Bob mumble, "I'm sorry, Frank."

Frank didn't say anything until we got in the pickup, then all he said was, "Man, this has been a bitch of a day."

The rest of the trip was made in silence. I had a thousand crazy thoughts going through my head and I knew he did too. He only drove a steady forty-five instead of his usual eighty or ninety, causing me to be a total nervous wreck by the time we reached town. I wanted to tell him to go faster but looking at his taut jaw, and a muscle jumping in his neck, made me keep silent.

When we finally pulled up to the two phone booths outside a grocery store, Frank grinned, "It's probably nothing. I haven't talked to her since I left and she's probably just lonesome." His voice was strained though, as if it was himself he was trying to convince.

At least I knew how I felt and I'd been saying the same thing to myself all the way to town but I touched his shoulder. "Sure, Frank, that's probably it." We walked to the phone booths.

The light came on when I shut the door, making me feel naked and exposed against the darkness of the night. I didn't have much change, so I called the operator and reversed the charges. The whirring clicks seemed to take forever, then I could hear a buzzing that told me the other phone was ringing. It rang five times before Sara's voice answered calmly then verged on panic when she told the operator she would accept the charges.

I was trembling when the operator gave me the go ahead. "Sara, this is Dave," I could hear my voice shaking.

"Dave, are you alright?" Her normal husky tone was shrill.

"Yeah, I'm fine." Then I almost choked. "How's Mom and Dad?"

"They're fine, Dave. Your mom's right here. You say you're alright?"

"Yeah, Sara, I'm fine. I just got worried about Mom---"

"You got worried?" she yelled shakily. "You little shit! You scared the hell out of me. Why the hell haven't you called or written, dammit."

I had to laugh. I could see her just then, her freckles standing out firey, reddish-brown, her eyes snapping like they always did when she was mad or excited.

"I knew I was alright, I just got worried about you," I said through my laughter.

"Well I didn't know you were alright, you little twerp," she said and I could see her smile. "Now, here's your mom."

"Davie," Mom said worriedly, "Are you alright?"

"Yeah, Mom, I'm fine. How's everyone else?"

"Oh, we're all okay. We've been worried sick about you though. Where are you?"

"I'm up in Colorado. We're camped outside a town called Holyoke."

"When are you coming home?"

"I'm not sure, probably another month or so. I'll be back in time for school for sure."

"Well just see that you do, young man. Have you been working? Do you need some money or anything?"

"No, Mom, I don't need anything. I'll be sending some more money home before long. Use it if you need it. Is Dad alright?"

"He's fine, but you could write or call a little more often. We've been worried."

"I'm sorry, Mom. I'll try to do better but I haven't had much time."

"It doesn't take much time to write a postcard, Davie. You do better from now on."

"I'll try, Mom. By the way, did Rocky get home alright?'

"Yes, he came in the day after you left. He had a black eye and said someone had beaten him up on the road."

I laughed, "that's too bad but I'm glad he got home alright."

"Well, we're running up a bill here and Sara wants to say something, so be careful and come home for school."

"I will, Mom. Tell everyone I'm alright and I'll see you in about a month."

"Okay, Davie. Here's Sara."

"Dave," Sara's voice was so low and gentle I could smell her and I felt a warmness spread over me. "You be careful, you little butt-hole, and if you're not better about writing or calling, I'll salt your hide when you get back."

I laughed, "I miss you too, Sara, but I gotta go. I'll see you in about a month."

"Dave," her voice dropped to a husky, almost whisper, "Please be careful," then the phone went dead. I looked at the receiver a second, feeling more lonesome and homesick than ever. Then I hung it up and walked back to the pickup. It was only then that a thought hit me. I hadn't even asked about Gayle. I'll write to her tonight, I thought. Really, I'll sit down and write to her.

Frank stayed on the phone almost another half-hour before he started back to the pickup. His face was drained of color and I remembered why we had come to town. He jerked the door open and dug under the seat, and something told me I'd better be careful. He found his bottle and took a gurgling drink then glared at me.

Not wanting to, I said, "everything okay at home?"

He glared at me even harder and drove away squalling the tires. He drove in silence to a bar just outside of town, stuffed the bottle inside his shirt and we went inside. Frank sat at a table with his back to the wall. I sat beside him so I could see the door.

The bar was nice and well kept. Eight men and three women were sitting at various tables and booths. Two more women sat at the bar. Johnny Horton blared, *The Tennessee Stud,* from the jukebox. The waitress, a trim brunette in boots and blue jeans, came to our table. Frank gave her a look that would freeze fire then said, "two beers."

She looked at me closely and said, "how about a beer and a Coke?"

Frank grinned slightly and nodded.

She smiled and walked away singing along with the jukebox.

I looked at Frank but he was staring vacantly at the table, gone somewhere in his mind. The girl brought the beer and Coke and went swinging away, still singing. He drank half his beer in a gulp then filled the bottle with whiskey. I felt a chill creep up my back as I watched him tear at the label on the beer bottle. He reminded me of the guy he'd pointed out to me back in Guymon, poised, coiled and dangerous, as if he could explode at any second.

Frank finished that boiler-maker and ordered another beer before he said anything. When he did speak, his voice sounded lost, low and full of pain. "This has been one bitch of a day, Dave." He looked at me real hard, "I mean, this has been a son-of-a- bitch of a day."

"Anything wrong at home, Frank?" I said feeling foolish for asking.

He nodded, "Yeah---But it's nothing I can control, so I reckon it's nothing I have to worry about."

I shook my head, wondering what he meant but I didn't ask. I'd seen people that looked like him before. A man would be a fool to bug Frank right now. Besides, if he wanted me to know, he'd tell me. *I Fall to Pieces*, by Patsy Cline came on the jukebox, a woman laughed and another sang along. A man and woman got up to dance. A crash came from the pool table as a man broke rack. Frank silently tore the label from the beer bottle. Finally, I couldn't stand it any more. "You going to have to go back, Frank?"

He shook his head. "Too late for that, Dave," then finished his beer in a gulp and ordered another round.

The same pretty waitress brought our drinks. I paid her. She smiled at Frank, saying, "you're gonna bust that bottle if you stare at it any harder."

When he didn't even look up, she shrugged and walked away singing, *Hello Mary Lou*, along with Ricky Nelson. A few minutes later she brought me my change and said, "what's wrong with Stone Face here?"

"Bad news from home," I said.

He face changed from mocking laughter to deep concern, "oh, well, I'm sorry I butted in, Mister," she touched his shoulder.

He looked up and said, "it ain't your fault, Babe, just go away now."

She frowned, then nodded, "sure, Bud, but I am sorry," and walked away.

He drank that beer and one more, finishing the whiskey, before we started for the door. The trim brunette stopped us just as we were walking out. "Look," she said to Frank, "I don't know what's wrong, but if you need some help. Well, I get off at midnight." She smiled then but her eyes were still full of concern.

He nodded and grinned slightly, "I appreciate it, Ma'am, but not tonight."

She smiled again, "I'll be here. I'm always here. My name's Linda."

He nodded, "I'm Frank and this here's Dave," and we walked out.

"How about that Wheatie," he said as we got in the pickup. "If I'd tried to put the make on that old gal, she would've called the law," he laughed. "And I'll bet she ain't been turned down a half-dozen times in her life.

Come to think of it, I haven't turned down a half-dozen in my life and none that looked anywhere near as good as her. I reckon all women got a little mother in them though." He laughed again, but it sounded like breaking glass.

"I kinda feel the same as her, Frank," I said. "If there's anything I can do."

He shook his head, "Dave, I don't think there's anything anyone can do about this. I appreciate the offer but I have to fight this bear alone." He went silent after that and stayed that way the whole time we drove back.

He made no move to get out of the pickup when we reached the tent so I just sat there with him, looking at the stars. A coyote hollered from a distance and another one answered him. I heard the dying shriek of a small animal from the field. The dry rustle of the wind through the wheat covered the death throes, then all was quiet again.

Frank's voice was startling loud in the silence although he spoke softly. "My daddy was a wheat farmer. He told me once that sometimes on quiet nights, he could hear the wheat grow. Sometimes he could hear it talk, even sing." Frank smiled in the dark. "I thought he was crazy then, but sometimes now I can hear it. Sometimes like tonight."

He went silent again and I listened as the wind played the myriad of dry stalks against each other in a rasping rustle that had as an underscore, a tinkling, almost musical sound. The coyote yapped again and was followed by a crescendo of yapping howls that drowned out the sound. A mosquito droned past my ear, then a whippoorwill called its lonely song. Frank moved slightly, then said low, "why don't you go on to bed, Dave."

"No," I said, "I'll stay out here with you."

He shook his head and said in a voice as old as time, "Dave, I'd rather be alone, really, go on to bed now. We got a bad day tomorrow."

There was nothing else I could do but go. My mind was in a turmoil as I undressed and lay down. Frank had said even he couldn't control whatever had happened and it was too late to go home, so I figured it was trouble with his ranch. At least that was the only plausible answer I could come up with. Then my mind drifted to home, but then, as it had in the more recent past, it drifted to Cloud Chief. Although it had been almost three weeks since the night with Mary Ann, each separate detail of that night was etched in my brain, the darkness of her hair, the deepness of her eyes. How she smelled and how she smiled. But then, as always, I saw her disappear into that mansion house and the crushing disillusionment washed over me, making me feel as if I had somehow been used.

But then I remembered how she looked when she said she loved me and how she felt in my arms. And I remembered she had told Gus, to tell me she lied. A warm feeling came over me and I smiled in the dark, then drifted off to sleep.

CHAPTER 22

Frank was sitting on his bunk the next morning when Bob hollered in the tent. I didn't know if he had ever gone to bed. He didn't look much different than he did yesterday, a little gray in the face maybe, maybe a little more quiet than usual. At least the hard stare was gone from his eyes but it had taken with it some of the light that had been there. The broken-glass laugh was the same though. I heard it when Bob asked him how things were at home, just before we loaded up to go for breakfast.

No one had much to say on the way in, or as we ate. When we got back to the field Frank climbed on his combine and hollered, "let's cut wheat," then drove away in a clattering roar, slowing to a snail's pace as he entered the wheat.

George and Bob followed him, the combines lurching and bouncing over the rocks and holes. Bill and I began checking out the trucks then we sat in the shade of one and waited. The sun had just barely cleared the horizon but it was already hot.

The field was a mile long and a half-mile wide which made it three miles around so I waited about a half-hour before starting after the combines. The ground was rougher than I had imagined. Even at ten miles an hour I was jolted and thrown around in the truck cab. George was stopped, working on his header, when I caught up with him and stopped to see if I could help.

"I just picked up a rock," he yelled through the window. "Had to stop to clean out the header. Go on and unload, Frank. I think he's ready."

I waved and drove on. Frank and Bob both were stopped. Frank had backed up enough for me to get under his spout and began unloading as soon as I was in position. I climbed out and on the combine.

"What's wrong with George?" He yelled above the clatter.

"He said he picked up a rock and had to stop."

Frank said, "Yeah, that's going to be a problem as short as this stuff is."

"How are you feeling today?" I asked, hoping maybe he would tell me what was wrong.

He shook his head, "I'm okay. Don't worry about it." The unloading auger began rattling. He lifted the lever, waved, I jumped to the ground and he drove away. I pulled the truck over closer to the wheat, waiting for Bob. When he got close, I made the catch on-the-go signal but he waved me off with the stop signal. I pulled alongside the truck and began unloading.

He waved me over and I climbed onto his combine. "It's too dangerous to catch on the go here," he boomed out.

I just nodded. There was no need to try to talk to Bob over the noise.

George had caught us by the time Bob had unloaded but his hopper still didn't make a load so I drove back to where we had started. Frank was just making the last turn when I stopped where he could unload. Bill had gone to sleep but that was alright. He didn't seem too bright. The noise from Frank's approaching combine woke him up and he walked over to me grinning.

"Man, what a dream I was having just then," he said with a nasal drawl. "I just had this old gal naked and was fixing to throw the meat to her.

I just nodded. "Sounds like a dream," I said. Somehow I couldn't see him with a girl, what with the cavities and pimples.

"Yeah" Bill said. "She was good-looking and had tits out to here," he waved his hands a foot in front of his chest.

"Yeah, okay. It sounds more like a dream all the time," I said and walked around the truck. Frank had started to unload so I climbed on the combine.

He looked out over the field. "Dave, this sucker's worse than I thought at first. I hit a rock back there that almost threw me off the rig. That's too bad, because I was gonna show you how to operate this thing." He shrugged, "Well, maybe up in Nebraska. I know that field."

The unloading auger started to rattle, he shut it off. "Take it on in to the elevator." I jumped to the ground and pulled away, noticing Bill pull into place to unload Bob.

The trip to the elevator was short and there was no line so I got back to the field even before Bill had half-loaded. This is going to be one long day, I thought, so I stopped by the tent and got my writing gear. It was something to do to pass the time and keep me from having to listen to Bill. I wrote a short letter to my brother back in Oklahoma and one to my youngest sister in California. Then I wrote one to Mom and Dad and enclosed the money order I had bought. I got real excited about that. Now I had almost six hundred dollars at home, more than enough for a really nice car and clothes for school. I even started a letter to Gayle, but after a while I realized it wasn't Gayle I was writing too. My mind was still in Colorado. Besides, it was my turn to load.

I mailed the letters I'd finished on my next trip to the elevator and never got back to the one I didn't finish. The rest of the day passed in a quiet blur. Bill took another nap. It was still light when we quit but Bob said, "it was getting too dark to dodge the rocks."

George agreed with him but Frank shook his head saying, "I don't think we cut fifty, maybe sixty, acres today, Bob."

"I know," Bob boomed, "And you don't have to remind me that it's my fault. I done enough of that today myself, every time I had to clean the rocks out of my header."

Frank didn't say anything back though. Enough had been said already. But he did smile when we got back to the tent and Bob stripped to take a bath in one of those half-barrels. I almost cracked up. There was more Bob than there was barrel and almost no water at all. But he managed. Then we all took our turn. The water was warm from the sun and, other than being uncomfortable sitting in the barrel and embarrassing because I could be seen for a mile, it wasn't too bad.

After that, we drove to town to eat and came straight back to the tent. Everyone was tired except Bill, but he'd slept most of the day. He talked all the way to town and while we ate, then all the way back, always about girls. They were all good-looking and all of them had tits out to here, and he described sexual acts I didn't even know existed. I hadn't heard anyone lie like him since the last time I saw Rocky. It was funny and sad at the same time. It was almost as if he was trying to prove something to us, or maybe to himself.

After a while though, when he hadn't stopped and we were trying to go to sleep, I didn't care what he was trying to prove. Neither did Frank. He looked at Bill disgustedly and said, "why don't you shut up a while. Everyone's tired of listening to you."

Bill looked shocked and snapped back, "What do you mean?"

Frank said, "I mean I'm tired of listening to you. In the past hour I've heard you tell of having sex with seven different women." His eyes narrowed, "Bud, I seriously doubt that."

"You calling me a liar!" Bill shouted, half-standing.

George smiled, "Well if he ain't, then I am." And he stood up, a full six inches taller and fifty pounds heavier than Bill.

A look of fear crossed Bill's face. "This here's between me and him," he said to George, pointing at Frank

George just smiled. "Bill, I'm giving you a break. Ole Frank there is just about seven-eight's bad and you was fixing to get yourself into some real trouble. Now a smart fellow would sit down and shut up 'cause like Frank said, we're all about sick of your mouth."

Bill eyed George carefully. "I ain't afraid of you nor him."

Frank smiled, "no one said you were afraid, Bill. It's just time to be quiet awhile." His tone was like cracked ice.

Bill nodded, "just so's you know I ain't afraid," he sat on his bunk.

George turned the lantern out.

I smiled in the dark, it had been close, real close.

The next thing I knew Bob hollered, "y'all gonna sleep all day?" And we were at it again. I stayed away from Bill as much as I could. He was shorter than me but heavier, and about nineteen or twenty years old. Somehow

I felt he would have something to say about last night, something about Frank or George, and I didn't want to hear it. I liked both of them.

We were just over half through when we quit the third night and no one was talking to anyone. It seemed as if the rocks and holes of the field were winning, beating all of us down. Bob stopped at a store and bought two cases of beer on the way back from supper and passed them around saying. "Boys, I want you to know that I've learned my lesson here." He looked at Frank and raised his beer. "I'll not ever say I'll cut a field again without looking at it first. And if I do, I hope someone feeds me half my combine."

Frank just nodded. "We'll finish up day after tomorrow and then it'll be done. Anyone can make a mistake and I got no hard feelings."

George nodded, "We'll get her cut, Bob."

I didn't feel like it was my place to say anything.

Bill was quiet too, for once. I think the trouble last night had scared him some. At least he'd been better since then, but after his fifth beer he started again. "I never will forget one old gal I screwed," he laughed. "I was laying up in bed, just throwing the meat to her when the phone rang." He stopped to take a drink. "It turned out to be her husband. He was working out of town."

Frank's head came up like it was spring-loaded and the light in his eyes went out. I started to say something but Bill never stopped, "I didn't even slow down just kept throwing the old pole to her while she was talking to---"

Frank came off his bunk with the speed of a shadow and kicked Bill in the face. Bill fell backwards, turning his cot over on top of him, and I think that's the only thing that saved his life. Frank grabbed at the cot and suddenly that terrible knife of his clacked open in his right hand. I stood up and stepped forward, but before I could yell, George grabbed me, and threw me out of the tent, just as Bob grabbed Frank from behind, pinning both of his arms to his sides.

"Frank!" Bob yelled and picked him up. Frank was fighting hard to get away but Bob squeezed him tight and yelled, "Frank!" again while Frank kicked at George. George grabbed his foot, holding it high and tight while Bob squeezed him even tighter. The knife fell to the floor and as fast as it started, it was over.

Frank went limp, George let go of his foot and Bob lowered him gently to the ground. Frank stumbled to his cot and sat down, holding his head in his hands, breathing raspingly. I picked up his knife and put it in my pocket. Bob watched Frank while George dug Bill out from under the cot. The side of his head was swollen and red and he was out cold.

"Must have turned his head just in time," George said. "lucky, if Frank had hit him square in the face that kick would have done some real damage,"

Frank was still calm so I went to the bath barrel and wet the towel we'd left there. Bill was just coming around when I got back, but he was real quiet. The look in his eyes was of total fear as he watched Frank like a man would a rattlesnake.

Frank finally looked at Bill, "I'm sorry, Kid. I kinda flew off the handle there for a minute."

Bill just nodded, still watching him.

Frank looked at all of us. "That call home I had to make the other day. My wife is divorcing me." He stopped for a second. "When Bill there said what he did about---another man's wife. I guess I went a little crazy." He stood, "but I'm alright now. And Bill, I'm sorry I kicked you. I haven't ever hit a kid in my life." Then he walked out into the night. A second later his pickup started and he was gone before I could catch him.

I walked back in the tent feeling more afraid for Frank than anything. Bill was still holding the wet towel gently to his face. He started to say something but I stopped him. "Bill, if you have anything bad to say about Frank, either don't---or stand up."

He shook his head. All the bluster and brag was gone from him. "All I was gonna say was I'm sorry. I didn't know that about his wife or I wouldn't have said what I did."

I sat back down on my bunk, "no one knew about his wife Bill, but you just shouldn't go on telling stuff like you have been. Not many people appreciate that kind of talk."

"Dave's right," Bob boomed out. "If I hadn't needed the help so bad, I would've sent you down the road the first day."

Bill nodded and Bob looked at me. "Dave, you think Frank is going to be alright?"

I shrugged my shoulders, "I don't know. He hasn't been himself since he made that call."

Bob nodded, "I asked him about that call two or three times. He'd just laugh."

"Me too," George said. "He'd just say things is fine, and go on."

"Well," Bob boomed. "He's a man grown, and I reckon he can handle his own affairs. I, for one, am going to bed. We got a long day tomorrow." He nodded and walked out.

George said, "How's your head Bill?"

Bill nodded, then grimaced. "I reckon it'll be alright. I got one helluva headache though."

George took the towel away. A vivid red mark stood out against the mottled bruise that was forming. "Don't seem to be anything broken. But it's going to be sore as thunder tomorrow. You're just mighty lucky you turned your head. If you hadn't, you might not have one now."

Bill moaned softly. "I never saw it coming. I guess I turned to look at someone. Man! He's fast."

George smiled. "I tried to tell you the other night. Frank ain't no one to mess with---Well, keep that towel on there the rest of the night. It'll help, but not much. I'm going to bed." He sat on his bunk and began undressing.

After a second Bill said. "You don't reckon he's still mad at me do you?" His voice trembled.

"No," George said calmly. "You're still alive. He ain't mad at you no more." He stretched out on his bunk and was snoring in seconds.

I shook my head, wishing I could go to sleep like that. Instead, I went outside. The night was clear and warm. The stars bright but fading in the rising moon. The wind played gently but the wheat was too far away for me to hear it sing. Even the whippoorwills had gone with the wheat. A coyote yapped some distance away and was answered by two more that were closer. I thought about going back in the tent, but there was no way I could sleep without knowing about Frank. So I climbed up on one of the trucks to wait.

I guess I went to sleep in spite of myself because the next thing I knew

Frank was pulling up beside the truck. I climbed down and got in the pickup with him. He smelled of whiskey and a really nice perfume and he grinned at me. "What are you doing still up Wheatie? We got a bitch of a day tomorrow. Excuse me, today."

"Couldn't sleep I guess."

He laughed. "You looked like you were doing a pretty good job when I pulled up."

"I hadn't planned on it though." I said. "By the way, Bill's okay."

"That's good. I'm sorry about that but it just hit me wrong. I guess I been acting pretty strange the last couple of days."

I heard the bottle gurgle. "We've all been worried. All of us except Bill. But then, he don't know you."

"I guess he does now."

"No, Frank," I said. "He still don't. Not like the rest of us. You feeling better now?"

He moved in the dark, the shadows hiding his face. "I don't know Dave. I'm really not sure." He laughed, "I may be some better, but I wonder. I went back to that bar. Remember the little waitress?"

"Linda? The good looking one?"

He grinned and nodded, "yeah. I took her home and wound up in bed with her."

"Here we go again, Bill."

He lightly punched me on the shoulder. "No, not quite. You don't get all the vulgar details. Besides, it wasn't all that good."

"It sure looked good."

"Oh, don't get me wrong. She was prime meat. It's just that, well, it was almost as if I wasn't there with her." He moved again and now the moonlight was on his face and I could see him frown. "And I guess, the worse part was that she noticed it too." He shook his head slowly. "She kept asking me where I was. And the hell of it is, I don't know."

Frank took a drink and offered me the bottle but I passed. Then he said. "I don't know why I'm letting this divorce get to me so. I knew it was just a matter of time. I've known that for some time, years even, but I still can't help feeling---I'm not sure how I feel. Part of me is mad. But part of me is saying, 'what the hell,' and other part of me is sad, maybe even hurt."

I didn't know what to say, what to tell him, how to help him, so I just sat there in silence.

"I guess," he continued, "I'm disappointed more than anything. It all seemed so right when we got married. But now that I look back on it, I'm surprised it's lasted this long." He held up the bottle. "And this is the only reason and I got no one to blame but me. Oh, Korea helped, the rodeo helped, and the harvest helped. But Dave, when I boil it all down, I got no one but me and the bottle to blame. And it's like I told you before, you can't go back. No one can." He opened the door. "Let's get to bed Boy. We got wheat to cut tomorrow."

I thought about it as we walked to the tent. I didn't know what or who to blame but Frank was my friend, more than my friend, and he was hurt bad. So I could sure blame the one that hurt him, whether he did or not.

After I lay down my thoughts turned back to Cloud Chief and Mary Ann. And I remembered the used feeling I'd had before. And I wondered if I had been used. I didn't think so. She'd said she loved me, but words are easy to say. But then, she'd called Gus the next day. My mind whirled over this and I could feel myself sinking into a depression fit. Then I realized I'd never really know for sure and anger replaced the depression. The more I thought about it, the madder I got until it was easy to hate her for what I thought she'd done.

CHAPTER 23

Frank seemed better the next morning but the gray in his face and the haunted look in his eyes hadn't completely left. Bill's face was purple and black and his eye was swollen shut. But he said he felt alright. Frank offered to stop at the little clinic we passed on the way to the café, but Bill said he would be all right so we went on.

Reynolds was waiting at the field when we got there and I could see Frank's jaw lock up as he got out of the pickup. He started toward Reynolds, but Bob stopped him saying, "it's my turn now Frank."

Frank nodded and waved all of us to the rigs, so I don't know what was said. But Reynolds didn't stay long.

We started to work on the shrunken field and when we quit that night, Frank said, "boy's I don't believe we'll have any trouble finishing up tomorrow. And if we really get after it, maybe as soon as noon."

I felt like cheering but I was too tired to do anything except eat and sleep. And everything looked a lot better the next day. Some of the swelling had gone out of Bill's face and Frank actually grinned as we started to work.

"This is it, Wheatie," Frank said later while he was unloading. "The last of this mess. And the last night in Holyoke." He laughed, "reckon I might go back to that bar and make a night of it tonight."

"Sounds like a helluva deal to me." I said.

He laughed again and said, "you want to go with me? She might have a little sister or a friend?"

I felt a stab in my guts, remembering my one and only blind date. "No, I don't think so. We have a long way to drive tomorrow and I'd just as soon do it sober."

Frank grinned his old grin, "damn pansy," he laughed. "Ain't I taught you nothing?" Then he clattered away.

He hadn't gone two hundred yards when I saw his combine lurch hard to one side. Bob was coming so Frank pulled out of the wheat to let him pass. I waved the unload signal to Bob, but he waved me off. So I drove past him to help Frank.

"Didn't see that damn hole there," Frank said disgustedly. Then yelled, "why me, Lord? Why am I ruining a twenty thousand dollar piece of equipment on a pile of rock?"

I laughed and knelt beside him, digging the dirt and rock out of the header with my hands. We got most of it out, and I climbed on the rig to start the header so Frank could check it. Bob waved as he passed. I waved back, pushed the header in gear and Frank started towards the ladder. I looked down just in time to see him twist and fall. His shoulder hit the solid part of the header guide, but he had stuck his arm out instinctively to break his fall and it went into the open end of the rapidly rotating paddle. I heard him scream.

I immediately killed the machine and honked the horn for Bob. He didn't hear it. I yelled at him. He drove on. Then I saw all the blood, the ragged flesh of Franks arm, still in the header, the whiteness of the protruding bone splinters, and I jumped to the ground.

There wasn't time to look at it, to wonder what to do. Frank was unconscious but bleeding bad and I knew he'd die if I didn't stop the blood and stop it fast.

I knew what to do, a tourniquet, like it showed in my Boy Scout handbook. I grabbed Frank and dragged him out of the header, his arm flopping, the blood spurting. I remembered I still had his knife and popped it open like he'd done, then split his good shirt sleeve from wrist to shoulder, cutting it off high. I wrapped it around his upper arm, below the big muscle, just above his elbow and tied it in a knot, a double. A stick! I had to find a stick. The blood, damn the blood, spurting, spluttering, splattering my shirt, dripping off my face. No time left to find a stick! The knife! I closed the blade, slipping the knife in the gap between the knots and twisted it tighter and tighter. The blood slowed, then stopped.

I tied the knife in place with the rest of the shirt sleeve and looked around for help but there was none. George and Bob were too far away. Bill was still gone. The truck was close. I opened the door, picked Frank up and fell forward with his weight. I picked him up again, this time keeping my balance and loaded him in the truck. I started the truck and headed for town, driving slow through the bumps and rocks of the field, until I hit the road. Then, all she would do.

I remembered the little clinic on the outside of town so I knew right where to go. I pulled in the driveway, across the grass, onto the sidewalk and ran inside, hollering for help. I was covered with blood.

A man sitting, waiting with his wife grabbed me. "No, you stupid ass!" I yelled. "Outside! He's outside!" I screamed again, but he held on to me. I twisted loose, shoving him away. "Outside," I screamed. "I'm alright. He's outside in the damn truck!"

Another man, wearing a white smock, came running. The doctor. I grabbed at him. The other man grabbed me. "He's outside!" I yelled and turned hitting the man under the chin with my left hand and, at the same time, in the chest with my right fist, knocking him against the wall across the room. The doctor looked at me, then at the man, nodded and ran out. I followed.

We gently unloaded Frank, carried him inside and laid him on the table at the back of the clinic. The doctor started hollering at a woman in white then began cutting the shirt sleeve off below the tourniquet, baring the mangled mess. I could see at least four pieces of bone sticking out. The elbow was twisted so that his arm looked like it was on backwards, only the thumb was left on the blood-covered stump that had been a hand.

The doctor looked at me, saying gently, "you better leave now. You've done all you can."

I walked out in the waiting area. The man's wife was cleaning up the blood on the floor. She smiled at me. The man, still rubbing his chin, came over asking what happened. I just looked at him and shook my head.

The doctor came back out some time later and sat beside me, putting his arm around me. "He's going to be fine," he said. "He'll be here for two or three days, maybe a week. But he's going to be fine. You saved his life." Then he handed me the knife. I looked at it, then put it in my pocket.

"I need to get some information from you now," he said. "If you feel like it."

I just nodded. The doctor looked up at the woman in white.

"What's his name?" she asked softly.

She has a nice voice, I thought, real pleasant tone, and replied woodenly, "Frank Turner."

"Are you the next of kin?"

"No, he has a wife in Burkburnett, Texas, Debbie. They own a ranch there. I don't know where. In fact, that's all I do know."

The door flew open just then and Bob came running in yelling, "what the hell happened?"

"He can help you more than I can," I said. "Can I see Frank now. Please?"

The doctor looked around, "Okay, but just for a second. He's still out but you can see him. Son," he added gently. "I had to take it off."

"Take what off? What the hell happened?" Bob screamed. I paid him no mind as I walked through the door. As it closed, I heard the nurse asking Bob how to get in touch with Debbie.

Frank was lying on a bed, a tube connected to a bottle was in his good arm. There was a large bundle of bandages just above where his other elbow should've been. I sat in a chair by the bed. He stirred slightly, then lay still. He looks smaller than normal lying there, I thought, reaching out, touching him. How quick it happened. How fast. On minute he's cussing, the next, almost dead. The doctor said I had saved his life. I felt something swell up in me, pride maybe. It deflated quickly when I thought about his arm. I was still sitting there when the doctor came back in. He asked me to leave.

"I'd like to stay with him if you don't mind." I said. "He might wake up scared."

He looked at me a second, "what kin are you to him Son?"

I thought about that a second, "he's the best friend I have in the world. I won't bother him but I would like to stay. He stayed by me once."

The doctor rubbed his eyes, then studied me and nodded. "Okay, just be quiet and call me if he wakes up."

"I will, and thanks a whole lot." I meant it.

I don't know how long I sat there, my mind blank, but it was dusk when I looked out the window. Vaguely, I wondered about the wheat. If they had gotten it all cut. Frank stirred then, his eyelids quivered. I went outside.

The doctor was there, just down the hall, he looked real tired. I could hear Bob and George talking through the door.

"I think he's coming around," I said to the doctor, then stepped back in quickly. Frank stirred some more, tried to move, then opened his eyes, looking at me.

He grinned, "Hello Wheatie," he said real weak. Then he raised his bad arm, looking at what was left. "I sure raised hell this time, didn't I?"

The doctor came in and asked, "how are you feeling?"

Frank said, "pretty weak and real dumb."

The doctor grinned, "I can help the weak. You hungry?"

"No, not really."

"Okay, in the morning then." The doctor looked at me, "Are you alright now?"

I nodded.

"Okay then, I'm going to give him another shot now. It will put him out for about four hours. You go get cleaned up and get some rest."

I looked back at Frank, he grinned weakly, "I'm okay Son. Do what the man says. You are a sight. You damn Wheaties are all alike, always nasty."

I reached out and touched him once more then turned and walked out. I walked down the hall hearing Bob talking. "Looked like someone killed a hog." He was saying. "More blood than I've ever seen. I found them fingers under the header, three of them. I guess the sycle got them. Looked like he stuck his arm in the end of the paddle wheel and them struts just chewed it up."

"Bob, shut up about it." George said tiredly. "That's about the millionth time you told it. I just wish you'd shut up about it. You're making me sick and giving me a headache."

"He fell into the paddle wheel," I said, walking into the room.

Bob stood, glaring at me as if he was going to hit me. "Well, why didn't you let someone know about it."

"I tried Bob," I said. "I honked and hollered both. You just drove on."

The doctor came in and looked at Bob, "The boy here did real good. If he hadn't been right there, knowing exactly what to do, and not going into a panic, that man would be dead. I figure he had a minute, maybe a minute and a half before he would've bled to death."

Bob looked at the doctor, then at me then back at the doctor. "You mean, this boy saved Frank's life?" he asked softly.

The doctor said. "I sure do, while you drove away, from the way it sounds."

"I didn't hear him honk or holler, either one." Bob said low.

"That's your fault," the doctor said tiredly. "They make hearing aids you know. You might---"

I walked out the door. I was tired of listening, tired of explaining, just tired. I drove the truck to the elevator, dumped the partial load and drove to the tent, completely exhausted.

I dug under Franks bunk and came up with the bottle we'd opened a couple of nights ago. I took a long drink, then another one, got my clean-up gear and a set of clothes and walked to the barrel-tub. My shirt and pants were stiff with blood. I put them in a bucket to soak and put myself in the tub.

I felt some better after the bath and clean clothes, so I drove Frank's pickup back to the café. I took the bottle. I remember eating, but I don't remember what I ate. By the time I got back to the tent, the rest were there. They didn't bother me or try to talk to me even when I started packing.

I lay on my bunk when I finished packing, drinking from the bottle, feeling dead, or at least not caring. I guess I slept but I'm not sure. I remember lying in the dark. Then it was gray, just breaking dawn. I was still dressed, still lying in the same position. I don't remember crying but my eyes were all crackly around the corners.

I walked outside, watching the sunrise. The entire eastern sky was bloody and dripping. The sun was like a giant drop of blood, hanging suspended between heaven and hell. Like me.

I took Frank's pickup and drove back to the clinic, parking beside a car with Texas plates. I took a drink, stuck the bottle in my pants, and walked in, straight to Frank's room.

There was a change. Now he had his left foot in a cast. He must have broken it when he fell, I thought. His arm was still gone. I hoped they'd burned it. I thought, it would be hell to be buried in two places. But what about the fingers? That made three---or four places. Bob only found three of them, and what did he do with---? To hell with it, I thought. What difference does it make where a man is buried or in how many places.

I sat close, touching him, trying to absorb some of the pain he must be going through. I knew he could handle the physical pain, that didn't worry me. But the mental pain of losing an arm was something I couldn't comprehend.

I looked at my own arm and hand and wondered what it would be like. My hand was something I had taken for granted, all of my life. It was just there, to be used for a thousand things each day. Then, to not have it? I shuddered at the thought. I knew, thousands of people had lost arms. One girl, back in Crane, was born without a left arm and they made it in life. I looked at my hand again, knowing it was the most intricate piece of machinery on the planet and I remembered what Frank had said the second day on the road. The day I had hit Rocky, *"You only got two hands and if you mess them up that's it. You don't get anymore."* Now what he'd said had come home. Now he only had one.

But I knew too that he was tough and resilient. I knew he'd make it if he had some help. He'd need help at first, someplace to go. But then I thought about the divorce---.

The door opened just then and a pretty, blond woman walked in. I stood up.

"You must be Dave," she said, her voice was clear, refined. "I'm Debbie, Franks wife." She held out her hand

I nodded, taking her hand, "I'm Dave, but how did you know?"

She said, "I know all of you, all about you." She smiled. She had a nice smile.

"How?" I asked, "Frank didn't tell you---" Then I really didn't care how she knew. "Okay," I said and sat back down.

She said, "The doctor told me you saved his life. Thank you."

I looked at her, then at Frank. "I'm not real sure I should've now. Now he's a cripple, with nowhere to go."

She seemed to cringe at the last part.

I didn't care, I wanted to hurt her.

She smiled. "He's alive. He'll be fine."

"Yeah, part of him is alive. The part that's left." I said

"The part that counts is still here. That's all that matters."

"Do you care?" I snapped. "You didn't seem to before."

"I care," she said low. "I care very much." She walked over then and kissed my forehead. "Thank you, so very much."

"Making out with my wife, Wheatie?" Frank said weakly, causing me to blush. I hadn't outgrown that yet. I hadn't known he was awake either.

"She's awfully pretty Frank," I said. "I might just steal her away from you."

He reached out his hand. She moved closer, taking it. "We've been talking all morning," Frank said. "Of course, I can't go on with the harvest. I'm going home. No, we're going home."

"Good," I said. "So am I."

Frank said, "I thought you might. When are you leaving?"

"Pretty soon. As soon as you're better. I came to give you this." I held out his knife.

He looked at the knife, then at me and he grinned. "Keep it, Dave. A one-armed-man doesn't need a knife. He's not going to get into any trouble and you need two hands to whittle. I want you to keep it. Something to remember me by."

My voice was thick when I said, "Frank, I'll never forget you, not as long as I live. I appreciate the knife, but I don't need it to remember you by. It ain't often a guy runs into an old boy like you."

He grinned again. "You either Dave, like I said a while back, you remind me of someone I knew---a long time ago. You keep the knife. It's a good one and, who knows. Maybe someday it'll get you out of trouble."

"Thanks, Frank. Like I said, I appreciate it." I slid the knife back in my pocket.

Debbie touched my arm then. I knew what she wanted. I could see the pain in his eyes being masked by the far away, drugged look. He was fighting to stay awake and would as long as we were there. "I'll see you later, Frank," I said. "I got something to do right now."

He just nodded weakly and I followed Debbie out the door. I looked back just before the door closed. He was already asleep.

I turned to go into the waiting room but Debbie said, "no, this way," and led me through another door into a kitchen. "This is where the doctor and his wife live," she said in that beautiful voice of hers. "They let us stay in here because the waiting room is so crowded."

I saw a man sitting at the table, a cowboy hat on the floor. He looked familiar for some reason, like someone I'd known a long time ago. He stood up. "Slim!" I hollered. Debbie shushed me

"Slim! What in the hell are you doing here?" I asked, not really believing it was him. I grabbed his extended hand in a handshake that meant more than usual.

He grinned sheepishly and pointed to Debbie. "That's a mighty good woman there Davie," he said.

We sat down at the table and I just looked at him, shaking my head. "What the hell? No, how the hell did you get here, Slim?" I said, still not believing it was really him.

He grinned again, "why, I drove Missus Turner up here from Texas."
"But, how the hell--"

He grinned again. "Let me start at the start Davie. After my trouble there in the panhandle, I run. I run for two days knowing they would catch me anytime. Then I got smart and dumped that car I stold. Dumped it in a deep lake. They won't ever find that car. Well, I figured then they'd never find me now so I started looking for work. I couldn't find any, so I went back to Wichita Falls to check with my parole man. While I was close, I hitchhiked over to Burkburnett to get word as to how y'all was making out. The little lady here sets me down and we get to talking and before I knew it, I'd done told her the whole story. All of it, about me killing that old boy and gouging that one's eye out and stealing the car and all."

Slim ducked his head, embarrassed. "And about me needing work. Well, she says. 'We got plenty of work right here. You just stay here with us and work.' Well, I wasn't sure. I didn't know about Frank and how he would take it. She says, 'He won't mind a bit.' So I stayed and I'm doing real good now. I don't go by Slim no more. I told her about that too. She says, 'Why if something is bothering you, just face it. You just got to face it down, and get it out of your system and then it won't bother you no more.' Now, I go by Ray Devers again, and it don't bother me no more when folks call me Shorty."

That was hard to believe. I'd Debbie all made out to be a bitch, a real dragon, fire breathing and all. But come to think of it, Frank had never said anything bad about her, only himself. "Have you seen Frank yet?" I asked Slim.

"No, not yet." He ducked his head. "I'm too embarrassed right now, me running off and leaving him shorthanded and all."

I had to laugh about that. "It turned out alright, Slim. We hired another guy the next day and he turned out to be a top hand. We did miss you though."

And the sequence of events ran through my mind. If Slims fight in the bar had never happened, I would have never met Mary Ann. Because we never would have hired Gus. It was then that I realized that all things in the world are connected and that a person's whole life can be changed in an instant, by something he has absolutely no control over and, by someone he has never met.

"It's good to know you just about got it all worked out. Your trouble that is, I'm real proud of you."

"Well, that ain't all I got worked out," he said proudly. "Missus Turner here," he beamed at her. "Done found out who owned that car I stold and I'm paying for it. And just about got it all paid for too. Don't I Ma'am?"

"You sure do, Ray. Just about three more payments." She smiled at him, and he beamed again. I could almost see him swell he was so proud. And, I thought, God help the man that even said a cross word to this woman. There would be no mercy from Slim and he wouldn't stop until she, and only she, called him off. If she didn't, Slim would kill him, or die trying.

A warmness came over me then and I felt better about the whole thing. I'd been worried about Frank, where he would go, what he would do. But not anymore, not now.

"Dave," Debbie said softly. "We still don't know what happened. The doctor told us some, Frank told me what he remembered. But we don't know."

I got me a cup of coffee, drank half of it, then pulled the bottle from under my shirt and filled the cup. I offered the bottle to Slim.

He looked at Debbie questioningly.

She nodded and he filled his cup.

I took a drink of Irish, leaned back, and told them the story. I didn't pat myself on the back either, I just told them the way it happened. When I got through, Debbie was shaken, the color of ashes.

Slim just nodded as if it had been expected of me. But then he said, "how did you ever get him loaded Davie? He must weight one-seventy or one-eighty. You won't go one-forty."

"I don't know Slim. I just did it, that's all. I had too, there was no one but me there. I did what I had too."

He just nodded, but Debbie leaned over and kissed me on the cheek.

Slim laughed when I blushed. "Don't embarrass him so Debbie, he's real bashful." Then he laughed and so did she.

About then my stomach growled, making me blush even more. Debbie grinned and I thought, how pretty she is, and nice. And I knew Frank would be alright then. She'd take him home and everything would be fine.

She stood then. "Let's go get something to eat. Frank will be out awhile. We can come back later."

Slim and I nodded as we stood. Debbie cleaned off the table, rinsing out the coffee cups, putting them in the drainer, emptied the ash tray and wiped off the table.

We drove to the café and ate breakfast. Then as we sat drinking our coffee, Bob came in. I waved to him. He walked over, looking at Slim, almost as surprised as I had been.

"Slim," Bob said reaching out a hand. "How the hell are you doing?"

"Real good Bob," Slim said as he stood and they shook hands. "Real good. Say, I'm sorry I left you shorthanded back there."

Bob said, "Don't worry about it." And I noticed he was talking in a normal tone. I noticed why then, he had on a hearing aid. He had finally broke down and bought himself a hearing aid. He spoke to Debbie and sat down then and all four of us talked until the café began to fill up. We left then, going back to the clinic.

I rode with Bob. He told me they were loading up, getting ready to move on north to Gurley, Nebraska. A little town just north of Sidney. He said they had fifteen hundred acres to cut there. He'd brought my suitcase to town with him though. Now he said, "so you're leaving for sure?"

"Yeah, Bob," I said. "I'm tired of it all. I'm going home."

"I figured as much and that's why I brought your suitcase in." He looked at me then. "Dave, you been a damn good hand. I wondered what Frank was thinking when he hired you, but you sure have made a hand. I hate to lose you."

That made me feel good and bad at the same time. Because I was leaving him shorthanded too. "I hate to leave Bob. But I just want to go home. I'd like to go on, but I better not. I'm just tired."

"Yeah, I know what you mean. This will be my last year too. I talked to Doris last night and told her I'm selling out. This is the last harvest. I might sell before I get home. Losing Frank just took the fun out of it. I sure hate to leave him here but I have to cut that field at Gurley---then I don't know."

"Frank told me it was a hard life," I said. "I just didn't know how hard."

"Oh, it's a bitch alright," Bob said. "It's sure a bitch and sometimes it's worse. Well, I got to hire some hands. Sure, you're going home now?"

It was hard for me to get use to him not hollering. "Yeah."

"Sure I can't talk you out of it?"

"No Bob. It's almost the first of August and school will start in a couple of weeks anyway. I better get on back."

"I figured as much when I found out how bad Frank was hurt. I got your time totaled too, including full pay for yesterday. It comes to seventy dollars. That sound about right?"

"It sounds good to me."

He counted out the cash in my hand laughing. "I lost about four hundred on this job. Many more like this one and I won't have to sell out." Then he held out his hand, "Well, good luck Davie," he crushed my hand when we shook. I'd forgotten the power of the man. "Ever you get out to Clinton, you got a place to stay. And if you don't leave today, you can stay in the tent tonight."

"I might do that. I might just wait and get an early start in the morning."

"Fine," he said. "We'll expect you. Okay?"

"Okay Bob, sure." I got out and he drove away. I went in the clinic.

Frank was still asleep so instead of bothering him, I went back outside. I still had Frank's pickup so I drove to the post office, bought a money order and mailed it home. I kept twenty dollars to get home on. It was enough.

Frank was awake when I got back to the clinic. He told me Debbie and Slim had gone to a motel to get some rest. They'd driven all night to get here. I sat with him the rest of the day. He was in a lot of pain and would come and go. The doctor said his stump was badly infected because of the dirt and trash he couldn't get out. He also said he might have to operate again, taking more off. But at any rate it would be two or three days before Frank could leave.

Slim came back to the clinic late in the afternoon. We all three sat and talked till Frank began to get sleepy again. Just before he went to sleep I told him I was leaving in the morning. "I hate to see you leave, Wheatie," he said. "I'll miss you."

"I'll miss you too Frank. You've been like a brother to me."

"Yeah, I know. You too." Then he handed me a piece of paper. "Here's my address and phone number in Burkburnett. You're welcome anytime, no matter what or when, anytime."

He didn't look so small now. Now, I knew he'd be alright. He had Slim and he had Debbie. He didn't need me. He was almost asleep when I walked to his bed. I took his hand and held it a second, then I walked to the door. I touched Slim on the shoulder, turned and looked back. "I'll see you soon Frank," I said, knowing it was a lie. I wouldn't come back to the clinic.

He smiled at me as I walked out.

CHAPTER 24

I drove back to the café and ate, then drove to Bob's trailer and gave him the keys. "I hired a new guy today," Bob said. "But you're still welcome to stay the night."

His normal tone still made me smile. "Only one hand? I figured you would need two."

"No," he said. "Slim is going to take Frank's pickup home with him. I won't need another until we get to Gurney. I'll probably have a better choice there." He shrugged noncommittally.

I nodded and sat at the tiny table.

"Too bad about Frank," Bob continued. "But it looks like him and Debbie might work things out."

"Yeah. I'm glad and worried at the same time. It seems like he lost more than an arm." Talking about Frank seemed strange, I didn't like it much.

Bob sighed deeply. "Something like that will take a lot out of a man. But don't worry about Frank. He's tougher than leather. He'll be down awhile but he'll be alright. And he's got Slim there too. He'll be fine, if he can just stay out of the bottle."

"I'm not worried about the bottle, he was doing real good there for a while. Now, he has a real reason to quit, maybe a couple of them.

Bob stood. "I hope you're right, but I've seen too many like him to make an early judgment. You going to stay here tonight?"

"Yeah, if you don't mind."

"No Dave, it's fine. We're leaving in the morning too. We can give you a ride to town."

"I would appreciate that."

"I just had a thought," Bob said. "You could stay and ride back with Slim and Frank when he gets out. Won't be but a couple of more days."

"I thought about that. But I've already sent all my money home."

"Well, if that's a problem, I could----"

"No Bob," I held up my hand. "That's not all. Frank has enough to worry about without me and I reckon it's time I started taking care of myself. I mean, I've been leaning on Frank every since I met him.

Bob smiled and scratched his bald head. "You've come a long way already Dave. I remember a scared kid that came to my house. I don't think you're scared anymore."

I had to laugh at that one. "Bob, I'm more scared now than I was then." I thought about it a second. "Then, I didn't know what to expect out of life and I guess, now I do. And believe me, it scares the hell out of me."

Bob seemed to age before my eyes and he sighed deeply. "There ain't no easy way to grow up Dave. But you've done a pretty good job of it this summer you've made mistakes but you learned from them and that's the best lesson a man could learn."

He paused a second, deep in thought. Then he said. "You see, almost everything in life is a trade-off and for the most part, it comes out even. Or at least you get something back for what you lose. Just remember that in some way or another you'll pay for everything in life. You make a mistake, you learn not to do that again. The trick is not to make the same mistake twice."

"You make it sound easy. But have you ever made the same mistake twice?"

He laughed out loud. "No more than a thousand times. We all do at one time or another. We all do. And for the most part it's over women." He laughed again and shrugged, "You've come a long way and you've been a good hand Dave. I'm going to miss you."

"I appreciate that Bob." He extended his hand and I shook it and walked outside.

The cut field looked dead in the moonlight, the rocks standing out like exposed bones through rotted flesh. All the animals, except the insects, had been driven away by the combines and trucks and the land was quiet, seemingly as dead as it looked. But the earth would heal and if Reynolds didn't plant wheat here again, grass would grow and the animals would come back. The field would never be the same again but life would come back. And life would go on.

I thought about what Bob had said about life being a trade-off. Frank seemed to have traded an arm for his wife and maybe happiness. I wondered about me, whether I'd gained anything from this summer. I knew I had. But mostly I wondered what I'd traded for it.

I went on in the tent then and lay down in the dark, hoping I could sleep, wondering if I would ever know exactly what I'd traded for this summer. I knew I would leave a piece of me here, in this wheat field, a part of me that I could never get back. But I'd traded that part of me for Frank's life. And that was good. It was what I'd left in another wheat field outside of Castle Rock that I worried about. I still didn't know what I'd gotten in return for that.

I wondered if I would ever know.

$$*\qquad*\qquad*$$

I don't remember sleeping, but suddenly Bob was yelling in the tent, "Y'all going to sleep all day? We got miles to go and we're late already."

We took down the tent and loaded by headlights, then drove to town. I was nervous, sad, excited and lonely at the same time. A light was on in the clinic as we passed and I said my last good by to Frank.

Breakfast was quiet. A few local people were there but we seemed to be the last wheat crew in this area. And now, we were leaving. I watched Bob and George while they ate. They didn't seem to realize how much I hated them right then. They were going on and I couldn't, not without Frank.

We said our good byes at the pickup and I felt a tremendous sense of loss as they drove away. They'd been friends, family and security for the last six weeks, but even with them I had felt alone. Now it was true, I was alone. I fought back an urge to run after them. Bob's still shorthanded, screamed through my mind. I still have a job. But without Frank?

The pickup disappeared into the growing dawn. I picked up my suitcase and started walking, south.

I stopped at a filling station that had just opened and got a road map then walked on out of town. I was a transient again, alone on the road. A migrant worker, without a job, in a country that frowned on such people. But at least now, I knew what to expect and how to head off trouble. I was well past the city limits before I stopped and sat on my suitcase. The rapidly growing light was fading the morning star when the first car stopped.

"Where are you going?" the man asked as I climbed in.

For some reason the question shocked me. I thought about it a second.

The man said, "well, Boy, where are you going?"

Finally I said, "south, I guess."

"Just south? That's all? That's a helluva an answer."

"Mister, that's the best I can do right now."

"If you say so," then he went silent, which was good. I didn't feel like talking right now. I didn't feel much of anything right now.

He let me out at Wray and turned east. Again, I walked out of town before I stopped.

The land had changed again. Where the wheat had stood, now the plows were at work, turning the straw and chaff under, causing great columns of dust to be carried high into the air by the ever-present, rushing wind. Where the plows hadn't been, the land had a naked look as if some great hordes had ravaged the crops leaving only barrenness in their path. The sun beat down and the rising heat gave a shimmering appearance to the distance where dust devils danced and played. The wind moaned around me coming steadily from the south. It seemed to be holding me, trying to carry me back with it, stinging me with the burden of dust it carried, for not going.

I caught another ride and the farther south we went, the heavier the dust seemed to be, sometimes limiting vision to a half-mile or so. But this ride was with a businessman in a suit and an air-conditioned car. He griped about the dust and the wind all the way to Burlington.

He let me out at the crossroads of Highway 385 and Highway 24. I stood there a second, studying my map in the buffeting wind, trying to make the decision that had been on my mind for two days. A car stopped. The man hollered out the window, "which way are you going?"

I couldn't answer and he drove away, south. Then I folded the map, laughing at myself. I had no decision to make. It had been made for me almost a month ago in a field outside Castle Rock. I picked up my suitcase and headed west.

It took me three rides to get to Limon and one more to get to the Highway 86, junction outside of town. I sat there for over an hour waiting for my next ride, wondering about something that had happened in filling station bathroom, back in a town called Bovina.

The door had been unlocked so I had just walked in. Suddenly I saw a man staring me in the face. His eyes were bloodshot, smarting from the wind and the dust, and had tiny wrinkles in the corners. His face was sunburned, lean and hard. His jaw was tight and the corners of his mouth turned down. His eyes locked hard into mine in a direct stare and I tensed for the attack I felt was imminent. Fear shot through me for a second. He looked rough and mean, like he would be a hard man to take.

I remember my manners then and said, "excuse me Mister. I thought the bathroom was empty." And started backing out. It was then I realized I was talking to a mirror, and I felt like a fool.

I smiled about it now but it bothered me some. I'd looked closer then, and realized, I really didn't know the guy who looked back at me from the mirror. He looked a lot like someone I used to know, but he had been just a kid.

The guy that now smiled at his own stupidity was no kid. He looked confident and sure of himself. I wondered who he was and just how he got so sure of himself when I was so confused.

And now I wondered, did I really want to go back and find out for sure what I couldn't stand to learn? Had I been used? Had I been experimented with by a little rich girl for a whim, because she knew I would be leaving and never come back? Or was I so sure of myself that I'd learn what I'd known that night? Would I learn what she had said was true. I believed it then. I wanted to believe it now.

"I'm not sure I want to know." I said aloud then looked to see if anyone saw me talking to myself.

A car turned off the main highway. I stood, held out my thumb and they stopped, a man and a woman. "We're just going a short distance up the road," the man said. "But you're welcome to ride."

I smiled and got in, "I'm not going far myself." And we talked about nothing for the thirty odd miles, but when we passed through Cloud Chief, the growing apprehension in me closed my throat. What was I going to say to her? Would she be happy to see me? Or embarrassed? All raced through my mind.

My clothes were dust covered, my boots scuffed and worn. I looked at least twenty-five years old and rough. I wondered if she had changed any? The month since I'd seen her seemed like an eternity.

Then the mansion house appeared on the horizon and just as suddenly, I didn't want to stop. Just go on! My mind screamed. She'll never know if you don't stop. But then I calmed thinking, I'll never know if I don't stop. And I heard myself tell the people, "I'll get out just up here, if you don't mind."

"Here?" the man said. "Son, there ain't nothing here but that big house up there."

"That's alright, I know someone that lives there."

"Well, whatever," he said as he pulled to the side of the road.

I thanked him and got out. He drove away and I was alone in the dusty wind, staring across the road at the white mansion on the hill that seemed even bigger than I remembered. The massive columns soared to the balcony of the second story. The pristine whiteness was off set by the lush green of the yard and the even deeper green, red, yellow, and white of the rose garden that seemed out of place in the rolling folds of dry browns and grays of the surrounding hills.

I remembered again how she looked in the moonlight. And I remembered how she had felt, naked in my arms. And I started up the crushed rock driveway.

Then I remembered how small I'd felt that night in front of this house, almost as if I'd entered someplace I didn't belong. And later, in Holyoke, the feeling I had been used, almost experimented with. I stopped and the wind moaned around me, bending the long grass of the prairie, making it point and wave back north, almost as if it were giving me a sign.

I looked up again, remembering the guy I'd seen in a mirror, and the house seemed to shrink before my eyes. It was just a house, I though, a big one sure, but just wood and nails, concrete and carpet. And I wasn't afraid anymore. A man had built that house. A man could tear it down. And now, I was a man.

I realized then that the house had become a symbol to me of something I couldn't overcome. And I thought, *HE* couldn't overcome it. He was just a kid, scared of the power and the position that this house wore like a mantle. But I wasn't him any longer. I was me. And I could overcome it. And I knew I could.

Then I saw the girl in the rose garden. Her hair was long and dark. She was taller than most girls, slender and willowy. I was still too far away to see her face but I knew she had deep, dark eyes that a man could drown in and a funny, sad, little smile.

I went back in my mind then to the wheat field and I could hear her voice echo inside my head. *I love you Dave, with all my heart,"* she had said. *"I will always love you."* And again, I looked into those dark drowning pools she had for eyes. Again, I kissed her, standing in front of this very house and I heard her say, *"I lied, I would have been happy in a shack, with you. I love you. I'll always love you."*

Now, I knew it was true. What I'd felt before had been only a reaction to my own fears. My own inadequacies, I had been fabricating reasons for me not to come back. But as I saw those eyes again, heard her voice again, I knew what she'd said had been from the heart. She did love me, truly and honestly love me. And she always would.

And I knew I loved her. And I knew I always would.

But I knew, just as sure, that it could never be. I had beaten the house. Now, I was bigger than the house. I had alleviated those fears and laid them to rest. But there was something else. Something nagging at me. My mind went first to Frank. He had said a truism, *"Love makes a damn small turd, when it's all you have to eat."*

And I knew what Mary Ann had said that night was also true. That it would work for a while, but then---? And that was the question. But then?

And the answer was, yes, she'd been right. Frank had been right. Even I'd been right. It was a hopeless situation. And if I left it, here and now, we would have each other for the rest of our lives the way we were that night in a wheat field outside Castle Rock.

My mind went to Bob then and what he had said about me. I had grown. I knew that now. I had seen life at its best and at its worse. I had seen death, mutilation and humiliation. But worse than either of them, I'd realized how ordinary day to day living itself can grind a man into the dust. And make him grow to hate the things and the people he loved the most.

But I had seen love too. I had tasted love and felt it, not just from Mary Ann, but from Frank and Bob, Debbie and even Slim. I'd been tested and, for the most part, I had passed the test.

Bob had been right about me but he had also been right about the trade-off. I remembered wondering, just last night, what I had traded for this summer. Now I knew that too. I had grown, but I'd lost something too. Something I'd had before had been missing from the guy in the mirror. And now I knew what was missing. And I knew I could never have it back.

I wasn't real sure the trade was even. But it seemed right.

I picked up my suitcase and walked back to the road. I sat down, my mind in a turmoil, not knowing which way to go. I thought of home but there was no real pull there. There was no one there I could talk to, no one there to help me understand my feelings.

I thought about Gayle but she was just a girl I had known, outgrown and left behind to her own dreams. Mine had been different even then. And now?

Now, I didn't know. I didn't dream much anymore. Even the car that I could afford now didn't seem all that important anymore. Nothing did. No one did. Frank had told me I couldn't go back and he'd been right about Mary Ann. Maybe he was right about home too.

The wind whipped the grass, moaning around me, talking to me, telling me to come, go with it, and I brightened. I can go on north, I thought. I can catch Bob and finish out the harvest. I can see where the wind gone. But then what? Then would I wind up with the road in my blood, like the old man had said. Or like Frank had said, *'just dust in the wind.'*

I heard a car coming and stood. It was a pickup driven by an old man, headed east. I stuck out my thumb. He stopped and I threw my suitcase in the bed. I waited just a second and looked back at the house before I got in.

The girl was still there among the roses. I didn't know if it was Mary Ann. It could have been a sister or even her mother. But I wanted it to be her so it was. I waved to her. She waved back as I shut the door and the old man drove away. I didn't look back.

The old man looked me over carefully, then said, "been on the harvest?"

"Yeah," I looked down the long, lonesome road.

"Figured so. You look like one of them wheat tramps."

I started to burn, but then I said, "that's right Mister. I'm a wheat tramp and damn proud of it too!"

He looked at me strangely, then nodded, "yeah Bud, I can see that. Can't rightly say as to why you're so proud, but I can see you are. Where you headed?"

I thought a second. "Home, Mister. I'm going home."

Then I thought of home.

Sara's there, I thought.

Sara's home.

I smiled as I thought of Sara.

The End

CPSIA information can be obtained at www.ICGtesting.com
Printed in the USA
LVOW12s0114020714

392632LV00001B/164/P